The Muzac Man

by

Thaddeus Hawthorne Grey

Volume I

Thaddeus Hawthorne Grey ©

DEDICATION

Thanks to those eldritch dreamers: Edgar Allan Poe, Howard Phillips Lovecraft, Clark Ashton Smith, Robert E. Howard, Robert W. Chambers, Frank Belknap Long, August Derleth, and Lin Carter, as well as to M.R. James, and Dennis Wheatley, who figure greatly in this work, I offer my sincere gratitude. And, to Lovecraft's contemporaries: Ramsey Campbell, Brian Lumley, Neil Gaiman, W. H. Pugmire, Caitlin R. Kiernan, Laird Barron, and Thomas Ligotti, among my favourites, to these authors, my most honoured regards, and to all the many twilight children that follow this shadowy world of cosmic horror, whether living or in death.

✠

Et pro praeteritis amicis praesens; et viventem, et mortuus est, hoc est liber fondly dicata. Nam amici mei J.V., L.A.M., T.R.K., M.D.K., W.B.G. Quia memoria narrat gaudium et gaudium amicorum. Denique frater meus G.C.J., qui sine intermissione spiritus taunts ultra, et quantum amari tribulationis — Reliqua frater — requiem in pace.

AUTHOR'S NOTE

The concept for *The Muzac Man*, originally titled: 'The Kmart Man,' came about with a lot of downtime, and by witnessing the social unrest in the streets and on social media platforms during the 2016 elections between Donald J. Trump and Hillary Clinton, a time in recent history that seemed to signify a distinct divide between the nation and its people. Then, when the SARS-CoV-2 (COVID-19) pandemic hit, the natural course of fear and paranoia followed, spreading like wildfire across the globe. It was a turbulent time for sure, though such emotions appear to be continuing despite a renewed feeling of hope in the nation. Certainly, there is still a noticeable divide that's hard to deny.

During this time, I had been working as a deputy medical examiner in the state of Virginia and had found myself inundated with more than my share of paperwork and other obligations. And though we took universal precautions when dealing with the dead, only high-profile cases were allowed, as the nature of the Coronavirus was still questionable within the medical community, leaving more mystery than fact. As such, I would assist the Chief Medical Examiner and other pathologists in performing examinations, but because the Medicolegal process had greatly altered the practice of conducting autopsies, my job description changed greatly for the next few years, so many of us were assigned secondary and even tertiary jobs. We were all understandably scared.

My wife, Gwen, was working with the federal government then, and so I was able to glean some aspects of her work that inspired me to write again. Having penned several nonfiction books under the nom de plume Greg Jenkins and G. Cledwyn Jenkins, the name of a deceased friend from college, I had decided that it was time to write a work of fiction using my own identity. It was in October of 2022 when I sat at a little café and outlined my first synopsis of what I was calling *The Kmart Man*, but after calling my attorneys about the title, they warned me to change it just in case someone wanted to get litigious about the brand name. Nevertheless, this was when my journey began.

The concept for the Muzac Man came while conversing with a federal agent after one of our more salacious medical inquests. I learned of one of his past cases involving a security guard, a strange man who worked in a now-defunct shopping mall in South Florida. Apparently, the man was practising magick in a long-abandoned Kmart department store attached to the mall where he worked. *Allegedly*, the man was conducting rituals and even sacrificing animals there. But as weird as this sounds, however, the man was much stranger than all that.

The agent went on to say that the strange man would sit and sometimes even live in the old, deserted Kmart that had departed the shopping mall years earlier. And though the department store was dark and damp, and strangely chilly, there was nonetheless power. As such, he would listen to old cassette tapes of Muzak that the store's past managers had left behind, along with an antiquated tape deck that would play one tape after another, again and again. The agent said that when police arrived to investigate reports about the man, they had discovered the odd security guard listening to outdated tunes while staring at a blank wall in the dark. But it wasn't until the agent pulled up a photo of the man on his iPad that I had an immediate epiphany. This was when *Patrick Allen Bush* was created, when the Muzac Man was born.

Now inspired, I checked to see if YouTube had any samples of old store Muzak, and sure enough, there was a plethora of actual Kmart Muzak there, and quite a bit of it too. Apparently, a former employee had kept these old cassette tapes when his store was closing and uploaded them on the social media platform for fun. He probably didn't know it, but he made an important, if not obscure, contribution to retail history in the process. And there are thousands of subscribers who, to this day, still listen to the antiquated Muzak of a lost era in America.

Three years later, I have eight volumes now completed for this series. Set in a timeline that doesn't exceed a decade from the date of this writing, it covers one possible environment and philosophy should a different political party have won and should that particular party have changed the world in the process. And though such may entice some to think it's about them, in truth, it is complete fiction with absolutely no distinction whatsoever. It is, however, an alternate universe, an aspect of the multiverse, if you will. Here, there *are* monsters, both human, daemonic, and cosmic. So please keep in mind that it's just a story.

Now, a few remaining items. First, the name 'Muzac' is misspelt on purpose. The Special Agent who told me about the odd security guard said that when he read over documents with the man's security reports and other writing, he had misspelled it. And because the proper spelling is still copyrighted, I decided to keep the odd spelling.

The second item may not concern people from Europe or the United Kingdom, but most Americans may find certain spellings and sentence structures that may appear somewhat archaic. This is done to emulate the style, at least some of it, of Howard Phillips Lovecraft (1890- 1937), the famous author of cosmic horror. Mr. Lovecraft was a staunch Anglophile and often antiquated in his thinking, an unfortunate earmark of his time. Regardless, I chose to honour him for his vision, which has inspired countless authors, musicians, and other dreamers of the nightside to explore and expand.

In the end, this work, should you wish to continue reading this saga, is for those who believe that there is yet so much more than what our philosophies dictate. This work is for the cosmic dreamer who can see beyond the confines of our mundane world. It's for all those who dwell within the obscure recesses of the fantastical and the grotesque. And it *may* be for people just like you. Cheers!

— *Thaddeus H. Grey, March 2024*

https://www.muzac-man.com/

PROLOGUE

The Land of Goshen
The Red Sea, Eastern Delta of the Nile

Saturday, October 9th, 1993, 11:11 A.M.

"Declare ye it not at Gath, weep ye not at all: in the house of Aphrah roll thyself in the dust. Pass ye away, thou inhabitant of Saphir, having thy shame naked: the inhabitant of Zaanan came not forth in the mourning of Bethezel; he shall receive of you his standing. For the inhabitant of Maroth waited carefully for good: but evil came down from the Lord unto the gate of Jerusalem…"

— Micah I: X-XII, KJV, 1611

By the time Nina Ari stepped off the Heliopolis Red Sea Tours shuttle bus, she had a good idea of the people she was ferrying on that brisk, bright morning. Though the dried lake beds had long since been abandoned by the majority of other tour groups that served inspired Europeans and a spattering of American Jews and Christians looking for religious reverence, Nina knew that the majority of her groups were no less fascinated by ancient history.

Today's group was larger than normal. There were Jon and Emilia Dieter from Amsterdam, Aaron and Bradley Kenner from Berlin, Germany, Rosalie and Heimlich Cronkite from Geneva, Switzerland, and Neal and Rebecca Stewart from Yorkshire, England. This rounded out the

Europeans. The remainder of the guests consisted of Robert and Marian Goldstein from Webster, New York, Jake and Liz Epstein from Boca Raton, Florida, and Calvin and Amie Clatterbuck from Conway, South Carolina. They were all retirees enjoying what Nina believed was one of the best tour lines out of Jerusalem. In addition to this were the four students from Dartmouth College, New Hampshire. They were on an extended study with the University- Without-Walls Program, set up by the Israeli Government for Jewish students to take part in a 'living history' event; all offering eight credits per semester. It was a solid plan, and the two students happily took advantage of it.

Sitting behind the Dartmouth students rested two elderly ladies, Helen Brocksen and Franny-Lou Myers from Lawrence, Kansas. They represented the East Lawrence Baptist Church, hoping to arrange for their congregation to visit the Holy Land. Nina would be the liaison for this larger group, and she was as pleased as a lottery winner to earn the commission. The last of this group consisted of two local students who had the day off and wanted to see a part of Moses' journey they'd yet to experience. For them, it was like a native New Yorker seeing the Statue of Liberty for the first time, or a native Floridian finally experiencing Disney World in Orlando. It was just something every Israelite had to do at least once in their lifetime.

The last man, an odd, lonely-looking American, lingered in the back of the shuttle bus. He was in his late twenties, perhaps younger. He never spoke so much as a whisper, though his eyes expressed choppy currents beneath still pools of pale blue. He held almost no expression at all, a reality that gave Nina cause for concern, though she had no idea why such a feeling would have existed at all.

This sad, sullen-looking man was listed as a foreign exchange student, an American, recently of the United Kingdom, and the University of Oxford. He was listed as a 'researcher' and was to be let off for one of the three-day excursion packages the tour company had offered, though typically, an offering that was reserved for five or more guests. Certainly, this pricy package deal offered a select few the chance to live like an archaeologist and camp in a fancy tent, while hobnobbing with professors and other experts on the Middle East. It offered a lofty introduction to the ancient adventures of the Israelites against Pharaoh and his doomed armies, though it was certainly a 'once-in-a-lifetime opportunity and encounter with history,' or so the advertisement flyer had proclaimed.

The guest paying for this excursion package would get the real deal, short of watching the nearby Red Sea part to reveal its secrets; just short of the twin lakes of Timsah and Tumilat coming back to life. In addition to the offer, Doctor Noam Isaac Hakimi, an expert in Hebraic history and folklore, and Professor Emeritus of Semantics from the Hebrew University of Jerusalem, would be offering a lecture for the foreigners, all for a mere twenty-five hundred Shekels for three nights in the wilds of the ancient land. There would even be 'authentic Jewish meals not unlike the feasts of King Solomon himself, or so the advertisement flier had continued to proclaim.

Don't hold your breath on that one, Nina thought to herself. She smiled in contempt of the flier's hook-line-and-sinker prose, though she realized the marketing scheme was a good idea. Regardless, she turned to gaze at the lonely-looking American again and frowned. She couldn't explain it, but the man continued to concern her, even when knowing Israeli Intelligence had cleared the man. She didn't know why, but there was just something about the man that gave her the creeps.

✠

Now, as the bus finally met its destination and the talkative group hurried to exit through the side door, the man waited until the cattle-like visage emptied out of the bus. The strange man, however, had departed the group without as much as saying adieu. He simply nodded briefly to Nina in thanks for the lift, but he said nothing. He was the only one staying for the three-day excursion.

"Remember, sir, we will pick you up here on Tuesday morning no later than ten, so please be prepared to depart here by then!" she echoed. She was loud enough so the strange foreigner could hear, though he didn't respond. The man simply nodded quickly in compliance and continued on to the camp. He remained cryptically silent as he flung his old, military-style backpack over his right shoulder, but his flippancy was anything but amusing or comforting.

Nina continued to watch the strange man as he made his way straight to the professor, who was conversing with a fair-haired woman in khaki clothing. She surmised that the odd American must have known the professor and his colleague, as he seemed to capture the scholars' attention almost immediately. They both sat down near the tent and began talking as if old friends.

Perhaps they know each other? she thought. *Perhaps this odd American is simply a student, an archaeology student … perhaps.*

✠

Perplexed, Nina sat in the shuttle bus and spoke briefly with Yaseen, the elderly driver. They talked about the group they had just dropped off, and of the strange American who had caused speculation for both of them. The little old ladies from Kansas and the retirees from New York and Florida were run-of-the-mill types for any tour service, that much was for certain, but Dr. Hakimi's four assistants had looked anything like scholars or students. They looked more like members of the military, though they were clearly European in nationality. This was also concerning.

Nina watched as the two Israeli kids began taking photographs and filming the surroundings. That wasn't a stretch either, especially for college students bucking for extra credit. But the strange American was something different altogether. She couldn't put her finger on it, but it was something about the way he acted; either his demeanour or the odd, almost otherworldly self-confidence he held as if he was the Chief Rabbi of all Israel — not arrogant as such, but silently commanding all the same. She couldn't explain it, but the man had frightened her.

Nina knew this wasn't the first time the strange American had been to the Holy Land or the Middle East, a fact made by the customary investigation by agents with the Israel Defense Forces. He'd encountered the ancient spectacle on several occasions, beginning in late 1992. He had trekked from Succoth to Etham, and from Baalzephon and Migdol to the range of Pi-Hahiroth. He'd camped alone in the wastelands of Nuweiba, and on the banks of the Gulf of Aqaba, though not even the jackals dared pass his camp. Certainly, today's mere four-hundred or so kilometre jaunt wasn't an issue to this man; this strange man who had known this land very well. Now, Nina just stared at the strange American with questioning eyes. She had considered that the man had had more than just a thirst for the Holy Land. Perhaps he knew its secrets.

✠

As the heat began to rise, Nina watched as the lone American left the company of Professor Hakimi and the fair-haired woman and sat alone on a rock near the location where the famed Pillars of Solomon, where the massive copper replicas of the Boaz and Jachin columns once stood. He was reading from several books he had pulled from his backpack. He'd look at one book and then another, followed by retrieving a little notebook, and then furiously jotting down unknown words into it. Then, he unrolled a small, grungy-looking map or scroll. He stood up with the books held tightly under his left arm and stared at the rock face and around the location of the first Pillar of Solomon. He did so with an unnerving reverence as if he knew what he was looking for. After a moment of contemplation, the strange man walked into the massive, dark opening of the eastern side of the cliffs and disappeared. Now, Nina just watched as a chill ran down her back.

Twenty, maybe twenty-five minutes had passed with no sign of the odd American. Nina was just about to walk over to the two people running the operation and inform them that she was worried for the tourist, but that would have been a lie. She had planned to politely interrogate them about the man. She was especially good at this and knew she could quell her fears of the odd man by doing so, but just as she was about to walk over to them, the strange American exited the dark orifice of the ancient temple and walked purposefully toward the two scholars by the tent. His expression was troubling, as if a silent rage had flowed through him.

As the man approached the open flap of the tent, he held a small box with both hands. It was no larger than a cigar box and appeared to be made of some form of white material, as if made of ivory and jet or 'oltu' stone. Nina couldn't see properly, but she was certain the box was lined with gold and something red, as if encrusted with rubies or other similar gems.

"Impossible," Nina mumbled to herself. "Those mines had been ransacked centuries ago, and again and again since the twenties. He couldn't have found anything in there … impossible."

✠

Now, Nina just watched silently as the strange man met with the two scholars. They had appeared joyful at the discovery of what she couldn't have known, but they were obviously delighted at the find. She continued to watch as the strange man opened a small, antiquated-looking wooden box delicately and then lifted out what looked like a small metal artifact, like that of a ring, or perhaps a broach of some type. The elder man only offered a look of sheer shock and amazement, quickly leaning in to examine the artefact. The thing glowed; it glowed in the sun, as if made of some blazing metal.

Nina continued to watch as the strange American touched the gem, then twisted its upper portion slightly to remove what must have been a secret opening. Now, the two scholars gazed at each other with shock, then returned their attention to whatever was within. The scholars quickly examined whatever was inside and then quickly wrapped it in what looked like a large piece of linen. Then, he placed that in some kind of metal box. Now, as the lady scholar held the box, the other man, appearing genuinely elated, as if the strange American had discovered some lost artefact of legend, had quickly hugged the man, and then put his arm around him. Everyone seemed happy, all but the American. He was as stoic as a statue, unmoved and seemingly dead to the world. The image was disturbing.

What the hell did he find in there? Nina thought to herself. *Impossible, he must have taken that thing out of his backpack, that's all … it's a gift for his doctor friend, that's all. Right, that's all it is … just a friendly gesture.*

Nina tried to explain the event as nothing but harmless pleasantries on the part of the strange American, but that feeling of doom continued. She couldn't explain it, but she knew the man was dangerous — she knew he brought trouble with him.

✠

The odd American and the two scholars continued to stare outward towards the lakebeds, and then out to where the sea had once crashed on long-dead shores. The American examined the cliffs that surrounded the area and then inspected his little map again. He looked as if a soul possessed, looking intently with eyes blazing like a madman. The strange American wasn't here to take photos of Egypt or the Holy Land or to collect bric-a-brac or other curios from street vendors. No, this man was here for a different purpose — *but what*, Nina could only inwardly question.

After a few minutes, the professor ambled over to the strange American, and again they began to converse as they both scanned the area. And as the professor pointed to the rock faces and the jagged cliffs of the Peak of Jabal al- Lawz, they spoke as if they were both on a mission, as if two generals preparing for some forthcoming siege. And then they both walked back to the professor's tent. The tent's flap closed, and then — silence.

Now, as dark clouds began to gather, and the distinct sound of rolling thunder began to race towards them, Nina motioned for the driver to go. And as they drove away, she couldn't help but get an awkward feeling that this man, this strange American, wasn't there for the sake of archaeological knowledge or for learning about Semitic history. She inwardly surmised that the man wasn't here to praise Moses for delivering the Jews to the Promised Land. She knew he wasn't here for any *good* reason. She felt it.

Despite her unsettling concerns, Nina just couldn't explain her feelings, now internally admitting that she found herself afraid of the man. This in itself was damning to Nina. She wasn't some lackey tourist agent. Nina Ari had served nine years in the Israeli Army, with three of those years battling terror cells in the Gaza Strip. She had earned the rank of Rav-Negad Mischne in the process and had commanded many troops at that time. Nina Ari didn't feed fear for anything, having faced more than her share of imminent threats in those nine years. She'd give her life for Israel without a second thought, and fight any man for the same sake, but this strange American, having done nothing wrong, had scared her all the same.

Instinctively, Nina reached for her clipboard and turned to the rear section. This is where each tour guide would have photocopies of each passenger, along with a clearance code by the Israeli government, and a remark offering that guide an overall opinion, such as 'cleared and in good standing,' or a warning, usually evident of past legal troubles as reported in each guest's home country. There were no such warnings for any of the guests, but this didn't ease her fears.

Nina turned to the last section in her clipboard. This is where a photocopy of the passports is, as well as photographs of each guest. Now, she examined the details of the odd American and read the date the passport was issued, which was the 4th of May, 1987. Then, she examined each and every location the man had visited. There was the United Kingdom, twice in 1987, and a dozen more times, from late 1992 to the present. Then there were the Netherlands, Belgium, Germany, and Austria, as well as several visits to Switzerland, France, and the Chechen Republic of Ichkeria. Poland and Moldova rounded out his most recent visits to Europe, with Israel being his current trip. Greece, Türkiye, and Egypt were listed on the man's itinerary. Now, she turned back to the man's photo and read the name beneath it.

"Patrick Bush," she muttered, then raising her gaze to the man again. "Patrick Allen Bush. Well, we're quite the traveler, aren't we?" she muttered again. She couldn't take her eyes off the strange man.

Now, as a coldness passed through her stomach, Nina began to wonder just what was allowed into her country. Whether a man or a monster, she didn't know, but her gut feelings were usually right. And right at that moment, her stomach began to ache.

"Mah—atah?" she muttered under her breath. "Mahi ha-matarah shel-kha?"

PART I

CHAPTER ONE

The Body

**J. McNeery Forest Preserve, DeKalb County, Illinois,
Thursday, June 5th, 9:22 A.M.**

Sometime in the Near Future

"It has been written since the beginning of time, even unto these ancient stones, that evil, supernatural creatures exist in a world of darkness. And it is also said man using the magick power of the ancient runic symbols can call forth these powers of darkness, the demons of Hell."

— Night of the Demon, prologue, 1957

"Like one, that on a lonesome road, doth walk in fear and dread, and having once turned round walks on, and turns no more his head; because he knows, a frightful fiend doth close behind him tread."

*— Samuel Taylor Coleridge,
The Rime of the Ancient Mariner, 1798*

It was overcast and muggy that early morning when John Hurst pulled up to the gates of the preserve. He was late again and feared he'd catch hell for it. His late-night benders always took a toll on him, and getting plastered like he was still in his glory days always proved painful the following day; the following three days, if truth be told.

As the old man drove slowly up the path to the main groundkeeper's building, he noticed that the ground was still saturated from the storm that ripped through the town the night before. Tree branches and leaves littered the gravel parking lot, as did an assortment of soda cans, paper cups, and plates from the overturned trash bins. It was a mess, and he knew he would spend the better part of the morning cleaning it up, but he was used to it. Nonetheless, this always made him gripe just a bit louder.

John wanted to wait a few more minutes before getting out of his truck, only until *Hotel California* ended on his newly installed Pioneer 200-EX radio system. The song had made him reminisce about better days when drinking, smoking, and hanging out with his friends back in the early 70s. It was the very meat and bones of his life. He mellowed to the tunes of the Eagles and Led Zeppelin; the Steve Miller Band, Pink Floyd, and a bevy of other awesome groups of the day; the ones that not only lit up the radio airways but had made history in the process. It was a stellar age, and he never stopped thinking about it. He longed to go back to it, to relive those glory days again, and to live in better times. But he knew that would never happen.

Now, John knew full well that those days were really gone for good, having faded away to an age of senseless redundancy, where the music consisted of cookie-cutter pop that would want to make anyone puke, or that violent, racist, America-hating rap, or the God-awful screeching vomited out by pink-haired, nose-ringed, overrated punks that could barely hold a tune. He hated them all, but most of all, he hated their music. It didn't matter if it was Katy Perry or Beyoncé, or Justin Bieber; he just couldn't stand the music of the modern day. For John Hurst, the music of his generation was over and done. For him, it was officially dead and buried.

"What a waste … what a total fuck'en waste," John burbled to himself, his head now shaking in disbelief as one of the Eagles' greatest renditions began to fade from his senses; just as the last of the guitars began to soften and disappear. Having always believed that the song was a story about a man taking a nightmarish journey through the hallways of some cursed hotel in some forgotten desert, or that it had been a poetic representation of the American dream gone awry, John found himself sad that the tune was actually about him and a life slowly being taken away. He felt defeated and empty. John believed — no, he knew that there would never again be great music like that — never again.

As the tune had finally transformed into a commercial, John Hurst switched off the ignition of his 1985 Ford F-150 pickup truck. He waited a few seconds to listen as the 170-horsepower V8 engine wound down. He loved that sound. It always made him reminisce about how much he loved classic cars and how much he loved his perfectly mint classic truck. Now, he smiled as he reached for a cigarette from an almost empty pack of Camels, placed it between his lips, and then lit it. He exited with a grunt of pain; his bones now beat and worse for wear. Regardless, the old man ambled to his grimy, creaky office space that shared a room with an old sit-down lawnmower, along with a dozen or so gasoline cans and an assortment of gritty tools that hung on equally dirty walls. Once inside, he sat down in his old chair and smoked the rest of his cigarette. He had hoped for just another uneventful day to pass, though somehow, he knew that wasn't in the plans.

John was getting up in years and fast approaching his sixty-seventh birthday. He just wanted to forget about it and relive at least a little of his wonder years. Now, he mentally planned for a night of drinking with his friends at Peg & Lou's Tavern down on West Lincoln Avenue. It was a shameless, dirty little pool hall that only bikers, construction workers and the downtrodden would frequent, but John loved the place and just hoped for the workday to be done so he could head on over for a few beers and a couple of snorts of Kentucky bourbon to finish yet another pointless workday.

Now, John found himself daydreaming of getting drunk and listening to the music of his life as he relit the cigarette that hung listlessly from his mouth. He knew that deep down, this was far more desirable than just staying home to think about all the things that were lost to him over the years; the wife who left him for another man, or his kids who wanted nothing to do with him, and even his old dog that barked too much, and who farted enough to clear a room of hardened veterans. He just wanted to go back to his wonder years when he was the high school football star; the quarterback that won not two, but three tri-county championships, when he could actually score with one of those hot, airheaded cheerleaders for a romp behind the bleachers. But that was all ancient history now. He knew it was gone forever.

There wasn't much left for John Hurst these days, and he knew it. Now, he just wanted to have another smoke and a little more coffee before he'd have to fix the old rider-lawnmower, an outdated piece of junk that he'd already repaired dozens of times over the past six months. As he scanned the little shabby shed-slash-office, the man stared at the grimy walls without emotion. Then, he looked inside his now-empty coffee mug; its stains and scratches and a dark brown chip near its rim. It reminded him of his life.

"What a waste," he mumbled sullenly. "What a total fuck'en waste."

✠

"Okay … let's just say no to any and all bullshit today," John muttered as he got up to fetch another mug of coffee. "No old ladies ask'n stupid questions about the ga'damn trees or the damn birds in the park; no damn kids screwing around and spray-paint'n on my shed again, and no sicko faggots creep'en around my bathrooms … I just want a quiet day with no bullshit, please."

John had no problem echoing his sentiments loud and clear. He was loud enough for anyone within twenty feet would hear, but he didn't care. "This old man just wants to breeze through the day, if you don't mind, thank you very much!" he publicly announced, as if someone or something was actually listening to him; as if someone or something would actually have cared.

Having worked for the County Parks and Recreation Department, mostly at the J. McNeery Forest Preserve for close to twenty years now, John was used to seeing a cavalcade of cars pull in through the front gates. Typically, he would watch school buses full of kids pull in, and drop off a dozen or so 'little shits,' as he always referred to children, along with their teachers to look at all the lovely flora and fauna of nature. And then there were the old farts who came in to watch the birds migrate and nest throughout the park. He had watched Little League teams come and go, either in loud cheers of victory or in the sad and gloomy faces of a lost game. He watched life come and go from the preserve, where most of it was benign and uneventful — most of it, anyway.

On occasion, there were others, however, who came to the park for more nefarious activities; those who fell outside of the wholesome families and children, or the old folks looking at nature, or those wishing to hit a home run. No, there were others who came there for nasty reasons; for sick and perverted reasons that only sick and perverted people could ever rationalize.

The police were well aware of the 'sexual' activities that occasionally occurred at the park, though arrests were seldom at best; far *too* seldom in John Hurst's opinion. He'd seen it all over the years, even in the act, no less. And he knew that such things were only going to get worse. He figured that the seal was broken now, that America was lost.

That kind of shit will probably be legal soon; protected by the fucking A—C—L—U, he thought to himself.

John Hurst thought he'd seen it all. He thought that the Vietnam era had been bad, and the twenty or so years in the Middle East were worse, the riots, the insane WOKE agendas, and the sick and twisted behaviour the world was forced to endure, but today; today would be the capstone of what the term 'having seen it all' really meant. He had hoped that Russia's so-called sanctions or special operations in Ukraine, Moldova, and Belarus would simply end, and the war raging in Poland and its neighbours. But he knew without doubt that World War III had already begun. John Hurst had seen a lot, but today was to be the day he would see far more than he would ever want to.

It was just about 9:35 a.m. when a teal-coloured Model 3 Tesla pulled in. Within seconds, an average-looking, plump little man exited from the well-maintained car. And as the thirty-eight to forty-something-year-old man walked — no, as he swayed from the car, gliding in a feminine manner and into the woodland's entrance, John had instantly known why the man was there. For some reason, when it came to this kind of lascivious behaviour, it didn't just rain; it poured.

Now, as the man entered the wooded area, he spoke with someone on his cellphone as he looked over his shoulder and back toward his car. He entered, prompting the weary groundskeeper to shake his head in disgust.

"For Christ's sake, I just said no problems today," John Hurst exclaimed loudly. "Fuck'en queers, always creep'en around my woods!"

Old John Hurst wanted nothing to do with it and instead had continued to scan over the morning's newspaper, though he'd occasionally check the parking lot where the Tesla sat. It gleamed in the light of the now fully risen sun. He knew what went on in the woods, just like the illegal behaviour that would occasionally take place in the bathrooms by the baseball fields. That kind of behaviour went on at least two or three times a week, despite the occasional presence of police vehicles driving through the park or when they'd stop to have their lunch when they parked under the trees at the north end.

If a cop actually got out of his car, and if the 'fags' caught a glimpse of him doing so, they would immediately begin their Hollywood-like acting routine. Most would start pretending they were reading a paperback novel or a magazine, or tossing a baseball to each other. Some would even pull out a camera and make-believe they're on a nature hike, interested in all the beautiful trees and flowers the state of Illinois has to offer. But it was all a well-rehearsed act. It was all a load of bullshit.

John tried to forget about it just enough to get to work and knock out the mandatory chores that were waiting for him in his old shed-slash-office. He nonchalantly scanned his cellphone for the latest news bits and the up-to-date predictions from the Weather Channel app. Now, hearing the slightest hint of thunder rumbling in the distance, he looked out the window again. He noticed that the sky was becoming darker as if a massive cloud had drifted over the park. Now, a wave of darkness seemed to quickly pass overhead, though John had enough time to see that there was a kind of tint to the cloud cover. It was strange.

Now cocking his head to examine the odd-looking sky, John just stared at the almost glowing hue of the day's clouds. There was a reddish-blue tint, not purple per se, but a red and blue colouring that seemed to coat the now overcast clouds. He shrugged off the sight as the oddly- tinted thunderheads formed from the east, though just as they did, the weird colouring simply faded away. Unmoved by the atmospheric oddity, he returned to his cellphone for the latest bits of news gossip. After this, he went to his YouTube site and listened as the unseen commentator of 'The Liberal Hivemind' ranted about President Damar and the state of America and how all was lost.

John laughed. Then, he switched to listen to Charlie Kirk, one of the last great Americans who actually loved his country. He smiled at that thought, sat down again, and just listened. He had earned the break.

✠

John Hurst was anything but politically correct, having mentally fought the exploits of loudmouth and corrupt politicians, mostly the Marxist Democrats that ruled his state with an iron fist, the ones that made the late Joe Biden look like a saint. For a time, he felt that he could finally breathe again during Trump's brief era. Even after the first assassination attempts that were propagated by the insane left wing, he thought he could speak freely in the new age that the Republican Party had left for him. This fleeting morsel of hope ended after the president was murdered, with the vice president shortly after that.

Even as the country was in disarray, Congress had quickly and most efficiently nominated the previous 2024 candidate, Kamala Devi Harris, as the 47th President of the United States. This, John believed, had been the beginning of the end. John believed that with the election fraud that was put into institution after the 2020 elections that the country would never be the same again. This was made evident once Harris's closest confidant, Fathiyya Hind Damar, the Democrat powerhouse from Michigan, had been made Speaker of the House of Representatives. And after the domestic terror attacks that took place after Trump's assassination, the whole world seemed to rally for America's demise. It *was* civil war, after all, even if it were a cold one.

Now, John sniffed loudly and then paused. He had remembered that in those days, the days before Biden, and a seemingly constant cavalcade of Democratic dictators who followed him, that there was still a chance. This all came crashing down once Donald J. Trump was no longer an option for the 2024 election. Now, all seemed lost.

In those days, John gloated at the fact that he didn't have to look over his shoulder every second to find angry, mentally corrupt liberal faces staring him down as if his penis was hanging out. Back then, he looked forward to the day when he didn't have to worry about these atheist weirdoes haunting his every step. He just wanted the day to come when he'd never have to hear the lib-tards telling him how to think or how to live; no more snowflakes or sick feminist whack-jobs debasing him for being a man, or some Black Lives Matter militant attacking him because he was white. Surely, he found himself hating his own country now.

John pondered his thoughts as he stared out the grimy window and into the woods. He just thought of how far his country had fallen now and slowly shook his head in disgust. He was a diehard Republican, and every time he'd hear of Obama in the news every now and then, knowing full well the man had been in his fourth and fifth terms without anyone ever suspecting, he could only cringe at the injustice. And then he'd be reminded of the past nonsensical ranting of the Marxist kooks that had taken over his state.

John hated people like Nancy Pelosi and Maxine Waters and their modern equivalents, but even with them out of the picture, their legacy had remained, and in full force. Today, he considered the bureaucrats as nothing more than traitorous audacities and nothing more, and the new ruling class, those like Harris and Ocasio-Cortez, or Tlaib, or Omar, they were the worst of the worst, all-out communists that were constantly trying to take over and destroy his America.

In the past, John Hurst had always been vocal. It wasn't just his way of venting; it was his American obligation. Now, he could actually be imprisoned for speaking his mind. Today, he could never be sure if change was on the horizon or if viewing a glimmer of hope for the future was even possible. He had always feared for the future of the country and believed he should offer his opinion as any good, red-blooded American should. Secretly, however, his world *had* forever changed, and he knew it.

Though John Hurst bled Republican red, he knew that with the day's mandated censorships and forced behavioural modifications designed and overseen by President Damar's newly formed Ministry of Etiquette and Oversight could change his life dramatically. He knew his opinions could get him arrested and jailed, sent to one of the new 're-education camps' or worse. John feared many things now, especially the president and her staff. She had made Hillary Rodham Clinton look like an inept child in comparison, and for good reasons. The world had changed for the worse.

Like many banana republic nations today, where a citizen with an opposing philosophy could quite literally vanish from the earth, so had many of the president's opponents. And though few would take what John Hurst had to say seriously, he, like many other Americans, had feared all the same — he feared for his very life.

✠

As he finished his second cup of Chock full o'Nuts coffee, John got up to start working on the old mower. He had to replace a filter and clean out the intake, but he knew he had to get it done that day, or he'd be stuck with that, along with the painting of the north field fence that week, so today had to be the day. These days, every day seemed like a heavy work day, just wishing he could retire and go fishing, but there was no such luck. He figured he'd die behind that old, grimy desk, probably while getting chewed out by his immediate supervisor, Barbara Kline. He figured that was the way he'd most likely go.

Now hearing the familiar crunching of wheels over gravel, he looked out the dirty shop window to find another car pulling up and parking in the lot. This time, it was an old, cream-coloured Honda Accord. And though the vehicle was at least an '83 or '84 model, it was in mint condition.

This guy must love the classics, too, he thought. He was impressed by the upkeep of the vehicle. He had respect for anyone who gave such loving attention to older vehicles, just as he did with his old F-150, but there was something odd about the man driving it.

John stood up and wiped the grease from his hands as he stared at the car. "Mint condition," he sputtered arrogantly, though it didn't take long to realize that the man in the Honda wasn't just another guy who appreciated old cars. "Awe, com'on," he muttered to himself. "Just another fuck'en faggot," he concluded. It was the way the man acted as he exited his car, the way he walked, and the way he quietly looked around as if checking to see if the cops were stalking the place.

Though John just stared at the man as he walked into the wooded path, a low rumble of thunder lightly echoed overhead. "Yup, this guy's up to no good," he echoed. His voice boomed throughout the old tin-roofed shed. "Just another ga'damn faggot."

✠

It was around 9:53 a.m. when John opened the overhead garage door. He was on his knees pulling the intake grill off the mower, and just about to begin to de-score the built-up lawn clippings and grunge that had accumulated on the intake's inner shell, when he heard a car door slam shut. Turning around to see who it was, he spotted the old Honda backing up just a bit too fast for a parking lot, and then speeding off through the front gates, leaving a trail of dust and gravel behind him.

"Whoa … that's fast enough, asshole!" John sputtered loudly. Then, he shook his head in disgust and went back to work on the mower. "Must have been a lover's spat," he muttered. This was followed by throwing his head back and cackling forcefully. He was proud of himself for coming up with that remark at a moment's notice.

By 10:26 a.m., John had finished with the lawnmower. He was just about to head over to the baseball field to cut the grass, a task he knew he'd have to get done before repairing the metal grate doors in the men's restroom, when the phone on his desk rang. He just knew it was the office with another request, or worse — a complaint.

Probably to plant some petunias or paint the whole ga'damn place, he thought.

Now, John looked at his cellphone and grunted. "Not even ten-thirty in the ga'damn A.M!"

The old, tattered telephone continued to ring with an impatient tone. It rang a bit too loudly for the battered old thing, which looked like someone had pulled it out of a garbage heap. A single, somewhat red light illuminated through a black, grease-coated button. The words 'Parks and Recreation Number 22' showed up on the display bar. It was the main office located in the downtown Federal Building.

"Morn'en, McNeery Preserve, John speaking," he said in his customary monotone voice, his customary style of speaking to management. It was met with a high, nasally voice that crackled through the receiver.

"Good morning, Mister Hurst, this is Barbara Kline from management … and that's J. McNeery Forest Preserve,' Mister Hurst … please state the entire name of the park when answering the phone."

"Ah, yes, ma'am," he retorted. "Sorry 'bout that."

"Two things; first, we just got a call from someone who didn't want to give out his name, which also came up as a private number on our phone, but he told us that the police need to get out there, and look in the woods, and to just send the police as fast as we can … not sure if it's a crank call or not … do you know what's going on? I just want to make sure there's nothing out of the ordinary taking place in one of our parks."

Not wanting to bring the subject of illegal activity that goes on in the park, and fearing that Mrs. Kline might want him to patrol the woods, he decided to keep still on the subject. There was also the possibility that she was a diehard Democrat, meaning she'd take offence to his opinions, so he quickly figured that remaining silent on the subject would be the better part of valour, and the best way to keep his job.

"No, nothing going on that I can see from here," he said. "There's nothing out of the ordinary … not really."

Barbara Kline took a moment to respond. "Okay, it's probably just a crank call anyway, but just to be sure, when you get a chance, could you please walk through the trails, just to be sure? And, oh yes, you'll also need to get your new insurance and benefits package updated and signed before next Friday, so when you can get that to me as soon as possible, that'll be wonderful … alright?"

"Sure enough, Mrs. Kline," John quickly replied. "I'll get that paperwork in tomorrow or the next day, and I'll check out the trails straight away."

"Very well, Mister Hurst, I'll expect that posthaste."

"Yes, ma'am, I'll call ya back if anything's going on here, but you're probably right; it's probably just some stupid kids playing a joke or sumthin' like that," John continued. He said goodbye and hung up the phone.

Now, John looked out the dirty window again and shook his head angrily. "Fuck'en assholes," he blurted loudly, though just loud enough for anyone within earshot could have heard. Today, he simply didn't care. He just wanted it to be a quick day without any problems, but now that wasn't going to happen. He just wanted everyone to just leave him alone so he could catch up on his work and go home without any incidents. He had hoped for that much, though for some reason, he just knew something was coming.

Now annoyed, John just couldn't help having that still feeling that the shit was about to hit the proverbial fan.

✠

It was just about noon when John decided he should take a quick look in the woods before he started mowing the backfields. As he began to exit his shed-slash-office, he reached for his trusty golf club, an old rusty and pitted five-iron he found in the pastures a year or so ago. He couldn't play golf to save his soul, but he knew he could bash someone's head in with it if it came to that. And though the old man walked at a quicker pace than usual when he carried it, for some reason, he just knew something wasn't right about the whole scene that day. Now, John found himself exhilarated, and perhaps a little frightened too.

A low rumble of thunder sounded as he was nearing the main entrance. He began to notice that the air seemed heavier than that of a normal summer's day, even in that part of Illinois. It could get hot in his state, contrary to what outsiders thought about Illinois. Something was just not right about the quality of the air that day. It felt like an open oven, like when you're cooking a roast at four-hundred and fifty degrees; when you stick your head in to see if it's done.

Damn ... it's oven hot, John thought to himself. It just wasn't right. In addition to the unnatural, sweltering heat, the sky was different, too. And as he looked up through the trees, he noticed the strange colour of the sky and clouds.

"Well shit ... the whole damn sky looks like mustard," he muttered to himself. "Jesus! It looks like watered-down egg yolks. Never seen clouds like that before … don't make a lick of sense."

Yellow sky and heat aside, John entered the wooded entrance and beneath the shaded canopy. He stepped on the old wooden trail and slowly walked in, and then stopped, and waited for his eyes to adjust to the darkness. The area was once a nicely manicured pathway, with varnished wood planks and benches. At one time, there were footlights along the boardwalk too, and flowers in little terracotta pots, but that was years ago. The place had certainly seen better days. Now, rotting and falling apart from age, the boardwalk glistened from the storm that had raged through the park earlier the night before, except for the parts that were covered with a thick, greenish-black mould.

Now, as John walked about a hundred yards or so in, the light that emitted from above and through the dense treetops began to die down. The whole place was taking on an entirely different feel now, as if something was coming or leaving.

Walking forward, John detected the scent of something that was completely unaccustomed to the park. The scent was otherworldly, as if a mixture of burning plastic and decaying meat, with just a touch of something acidic.

"Pee-yew … what the hell is that?" the old groundskeeper muttered to himself. "It smells like swamp gas and … and smoke, and … and rotten eggs." John figured it was just that, swamp gas rearing itself up from the extra hot day, and maybe a dead animal mixed in for extra measure, but he just couldn't be sure.

Now, in what seemed like a haze descending through the treetops, or coming up from the ground, John began to notice that the yellowish tinge of the day was beginning to get duller, and duller. Within a few seconds, everything became darker, except for a strange glow that seemed to linger about the wooded trail. Then, the atmosphere began to change too, as if an oven door was shut, and a freezer door had been opened in its place.

"It's, its frigging cold as hell in here; freezing … geez," he grunted loudly. "What … what's it … is it going to rain now?"

After standing in that spot for what seemed like forty minutes, John walked another twenty feet or so within the woods. He noticed that the gold and brown leaves that usually covered the ground beyond the wooden plank path had been disturbed, scattered, and muddied with the foot traffic from something, as if a scuffle had taken place there. He immediately figured that this is where the 'fags' met to do their dirty deeds; figuring that something might still be going on back there, behind the trees. What's more, he figured that the guy who took off may have been on the up- and-up the whole time and called the number on the exit gate to report such dirty deeds in question.

Sure, that's gotta be it, John thought to himself. *Someone's back there monkeying around. It's probably a couple-a faggots back here, here in my park.* Now getting angry at the thought, Old John Hurst's expression had changed from that of a scared teenager to the look of an authoritarian. He straightened up, pulled his shoulders up, and took a step forward.

"Yeah, your number's up asshole," he muttered. "This time I'm turning you into the cops myself."

✠

John Hurst made his way past the first patch of trees, just beyond the wooden path. He ambled slowly on the wet ground as he scanned the area, but it was too dark. The steam rising from the wet leaves from the heat had obscured his sight, forcing him to squint just to see through the darkened woods. Now, he saw only the twisting of native trees and vines and a collection of soda cans and paper cups from various fast-food restaurants.

"Jesus ... it's a fuck'en mess back here," he snorted, followed by the typical sarcastic quip that was totally commonplace for the man. "I wonder who's gonna clean this crap up?" he continued. "I can guess who ... and how the hell am I supposed to get things done around here when there's always some bullshit I gotta deal with? For God's sake, can't I just have one day without this shit!"

John tried to manoeuvre off the muddy patch as his feet began to sink into the mud. For a minute, he thought he saw the twinkling of tiny lights as if someone was looking at the face of their cellphone from within the dark thickets. For a minute, he thought he heard the fluttering of wings, like the tiny wings of small birds or maybe bats. John knew what bats sounded like, having visited his little brother Tom in Arizona. He remembered the mass of bats that had nested under a bridge near his house. He remembered the ammonia-like smell of guano, too; a scent that may have explained the swampy smell he'd been treated to that morning.

"Fuck'en creepy shit, man," he quietly grunted. "There better not be bats out here … I ain't be'n paid enough to deal with that."

Now, as the fluttering or squeaking sound faded away, he continued to check the surrounding area. A moment later, he saw what looked like a light again; a very soft, pale violet light coming from behind a mass of trees. And just as he cleared a path just enough to see more of the odd light, it started to shrink to a tiny mass or cloud of dull illumination just as he was beginning to get a closer look at it. And in seconds, it had vanished just as quickly as he had seen it.

For an instant, he thought he saw the shape of a man, like a large, black figure standing behind a thick tree, but it too had simply vanished from sight. For a second, he thought he saw the flash of two tiny eyes glistening from a scant ray of the sun, but that too winked away. Whatever it was, it was gone.

After a few seconds, the sound of low, rumbling thunder echoed in the distance, prompting John to just stand in place, dumbfounded, but curious. He watched as tiny specks of light spun around, like a miniature vortex or tornado spinning with grey or blue, illuminated particles of what seemed to be glitter within its mass. And then, the weird funnel-looking cloud just faded away, as if simply dissolving into nothing. Within seconds of this, the yellowish, misty haze that had enveloped the woods had suddenly lifted.

Now, John just stood there a moment and considered the event. It was as if someone had opened a window and let out smoke from a room; as fresh air had just blown out a cloud of dust, even though this dust had almost glowing particles spinning along with it. And in the seconds following this, it had become eerily silent under that dark canopy. Not a chirp from any bird or a squeak from a squirrel could be heard. It was as if all of nature had quickly gotten up out of their nests and underground holes, and took off in fright. The place was as quiet as a tomb.

"Well shit," John muttered, "Must have been mosquitoes or gnats or sumthin' … no big deal, I guess … unless it's bats." John was still worried, and there was no doubt that there was a hollow feeling in his gut. Now, he felt his flesh creep ever so slightly.

✠

As John slowly furthered his step, looking for any sign of the spinning bugs and the strange light, he could see what looked like a pair of fancy, cream-coloured sneakers, with the toes facing upward, as if someone was lying on the ground. At first, he thought it was a man lying on his side with his pants pulled halfway down, exposing his fat buttocks, but he couldn't be sure.

"Oh, that's just nice, you … you scumbag," he said in a low, yet authoritative voice. "Hey! Hey! Get up, dude! Com'mere, buddy! What the hell are you doing? Now, get the hell up! Get—uhh—"

John's voice ceased with what his mind finally deciphered from a visual fantasy he only thought was his imagination. He stood still there for a moment or two and tried to fully comprehend what he was seeing. Now, he had to squint in order to get a full view of what lay on the ground ahead of him. And as his feet began sinking even deeper into the wet mud, he finally realized what he was seeing — pure, unadulterated horror. The man on the ground was dead.

The shape on the ground, the human shape that lay outstretched and with one leg lying over the other, had all been stained with a mass of blood and gore covering an off-white or light-green shirt. And his head; his head faced John with a horrendous expression on its face, as the rest of his body was twisted like some kid's discarded toy, its lower half looking as if it had been twisted completely around, and then back in place to its side. The image was simply horrible and utterly surreal.

Reminds me of … of that Stretch Armstrong doll we used to play with, He immediately thought to himself. *No, no, that was Tom's Stretch Armstrong doll … all twisted and … and, and all bent outta shape … Jesus!*

John just stood there; he stood there for what seemed like another forty minutes, but what was in truth only a few seconds. He couldn't stop thinking about his brother Tom's Stretch Armstrong doll, imagining this guy was stretched and pulled just like that old doll was, way back in the early '70s. Then he let out a sound, like that of a gasp or a scream that was cut short as if he had just gotten a slug to the gut. John truly realized what he was seeing now. He was scared — no, he was terrified — he was completely, and utterly terrified.

CHAPTER TWO

Once the old groundskeeper came to his senses and realized just what he was seeing, he took off as if his life depended on it. Now, he ran for dear life, haphazardly following the muddy trail path and having to repeatedly pull his work boots out of the thick muck and sludge. Once onto the wet, wood-plank path, he slipped and fell to his knees in the sprint. This was followed by a cracking-thud sound. No matter the pain, however, he got up as fast as his old bones would allow him and hobbled as fast as he could back to the old makeshift office.

"What the hell! It's freezing again and, and everything's blue, like … what's this blue light shining over everything … what the hell's going on!?" he grumbled loudly. Even though he was in considerable pain, he hadn't sprinted like that since 1974 when he was able to outrun Mike Flanagan, Riverside High's best quarterback. That was the first time he won his first tri-state championship, but instead of running to win, the old man ran to escape a similar fate to that of the twisted and gorged body lying in the woods.

Jesus, I wish I was there, back at school right now, he thought.

John knew he had that old magic back again, even if it only got him back to the old office. When he finally reached the open garage door of the shed, he looked behind him to make sure he wasn't being followed. And it only took a second to pull down the overhead door as fast as he could, lock it, and then jaunt to the front entrance, scrabble in, and shut the heavy door. In haste, he pulled the bolt over and locked it. Now out of breath, he just stood there and panted while a cold sweat ran down his face.

"I just saw a fucking dead body ... Jesus!" he yelled with the full range of his lungs. "What the hell's go'en on here?" He stood there a moment and began to shake just enough to notice it. He looked around to make sure no one was in there with him, knowing full well that a little paranoia might just save his ass. "The cops!" he blurted. "Oh, no shit ya old fart, of course, the cops ... I need to call the cops!"

Picking up the old, outdated telephone, his first thought was to call Barbara Kline back at the main office, but then, coming to his senses, he quickly smashed the quick dial button for 911. The receiver rattled in his hand as the dispatch operator answered, but John stumbled with his words. After a few seconds, he cleared his throat and sat down hard on the edge of his desk.

"Yes, yes, my name's John, ah, John Hurst!" he bellowed into the phone's receiver. I, ah, I work with the Department ... ah, the Department of Parks and Recreation ... with the county, at McNeery Park! ...um, ah, I have, I think I found a body, a dead body here, here in the woods, on the path ... near the pathway ... at the McNeery Forest Preserve Park!"

The operator asked John to calm down, and then began to ask the typical questions: when and where, and what did he see, exactly, and questions like that. She then told the frightened groundskeeper to stay away from the body, which, from the description John had given her, was clearly a crime scene. She told him to make sure no one else goes in that area. Then, she asked him to secure the front entrance to the woods if possible, so no one would touch anything, and to watch for anyone trying to leave the park. She told him not to try and stop anyone, but to get as many details as possible, and to get any information as he could about any person or persons leaving the area; all cars, makes, and models, and things like that.

The police dispatch officer went on to say that he should close the main gates until the police arrived, that patrol units had been notified, and that they were on their way. John wasn't comforted by the operator's reassurance or orders. He just couldn't help thinking that he might be the next victim, like one of those poor saps in one of those slasher movies from the 1980s, the ones where some guy who wore ratty overalls and a dirty mask would hunt you down and start stabbing you with a huge butcher's knife.

"No, thank you, ma'am!" he said aloud. "I'm, stayin' right here if you don't mind!" Now feeling a cold shrill pass down his back, the old man picked up his five-iron and nervously fondled it. "Ma'am, I'm stayin' right here in my office till the cops come, okay?"

The operator agreed and said she'd notify the officers en route. And with that, the old groundskeeper hung up the phone and kept vigil by the window. Now, he would keep one eye on the front gates and the other on the wooded entrance. His whole body shook at the thought of some crazed killer racing out of those dark woods, and it showed.

✠

At just about 11:20 a.m., two DeKalb County patrol cars pulled up to the front gates. Quick like, John ran over to them as fast as he could, feeling like a swimmer trying to out-swim a fast-approaching shark. He constantly looked over his shoulder as he ran, as if the killer was right behind him, running for dear life. When he reached the gate, he pulled the bar back to release it and swung the metal gate inward with considerable force. No time for the padlock that slinked to the dusty rubble beneath the gates. Instinctively, John jumped out of the way for the cars to pull in, impatiently waving his hands to direct the police in.

For the first time in the last thirty minutes, or was it the last thirty years, John had felt safe. Now, he was somewhat relieved knowing that the police had arrived, but he continued to shudder and shake like a child lost in a big city.

As the first police officer got out of his patrol car, a young man around the age of thirty-five to thirty-eight quickly represented himself as Officer Matt Culberson. John introduced himself and then began telling the officer what he had discovered. The young officer quickly followed by asking the most obvious questions. He wanted to know where the body was, if anyone else was in the park, if he had seen anyone in the area, and questions like that. The young cop was one hundred percent serious, but as cool and as unmoving as a statue.

Pointing towards the southeast section of the forest, John waved his hand towards the wooded section where an opening could be seen. "It's on that path, just around fifty or so yards in; towards the right, and behind some trees there," he yelped. "You can't miss it … but I, I'm not going back in there!"

Officer Culberson, looking in that direction and then back at John, asked him exactly what he'd seen. John just offered a confused look, most likely trying to understand why the cop wasn't running back to the crime scene.

"Ah, there's a dead man, ah, a body lying on the ground just past the trees a ways," he said. "He's covered in blood and his head; Jesus, his, his heads bent all funny … there's no way this guy's alive … no way, no how!"

Officer Culberson waited and listened to the groundskeeper. And within seconds, his shift supervisor pulled in through the gates. Sergeant Jacqueline 'Jackie' Stearns quickly stopped her patrol car. She gave John a hard look while talking on the little radio she had attached to her right shoulder, but showed little emotion. Sergeant Stearns was a dark-haired woman of about thirty to thirty-five or so years of age. And though she was official-looking, she radiated a beauty few female cops could rival. And when she got out of her patrol car, John could quickly surmise that although she was thin and graceful, she also had that *fuck with me and you're toast* kind of look. This, John knew for sure.

Sergeant Jackie had prompted almost forgotten emotions in the old groundskeeper. He had actually found himself becoming slightly aroused by the official-looking woman. Quickly, however, he turned to face the other officer in embarrassment. Now, Sergeant Stearns breezed over to where Officer Culberson and John Hurst were standing and quietly and quite eloquently began asking questions of her subordinate.

"What's the story, Mike ... what do we have here?"

Officer Culberson walked up to his superior and began to whisper something to her. He'd look back towards John Hurst every few moments but made it clear that he wanted to say something in private. Then, he turned to the old groundskeeper and asked him to close the gates behind them and to make sure that no parkgoers or anyone else were to enter or leave the area and that he was only to let in the other police vehicles when they arrived. Then he asked John to wait over by the two patrol cars. The man grumbled something but complied with the orders.

As he began meandering toward the vehicles, John continued to watch silently in the wooded area. He didn't see anything even overtly frightening, but he just knew that someone could still be back there, waiting and preparing for another kill. This had sent yet another cold chill down his back, but he had faith in the police. And besides, they were so close.

After a few minutes, Sergeant Stearns walked over to the old groundskeeper to begin her interrogation. He just watched as the beautiful woman sauntered slowly and quite seductively over to him. And with her notepad in hand and a serious, though sexy smile on her face, the old man had felt a warm flush pass through his stomach.

"Mister Hurst, can you tell me if there are any other people in the park?" she asked.

"Ah, no, it was still too … was still too early at the time," he said. "Well, no, wait a second, just the two cars, the two people that got here about nine or so … the guy back there and another guy who took off like a bat-outta- hell!" He pointed to the new Tesla parked in the east parking lot. "That's the one over there, the sissy car, but the other one took off as I said!"

Sergeant Stearns smiled at the comment and cocked her head slightly. "Like a bat-outta-hell, Mister Hurst?" she asked. This was followed by a slight smile.

"Ah … yes, ma'am."

"I see. And what do you mean by a sissy car, Mister Hurst?" she asked with a questioning look.

"Well, ah … you see … weird things go on here from time to time, Miss, ah … Sergeant … that ah, well … men meet here sometimes to do things in our bathrooms and in those woods, you know?" John was clearly feeling a little nervous now, especially as he almost busted out the word 'faggot' or 'queer' to the cops. He didn't want to believe it, but had quickly surmised that Sergeant Sterns might actually be a dyke herself. He figured he'd have to use a little decorum just in case.

"Please continue, Mister Hurst."

"Well, ya' know …gay things," John said in a low, shaky voice.

"I see. Alright, Mister Hurst," Sergeant Sterns said with a struggling grin. "Could you show us where the body is?"

Now, John was still a bit confused, but pointed towards the wooded entrance. "In that opening, over there," he quickly blurted. "It's, I don't know, maybe a dozen or so yards in, and then, ah, at the right side, just a bit!"

Understanding that the man was scared, Sergeant Stearns just nodded at the man. "Alright, Mister Hurst, just stay here, please. When the other patrol cars arrive, just open the gates and instruct them of our location ... and please ... make sure you close the gates after they're in, understood?"

John nodded his head and watched as the two officers proceeded towards the entrance and then disappeared into the canopy of the dark woods. He watched as the lady Sergeant walked away, as she seductively fanned away from him.

Lord, hope she ain't no lesbo ... she's just plain, outright sexy, he thought to himself, now with a noticeable leering expression rising on his face. It was then that John noticed that the sky was normal again, not a sickly yellow or a royal, day-glow blue or red or purple; it was just another hazy-blue sky with the typical, billowy clouds that slowly drifted by. Now, he leaned up against the gate and arched his head back to examine the sky. It wasn't as hot as an open oven, nor was it as cold as a walk-in freezer; it was just as normal as it was before the day had started, before all hell broke loose.

John Hurst had remembered the other things he saw in the woods, like the twisting and turning of some kind of glowing particles, but that was probably just gnats or mosquitoes buzzing around. And then there was the big, black shadow of a man, or what he had thought was a man, standing behind a big oak tree, but he figured he'd keep that to himself. He couldn't explain the vision, but he knew that it was human-shaped, and more than that, he thought he had seen the dark man's eyes glistening through the misty haze of that mouldering grotto.

Regardless of what he saw, or thought he saw, he knew that the hulking black shape that seemed to loom in the darkness didn't just appear there by magic. And yet, he just knew it couldn't have been a man — it just couldn't have been.

✠

By 12:05 p.m., another patrol car pulled up to the gate, with a police van close behind it. On the side of the van, large blue letters spelled out the words: *DEKALB COUNTY POLICE CRIME SCENE INVESTIGATION.* Now, John Hurst stood by the gate and just shook his head at the sight of the activity. He quickly realized that it wasn't only going to be a busy day but that his plans for leaving on time were simply shot.

Looks more like one of those fancy, private electricians' vans, he thought to himself. *Like something a high-priced journeyman from Oak Park might drive.* He thought it looked out of place.

Once patrol unit number eighty-six had stopped and parked next to the other police vehicles, with the van parking more towards the wooded area, John quickly closed the gates behind them and just stood there. Soon after that, several cars and yet another van were quickly making their way towards the park, leaving a cloud of billowy, grey dust behind them as they sped towards the gate. But they were clearly not with the police; at least, that was the first impression John had received.

The van that followed had WKAX CHANNEL 13 stenciled on its sides. It was one of the local Chicago news services. John figured it might have been affiliated with one of those major liberal outlets, like CNN or MSNBC, but he didn't care. He wanted to tell his story all the same. He needed to tell someone.

Fuck the lib-tards, he thought, *I'm gonna be on the ga'damn news tonight! People gotta know about this shit!* Now, he opened the gate and walked out, then closed it behind him. He adjusted his belt, tucked his shirt in, and patiently waited for his big opportunity. Meanwhile, Officer Culberson and Sergeant Stearns had made their way to the scene with little hindrance.

They found it just as the groundskeeper had described it. The body was mangled, and the head was facing them, towards the old boardwalk. The neck was obviously broken. And though they had maintained a good distance from the wet ground where the body lay, the young officer had seen more than his share of dead bodies, though not as strange as the one he was inspecting at that moment. This one wasn't only out of place — it was downright bizarre.

Officer Culberson was young but had served a little over five years with the United States Army and had made it through two full tours in the Iraqi Civil War, primarily in the

Anbar, Al Qaim, and Fallujah campaigns. But it was just after being deployed with the 11th MEU in the Syrian region of Manbij that he was medically discharged for a serious, though manageable bout of colitis, a condition that reared its ugly head just when things were becoming interesting for him. Nonetheless, he had seen combat up close and personal and had known the effect of ballistics, as well as what humans could do to another human. What lay ahead of him, however, had not been done by either of them. That much, he knew for sure.

Though Officer Culberson only completed a 'stint' in the service, as he put it, his military experience was exceptional. His history clearly told of an experienced and well-trained soldier who had seen and done what civilian society never sees and never does. Nevertheless, having served with the Rangers' First Battalion during that time, towards the end of his career, he had more than enough understanding of human anatomy as far as how to *properly* kill a man. And as he surmised what was lying before him that afternoon, he at least knew that it wasn't an ordinary homicide.

Though he was relatively green as a police officer, Officer Culberson understood full well that snapping a man's neck like that wasn't as easy as it seemed, especially as depicted in the movies or on a television crime drama. No, breaking a man's neck took far too much effort and was surely not the first choice when endeavouring to kill a man, not for a smart killer, that was for sure. Now, he just exchanged a glance with his sergeant.

Sergeant Stearns crossed her arms and then made a low grunt. "Whoever did this either had unbelievable strength, or it was done by more than one person," she said.

"Yeah … it looks that way, doesn't it?" Officer Culberson mumbled as he began to take notes. "This scene doesn't make sense, not for a typical homicide, anyway; not from any typical, random murder," he concluded. Sergeant Stearns just nodded her head, but she didn't say anything. She just continued to jot down her take on the scene and then began to take photos of the area with her cellphone. Just after she took her first photo, her cell vibrated in her hand. This had effectively jolted her senses, as well as her ad hoc photo session. For a second, Officer Culberson could have sworn that his sturdy supervisor had jumped a little.

"You all right, boss?" he asked cautiously.

She just looked at the man with a serious expression and nodded. Then, she answered the call. She just listened and lightly grunted that she understood. She disconnected the call and then just stared at the body. She seemed perplexed.

"What is it, sarge?"

Sergeant Stearns just shook her head. "Dispatch advises us not to have anyone remove the body, nor is CSI to tamper with anything until an FBI representative gets here," she snorted in disgust. "And that's not a request." She looked over to Officer Culberson again, this time with a half-hearted smile. "Typical, isn't it?" she grunted. "The feds always get to muck things up for us, don't they? You'd think we were incompetent morons or something."

"Ain't that the truth?" Officer Culberson mumbled back.

"Alright, let's just secure the area, drop some tape, and we'll work the report together, sound good?"

"Yup, sure ... whatever you say." Officer Culberson continued to stare at the body. He looked around the whole area, trying desperately to figure the whole crime scene out for himself, but the layout didn't make sense. There were footprints and some scattered leaves, but not in a fashion to suggest a fight had taken place there. And if the body was tossed, it would have had to have been at least fifteen feet from the boardwalk, and then around a large tree, so the entire scene just didn't add up. None of it gelled for the young cop. He'd seen lots of horrible things in his brief military career, but this was anything but typical — anything but normal.

The two officers began putting crime scene tape around the posts that line the wooded trails and then radioed the other units of their progress. By the time they started writing notes for their incident reports, however, the buzzing of the news crews became obvious. Now, a selection of reporters had kept watch from behind the gates but had kept their distance until they would *officially* be given the scoop. The news crew, however, had quickly, though incorrectly, assumed that the scene appeared cut-and-dry to them, like any other death or homicide, though it was the police activity that made them think differently.

Even though none of them had yet seen the carnage that lay sprawled in the thickets just off the wooded path of the park's nature trails, they all figured that it was either a drug deal that went wrong or something as simple as an old man having a heart attack. They hadn't seen what Officer Culberson and Sergeant Stearns had seen, not what the old groundskeeper, John Hurst, had seen.

Back at the front gate, the newshounds with WKAX Channel 13 were relentless, actually setting up their own yellow and black 'Do Not Cross' tape around the posts, just in front of the main gates. The yellow and black-striped tape fluttered in the breeze, while a busty blonde beauty stood before a camera waiting for the red light atop of it to begin glowing.

Immediately, a chubby man with curly red hair gave a countdown with his fingers, just as the blonde beauty shifted her skirt and adjusted her breasts. John just watched the whole scene as the news teams set up their own little portable studios, while the red-haired man gestured the number three, the number two, and then the number one with his fingers. Now, the little red light atop the camera went on, and the show began.

This guy looks like that comedian from Freaks and Geeks, or maybe that fat guy from the 40-Year-Old Virgin, John thought to himself. The thought had let him crack the first smile he'd had that whole day.

Now, the blonde beauty chimed in with an official tone and demeanour. "This is Channel Thirteen News, and I'm Gloria Severn with a live report coming to you from the J. McNeery Forest Preserve, where an apparent homicide has taken place in this quiet neighbourhood park ... in what sources report as a grisly murder. We wait for police correspondence to keep us informed of the latest information ... please stay tuned for further updates ... seen here, only on Channel Thirteen."

As soon as the little red light had turned off, the burly man tilted his head away from the camera and silently nodded to let her know the take had gone well and that the shot was clear. Now, the blonde beauty, her smile now dimming to a frown, and with her hands resting firmly on her hips, just stared at the Seth Rogan look-alike cameraman with a disgusted look.

"How are we supposed to do this right when I haven't anything to report on, Ryan? I don't have any details on this; nothing at all ... nothing from the station yet, and the police aren't helping either; there's not a bit of info to work with. Look, we're gonna need more if I'm going to get this in time for a news alert, and maybe not even by five at the rate we're going. I'm telling you right now, somebody's gonna have to spill, or we're gonna be finished here, and that ain't happening, Ryan ... not on my shift!"

"Right," the burly man retorted unemotionally. He pulled out his cellphone and then waited for the agitated woman to give him his orders.

After a few moments of stressed contemplation, the blond beauty adjusted her breasts again, scratched her chin, and then exhaled loudly. "Call the station again, Ryan, and then go grab the makeup kit, please ... I probably look like that stiff in the forest ... Christ!" she barked.

A few seconds later, the white coroner's van was seen driving on the dusty road, followed by a pale blue- coloured car with dark windows. Behind them, two or three other police vehicles followed, with their blue and red lights letting everyone know that something big was going on, while in the distance behind them, two other news vans, WKAB CHANNEL 2 and WINS CHANNEL 9, were quickly approaching. They were almost completely hidden in the dust cloud made by the vehicles ahead of them.

John Hurst continued to wait patiently for one of the newshounds to question him about his experience, but they had caught a glimpse of the approaching vehicles and were fumbling over themselves to get as much information as they could get out of them once they parked. Such was the nature of the news business.

Now a little rattled by all the attention, John tucked his shirt in and made sure his pants zipper was up. He normally didn't like commotion or too much activity in general, but he *was* the first one on the scene, after all.

Channel Nine ... oh yeah. Hopefully, it's that redheaded broad with the big tits, he thought. *Yeah, that'd be sweet enough for me.*

✠

The vehicles pulled in just after 12:25 p.m., parking at the farthest section of the park, near the CSI van. Within seconds, two men exited the rear doors of the coroner's van, while a young woman exited from the driver's side door.

This is just like one of those cop shows, John muttered to himself, as he stood frozen by the front gate. He watched the scene while at the same time keeping a close eye on the busty blonde beauty. "God, I wish she'd bend over or something," he softly muttered. "I'd love to see that sweet rack of hers."

The men from the coroner's van pulled out a gurney, carried it above the gravel parking lot, and then placed it on the wooded pathway that juts from the trail's entrance. The woman, a girl no more than twenty-two, twenty-four tops, began making a call on her cellphone. The bystanders, of course, might imagine the fantastic, but for the coroner's technicians, this was just another pick-up ... just another cadaver to schlep back to the county morgue.

John just watched with his mouth ajar, trying to disbelieve the audacity of the news outlets today. He watched as the busty blond beauty went over line after line of made-up nonsense about the body, a body that none of them had even seen yet. Now, he could only snicker and leer as he watched the spectacle.

"What the hell ... why would they just push out bullshit like that?" John silently reflected. "They didn't even talk to anyone ... not the cops, not to me, nobody ... what the fuck is this shit?" John just watched in disbelief as he shook his head. "Ga'damn fake news ... ain't anything real anymore?" he muttered. "Anything at all?" He looked down and then up again in a sad look of disbelief and continued to slowly shake his head.

As John gazed towards the section furthest from the front gate, he could see the mobile antenna tower lifting from the roof of one of the news vans. Another news van was parked a few spaces down, with three or four people buzzing around setting up their own little makeshift studios. The scene looked like a hornet's nest after being hit with a rock. And after a few minutes of watching the spectacle, John found himself disgusted by what he was watching. It was insane.

Now, John believed that all those homemade videos he had watched on YouTube had been the truth after all. He figured that there are conspiracy theories and then there's the truth — but now he knew that what was going on now was nothing but bullshit.

After a few moments of trying to figure out just what was going on around him, John noticed movement in the plain white patrol car that was parked closer to the gates, the one with no blue and red lights on top of it. The doors finally opened, and two young men no more than forty years of age got out. "These guys must be the detectives, with their fancy suits and their department store ties … and spiffy shoes," John mumbled with a smirk.

The two men quickly walked over to where the other police officers were mingling together, quickly scanning the whole place as they did. After a few minutes of speaking to each other, they quickly walked onto the wooded trails and disappeared into the darkness.

"Now they'll see what I was talk'en about," John mumbled. "Shit … they'll see that I wasn't exaggerate'en."

✠

By 12:35 p.m., the driver's side door of the light blue Crown Victoria finally opened. It had been parked next to the coroner's van since they had all pulled in, but whoever drove the car just waited. John suspected he might have been another detective or maybe some kind of field supervisor, but he couldn't be sure.

Some kind-a big-wig with the cops must be on the scene now … probably been making a phone call to his superiors or something, he thought. He watched as the latest pair of cops to arrive on the scene walked over to the remaining police officers. There were six of them now, all huddled together like football players just before a big skirmish.

The cops talked and then chuckled at something that must have been funny. Officers Frank Dumont and Rebecca Manning both had corporal ranks on their collars, and they had commanded the experienced look so commonplace with cops who have seen it all. With Officer Manning, her thumbs securely hooked under her utility belt, and Officer Dumont, with the way he looked around with profound seriousness, the whole scene gave off a crime drama feel.

Maybe I should wait for that David Caruso character to walk in with his fancy sunglasses, John thought to himself, now clearly laughing behind what was left of his yellowed teeth.

Within a moment, the man from the Crown Victoria exited and stood up from his car seat, shut the door, and slowly approached the huddled cops. He pulled out a little black notepad from his jacket pocket and then a pen from his shirt pocket. Now, the cops all began turning their radios down as they watched the man approach, waiting desperately to see what the mysterious gentleman had to say. And just as the gaunt and prematurely grey man had quickly flashed a badge, the private conference commenced.

Meanwhile, the news reporters quickly began swarming the gate where John Hurst was standing. They began asking him who he was and who he was affiliated with, and questions like that. One of the news team interns in the Channel 13 van had called the station to see if they could get any answers by running the plate on the light blue Crown Victoria, but they couldn't get any information. The grey-haired man was a mystery, and the newshounds didn't like being left in the dark, especially when a potentially huge story was breaking. Unless they could scoop it and report it before their rivals did, such would be a failure for any reporter, and it didn't take long for the busty blonde beauty to begin grilling John Hurst for information.

"Sir ... who are you? Do you work here in the park ... sir?"

John just stared at the lovely image before him. *Damn, she's got big tits*, he immediately thought as he tried desperately to maintain his attention to her eyes instead of her breast, answering her with what he thought were simple enough responses, like giving his name and his position at the park. Thankfully, it didn't take long for Officer Culberson to see what was going on at the gate and abruptly call out to the man as the military-looking cop quickly walked toward them.

Officer Dumont turned his gaze to the blond beauty and barked out at her as if he were her drill sergeant.

"You know better than that, Gloria ... and you already know the drill ... when we have something for you, we'll get that information to you and not before ... okay?"

"C'mon, Frankie, what's the big deal?" the now agitated newswoman yelled back. "You've helped us out before ... just give me something to report, just a little meat ... I can make that last all night with just a little info, what do ya say?" She knew Frank Dumont well enough to know that he liked her body, catching him on more than a few occasions checking her out when he thought she wasn't looking, and even when she was. "What do ya say? Just give me a few details, Frankie ... is it, is it one victim, two, or more?"

The busty blonde had unbuttoned her blouse when he looked away for a moment, figuring that a little cleavage could go a long way, and then she asked one more time; this time, in a less demanding tone. "C'mon ... is it a homicide, an accident, or what?" The attractive newshound was trying as best she could to get anything from Officer Dumont. Despite her soft wiles and extra-exposed cleavage, she was failing miserably. This was practically unforgivable for any woman, especially when knowing that her smok'en hot body wasn't working.

"Ah ... you got to be kidding me," she burbled.

"I have my orders, Gloria!" Officer Dumont snapped with a smile. "But ... you'll be the first to know when we get the go-ahead, I promise. Now, you'll have to leave Mister Hurst alone, okay? He's got nothing to say to you, not right now, understand?"

The attractive reporter looked depressed, with a half-sideways smirk on her face. "Okay," she said, "just, just please flag me down when you have something for me ... please?" Then she started walking away, halfway backwards, making one last attempt to sway the young cop. "Maybe we could have a drink," she said softly, "maybe later on, you know … just, ah … just let me know, okay?"

Officer Dumont smiled, turned quickly, and walked away. He smiled because he knew full well what she was up to. "What a frigging tease," he mumbled as he walked away.

John Hurst held his tongue now, figuring he'd blown it, talking to the press and all. He figured the blonde beauty, though attractive and having larger than average breasts, was just about to squeeze him and twist his words all around. He didn't want to believe it, but he remembered watching CNN as one of those horrible female commentators made jokes about Donald Trump back before the 2024 elections. They were monsters.

John remembered Rachel Maddow and Joy Reid, their evil laughter, and how utterly unprofessional they all were. They claimed to be unbiased journalists, too, but when they laughed at his assassination, that was the wake-up call. No, this woman standing before him could be like that bitch on CNN.

Maybe she'd even implicate me in something … maybe even link me to the murder in the woods, he thought, his mind now reeling because he had fallen for what had to be a lie. Now, he believed that the blonde beauty was just taking advantage of him. He felt used.

✠

Officers Culberson and Dumont were talking with the cryptic-looking, grey-haired man from the light-blue Crown

Victoria. The men remained silent, ignoring the annoying press slugs for what they were: nuisances and authors of the worst kind of yellow journalism and nothing more. The image was amusing because the police officers had all known that feeling and the gesture that typically followed. As such, they couldn't help but chuckle a little at the snubbing.

Now, as the three men approached the main gate, Officers Culberson and Dumont began giving the standard orders of the day; orders for the press to keep calm and to stay out of the way. Meanwhile, the grey-haired man flashed his badge again, but only to John Hurst.

Federal Bureau of Investigation, John repeated in his mind. The badge had looked real enough, but he quickly inspected it again just in case. Then, he looked up at the man, now with a scared-straight expression. Despite this, the federal agent smiled to ease the old man's nerves.

"Mister Hurst?" the agent said politely. "I'm Special Agent Le'fadden, and we're investigating a few similar incidents like the one you stumbled on this morning. I'm going to need some information if you don't mind."

"No, no, of course, ah … whatever you need, sir," John Hurst mumbled back. It was as if he were in shock, but the man seemed calm and unaffected by the events of the day. And as the agent gently placed a hand on John's shoulder, he slowly led him away from the clamour of the now-chattering journalists.

Special Agent Le'fadden and John Hurst slowly ambled away from the agitated reporters, even though they continued trying to capture the old man's attention.

Regardless, the grey-haired agent continued to ignore them; knowing full well that this would really piss off the press, depriving them of the information they so desperately coveted. And though the man was certainly a mystery, Special Agent Le'fadden always took pleasure in snubbing the overly 'in-your-face' newshounds. It was a sinless pleasure for him, but he enjoyed it all the same. Now, he began speaking quietly to John of his intentions while motioning for him to walk away from the now busy gate.

John had noticed that the man's face was like a painting, unmoving and serious, with eyes securely hidden behind dark Ray-Ban sunglasses. The agent gave off a look of professionalism but also a look of some secretive purpose. Despite the overuse of aftershave and wearing seriously outdated clothing, John found himself unnerved by the man. Despite the first impression, however, Special Agent Le'fadden was polite when he asked about the events of his morning, how he discovered the body, and what time he discovered it.

The agent jotted down notes in his little black flip notebook, looking up at John every few moments while writing. The agent then asked questions that didn't make a whole lot of sense to him. Of course, John expected to get grilled by the police, but surely not by someone from the FBI. Now, he figured the incident in the woods must have been very important.

What kind of questions are these, John thought? *Man ... weird questions for a Fed to ask ... I don't get it.* Thinking that it's one thing for the FBI to be there, which was weird enough, but with his particular line of questions, such had made the old groundskeeper even more nervous, forcing him to contemplate why the weather and the temperature could have anything to do with the dead man in the woods. And more than that, why the absence of animals or birds would have been important to the FBI.

In a moment of clarity, John began to understand. The questions the stalwart-looking, grey-haired agent had asked were not only pertinent to that morning's horror show — they were spot-on. John just looked at the agent with questioning eyes, thinking it all might have happened before, or maybe that there was some kind of weather- altering disease causing it, or that there might be a serial killer loose in DeKalb. His mind raced with what-ifs.

With this new reflection, John then related what he had experienced in full detail.

The man felt a little stupid, of course, but he told the truth. All of it.

After John Hurst offered the morning's events to the grey-haired agent, and in detail, the agent had learned of the weird atmosphere: the watered-down, egg yolk-coloured sky, the day-glow blue and reddish-haze, and the darkness that fell over the woods immediately after that. And it had been obvious that the old groundskeeper was earnest about the events, as his agitation had proved.

The man continued to relate how he couldn't forget the intense heatwave that had suddenly occurred, and then the frigid blast of cold air that took place only moments after that. John even recalled the fact that the wooded area of the park, which was usually filled with birds and little animals like squirrels and raccoons, wasn't there the time he was on the pathway; the time he discovered the body, when the weather went all funny.

In an instant, John wasn't scared anymore — he was utterly terrified all over again.

✠

Agent Le'fadden thanked John for the information and shook his hand. He asked him to keep quiet about the details and that the press would likely be breathing down his neck for the next few days. He told him that the newspapers might be calling him at work or even at his home and that he might actually be stalked by reporters for information. As the agent walked away, he turned and smiled at John and offered some sound advice —

"Stay vigilant, Mister Hurst," he grunted. "Law enforcement will be watching this area more closely now ... so please be sure to keep this incident to yourself. If you remember anything you might have forgotten or that might help us in this investigation, please ... please inform us."

"Yes, sir, I surely will," John barked back.

"And if anything else out of the ordinary occurs here again ... you know what to do." John just nodded as he stood there dumbfounded, not knowing how to take the whole affair, the meaning of the agent's warnings, or the as- yet-to-be-solved murder of a man lying dead and mutilated in the woods. Now, he slowly meandered back to his grungy office. Certainly, there was no doubt now, he was beginning to seriously consider early retirement. It had been a long day.

It isn't even my lunchtime yet, he thought. *And what did he mean by if anything else out of the ordinary occurs here again?*

As Special Agent Le'fadden walked towards the remaining group of police officers, while looking at his cellphone, he stopped in his tracks and turned away from anyone who might see his face. The agent devoted a few moments talking to someone on his cell, but quickly ceased his conversation and turned back to the group. He was approaching Sergeant Stearns, the lovely cop who seemed as serious as himself.

By now, Special Agent Le'fadden was ready to leave the scene, a testament that was clearly written across his face. He curtly asked where the body was and received a pointing finger from both police officers. And then they all walked together into the wooded area and into the darkness under the leafy green canopy. Now, they had blended into a night-shrouded blackness where the man lay sprawled, twisted, and dead.

CHAPTER THREE

It was just around 12:53 p.m. when Officer Culberson, Sergeant Stearns, and Special Agent Le'fadden emerged from the woods, along with the two detectives behind them. Sergeant Stearns waved to Officer Dumont to tape off the entrance to the trails while the three discussed the situation together: the day's findings and what had likely occurred that morning. Shortly thereafter, the last four police officers to have arrived on the scene had begun walking in two-by-two teams into the woods. They were armed with heavy-duty 1,000-lumen flashlights, with one of the officers leashing his two German Shepherds. No stone would be left unturned.

Now, he was to begin a survey of the farthest parts of the woods. They were to make sure no one else was on the trails or anyone who might have walked in unseen by the groundskeeper. They had considered the possibility that the killer or killers might still be in the park somewhere, and because the outer roads had been under constant watch, escape would have been impossible. Now, everyone was alert and ready for anything.

While the search team began exploring the wooded trails, the two young men John had watched earlier were leaving the group of cops and were now approaching him. The first man was Asian, and the second was a large man of either Italian or Latin heritage. The last one had a gut on him. Now, once again, John had braced for retelling his story for the fourth or fifth time. The imagined glory of the day's events had faded, prompting the old man to wish he could just go home. And as the Asian man approached, John watched as the man smiled and pulled a notepad from his jacket pocket.

"Good afternoon, Mister Hurst, I'm Detective Wong with the DeKalb County Police Department, and this is my partner, Detective Merino," he said. "We'd like to speak with you for a few minutes if that's okay?"

"Oh, ah, sure, of … of course … I already gave my information to the other police officers, though," John quickly replied.

"Yes, I understand that, sir, but we just need a few more details, if you don't mind. So, as you told officers Stearns and Culberson, you didn't see anyone else in the park at the time you opened … is that correct?"

"Yeah, yeah, that's right … there's really no way in by car unless you cut the chains, but someone could get in just by jumping the fence, either from here or back by the northeast parts of the park … there's no fence back there, so all you'd need to do is walk through a little water; through the creek to get inside."

"I see," Detective Wong said as he began to write in his notepad. "Tell me about the general area and the footprints we see all around the crime scene … is that common back there, and if so, is there a reason for so much foot traffic in that area?"

"Oh, ah, I thought, I thought you'd know about all that, being detectives and all." Old John Hurst said this with a confused look, but he knew he might have slipped up in his words. Now, he feared he had opened a can of worms.

"Know about what, Mister Hurst?" Detective Marino chimed in, now looking extremely confused by the man's comments. "Know about what, sir?"

"Well, I thought for sure you'd all know about the queer, ah, ah, the gay, the, the homosexual things that go on back there ... not that I'm a hundred percent sure, you know, but we all kinda figured that's what goes on back there," John said. "I've even caught a few dudes going at it in the bathrooms once ... geez, it ... it was ... it was totally gross, you know?"

"I see," Detective Wong said, now with a slight grin beginning to rise on his face. The other detective just looked at the ground, now with an obvious smirk taking over his former, serious expression. He couldn't help but laugh at least a little at the groundskeeper's comments. Then, he quickly looked over his shoulder so as not to make eye contact with the old man.

"You should have called us," Detective Marino said, now feeling comfortable enough to chuckle aloud.

John Hurst now sported a face that betrayed his embarrassment. "Well, I, ah ..."

"Don't worry about that, Mister Hurst," Detective Wong said. "We've recently been notified of such activities here, not to mention in Winnebago County and in other parks, too. The problem is the man-hours needed to investigate the claims and just to delegate our time to it. We're busier than ever these days ... you understand?"

"Well, I didn't want to get too involved, you know? John returned. "I thought that, well, you know, with so many liberals in office these days ... that I'd get in trouble or something you know, these days you'd end up in court just for calling a tranny, well, you know what I mean … a *man*."

The two detectives just looked at each other and smiled. They chose to stay away from that subject, though both men were clearly holding back emerging grins at the same time. Regardless of political correctness or the insane WOKE agenda of the day, both detectives did indeed smile back at John and nod their heads in confirmation. That moment of levity, however, was quickly overtaken by the Cessna Police helicopter that passed overhead. As it quickly began making its rounds around the perimeter of the forest and the outer regions of the park, it had become obvious that the day would only drag on. For old John Hurst, he just wanted to go home.

Now, the three men just stared at the helicopter as it began to hover near where the body was, and then watched as teams of police officers canvased the nature preserve, as the police dogs sniffed in doubtful suspicion. The dogs were clearly frightened. In the distance, an ever-so-light rumble of thunder gently sounded.

God, this is getting bigger by the minute, John thought to himself. *I just wanna go home.*

✠

It was already going on 2:15 p.m. by the time the police patrol cars were beginning to leave, and the medical examiner crew was finally able to get the mangled body out of the woods and into the van. John had thought the damned thing would be lying in there all night, and that he'd have to stay all night to keep an eye on things. It was an irrational thought, but the man was more than unnerved — he was thoroughly spent.

"We're almost done here, Mister Hurst," Detective Marino said.

John looked relieved. "So, who … who do you think could have done this, like that to that guy?" he asked.

"That's the sixty-four-thousand-dollar question, Mister Hurst … but we'll find out, you can bet on that," Detective Wong said with a matter-of-fact tone. "Okay, sir, can you tell me exactly how your morning started, up until the time when the first officers arrived?"

Once again, John relayed his story exactly as he had the first four or five times that day. He figured that this would be the norm for the rest of his day and maybe after that, too. And as the two detectives listened to his description of events, along with the weird weather and how it got blazing hot one minute, and then freezing cold in a matter of seconds, the faces of detectives Wong and Marino became rigid and questioning. This was followed by looks of disbelief, like you might see when someone tells you they were abducted by space aliens, seemingly honest and true, but crazy all the same. Now, John felt like the village idiot.

"Just one more thing, Mister Hurst," Detective Wong said. "I see the park has a camera system … are they up and running?"

"Oh, Christ, I completely forgot them … I'm a complete dipshit! Of course, yeah … come with me a minute."

As the two detectives followed the old groundskeeper into the maintenance shed, John looked over his shoulder, now with a half-smile on his face. "I can't believe I forgot that … here, let me get it, it's in the cabinet over here … it records continuously for three full weeks, and then ejects the disc when it's done … it still has a few days left, I think … it's, it's on a fast setting."

"How many do you already have saved?" Detective Marino asked, now in a more serious tone.

"Ah, I have a box here, from the last; the last five months or so … I've got to get this downtown soon."

Detective Wong shared a glance with his partner and then smiled. "We'll just take the box, Mister Hurst, and review them ourselves," he said. "Once that's done, Parks and Recreation can have them back."

"Ah, sure, whatever you say, detective … just let me get these ready, and put a fresh disc in." John handed over the box of recorded discs to Detective Marino and continued to replace the old disc with a new one.

"Excellent, that'll do, Mister Hurst," Detective Wong said. "Alright, sir, I think that'll do for now. If we need to speak with you further, we'll call you at the number we have or stop by here, okay?"

"Yes, sir, I'm here Monday through Friday, sunrise to sunset!"

"Very good, Mister Hurst, but you need to be aware of the press. They're going to be hitting you up for any information about all this, so just keep your composure. You have every right to talk to them, of course, but we advise you to remain still on the subject until we can sort all this out ... do you understand?"

"Oh, ah, of course, detective! I'll, I'll be quiet about it!"

"Very good. We'll be in touch. Thanks for your time."

✠

As the two detectives walked away, both with official-looking grins on their faces, John just watched as the two remaining police vehicles slowly drove around the entire park, inspecting every place their eyes could scan. He watched as they checked the bathrooms, all of which were still locked because he had never had the chance to unlock them yet, not before everything went to hell.

Other cops checked the baseball grounds on foot, as well as the snack bar below the commentator booth and the booth above that. The surrounding woods at the northeast end were clearly fenced, except for that one section, which was cut off by a shallow stream. This area was being checked by the other foot patrol, which then began inspecting a small maintenance shack. It was locked, secured by a huge Master padlock. No one was seen under the pavilions that were situated around the baseball field and the T-ball field beyond that. The nature preserve seemed as dead as the man lying in its woods. For sure, park-goers didn't have a chance to get in that morning. And the two games scheduled that evening, the Kingston Tigers from Rolland B. Holmes High School and the Cook County

Gamecocks, the regional tri-county champs, wouldn't be playing that night. More likely than not, the DeKalb Middle School's all-girl softball team, which was scheduled for the following day, would be cancelled too.

Now, John just watched the police converge on the park, thinking that the whole affair was just too bizarre to comprehend. He stood at the gate's furthest post and just watched the strange affair. He hoped to figure out just what was really going on, thinking that tonight he wasn't going to have a few beers after all. Tonight, he knew he'd be drinking as if it were 1976. A slight smile rose on John's face as he immediately recalled his nearly perfect physique, his long hair, and all the hot girls he'd known. He remembered the days when he'd listen to cool tunes on the record player and just chill to the scent of African Violet incense and marijuana. Back then, he could just drift away from the bullshit, and just chill out. Just cool, psychedelic vibes, awesome tunes, and no worries. But now, he knew those days were gone — gone for good.

I'm gonna get shitfaced beyond belief; totally and completely shitfaced, he thought. John figured he deserved that much. The world just wasn't the same anymore. Now, it was a crazy world of angry sub-humans and senseless philosophies, where preschool teachers wanted their children to be gay and trans, and where politicians fought for the rights of devil worshipers while condemning those who loved God. Today, foreign terrorists could actually invade his country and do so legally, thanks to crooked politicians and evil lawmakers. No, John just wanted off this nightmare merry-go-round. This night; he figured he'd deserve to piss his way into oblivion and sleep late the next day, thinking the park would be closed anyway. He deserved at least this much.

✠

Knowing that the police had taken over the scene and knowing that it was impossible to mow the grass in the back fields, John Hurst decided to head back to his shed-slash-office and have something to drink. This time, though, it wouldn't be Chock Full o'Nuts Coffee. This time, he'll dip into his private stash he keeps in the back of the bottom drawer, under a tray of assorted screwdrivers, nuts, and bolts. This time, he'd reach way back in that drawer and detain a now most-coveted bottle of Evan Williams Kentucky Straight Bourbon, Green Label.

"Oh-so needed right now ... oh-so-needed," he muttered a bit too loudly. "Sweet Jesus, I need this more than a keg of ga'damn beer."

Old John Hurst sat back in his raggedy and far-too-old office chair, a chair that creaked and squeaked as if it would bust apart at any moment. "No, Mister Williams, you're my date tonight, yes-sir-ee!" He muttered. Now laughing, he remembered the callous comment he made earlier that day when the faggot in the Honda drove off in a hurry ... "Hot-to-trot ... lover's spat!" he blurted aloud.

Now, a grimy smile crept over the old man's face. A second later, John began to bellow out with laughter again, relieving at least a little of the man's tensions. The old man's cackles could be heard throughout the old shed-slash-office and in the parking lot. John Hurst needed to laugh; he needed to laugh a lot.

✠

By 3:35 p.m., the body was finally removed from its location, and the coroner's van had departed the area, along with the WKAX Channel 13 News crew. The other news crews had packed up and departed a few minutes later, with the mysterious, grey-haired federal agent rolling out of the park in his Crown Victoria Cruiser just after that.

As John Hurst sat at his desk, now more than a little in his cups, he lamented on his day. He had hoped that he could get out of there before five, but he had his doubts. He wanted it to be over quickly and without incident, but there had been far more incidents than he could have ever wanted. Now, John had his nip, maybe two or three nips from his green-label bourbon, and it helped a bit. And yet, he figured he deserved the much-needed libation.

Silently, John figured he deserved much, much more than that, especially on that particular day. The old man just sat and thought upon the spectacle that was his life as he gazed out a dirty office window, as he watched the 'meat wagon' pull out of the front gate, and as the remaining news crew scurried and flopped around like angry wasps to follow it.

It was just after 4:22 p.m. when Sergeant 'Jackie' Stearns walked up to the old shed-slash-office where John sat. The dark-haired, exotic beauty, with her thin, almost Egyptian-looking features, entered the now-open overhead garage door. John didn't see the policewoman enter because a tune from the office radio played a familiar melody, a melody which had echoed softly throughout the garage. It was Led Zeppelin's *Stairway to Heaven*.

"Oh Lord," John chimed, "Zeppelin … ah, Jimmy Page. Man … best of the best." He was halfway into a dream when he snapped out of his buzz-like state. As he looked up to the official-looking, goddess-like police officer, he found himself having a sexual fantasy about Sergeant 'Jackie,' though fleeting as it was. Nevertheless, he quickly, perhaps awkwardly, snapped out of his daze, knowing that it could never have been.

"We're done here for the day, Mister Hurst," Sergeant Stearns hastily replied. "But I'll have to keep this area closed until tomorrow, likely for the whole day … just as soon as a separate forensics team can take a closer look at the area. I'll need you to lock up the gate once we're out of here. Also, we're going to leave an officer here throughout the night to protect the crime scene and to watch the area, so please, please see that when you leave, you'll give that officer your key, or a spare to the gate lock. Otherwise, we'll have to call you at your home or cut the chain, and we don't want that … okay, sir?"

"Ah, yes, of course," John replied. "I have a spare key here for the police officer … but will I be able to go home tonight?" John asked haphazardly, complete with a sad, puppy-dog face.

"Yes, certainly, Mister Hurst," Sergeant Stearns returned, now with a slight smile on her face. "Just give the key to the overnight officer, and he or she will return that to you in the morning, alright?"

Unnerved and maybe a bit infatuated, John replied as best he could. "Absolutely; whatever you say, sir, ah, ah ma'am … officer."

Sergeant Stearns just smiled and walked away and into a new, bright, and gaudy day. She vanished like one of John's memories, like a memory of his glory days, like something that could have been but never was. The dark-haired beauty, like a vision that only Glenn Frey could have immortalized, had walked away. She walked away seductively, seemingly on purpose, but she definitely walked away.

Instantly, the old groundskeeper felt a bit younger as she ambled away from him, though a cord of pain echoed deep inside. He lamented on his ever-steady cascade of failures and losses, but he'd always remember his triumphs, and if it were 1976 again, Officer Jackie would have been a victory.

Now, the old man just smiled. *Oh my God … what am I, fifteen years old again, Jesus,* John thought to himself. *I'll have that beer anyway, No … I'll have more than that.*

✠

Shocked by forgetting, John knew he had to call the main office; he had to notify Barbara Kline of what was going on. "This is going to be a lot of fun," he burbled loudly. Then, he picked up the receiver and pressed the number eight button, which was the speed dial to the main office, and then sat back in his chair. The phone only had to ring twice. This was very rare for the main office, as it usually rang two dozen times before anyone would pick it up. Typically, it was more like calling the electronics department at Walmart, where the phone would just ring, and ring, and nobody ever answered. But this time, the phone was answered; this time, it wasn't Barbara Kline's twenty-something-year-old secretary who answered the phone. This time, it was Barbara Kline herself.

Son of a bitch! John thought as she answered the phone.

"Hello, Parks and Recreation, main office," a nasally, stressed voice chimed.

"Ah, hello, Mizz Kline, this is John at the Park, ah, over at the McNeery Preserve."

"Mister Hurst ... we've been trying to reach you for hours now ... you obviously don't have your answering machine turned on, and your cellphone number just goes straight to voicemail," the now irritated park's manager snorted.

Trying to answer as fast as he could, John blurted a quick apology: "I, I'm sorry about that, ma'am, but I haven't had a chance at all this morning ... it's been extremely crazy here, I—"

"Now listen," the woman interrupted. "We've already been notified about the situation, having been told by a representative with the police department ... but could you please give us a little more information about all this? I have about ten people breathing down my neck about this ordeal. In short, what the hell is going on out there? Do we have a lawsuit to worry about?"

"Um, no, I doubt that very much," John quickly answered, knowing that the park couldn't really be held responsible for someone killing another person. "No ma'am, there wasn't an accident … nobody fell or anything like that … this was a murder, I'm almost a hundred percent sure of that," John said, his voice now cracking. "All I'm sure of is what I've seen … a twisted body of some dead guy and another person that took off in his car … but the cops are on it!"

"Well, that's certainly enough, don't you think?" Barbara Kline blurted angrily. "City attorneys are looking into this, and they haven't given us any response yet, so we're all pretty shaken up over this … so here's what's what. You're to get down here as soon as they let you leave, so you'll have to fill out an incident summary while we're all here; while your memory is clear, okay, Mister Hurst? Right away, Mister Hurst, as soon as you're free to leave!"

"Oh, ah, absolutely, Mizz Kline, I'll be right down A—S—A—P!"

"Alright then, we'll be here, and we'll expect you post-haste … and you'll likely need to speak with the city attorneys, most likely with the assistant to the mayor, maybe the mayor herself." Barbara Kline continued to grunt out commands and threats as if angry at the old groundskeeper.

"Oh, ah, yes ma'am, I'll be right down there!" John yelped.

"As soon as possible, Mister Hurst, please," the angry woman grunted again. This was followed by the obvious clicking sound of a phone receiver being slammed on its base. Now, as John hung up the phone with Barbara Kline, he slowly placed the receiver back on its base and sat back in his chair again.

"Damn it!" he yelled. It was loud enough to catch the attention of the cops huddled around the front gate. "Well, so much for this evening's cocktails ... sonofabitch."

As the last patrol car pulled out from the main gates, John rushed out to speak with the last police officer who was just about to pull away.

"I'll be parking over here, beyond the gates ... under the trees until my relief arrives," the officer said." So, if you need me, I'll be here most of the night."

"Yes, sir!" John quickly replied. "I just need to get my truck out, and I'll give you the main keys ... um, they'll get you in the front and rear gates, and my office, and the restrooms too, okay?"

"Sure enough," the officer said with a smile that told John that he understood him, that he understood his feelings by having his life temporarily overturned. "You'll get out of here soon enough, Mister Hurst. Just remember to do what the detectives say, and if they come back to talk to you tomorrow, don't hold any information from them, okay? That's always the best plan ... even if you think the information is unimportant, just tell them everything you remember, alright, Mister Hurst?"

"Oh, yes sir, I surely will!" John confirmed. He quickly realized that the parks would be closed tomorrow, and grumbled to himself as he ambled to his old truck.

Sonofabitch, he thought to himself. *Straight to hell I swear I can't get a break for anything ... when this shit's over, I promise, I'm taking a vacation, no matter what that bitch says. I deserve it!*

✠

By 5:50 p.m., John Hurst had his old Ford F-150 outside the gate, with the padlock secured to a chain that was wrapped tightly around the gates. Now, he turned to inspect the sign on the front gate. The mildly battered sign facing him read:

J. McNEERY FOREST PRESERVE AND PARK – HOURS – DAILY 9 A.M. to SUNDOWN

John spotted the police officer who had parked at the furthest section of the road, under the shade of the tree's leafy canopy, and promptly walked towards his truck. He couldn't wait to get out of there — he needed to get out of there.

Nodding at the officer sitting in his patrol vehicle, with the cop nodding his head back at him, John got in his truck and drove off. He dreaded having to drive all the way to the federal building downtown, and worse, having to deal with the city's officials, and even worse than that, having to deal with Barbara Kline. He sighed, knowing that the park would never be the same now, knowing that the events that occurred there that day would never leave his memory.

John just wanted a drink now — no, he wanted more than a drink; he wanted to drink until he could forget that day — until he could erase that day from his mind.

CHAPTER FOUR

The Autopsy

Friday, June 6th, 9:45 A.M.

The following morning was bright, though a light rain fell across the county. Once again, it threatened a hot and muggy day ahead, as foretold by the curious sun shower that promised a taste of what was yet to come. And like the curious sun showers, the events that occurred the day before had shaken the top advisers with the Department of Parks and Recreation, as it did the city planners and the mayoral staff. And though the general populace was still in the dark about the gruesome affair in the nature preserve, people were noticing that more police vehicles were patrolling their neighbourhoods, the shopping centres, and around the many parks and public gathering places throughout the county. Everyone knew that something had happened.

As Police Captain James Holzer pulled into the parking lot of the DeKalb County Medical Examiner's Office, he watched as his friend Bob Ketchum, the county's chief medical examiner, ambled out of the main door. He had a raincoat draped over his head and shoulders as the rain pelted down on him, while the parking lot emitted waft-like steam as the cold drizzle hit the pavement. Captain Holzer found the image somehow charming, almost like the setting of an old film noir. Despite this, he knew what lay within Dr. Ketchum's house of horrors, and had quickly detached the misplaced romantic aspects of that fading thought and thrust his senses back to a more mundane, horrific world where he had found himself. It was the way his friend was walking that added to his already sour outlook. Captain Holzer knew that something was out of place — that something was wrong.

James 'Big Jim' Holzer knew better than anyone that Bob Ketchum was probably the most by-the-book city official he'd ever known in his thirty-three-year career as a cop, and for Bob to walk out and meet him at his car, not to mention that he was wringing his hands together like a schoolboy being sent to the principal's office, was completely uncharacteristic of the man. Besides, Bob Ketchum was a career pathologist, having worked with the Cook County General Hospital's Pathology Department since 1983, up until 1991, and then with the DeKalb County Coroner's Office ever since. Dead bodies didn't spook Bob Ketchum; dead bodies were his stock and trade. Sun showers aside, today, things were very different, and it showed on the man's face.

Captain Holzer knew that Bob Ketchum was an expert in his field; a man who had seen everything, from murders, suicides, plane, train, and auto crashes galore. He'd been an expert witness for the court system throughout the states of Illinois, Wisconsin, and Indiana and had served as the Vice President of the National Pathology and Forensic Sciences Commission for the past four years. The man was a pro, through and through, yet this case confused him, just as it did himself.

The stalwart captain had surmised that because his friend didn't have any definite answers, or because the circumstances just didn't add up, the typically unfaltering medical examiner was stumped, and being stumped simply wasn't in the man's job description. After all, Bob Ketchum was practically as famous in his state as other medical examiners who excelled in his field. Indeed, he matched the wisdom of Thomas Noguchi of Los Angeles and Michael Baden of New York City and shared the professional charisma and candour of Jan Garavaglia from Orlando and even Alexander Phaeton from Boston with considerable ease. For the citizens of greater Illinois, it was common knowledge that Bob Ketchum was a wunderkind of equally matched skills. Today, however, the man just looked plain stumped.

Dr. Robert Kilpatrick Ketchum, Chief Medical Examiner, and Captain James Elijah Holzer of the DeKalb County Police Department didn't like mysteries. They didn't approve of the nature of the homicide, nor the manner in which the details of this particular case had ruffled more than a few feathers in the process. It was, to date, the granddaddy of all mysteries for their otherwise sleepy community, and it had dropped right in their laps.

The two men approached each other, expecting to follow through yet another homicide in their city, a homicide that had not only befuddled local law enforcement but even had the FBI creeping around. This was a reality that didn't sit well with either of them. It was to be a long day, after all.

"Morning, Bob ... looks like you got an early start," Captain Holzer said. He had offered a sideways smile with the greeting.

Dr. Ketchum just snorted. "Unquestionably ... that's my lot in life," he returned in a curt and somewhat anxious manner. "I've already had a preliminary look at the body. In fact, I didn't get out of here until almost three in the morning. And to top that, I had two gents from the Bureau here with me!"

"The Bureau ... the FBI was here?" Captain Holzer asked with a dumbfounded look. "Why would they be here last night? One was on the scene yesterday morning, I know that, but I didn't expect them to follow you here ... not until late afternoon today, anyway. The Chicago office did verify that an agent would be here to crosscheck any similarities to past crimes, but they said they'd be here late today to get a transcript of your findings and maybe poke around the nature preserve, but nothing else."

"Right ... nevertheless, they were here; three of 'em, and I don't think they were as surprised by this mess as much as I was, considering," Dr. Ketchum said. He was clearly agitated.

"Well, what do you mean? Considering what?" Captain Holzer barked.

"Considering the fact that they were here when the body came in, along with Agent Le'fadden and his partner, had annoyed me a tad. Both had arrived just after the FBI's medical examiner, a doctor named Straub. At any rate, he gave the body a once-over, took photos, took notes, and ordered it wrapped up to be sent to the National Lab in D.C."

"Huh," Captain Holzer grunted. He had an expression that dictated anger and confusion at the same time.

"And the other two ... well, they stayed here until I finished my cursory exam, along with my lab boys," Dr. Ketchum continued. "I mean really, they stayed that whole extra shift here with me, and then having to come back at seven this morning is a bit taxing ... even for me."

Captain Holzer nodded in confirmation. "I hear ya, my friend, and I can relate to it, no doubt about that," he said, now with a slight chuckle in his voice.

"Goes to show you I don't have a life, Jim. And if I continue with this particular brand of dedication, I probably won't have a wife either."

Now, with a slight titter, Captain Holzer shut the car door and locked it. He kept an eye on his frustrated friend as they started to walk to the main doors of the building. The tension brought on by the unannounced federal inquiry the night before had faded to the typical bullshit session so common for the two friends of many years. And with light talk that revolved around such topics as baseball, their wives, and the grandchildren, the moment seemed a bit less stressed. But the lighthearted banter didn't last, and they both knew that they had a big day ahead of them.

"Do ya have any coffee made yet?" Captain Holzer inquired.

Dr. Ketchum smirked and nodded his head. "Dumb question, Jim. I'm practically floating away as we speak," he chimed, now with a little levity to his voice. They passed the receptionist, through a pair of dull-white swing doors, and then down the long corridor. Now, the fluorescent lights flickered and hummed ominously, while the white, medicinal glare of the stark light illuminated the place like some mad doctor's surgical arena. And though it had created an unnerving feeling that only enforced a sense of dread and foreboding, such a description could have fit any morgue around the world.

Captain Holzer had become accustomed to visiting his city morgue on more than a few occasions, though he never really learned to accept it as much as his friend and colleague, Bob Ketchum. There was always a smell to the place, like the uncanny scent of flowers that had wilted and decayed, all existing within a bleached environment. He'd seen far too many innocent people lying on those stainless steel and aluminium slabs — far too many people that didn't deserve being there — far too many children. Secretly, he hated the place. It always gave him the creeps.

✠

As the two men made a turn down the east corridor, they found a lone police officer sitting outside one of the main autopsy theatres. As the rookie cop was reading the morning paper, he was startled to see his captain filing down the hall toward him. As the officer stood in front of a set of double doors, now folding his paper into neat squares, he immediately recreated his best image, as taught to him by the police academy only a year earlier.

"Morn'en, Mister Paige," Captain Holzer said.

"Good morning, sir."

"Who did ya relieve last night, son?"

"Ah, I relieved Officer Metz at three-thirty this morning, sir."

"Would you locate his D.A.R. for me, please … I want to get the names of those federal officers that were here last night … I'm curious who their medical examiner was, too, and why they have their own investigation into this."

"Yes, sir, just a moment," Officer Paige said as he fumbled through the manila folder that rested on the chair next to his.

Captain Holzer exchanged a glance with Dr. Ketchum. His expression was one of being perturbed. "Don't like being kept in the dark, especially in my own house," he murmured. Now, sounding more official, Captain Holzer waited for the rookie officer to shed some light on the mystery.

"Yes, sir, his daily activity report is right here … here it is, sir."

Captain Holzer visually scanned the documents and found the names he was looking for. "Ah, here we go," he mumbled. "We have a Special Agent Martin S. Le'fadden … and a Special Agent Keith A. Straub, M.D., the medical examiner, I'm guessing. And there's another agent listed as V.W. Rovina. Mister Paige, are there any other documents that the FBI gave you or Officer Metz?"

"Ah, no, sir, and Officer Metz didn't pass anything else down to me … only that I was to make sure no one entered the autopsy room unless it was Dr. Ketchum himself or other federal agents … sir."

"Other federal agents? Huh, well, I just don't understand these shenanigans," Captain Holzer erupted. "There's supposed to be a certain level of etiquette between law enforcement officers, despite the nature of the crime being investigated or the obvious secrecy involved … this is a load of horsepucky if you ask me."

Dr. Ketchum just nodded his head. "It might be easier to explain it when you see the body, Jim," he said, now in his most authoritative voice. "When you see the body, I think you'll understand … and also, according to what the head agent said last night … that according to this Agent Le'fadden, this wasn't the only killing with similarities to this one. Apparently, as per that agent, there were others who had died under highly irregular circumstances that matched this one; some similar, some a little different, but all of them completely out of the ordinary.

There had been quite a few others like this poor sap out there over the years to have died in a similar fashion … and in different states, too. This is what the other agent, the younger one, told me when we were out of earshot of Le'fadden and Straub."

Now thoroughly disrupted by being denied such pertinent information, Captain Holzer was beginning to see red. "It isn't just a matter of official business being kept from my eyes, Bob; they must realize that a homicide in DeKalb County is my domain."

Dr. Ketcham just nodded to his friend's dismay. "I understand, Jim, it was bad etiquette, that's for sure," he retorted. "But I think something else is going on, especially with so many feds snooping around, wouldn't you say?"

"Bad etiquette my ass. Such information is not to be pilfered and hoarded in secret by anyone, including the feds!" Suddenly, Captain Holzer's cellphone began to ring. "This is Holzer," he barked into the phone. "Yes, yes Chuck, what do-ya got for me? I see … okay, okay, alright. Go ahead and run both of 'em, and then call me back as soon as NCIC updates you. And that's great work, detective. I'll be waiting for your call."

As Captain Holzer ended the call, now looking a bit less perturbed as he pocketed his cell, he offered a half- assed smile to his friend, Bob Ketchum.

"That was one of my detectives, Charlie Wong," he said. "And he tells me that they were able to match the vehicles in the video, the old groundskeeper at the park gave us. Turns out their surveillance system is pretty damn good after all. It also turns out that there have been several arrests with cars matching those vehicles, too … we got the plates from both vehicles that morning. And, oh yeah, both of these guys have been in the park on more than a dozen occasions, so we have the office and NCIC working on it. We'll get a little more info in a few. Now, some of that coffee would be great right about now, Bob."

Turning to walk back down the hall to the main autopsy arena, Captain Holzer continued to gripe about all the secrecy and having been left out of the FBI's information-sharing loop. His voice echoed through the hallways. "I don't give a damn about any federal *eyes-only* nonsense!" he chimed. "And I want to see their files, their findings and what- have-you, and A–S–A–P!"

Officer Paige; still standing guard at the doorway began to worry that somehow, somewhere, he had screwed up the night before. The loud murmurings of his captain had the man figuring that he might have *screwed the pooch*, a slang term that Captain Holzer was accustomed to throwing out when he was about to crucify a rookie that seriously screwed up. Now, he stood in place, waiting for the inevitable.

"You're relieved, Paige. Go home and get some rest," Captain Holzer barked as he turned the corner.

"Thank you, sir … but if you need me to stay, I'd be happy to help out."

"No, that's alright, son. You go and get some sleep."

Officer Paige smiled, tucked his folded newspaper under his arm, picked up his now-empty thermos, and quickly left the area before his superior could change his mind.

Now, as Dr. Ketchum and Captain Holzer reached the coroner's inner office, the scent of the slightly over-cooked coffee and bleach filled the air. Seconds later, one of the overnight intake specialists walked in with a stack of manila folders in his hand.

"Here you are, sir … I'm gonna stay a little over my shift and finish filing my work before I go home, so I'll be in the back if you need me," the man said.

"Um, wait a minute, Brian."

"Yes, doctor?"

"You worked the third shift last night. What went on here after I went home? Did those federal officers come back? Did they talk to you about anything, anything at all?"

"No, sir, but they did tell me to keep an eye out for any other officers if they arrived here, but no one else came."

"Okay, Brian ... thanks ... we'll see you tomorrow."

"Yes, sir, goodnight, sir," the young man returned.

As the technician turned to leave, Captain Holzer, now looking stern again and a bit flustered, began checking his cellphone for any missed messages. Seconds later, he phoned someone and walked out of the room into the vacant corridor. As he did, Dr. Ketchum began scanning through the folders for anything out of the ordinary. The case files were proper and without noticeable irregularities, but they were sterile and far too cut-and-dry. Dr. Ketchum knew better — he knew something was out of place.

"There's simplicity, and then there's simplicity, but this is ridiculous," Dr. Ketchum mumbled to himself as he continued to read over the documents. "This is nuts ... where's the beef?" he muttered again, now a bit louder. "This is typical of a first-year student's final for Christ's sake, a gross anatomy midterm at best ... not what we should get from a seasoned physician, a physician with the FBI no less."

Disconcerted, Dr. Ketchum leaned up against a long metal table that stretched the length of the autopsy room. He continued to resonate with outsiders taking advantage of his personal workspace, not to mention his personal office, which they had used in his absence after he went home. He suddenly realized that there are work ethics to be respected, and just as quickly, he knew something was definitely going on, something much bigger than what he was being told, and much bigger than what he understood. Whatever it was had to be bigger than what his long-time friend, Jim Holzer, even knew.

Moments later, Captain Holzer walked in, quickly pocketing his cellphone into the flap of his windbreaker. He offered a look that embodied a mixture of rage and confusion that was not necessarily a rare event for the career cop who had dealt with situations like this before. But something was different. And though he had indeed seen it all, and in spades, something was just out of place. Whatever was going on the day before had caught the attention of the Federal Bureau of Investigation, and evidently, whatever was going on had caught the attention of other entities too, a fact that had made all the difference in the bizarre homicide case that lay before them.

As for Captain Holzer, an experienced career cop, a man who'd seen it all, he had known that he was seeing something different, and somehow, he knew this particular brand of craziness was far from over.

"Here, let me make a fresh pot, Jim ... it'll only be a minute," Dr. Ketchum said.

"Sure, but that can keep, Bob ... what I really want is your take on this whole thing. I just want to know what the story is here ... I mean, what makes this case so damned unusual anyway, and why would the Bureau be involved in it? There's no doubt that you and I have seen more than our fair share of nutty things over the years, haven't we? I mean, we had that William Potter case back in what … two thousand and five?"

"February of that year," Dr. Ketchum returned.

"Right. Well, that was some pretty crazy nonsense if I remember correctly … the guy's beheaded while driving his convertible … sure, it was while standing and driving at the same time like a moron, and then having his noggin whacked-off by an overhead bar from the South Street Tunnel. But when his headless body falls back into the seat, and then the blasted vehicle pulls up and stops at the bloody red light on Fourth Avenue… Jesus, what more weirdness could you ask for?"

Now laughing and shaking his head, Captain Holzer just stood there with his now quintessential *what the fuck* look on his face. "And then what about that kid that washed up on shore last year, with his face frozen with that god- awful grin as if he just spotted a naked girl on his bed for the first time?"

"Oh, yeah, I remember that one," Dr. Ketchum blurted, now with a grin. "Right, that actually *was* pretty odd."

Captain Holzer just nodded with raised eyebrows. "What was he … fifteen-or-so years old, and underwater for more than a month, and he's still fresh, remember, Bob? He looked a bit blue about the gills, yeah, but still fresh after a month's time in Lake Michigan; you remember that too," he asked with a sigh. "For God's sake, Bob, isn't *that* weird enough?"

Dr. Ketchum nodded. "I suppose so," he said. "But I've seen my share of weirdness, too."

Now, Captain Holzer crossed his arms and began to walk around the room. He looked as if in deep thought, or as his wife would say, that he looked like he was constipated. Captain Holzer was never amused by the reference, even though the reference was largely true.

"Look, this mess in the woods out there in the McNeery park is bad, I understand that," he continued, "but the manner in which this man had died just couldn't have been accomplished by one man alone. It almost looks industrial to me."

"What do ya mean by industrial, exactly, Jim?"

"Meaning that it was likely done by some kind of … I don't know, as if from some kind of machine. Ya' know, Bob, I'm about open for just about any answer right about now, so please … don't spare any details. I'd like to wrap this thing up as quickly as we can … I just don't want any more aggravations."

"Alright then," Dr. Ketchum said with a grunt. "Let's get started."

✠

The two men just shook their heads in disbelief, though now with a certain amount of levity interjected. Dr. Ketchum finished putting the coffee grounds in the Mr. Coffee and pushed the button to start yet another pot of extra-strong, though much-needed brew to begin the long day ahead. They had indeed seen it all, both of them. But this case, no matter how strange, was a case that still needed to be solved, regardless of the FBI's involvement and their lack of sharing information. It was still Bob Ketchum's case — it was still Jim Holzer's case.

"Just a minute, Jim; hold on a sec," the now less agitated medical examiner said. Picking up the phone, he hit a button and called for the assistant medical examiner over the P.A. system. "Doctor O'Conner, please report to arena five; Doctor O'Conner to arena five, please." When he hung up the intercom phone, he offered Captain Holzer a sideways smile. "Let's have my second-in-command answer some questions first. He's a former Navy Corpsman, Desert Storm, and he has his Ph.D. in physical anthropology. He's a pretty bright kid and pretty much an authority in all things of a forensic nature, believe me. I think he might shed a little light on this situation ... hopefully."

Now, as the Mr. Coffee gave off sounds of life, the scent of the dark brew overpowered the customary smells that are commonplace in any morgue around the world; even the industrial scent of chemicals seemed to linger a bit less from the doctor's cherished Green Mountain Coffee blend.

"This is called Dark Magic, Jim ... I think you'll like it."

"Great ... I'm gonna need it." Captain Holzer removed his cellphone from his jacket's pocket flap while at the same time, methodically taking off the now uncomfortably hot windbreaker.

As Dr. Ketchum poured coffee into two bone-white mugs, both men appeared more at ease now than they had earlier that day. "Let's have a cup," he said ... then we'll review my files from last night and then listen to Doctor O'Conner's findings. sound good?"

"Sounds good," Captain Holzer said. "Then I want to have a look at the body myself." Dr. Matthew O'Conner entered through the double doors of the arena and headed for the back office. "Smells a little better in here, Doc," he chimed loudly. "Come and get a cup, Matt. You know Captain Holzer, don't you?"

"Yes, yes, we met briefly a few years ago on the Patterson Case back in July of twenty-three, I believe ... good morning, sir."

"Good morning, Doctor O'Conner. Good to see you again. Wish it were under better circumstances, of course."

"Yes, sir, that's always preferable, but rare in our business."

As Dr. O'Conner helped himself to a cup of 'Doc Ketchum's Black Magic,' as he called the now well-established coffee at the morgue, he took a seat at the corner of the large metal desk and waited eagerly for the first round of questions.

"Now that we're settled in for a bit, we can play back last night's recording. We don't have all the transcripts finished as of yet, of course, being down on one of our file clerks this week, but I think we have enough to get started. Our head secretary, Mrs. Krenshaw, is in Georgia visiting her grandkids. Besides, you'll get to hear my best Doc Hammerback impressions, Jim."

"Doc Hamma-beck?" Captain Holzer asked, now with an expression of confusion and annoyance.

"Doctor Hammerback ... from CSI ... New York? You know, the TV show?"

Captain Holzer offered a sour look. "Nope, don't watch it ... got enough crime drama every day already, and I don't need some Hollywood dipshit playing one of us for entertainment."

Dr. Ketchum just laughed at his friend's comment. "Gotcha, Jim. All right then, let's see what we got here."

As Dr. O'Conner sipped at his coffee, he reached for a small box he had taken from the receptionist's desk and began shuffling through a collection of micro-cassette tapes. He quickly found last night's tapes and inserted one of them into the tape player.

"This reminds me of *The Collected Poems* by Langston Hughes," he said as he looked over towards the locker where Nathan Prud was stored. "*Life is for the living. Death is for the dead. Let life be like music, and death a note unsaid.*"

Dr. Ketchum smiled at his colleague's taste for the arts, regardless that he thought poetry belonged more in the arena of hippies and the beat generation of his youth than that of a medical examiner. Nonetheless, he nodded and smiled. "Very nice, Matt ... and appropriate, I suppose," he said. "All right, gentlemen ... let's get this ball-a-roll'en."

✠

The distinct sound of the audiotape began to play with the now ever-recognizable voice of Bob Ketchum echoing throughout the auditorium. "DeKalb County Medical Examiner's Report

June six; eight-forty-five a.m. Postmortem case number is twenty-twenty-dash-eight-ninety-four-dash-C. Date of Autopsy: six-six-twenty … ah, wait a second, Jim, let me get past the preliminaries here," Dr. Ketchum grunted as he hit the fast-forward button on the tape player.

Captain Holzer just smiled. "Still using old tape cassettes in the twenty-first century, Bob?" Captain Holzer asked sarcastically. He had cracked his first joke for the day, which had proved hopeful. He often poked fun at the much-too antiquated medical examiner, knowing full well that he was almost identical in his mannerisms.

"I'm afraid so, Jim," Dr. Ketchum returned with a smile. "As you already know, I'm just an old geezer that doesn't like the constant change in technology … just a way to bilk more money out of us. Besides, I trust what works, not those iced tea coasters that get scratched or read errors every time I use one … okay, here goes."

Now, the three men settled back, Dr. Ketchum in his chair, and Dr. O'Conner and Captain Holzer, now leaning on the stainless-steel table. There was a distinct hum emitting from the fluorescent lights overhead, just as the sound of distant thunder could be heard outside. The rumble lasted at least a minute, as if promising another day of stormy weather.

"Medical Inquest case number sixty-two-three-dash-eight; autopsia cadaverum … time initial start: twenty-hundred hours and forty-five minutes," the echoey voice of Bob Ketchum continued on the little tape player. "DeKalb County Coroner FOIA Officer Maynard F. LeRay, M.D., Administration, twenty-two-fifty-three, West Wood Street,

DeKalb, Illinois. Presiding medical examiners are Robert K. Ketchum, M.D., Chief Medical Examiner, and Doctor Mathew Dean O'Conner, Ph.D., secondary charge. The subject's Name is Nathan Nicholas Prud, with identification on file. The subject's last known address is listed as eighty-eight-ten, East Bungle Street, DeKalb, Illinois, sixty-one-fifteen ... occupation ... *formally* was a college professor; adjunct with Nimbus University ... he was also a freelance writer."

"You said Nimbus University?" Dr. O'Conner asked.

"Correct. He's been there for these past sixteen years," Captain Holzer returned. "Continuing ... date of birth is October twenty-two, nineteen-eighty-four ... race, Caucasian; white, sex ... male ... body identified by one Marsha E. Prud, wife of the deceased ... case number is twenty-twenty-dash-eight-ninety-four-dash-C, photograph batch number is twenty-twenty-dash-eight-ninety-four-dash-forty-two, consisting of forty-two colour photos, plus one video of general location with cadaver placement, and crime scene details ...."

As Dr. Ketchum lifted his glasses to rest upon his forehead, temporarily forgoing the use of putting on his reading glasses, he stammered to find the fast-forward button on his micro-tape recorder.

"Why don't you just get bifocals, Bob?" Captain Holzer snapped.

"Damn things make me dizzy ... just wait a second ... alright, let's get past this too," Dr. Ketchum snorted as he held down the fast-forward button.

"Oh, here's the print-out of the entire proceedings so far, minus those of the federal agents, of course," Dr. O'Conner said. "Captain Holzer, if you want to take a closer look at the details, you're welcome to, of course. They only reflect our preliminaries, you understand, and not the official transcripts, so please just ask if you have any questions for us, okay?"

"Will do," Captain Holzer returned as he tipped the last of his coffee down his throat.

"Let's see what we have here," Dr. Ketchum said. "The tape's rather long, Jim. Do you prefer to read the report or keep listening?"

"No, no, let the tape go on, I can get more out of the tape than just reading ... but I'll probably ask about something ... you know me," he said with a smirk on his face.

"Oh boy, do I ever," Dr. Ketchum retorted with a laugh. "Continuing ... evidence collected consists of one green and white short-sleeve shirt, size extra-large, with body fluids positive ... one pair of powder-blue pants, size forty-two, also positive for body fluids. One gold wedding band, one wristwatch, a Cartier with a black band, and one man's black leather wallet. There's also a one-and-a-half- inch wide black belt with a brass belt buckle, and one Apple iPhone SE-Seven is also listed, but recovered by P.D. upon removal. This batch includes postmortem imaging results, CT scans, MRIs, and X-rays. The victim's personal effects are in locker number six."

As the tape player continued to recount the previous night's events, a low yet deep rumble of thunder could be heard resonating from outside. A second later, a loud crack of thunder followed a bolt of lightning, which was seen through the small high windows from Dr. Ketchum's autopsy room. The vibration of the thunder had caused the instruments on the metal tables to rattle, creating a tuning fork-like sound throughout the large, medicinally-white medical arena.

"The body is presented in a black vinyl bag with a list of all articles discovered at the crime scene, and is attached to the bag," Dr. Ketcham continued. "All official signatures are present. There are also four large specimen containers with bio-matter in them. Upon initial observation, the limbs are equal in length, symmetrically developed, and show no evidence of major injury, minus some minor abrasions, likely from the scuffle. The fingernails are of normal length, and the fingernail beds are slightly blue. Note that the fingernail on the fifth digit of the subject's right hand is painted black, the victim's belt is found partially torn, and the pants were found halfway pulled down. The opposite end of the belt appears to have been torn by a considerable force, indicated by a tear and frayed fibres. The body was found with sunglasses close by, but not affixed to the head."

Dr. O'Conner had pointed to a sheet of paper, prompting his superior to shut off the tape player. "Don't forget the differentials," he whispered.

Dr. Ketchum smiled and then nodded silently. "Right you are, Matt. Jim, the cadaver had its temperature taken at the scene, and upon arrival, an algor mortis was recorded, and it read seventy-nine-point-eight degrees.

Upon arrival and during the initial autopsy, the body is at seventy-point-one degrees per one-point-five degrees Fahrenheit ... that's at a zero-point-three-degree decline."

Captain Holzer cocked his head slightly. "And what does that mean exactly, Bob?" he asked. "That means that the body had cooled significantly during the period of time when the park gates had opened and when the body was first discovered, so basically, it means there's a discrepancy here."

As Dr. Ketchum's voice continued to sound from the tape recorder, Dr. O'Conner handed Captain Holzer a packet with the crime scene photos and then pointed to the yellow sticky note attached to the first photograph. "Look at the temperature, captain, and then refer to the times the victim had likely expired and the time from the body's removal," he said.

Captain Holzer wrinkled his nose at the information. "I don't get it. Outside temperature reads ninety-eight-point-five degrees. And the body temperature was recorded at what ... sixty-eight to seventy-two degrees Fahrenheit? What does that mean exactly, doctor?"

"It means that our body here had cooled significantly in a very short amount of time," Dr. O'Conner interjected. "It was almost a hundred degrees yesterday, and with the body being discovered less than thirty minutes after death ... these numbers are way off. Just wanted to let you know that, captain."

Captain Holzer looked at the notation and then at the photos while the tape recorder continued to echo with the now customary voice of Dr. Bob Ketchum.

"The body is that of a normally developed, however, slightly overweight white male measuring seventy-point- zero inches and weighing two-hundred-and-fourteen pounds," the echoey voice continued. "His appearance is consistent with the previously stated age. The body is cold and unembalmed; cadaveric rigidity appears normal, and lividity is fixed in the distal portions of the limbs. Note that the eyes are partially open and are partially glazed."

"Hey, can you pause this for a few minutes? I've got a call," Captain Holzer barked. "Sure, Jim, we'll go over a few things while you're busy."

As both doctors reviewed the written transcripts, Captain Holzer discovered the criminal history of the J. McNeery Forest Preserve cadaver, as well as the other man who had fled the area. While jotting everything down in his notebook, his typical 'ah-ha' look fell over the man's face.

"Mister Nathan Prud and a Mister Andrew Lynch … gotcha boys!" he blurted loudly.

In addition to the report by the National Crime Information Center, the video recordings from the park were clear enough to reveal the license plates of both cars on the morning of June fifth. This gave the police captain more than enough information to go pick up the driver of the Honda, who has been identified as thirty-three-year-old Andrew Michael Lynch of Aurora, Illinois. He and Nathan Prud had substantial police records, and both had been in the park on numerous occasions — all occasions that likely validated the bulk of their arrest histories over the years. The information made Captain Holzer feel like a kid on Christmas morning.

Now, as the stalwart police captain entered arena number five again, both doctors ceased their laughter from the previous 'dumb blonde' joke Dr. O'Conner had laid out. They were both surprised by the captain's now juvenile-looking grin.

"We were reminiscing about the last receptionist, Jim," Dr. Ketchum chuckled. "You remember her? Connie ... ah, Connie Cooper-Snyder? You know the one, the bleach-blond who thought the place was haunted ... and, and she quit because she thought ghosts were following her home every night ... you remember that, right?"

"Yeah, yeah, I remember ... dumb blonde. But I've got better news," Captain Holzer chimed. "We've finally got something on our corpse, as well as the guy who called the park yesterday; the guy who made that anonymous report to Parks and Rec. Now, listen to this ... Nathan Nicholas Prud, with aliases that include Nicky Prud, Nat Richards, Nathanial Prude, Paddy Dunn, and get this ... Nicky Puddles!"

"What, was he a gangster or something?" Dr. Ketchum playfully snapped.

"No, just you're run-of-the-mill pervert dirtbag. Apparently, he liked getting urinated on. According to Marino," Captain Holzer returned. "And to top it off, we have the wife, Marsha Lizbeth Prud, down at the station ... again. This time, she wants to talk about their alternative lifestyle, whatever that means, and to clear her husband's *good* name. Detective Wong says I should listen, so why don't we finish the tape or as much as we can ... I want to get a foothold on all this before I go downtown, okay with that, Bob?"

"Of course, of course, I'm here the rest of the day anyway … who needs sleep? Now, how about a little more coffee for the road?"

"That's alright; I've to get back pronto, so let's just finish this thing so I can get." Pushing the button on the tape player again, they continued to listen to the report, while the captain jotted down the various particulars that he'd need to formulate a motive, if possible.

"The irises are brown, and the corneas are cloudy," the voice on the tape player continued. "Petechial haemorrhaging is present in the conjunctival surfaces of the eyes. The pupils measure zero-point-three centimetres… the hair is dark brown, straight, and receding, with slight balding at the crown. The body reveals what appears to be a grip mark, though this description has not been verified. This will be known throughout this report as 'Grip Mark A,' which is located on the neck below the mandible. Grip Mark A consists of four unnaturally large markings like those of fingers, though this is just an observation due to the irregular size and shape … each *finger-like* marking is approximately four-point-five inches wide, and at least nine inches in length."

Dr. O'Conner pulled out several hard-copy photographs from a folder and showed Captain Holzer one of them. He pointed at the so-called grip marks.

"These grip marks encircle the neck in the form of a large grasp, with what appears to be four distinct finger-like marks on the anterior of the neck and having an inverted, or otherwise large grip on the posterior of the neck," the taped voice continued. "This is consistent with strangulation and, or hanging, though at this time this aspect of the exam is still cursorily pending a secondary investigation. Please note ... these grip-like marks appear to be burnt into the skin, though without damage to the muscle tissue below the second layer of the dermis, and does not support any known ligature mark on file."

Now sporting a look of utter disbelief, Captain Holzer just fiddled with his chin and then started rubbing his lower lip. It was the way he stared off into space that announced that he was desperately trying to figure out what the grip marks had meant — what the oversized grip on the body really was and how it was put there. Captain Holzer understood that certain methods used by killers can sometimes cause irregular marks, making the crime scene appear strange, but there would always be a logical answer behind it, eventually. He knew that a good cop would figure it out, one way or another.

"Wait a second, Bob," he blurted. "Explain this to me ... this gripping issue, and ah, the burned skin."

"I really wish I could," Dr. Ketchum returned. "Fact is, I don't know of any weapon that could cause such marks, let alone a weapon that could scorch the skin like this. It looks like maybe ... *that's maybe*, but it looks like some kind of tool might have done this, you know, like those small Bobcat tractors ... the kind construction workers use ... the ones with claws on them instead of shovels? Maybe it was something like that, only a little smaller ... and it could have been hot enough from the day's sun or from something mechanical to leave a slight burn on the skin. In this case, more like a welt than a burn … but I'm not satisfied with that hypothesis as of yet."

"That sounds fine to me, Bob, but the groundskeeper watched as Prud drove in, and it only took about … well, less than forty-five minutes to be killed. And there was no such construction equipment or vehicles on the property, except the groundkeeper's riding lawnmower. It just doesn't ring true."

Dr. Ketchum raised his hands in front of him to express that he was stumped. "Well … it was just a guess," he said. "It's a mystery, that's for sure. Alright, continuing … there are minor abrasions and contusions present in the area of Grip Mark A, including what appears to be sharp, five-point-five-inch-deep impaling-like punctures on the lateral side of the clavicle region. There's slight haemorrhaging surrounding this region, as well as said burn marks, all of which indicate this injury to be pre-mortem. Upon removal of the victim's clothing, I find that the body is excessively hairy, including the arms and legs. A yet-to-be-determined odour emits from the cadaver, an odour resembling that of rotten eggs and … and perhaps charcoal or burning wood? Areas of the body had been swabbed for submission to the lab for detection of any organic or inorganic chemicals."

Captain Holzer cocked his head and furrowed his eyes when he heard the last remark on the tape player. "Hum … what could have caused that, Bob?" he asked.

"Could be as simple as a chemical having been placed on the body, or it could be environmental, significant to that location only … we'll find out once those tests come back. You might want to recheck that area, Jim."

"Right, right … go on, Bob."

"Following the removal of the shirt, we find a massive wound; I believe the primary wound resembles a deep gorge. This will be known as 'Wound B.' This wound is observed on the cadaver's abdomen, within the lower extremities, below the thoracic region, and measures approximately thirteen to fifteen inches in diameter, crossing the anterior midline of the stomach. This is slightly above the navel. A T-shape incision was made on the anterior region, starting at the tips of both shoulders and extending to a horizontal line across the region where the clavicle meets at the sternum … this follows a single vertical cut made at the middle of the neck. The initial appearance is remarkable."

As the tape continued, Dr. O'Connor reached for the photographs taken during the autopsy. He pointed to the areas that were being discussed. Though Captain Holzer could have sufficed with the verbal descriptions, the photos had nonetheless proven Dr. Ketchum's process in nauseating detail.

The room seemed to be colder now, a reality that prompted the sturdy police captain to put his jacket back on, while Dr. Ketchum pushed the button on the tape player again. "I am now removing the first layer of fat," the little tape player echoed. "Here, and I can see a collection of massive haematomas that are obvious around the Platysma muscle area. Please note that there appears to be an increased focal swelling in this region. This is consistent from the lateral, medial, posterior, and anterior aspects of this region," he concluded.

Now, as a low rumble of thunder echoed throughout the large autopsy arena, followed by a flash of lightning through the high windows, Dr. Ketchum leaned back on one of the tables and perused the photographs. He picked one and turned it to face his friend, Captain Holzer. "This, this Jim ... this is a problem for us," he said.

Captain Holzer just stared expressionless at the so-called grip marks on the neck of the lifeless body of Nathan Prud, and then he turned his gaze towards his friend.

"Problems?" he muttered.

"Yes, problems that will make it very difficult for me to sign off on this thing. Pure and simple, they're just too many damn discrepancies I just can't explain in order to do that ... not honestly, at any rate." Dr. Ketchum took in a deep breath and exhaled rather loudly as he placed the photograph back on the table. Something very strange is going on here, Jim, and I don't like it. No, sir, I don't like it one damn bit."

A loud clap of thunder echoed from the west of town. A storm was coming, and everyone in the room knew that more problems were coming with it. Everyone shivered from the cold, and everyone felt a chill run down their spines.

✠

In the time it took to explain the various details of the autopsy, the first impression by Captain Holzer was that the case wasn't as bizarre as it had first seemed. Nor were there any particulars that should have raised any eyebrows, even with the so-called 'odd' scent of rotten egg and burning wood that had been detected by the old groundskeeper at the nature preserve, or the scent that had still permeated the body. Captain Holzer believed it could all be accounted for in natural and down-to-earth ways. He believed that there was nothing spooky about the events, only that the killer or killers were extremely well trained. He believed it could all be explained, and not necessarily from the point of view that would suggest anything out of the ordinary. He just couldn't prove it.

The rumbling thunder had continued to roll to the west of town as Captain Holzer had explained that the situation was something more *typical* in nature than that of a high-profile case that had involved the FBI's presence. Now feeling suspicious, he was beginning to think that this was just another homicide the Federal Bureau of Investigation was trying to conceal, for whatever reason. He was becoming more suspicious by the moment and had vowed to find out the truth.

"Let's stop here for a second, Jim," Dr. Ketchum said, just as he clicked the tape recorder to stop. "I think it'll be better to play this as we point out the incisions and wounds as the tape plays. That'll be better than Matt showing you the photos, alright?"

"That's fine with me," Captain Holzer said as he looked at his watch. "But let's make it quick."

Dr. O'Conner walked over to the east wall where the bodies were stored and pulled out drawer number six. It halted with a heavy clicking sound. The body was still in its shroud and unzipped, though the top half was only flipped over to cover the face and chest. Now, he pulled back the sides to reveal its gruesome interior. Nathan Nicolas Prud lay in state, his head almost twisted all the way around, and the cuts from Dr. Ketchum's scalpel, now fully apparent to the eye, had created an almost unnatural vision before the police captain. The body did indeed emit an odour that everyone in the room could detect, but none of them was able to identify the source of the odd scent.

"The man wasn't just killed," Dr. O'Conner said. "This guy looks as if he was executed in a manner that might have been seen five hundred years ago; something from the Tower of London, perhaps … but surely not here
… not in modern-day Illinois … not in the middle of some park. Here, just let me pull the shroud down, and I'll show you."

"No … no, it sure doesn't look typical," Captain Holzer returned. He held one finger under his nose in hopes of diverting the cadaver's odd scent.

"Okay, just follow my lead, Jim," Dr. Ketchum said. "As I point out the entire process, I'll follow my observations as I see it … and I'll make it as quick as possible."

"Appreciate that, Bob."

"Okay … Wound B exhibits a depth that varies between eighteen-point-three and nine-point-two inches. It appears to have penetrated the Aponeurosis region and through the Linea alba and Umbilicus in this region … right here, Jim, just above the navel. There had been a removal of approximately three to five feet of the small intestines ... the Duodenum, the Jejunum, and at least five inches of the Ileum. But that's not it ... these wounds appear to be secondary, or perhaps accidentally ... look here, Jim—"

"Jesus!" Captain Holzer interrupted. "Do ya have to put your whole hands in there?" Dr. Ketchum just smiled as he pulled the fatty tissue back with his gloved hands. "See, whoever did this was someone who was able to reach under the ribcage and effectively and quickly pull out the bulk of Mister Prud's heart ... almost completely out. Mind you, whoever did this was able to pull it out of the body with what appears to be from one large ... forgive me, but from what appears to be from one large hand. Keep in mind, Jim, that in order to do this, you would have to have incredible strength, no ... impossible strength!"

"What ... what do ya mean by impossible strength, Bob? Are you supporting the theory that someone had used a mechanical tool of some sort?" the captain asked.

"Well, first of all, the aorta is a very thick, husky tube that's practically the size of a garden hose, and about a half-inch thick and close to a foot long from the heart ... you just don't pull it out, Jim, it'll stretch before it breaks. And secondly, the man was alive at this point, with blood flowing. This is a fact. Basically, it creates a suction effect, making it even more unlikely because of such suction ... you with me?"

"Yeah, yeah, go on," the now thoroughly befuddled police captain barked. "Do ya have to play with it with your hands though?"

"No big deal," Dr. Ketchum shot back, now smiling from his friend's reaction.

"It's like pulling a knife out of a living person, captain," Dr. O'Conner broke in. "You've seen that before, I've no doubt … well, if you did pull it out, you'd pull out a few inches of tissue along with the knife … that's the suction part. Well, the same physics work here, too. Half of the guy's guts should have followed with the heart. If someone wanted to do this, they would only pull out pieces of the organ, and not the whole thing, snapping the valves, the pulmonary arteries, and veins, and it wouldn't be so … so perfectly done. Do you understand what we're saying, sir?"

"Yeah, yeah, I understand."

"Plus, you can clearly see a slight burning on the inner sections of the tissue, too."

"Um-hum, that's right, Jim," Dr. Ketchum blurted. "The kid's got it right. It'd be impossible to pull out. Listen, Jim, this wound, if made while Prud was alive, tells us that not only was there an immense amount of strength needed to accomplish it, but the size of the … *the hand* … if you will, is simply impossible. Firstly, it's too damn big, even if coming from a huge man. Secondly, it would be like pulling your foot out of four feet of almost hardened cement. Understand what I'm saying?"

"Right, right, lots of suction … I get it," Captain Holzer snapped back.

"In addition to this, the Fundus of the Gallbladder had been pulled out too," Dr. Ketchum continued. "And we can see that the Transverse Colon has been pierced or punctured, as yet from an unknown source … and there was haemorrhaging in the surrounding areas, measuring approximately five to eight inches. The liver, however, appears undamaged. The duodenum, jejunum, and the ileum, which have also been torn out, are all still missing. So, I ask you … how much more of a mystery do you need, Jim?"

Now posing a question not yet answered for Dr. Ketchum, he stopped the tape. "I'm glad I just reminded myself, Jim … have your people found any tissue or organs like this, any fleshy matter in the area as of yesterday or, or today? It doesn't matter if it can't be identified as human or animal; if there's any tissue whatsoever, we're going to need that as soon as possible."

"No, not that I'm aware of. And your people spent most of the day out there yesterday, and a team is there this morning too, so if there is, they should've discovered something; both my people and Cook County's people. CSI should be there now, along with Detective Marino, who'll be overseeing the process. And old Ferrell Pastor's cadaver dogs are there too, so if they find anything, we'll hear about it soon enough."

Dr. Ketchum silently nodded his head. "More than anything, Jim … it's the whole heart issue that has us really stumped here. No one … and I mean no one man can do that, not one man alone, that's for sure. And even if a few men had managed to pull out his heart, it would have fallen apart in their hands. Then there are the burn marks to remember, burn marks that were found on the inner circumference of the chest cavity. Even if slightly, it just doesn't add up for us."

"It doesn't add up for you?" Captain Holzer blurted sarcastically. "What do ya think this crap is doing for me?"

Dr. Ketchum just smiled, and then pulled back the skin flap on Prud's chest, and then removed a ten-by-ten-inch portion of the ribcage. "Here, look here, Jim," he said. "The inner cavity of the cadaver's chest revealed an empty socket where the lungs had been removed and placed on a large specimen tray. The obvious gash where a heart should have been was plain to see, along with what looked like dark red and black scorch marks as if from something blazing hot — something unnaturally hot had been inside the man's chest.

Dr. Ketchum pulled back more tissue and then offered the captain an inquisitive look. "See, look at the trauma here, beyond the cauterized markings ... the entire outward sections. You can see that the remains of the heart's coronary sinus, the inferior vena cava, and what's left of the aorta all show evidence of massive trauma."

"Yes, and over here too," Dr. O'Conner said as he shined a small penlight within the cavity. "Basically, it must have been pulled down and outward, and with one quick thrust. It must have been done very quickly because it only has a slight discharge of tissue, meaning it was done quickly enough to have avoided having pulled out only parts of the heart, instead of the majority of it, and more importantly ... without stretching the aorta."

"So, what you're saying is that some kind of machine might have done this?" Captain Holzer asked.

"Possibly. We're just not sure, Jim."

Dr. O'Conner nodded his head to his superior's statement. "And as suggested before, we think that it might have been a tool of some kind," he said. "Maybe … just maybe, it could have been a surgical tool that has been modified as a weapon of sorts. We just can't be sure."

As the three men pondered on the suggestion that some kind of exotic surgical tool might have been used to kill and mutilate Nathan Prud, a clap of thunder sounded again, followed by the lights flickering ever so slightly. The atmosphere of the autopsy arena had taken on a dull luminescence as if the lighting had been damaged. And with the realization that a crazed serial killer might have been responsible for the strange homicide, the now cold autopsy room had become even more unsettling.

✠

Dr. Ketchum and Dr. O'Conner continued to testify that some kind of mechanical or surgical device had to have been used to remove Nathan Prud's heart and that it was likely done by more than just one man. Despite their hypothesis, however, it only made the mystery more implausible than clarifying any logical method, let alone offering a possible answer to the details of the crime. There could be no doubt now, the mystery was only becoming deeper by the moment.

Now, as Dr. Ketchum pointed to the tube-like structures towards the cadaver's neck to exemplify this, he tried as best he could to explain a probable methodology of an attack. He reached into the chest cavity and fumbled with the tissue. "See, look at these remaining segments here," he said. "The left subclavian artery is intact, having been torn here, though almost resembling a cut, see? That's not a cut, just that the heart had been pulled out with such veracity it only appears that way … and as you keep looking, you'll see that the descending aorta shows the same thing."

Dr. O'Connor interrupted by clearing his throat. "Frankly, we don't know of any tool that can do this," he said. "The ascending aorta, right here, and the coronary arteries … well, the pulmonary valves alone have very sturdy cusps to them. Its job is to offer a steady flow of blood throughout the bodily system. This is for regulation, you understand, but above all, it's profoundly strong … the arteries as a whole, I mean. I'm just saying that both the superior and inferior vena cava have tensile strength to them, much like a spider's web."

"It's highly irregular," Dr. Ketchum added. "This should explain the reason why we're kind of up in arms about this … from a medical point of view." Now, Dr. Ketchum placed the cut section of ribcage back in its place and then closed the flap of skin over that. He pulled a glove off one hand, balled it up in his other gloved hand, and then pulled them off as one. Then he tossed it in the red medical waste bin.

"Alright, two points, Doc!" Dr. O'Conner chimed enthusiastically.

"Um, just making sure about the tissue," Dr. Ketchum muttered. "It's not typical to simply have that much tissue matter just go missing like that unless the perpetrators took it with them, or perhaps your men missed it yesterday, or maybe wildlife ate it. That's not uncommon, I'm afraid. It's just strange, that's all. Ya' know, Jim, you remember we had that cult-related murder back in ninety-nine when that woman's heart was cut out ... on the outskirts of Chicago, you remember?"

"Yeah, I remember," Captain Holzer snorted. "What about it ... do you think there might be a connection?"

"No, but there are aspects of that crime that need to be observed. For one thing, sub-humans like that like to boast, Jim ... Satanists and what have you. That case was fairly cut 'n dry, but this case is extremely odd by any definition. These killers are human after all, and they make mistakes. And even if they know human anatomy and physiology, they wouldn't be able to pull something like this off, especially in the middle of a family park at midday... it just can't happen that way, Jim."

"Right," Captain Holzer quipped, now looking at both men with an emotionless affect. "I'm gonna do a cross-reference later on to see if there are others like this. I'll try Chicago and Indianapolis first ... I'll start there."

Dr. Ketchum just smiled. "Now, I'm no psychologist, Jim, but major organs like the human heart would be hard to just let go, especially if it's intact, though I doubt this very much," he said. Then, he balled up his fist and held it up. "Basically, it's about this size and weighs about three hundred to three-fifty grams, tops. The other organs, the jejunum, duodenum, and ileum, well, they're just too obscure for your average devil worshipper or other cultist to even know about unless he's also a surgeon or a professor of anatomy … or maybe if the perpetrators were just grabbing at anything."

"Yeah, that's what it looks like to me," Captain Holzer retorted.

Dr. Ketchum nodded and smiled at the comment. "It kind of does, but maybe figure it like this, Jim. These parts of the intestines are not unlike radiator hoses from a car. They're important to sustaining life, but outside of that, after death, they're pretty much useless. And to the untrained eye, it's just going to look like a mass of pink goo, like chicken guts. There's just no logic that we can find. It's just really bizarre, Jim. Definitely, I think this is one of the weirdest ones you've sent us yet."

"I'll second that," Dr. O'Conner said.

"Bizarre … weird?" Captain Holzer exclaimed. "What part of this mess *isn't* bizarre and weird?"

"Yes, yes, you have a point … but let's continue just a bit further, shall we? I think we need to explore just a bit further in order to put some logic to it. Just a little more, Jim," Dr. Ketchum pleaded. He proposed the question with a smile, just as he pressed the button on the tape player again.

Now, as the low, vibrating thunder continued to rumble in the distance, the lights flickered three times again, just as the temperature dropped another few degrees. Ever so lightly, the scent of burning spices had filled the air, as if from some ancient temple of history, or perhaps from a restaurant nearby. And though no one mentioned the odd scent, everyone, including the robust police captain, had looked around with a confused look. There could be no doubt now that the day was quickly becoming stranger by the minute, as if the autopsy arena had become a different place — a place of imminent danger, as if someone or something was there watching them — watching their every move and action.

✠

As the three men just gawked at the cadaver, trying desperately to piece any logic to an otherwise illogical manner of execution, it was determined that it certainly *was* a case of execution, in that Mr. Prud, despite having meandered into an otherwise safe location, free of wild beasts and hazardous machinery had died in a manner that made absolutely no sense. The fact that human tissue may have been lost at the crime scene, either by being taken by the perpetrators or by being ingested by animal life, had made little difference to the overall case. The primary difference was the method of death, which at this point remains at odds with both medical examiners and Captain Holzer. One thing was for certain, however. Each of the men knew that they'd have to spend a lot more time before any logical answer would be found.

"Alright, let's finish up," Dr. Ketchum said. "The subsequent autopsy shows a broken hyoid bone. There was haemorrhaging from Grip Mark A, which had penetrated the skin and subdermal tissues of the neck, creating subcutaneous emphysema in the process. Here, we can see swelling when we look at the lining of the throat and stomach, however, the oral cavity and such, and the mucosa and the wall of the lower esophagus are intact and with no remarkable injuries. There is a normal, greyish-pink hue to the tissue, and there are no lesions or apparent injuries to the adjacent region. The gastric mucosa is intact, and there are no obvious injuries to said organs. In the stomach, however, we find typical fluids such as water, coffee, and partially digested food consisting of bacon, eggs, and bread. There appears to be a fruit, possibly an apple or melon, or what have you. There's also an unknown fluid here. We believe this is semen due to consistency and PH testing ... we're just awaiting labs to come back on this."

Captain Holzer looked at his friend with a *no-shit* expression on his face. "Yeah, that's a no-brainer, Bob. This guy and the other fella we're picking up now are likely to have a lot of that stuff in their gullets ... they're both card- carrying deviants, and both have extensive records to prove their extracurricular activities."

Dr. Ketchum turned the tape player back on. "Continuing," he said. "Stomach contents have been saved ... the colon and rectum are both intact, though there appears to be evidence of human papillomavirus. There also appears to be long-term trauma to the anal region and partial tract ... the sphincter is slightly prolapsed ... this is likely the result of sexual; anal intercourse over a period of many years. Again, testing has been ordered. The genitalia are those of an adult, uncircumcised male, and there is no evidence of injury. However, there is evidence that the subject had several bouts of genital warts, as evidenced by scar tissue. Pubic hair has been partially shaved within six to twelve hours prior to death—"

Dr. O'Conner took the stack of photographs and placed them on one of the empty autopsy tables. He spread them out in the shape of a fan and then pointed to a series of images. This was followed by Dr. Ketchum shutting off the tape player.

"Outside of there being no residual scars or markings in this region; outside of an understandable number of hematomas, that is, there is one small tattoo, and what appears like burn-like scar tissue, which may or may not have been there before the subject's death," Dr. O'Conner said. "You may want to view it for yourself."

Captain Holzer offered a brief glance at his friend and then at Dr. O'Conner. "Alright, let's see it," he said.

"Right here, Jim. You can see this tattoo is that of a human penis and scrotum, with what appears to be a gold-coloured earring through the balanitis, with the word 'Bobby G.' inked in black on the shaft of the image."

Dr. O'Conner handed Captain Holzer another set of photographs and pointed to several other images of it. "The tattoo is located on the inner thigh of the left-lateral leg, approximately four-point-zero centimetres below the image," he said. "It measures approximately two-point- eight-by-four-point-six inches in size. The colours are flesh tone, pink, black, and yellow ... but it's the name that stood out to us, captain."

Dr. Ketchum nodded his head in agreement. "True, but there's the other tattoo or scar you should look at, Jim," he said. "On the cadaver's lower back, on his left side, and just above the waist is a small scar or burn. It's possible that it was made pre-mortem, but it is yet by an unknown source. Photos are on file. Next, we'll begin with a brief overview of the labs and see what we can find there. Okay with you, Jim?"

"That's fine … let's get this over with. Maybe I can finally have some answers," Captain Holzer returned gruffly.

"Alright then, let's try for that, Jim. Let's see if this Doctor Straub missed anything, shall we?"

✠

Dr. Ketchum and his assistant explained the possible reasons for the abrasions and the cursory wounds found on the body. Though most of the procedure exemplified what should have been the result of a homicide having been committed at another location and then dumped at the nature preserve, the fact that the old groundskeeper had seen the man alive and well only minutes before being discovered dead had only confounded the medical examiners. For Captain Holzer, however, the questions regarding the case were only mounting instead of being explained. This was not appreciated or typical for any of the men in the room.

Despite the thoroughness of the medical examiners and the top-notch police work that oversaw the Nathan Prud case, not one of them could devise a logical answer for the body that lay before them. To add insult to injury, the fact that the FBI had already been at the crime scene before the event could even be properly reported and that a team of them had already taken part in the cursory exam of the body went far beyond the concept of 'bad form' for both Dr. Ketchum and Captain Holzer. It was simply the wrong thing to do.

CHAPTER FIVE

As Dr. Ketchum continued to position and reposition the cadaver in order to prove his point, both Dr. O'Conner and Captain Holzer began scanning the notations left by the federal medical examiner from earlier that morning. They flipped through the pages, while both had sported looks of being confounded. This was followed by preparing the lab reports that had been rushed on the case, neatly laying them out for Dr. Ketchum to inspect, as per norm. What all three men would discover, however, was that the findings on those documents would not match. There were gross discrepancies.

Now appearing highly suspicious, Captain Holzer just leaned against the vacant examining table with a hand cupped over his mouth. He just stared at the cadaver before him and tried desperately to figure out the mystery. He just scratched at his full, salt-and-pepper moustache and grumbled under his breath. His eyes never blinked.

"Do you have any questions for me yet, Jim?" Dr. Ketchum asked.

"No, I'll hold any questions to the end. Seems cut and dry as to this guy's lifestyle, as our reports clearly suggest, that's a no-brainer. I'm just waiting for the big revelation as to what this is all about, and how this guy died beyond the obvious looks of 'em. I want to know how this happened, how someone could have done this, physically, I mean, and if there was more than one man doing it ... I'm just trying to understand how it could have been done in the first place. You get what I'm asking for, right, Bob … Doctor O'Conner?"

"Of course, we do," Dr. Ketchum said, understanding full well that the mystery that lay before them should have to be concluded with a logical and *acceptable* answer from both of them. This was obvious by their general lack of having ready answers, where instead, only questions lingered. Dr. Ketchum just folded his arms and sighed. "It's just that we don't have any definite answers to offer you yet," he continued. "And more importantly, those missing organs would certainly help us. The bottom line, Jim, is that we just cannot navigate properly with what we have here, you understand … and with the discrepancies on the FBI's reports, the lab reports, and our own findings simply don't match. Right now, until we get to the truth of the matter, it's gonna remain too subjective to put a definite cause to this whole thing."

"Yeah, I understand that, and as I said, I have had two separate teams out there, but again, nothing stands out for us, and definitely, no human flesh was found. And the old groundskeeper at the park wasn't able to give us anything useful, not really. He only found the body after he was ordered to check out the woods that morning. His superiors got the call from Mister Lynch … the guy who took off from the scene, so the groundskeeper is pretty much useless. This Andrew Lynch, I think, will shed some light on this … I'm just waiting to hear back from one of my detectives … he's interviewing him as we speak, so let's just finish this; wrap this guy back up and let me get outta here."

"Alright, that's fine with us ... just let me cover the toxicology report from Amanda Provost, our friend from the University of Chicago ... this came in about an hour before you did, so I'll just breeze over the report here. I have to stay on track, Jim, and it'll only take a minute."

While Dr. Ketchum continued with the tape's contents, Captain Holzer and Dr. O'Conner topped off their coffee cups with a little more of the *Dark Magic* and then returned to the fixed gaze that usually takes over Holzer's face when a medical examiner spins off a reel of overly-charged medical lingo. He tried not to appear as if he were stupid, but the simple retelling of the drug screening alone was beginning to give him a headache. Captain Holzer, however, just leaned against the metal table with folded arms. His head slowly wagged from left to right in silent disapproval.

"Drug Screen Results ... urine screen immunoassay was negative," Dr. Ketchum blurted as he read from a sheet of paper. "Ethanol is zero-negative, blood to heart, which would have been vitreous cerebrospinal fluid culture. And sensitivity wasn't found, and the gram stain was largely unremarkable and for obvious reasons ... no growth should have been found after a forty-eight-hour period, *typically*, but since there's no heart—"

"I wouldn't have figured that one out, Bob," Captain Holzer grumbled sarcastically. "Right," Dr. Ketchum returned, now offering a slight smile to his friend's typical candour. "Continuing ... the cerebrospinal fluid bacterial antigens are unremarkable. Hemophilus influenzae B shows a trace-positive result, and

Streptococcus pneumoniae is negative. Meningitidis shows negative, and Neisseria meningitidis and coli k-one all read negative as well. Okay then, that's that ... now hold on a sec," Dr. Ketchum burbled as he flipped to the second page. "Now, this section reflects finite reviews ... x-rays and such. We did this, along with a CT and MRI last night ... alright?"

"Oh, what joy," Captain Holzer cynically returned, now shaking his head as he perused the photographs of the victim's perverted tattoo.

"There's damage to the clavicle region, along with profound swelling and displacement of vital organs in the neck," Dr. Ketchum continued. "Specifically, the trachea and esophagus region is compromised. And though the haematoma is visible on the X-ray, the bone structure throughout the remainder of the body shows no damage or relative trauma. Regarding the external examination, there does, however, suggest petechial haemorrhaging, thus stating that strangulation is of yet from an undetermined cause.

"In addition to this, a CAT scan shows a massive pooling of blood throughout the neck region, which is evident, exhibiting fractures resulting from high-force impact or localized stress," he continued. "This is, however, not determined pathologically, and bone structure throughout the remainder of the body shows no damage or trauma. To that end, our scans exhibit evidence of profound hematoma to the soft tissues in the neck region, as well as to the anterior section of the mid-frame area. This includes the patency of the trachea and carotid arteries ... and bone structure throughout the remainder of the body shows major damage resulting from yet unknown trauma."

Now, Dr. Ketchum briefly looked over the written reports and then stopped the tape player. "The rest of this appears straightforward enough to me, Jim. I just need to retest a few things later, but otherwise, there's no major discrepancies in the labs. Now, Doppler ultrasonography, however, does prove some stagnation, which is evident in pre and postmortem observation. And angiography right on down to a full esophagoscopy was not performed."

"Bottom line?" Captain Holzer grumbled loudly. Now, Dr. Ketchum took a breath, and lowering the written report to his lap, he began to offer his best explanation as to the cause of death.

"Jim, it is my general opinion that the immediate cause of death, the primary cause of death, was by extreme trauma to the upper thorax region, specifically in the removal of the victim's heart. This, along with Wound B, the trauma in the lower stomach region, constitutes the secondary cause. As for Wound B, there is no logical ... I should say no reasonable explanation for such a wound, other than it may have been caused by as yet an unknown weapon, as already suggested. The third and acceptable cause of death could have been acute asphyxia due to intense strangulation, but I doubt the man lived long enough for that."

"Go on," Captain Holzer said. "What else is there?"

Dr. Ketchum returned to the body and once again pulled down the shroud. He repositioned a flap of cut tissue and pointed to what looked like a mass of pink goo.

"This area right here," he said. "This caused significant damage to the carotid sinus reflex. Specifically, this region had likely caused the bradycardia and acute hypotension as found throughout this entire region. Simply stated, the man was strangled like a rag doll while at the same time having something quite hot inserted in his lower stomach region, and then literally having his entire heart, along with other organs, ripped down and out of his body. Then, he was slammed against a tree with profoundly excessive force, enough force to cause the damage we now find. This was an extremely violent death, Jim."

As Dr. Ketchum related his personal opinions, he admitted that the blunt force it took to slam an over two-hundred-pound man against a tree was indeed the cause of the fleeting looks of amazement from both Captain Holzer and Dr. O'Conner. Dr. Ketchum had described as best he could the nature of the wounds on the corpse, though any finite reasoning had eluded him, just as it did for the DeKalb County police detectives and their Crime Scene Investigation team. The mystery was only becoming more of a mystery.

✠

The three men considered that, though not the primary cause of death, being typical strangulation, whether by ligature, such as by hanging, or manually, such as by hand, each of them knew this wasn't the case. This opinion was due primarily to the grip marks left on the body. Each of them realized that such would require a lot more strength in order to cause such ligature marks, as well as in causing stomach and chest wounds, let alone the removal of the victim's heart.

Captain Holzer would walk away with more information than he had when he walked in, but the answers were not what he had expected — or had wanted.

Now appearing in deep thought, Dr. Ketchum turned to his colleague and raised an eyebrow. "Matt, how would you calculate this ... what specs could you offer; overall, that is?" he asked.

"Well, considering the extent of the damage, I had to use less-than-standard techniques to round out any kind of typical answer. So, I measured as best I could and then called our friend Marion Gonzales at U of C to get a viable number from her. She's a lot better at this than I am. And from the numbers, she came up with ... hold on a sec ... here, I'll read it:

There's at least four-point-nine PSI; that's pounds for square inch measured, which would be about thirty- three thousands-seven-hundred and eighty-four-point-three Pascals, which in turn would equate to about three-point-four NCM-squares."

Captain Holzer just shook his head and exhaled impatiently. "Ah ... what the hell's an NCM?" he asked. The man was clearly confused by the medical jargon.

Now, Dr. O'Connor offered a slight smile and leaned in to explain. "That's a Newton per Square Centimetre, captain. It's a form of measurement; in case you didn't already know. Well, anyway, in order to cause significant damage to the jugular and carotid arteries, around thirty-two PSI or twenty-two NCM-square would cause similar damage to the trachea, but we think it's more than that. Frankly, the numbers would be off the charts, ya' know? Basically, it would be more like seven-thousand-four-hundred and forty-one-B-Fs to the second power, or fifty-one-point-three MP-A of tension. Definitely, it would be an enormous amount of—

"Whoa, whoa, slow it down a bit, Newton!" Captain Holzer yelped. Now, he just stared at the young doctor as if he were a space alien trying to communicate with him. "So, ya think you could dumb it down for me a bit more for me, son? How much strength or force are we talking about?" He asked this as he held his hands like a waiter holding two invisible trays. "Seriously, do I look like a scientist to you? My God, son, I became a cop so I wouldn't have to listen to these high school science lectures … just give me the short and skinny of it … just dumb it down a tad."

In the time it took for Captain Holzer to express his sentiments, and at the risk of making the man appear stupid, both doctors Ketchum and O'Conner gave out a much-needed round of laughter. And at the chagrin of the now weary police captain, the two men couldn't help the levity. Regardless, it only took seconds for the normally irritated police captain to take part in the laughter.

Now, Dr. O'Conner stood up, ceased the majority of his chortling, and then explained the otherwise obscure form of measurement to the captain. "A Mega-Pascal!" he blurted loudly. An MPa is an abbreviation for a Mega- Pascal. It's a basic measurement for a unit of pressure or, in this case, of tension. It's a standard in the International

System of Weights and Measures, and we use it all the time."

"So that's a lot, I take it?" Captain Holzer returned.

"Such would normally be improbable for such ligature markings like those found on Grip Mark A," Dr. Ketchum interjected, now ceasing his laughter. "In effect, the number my esteemed colleague gave you is certainly a lot of strength. But if it were applied to water pressure, let's say from one of those water pressure hoses that clean driveways and such? Well, that could be enough power to literally cut your arm, Jim."

"Jesus," Captain Holzer mumbled to himself.

"Normally, where such pressure would need to be considerable, that seems to be the case here, Jim."

Now, Dr. O'Conner nodded at Dr. Ketchum's remark and then raised a finger. "Well, in short, captain, that estimated PSI was at least seventy-eight to eighty … or as the report says in black and white, fifty-five points," he said. "Let's just say whoever did this … *whatever* did this, is not within the spectrum of human capability. It wouldn't be human. In fact, in my opinion, if you had five Dwayne 'The Rock' Johnsons all squeezing the man's neck at the same time, they wouldn't have caused this type of damage. Perhaps a nine-hundred-pound, Silver Back Gorilla might make these numbers, but only if it was really, really pissed off."

Both Dr. Ketchum and Dr. O'Conner nodded at each other in agreement, though the police captain was still very much in the dark. There had been no logic to the bizarre crime, especially in explaining the bizarre death of the cadaver lying before them. Despite the science or the determination of either of them, however, a definite answer simply did not exist. For Nathan Nicholas Prud, he would remain the quintessential conundrum.

✠

"Alright, just the basics then," Dr. O'Conner said. He pointed to the neck region on the cadaver and repositioned its neck to best illustrate his findings. "Okay, look here," he said. "Basically, we can conclude … we might conclude, I should say, that by the occluding and fracturing, and the crushing of the hyoid bone, along with this section of the spinal column, proves the lion's share of the damage to the pharynx, including the oropharynx, and hypopharynx. And then there's the crushing of the arteries, captain, specifically the carotid arteries and the jugular vein…

This is where the majority of blood vessels were found highly traumatized. Because of this, we can at least verify the damage directly. Beyond this, even though we can't honestly establish a direct cause at this time because of the body's condition, outside of his body temperature or the nature of this particular wound does, however, suggest at least a possible source …we just have to identify it. Either way, both wounds are pre-mortem in nature; we know that for sure."

"So, you're saying that this guy was strangled with excessive strength, an … an inhuman strength?" Captain Holzer asked.

Dr. Ketchum nodded in confirmation. "Yes, excessive to the point of being redundant," he said flatly. That's to say, by hands more than one; surely by someone or something far greater than one man, which is why we're entertaining the idea of a weapon of some sort. It would have been impossible for one man to do this, Jim, pure and simple. The pressure it would take to cause this amount of damage, this amount of pressure-per-square-inch, is simply beyond human strength. What I mean by this is that it would take something more like a hydraulic vice grip to cause such damage. But we have to remember that human skin, being very pliable, didn't rupture by the strangulation. This … this just isn't feasible here. The skin should have been torn to ribbons by such a force … unless."

"Unless what?" Captain Holzer asked impatiently.

"Unless a somewhat soft and extremely large device could have gripped the victim and squeezed with tremendous strength … as if a giant hand had done this. You just can't fake the numbers; can't falsify simple physics or the math … it's just not possible, Jim."

"You realize you're not helping things … you know that," Captain Holzer blurted.

Dr. O'Conner looked at the captain, deciding to offer a little more information to round out his mentor's presentation. "So, what we have here is a very large hand, a *human-like* hand, captain, an immensely hot, human-like hand that squeezed this guy as if he were a burrito from Taco Bell. He or whatever did this to Mister Prud had done so until his neck snapped like a handful of crackers, and then twisted it, from what appears to be one giant, albeit oddly-shaped source … almost like a great big thumb had simply snapped his neck. It's as if whatever had done this had twisted his head, almost to its backside. Now, absolutely none of this makes sense, I know, but if you mentally envision it and then look at the cadaver before you, you'll see it too."

"It probably was very quick," Dr. Ketchum added. "If that's even imaginable, but everything you're looking at tends to point to that idea, regardless of it sounding ridiculous."

Captain Holzer just shook his head slowly, as a slight smile began to rise on his face. "So, you're telling me that the Jolly Green Giant swooped down from out of the trees and slapped this guy around until his head went all funny, and then shoved his red-hot hand into his belly and pulled out a sample just for fun, is that what you're telling me?" he asked, now with the unmistakable look of being played a fool."

"In short," Dr. O'Conner added, "this guy was picked up off the ground and had his stomach gouged by what appears to be from a large scoop that was hot enough to cauterize some of the organs and tissue. Then, his heart, along with parts of his intestines, was ripped out. After that, he was tossed against a tree with a tremendous amount of force and left for dead. With that, it was a simple, quick killing, in and out … assassin style, if you will."

Captain Holzer just stared slack-jawed, exchanging looks of disbelief with both men. He didn't say anything.

"Captain, I've seen my share of killings, maybe a bit too many," Dr. O'Conner continued, "and I've seen what a man can do to another man, believe me. But this ... this is way out there. No, sir, no single man could have done this; there's absolutely no way of that. I'll state my reputation on it."

"Me too, Jim," Dr. Ketchum interjected.

Captain Holzer just scratched his moustache again. "Well, I agree with you, son, and I've seen my share of murders over the years, too, and this one's for the books, that's a cinch," he said. "But I'm gonna need more than this. I'm gonna need to hear something from these FBI boys, whether they like it or not."

"Oh, yeah, there's one more thing ... I almost forgot. Remind me to put it on the report," Dr. Ketchum said to Dr. O'Conner. Then, he looked squarely at Captain Holzer and then began to lift the body to its side. "Help me here, Matt," he asked.

The two medical examiners moved the body to its left side and then rolled it over, almost to its front. Dr. O'Conner closed the vinyl flap in order to hold the cadaver's innards in place so Nathan Prud's sawed-off chest plate and intestines wouldn't spill out. Then he pulled down the back section of the shroud just enough to expose Prud's lower extremities.

"I almost forgot about this, Jim," Dr. Ketchum said. "If you take a look here, you'll see what appears to be a scar of some sort ... see right here?"

"Yeah ... what is that?" Captain Holzer offered a look that reflected a man who was truly mystified, like a man who was trying to remember something. "It looks like a burn of some sort, like something was burned into his skin, doesn't it?"

"That was our idea too, but if it was burned, as it appears to have been … then there should be some redness around it unless it was done after a period of time, post-mortem, though that doesn't really gel either, Jim."

The men stared at the strange marking, a marking that looked as if it were either burned or cut and then burned at the same time into the man's flesh, like a rancher's cattle branding iron. The scar was raised just enough to authenticate this hypothesis. Captain Holzer recognized the mark as possibly being significant in either gang or occult terms. He realized that gangs would sometimes initiate new recruits with cuts or burns, and satanic cults often did the same, though this seemed different, almost natural in origin. Nonetheless, for these people, it was necessary to mark their victims in a similar manner. Now, he quickly snapped a photo of it on his cellphone and then stood back as the two doctors returned the body to its original position.

Dr. Ketchum explained that the strange mark could have been a result of three possible causes. One, that it was made as a form of tattoo before the man's death; having then turned to semi-ridged scar tissue over a period of time, or two, that it had occurred as a result of the body being thrown against the tree, somehow making that mark from that trauma, and three, that someone had placed the mark on Prud's body after he was killed. The third possibility appeared to be the most plausible, as agreed upon by both doctors. Captain Holzer, however, had retained his gut feelings on the possibility, believing it was gang or cult-related. Despite the logic, the captain's theory had prompted him to make a quick sketch of it in his notepad in order to show Nathan Prud's wife, just in case she knew of its origin.

Dr. Ketchum went on to explain that the strange burn-like marking had been chemically tested for any caustic residue, meaning that it might authenticate that some kind of inorganic acid might have been used to make the marking, but this, too, was still only conjecture. Regardless, he assured the captain that the mark was likely made by another source, such as from something red-hot, such as from a branding iron, though there was no certainty in that hypothesis as of yet.

For Captain Holzer, however, he had made it clear that such a wound might have been placed there as a calling card from an enemy and was now a major link in the homicide. He believed that this was the most plausible answer. Now, the suspicious captain would keep the possibility of an occult-related murder as the most probable cause, where the strange marking was left as a warning to someone, possibly for another cult, perhaps a rival cult.

This was no surprise to law enforcement. It was, as Captain Holzer had believed, a common behaviour with many homicidal occult orders. Silently, he assigned himself the task of researching this idea for a later date and in detail. For the moment, however, he would look for answers elsewhere. He knew he'd have a long week ahead of him.

"It's just that it looks so familiar to me for some reason," Captain Holzer blurted, as he closed his notepad. "Is there anything else, Bob?" he asked.

"Pending outside review of toxicology screening, MRI-C scans, polymerase reactions, and DNA fingerprint testing, I have no choice but to list this case as open until further notice, with my findings typed as death from unnatural causes," Dr. Ketchum stated emphatically.

Though looking confused, Captain Holzer just nodded his head to agree.

"The short and skinny of it, Jim ... well, I'm gonna have to list it as a G.O.K. for the time being, at least for now."

"G–O–K?" Captain Holzer snapped. "What the hell is that?"

"Oh, that's old coroner slang, Jim. It stands for *God Only Knows*, and that, my good friend, until further notice, is the truth ... no doubt about it."

CHAPTER SIX

"How are we to understand this dance of death, and the further legend of her tossing bodies into the air for amusement?"

— Moncure Daniel Conway, Demonology and Devil-Lore

It was a quarter to noon when Captain Holzer had decided to end the impromptu meeting and the diminutive autopsy that had left more questions than answers, more questions than there were facts. Nonetheless, he figured that he had all the information he needed for the time being. The whole concept of 'God Only Knows' baloney was not to be in any cop's dictionary, only cold cases, which he'd be damned if the Nathan Prud case became. The stalwart captain demanded answers and absolutely hated not having them. He was certain that there was a much more plausible answer to the mysteries at hand and, more importantly, his homicide case. This was still his township, and he wasn't finished with this case — not by a long shot.

By noon, Captain Holzer was on his way downtown to interview Mr. Andrew Lynch, the gentleman who had more answers than he was admitting to, a man who, more likely than not, had the answers he would need in order to wrap the case up quickly and neatly. And with that, he stepped on the gas just a bit harder than usual.

By 1:23 p.m., Captain Holzer had finished his briefing with detectives Wong and Marino. They had furnished him with enough information about the victim and the potential perpetrator, Mr. Andrew Lynch, of

Aurora, Illinois. Both Prud and Lynch had their share of legal problems over the years, specifically Mr. Lynch, who had a propensity for indecent exposure and public masturbation, a problem that had him serving thirteen months at the Cook County lockup. He also had his face and address smeared across several newspapers as a result. In the end, Captain Holzer realized that the man wasn't the most infamous in his circle of perverts, though his crimes were consistent enough to place him on the Illinois State Sex Offender Registry.

After reviewing Mr. Lynch's past, Captain Holzer had learned that he had once worked as an assistant coach for the junior varsity football team at a high school in Quincy but was let go on suspicion of *inappropriate behaviour*. He had had the 'problem' since he was a teen, having been a victim of child abuse, he said. But Captain Holzer wasn't interested in his life story. He just wanted the facts regarding the body lying in the county morgue.

Regardless of Mr. Lynch's legal history, however, his sexual preferences, and perverted desires, he had offered practically no information other than finding the body, just as the old groundskeeper had less than an hour after him. The man just wanted to get out of there, wanting nothing to do with the dead body that lay in state in Dr. Robert Ketchum's morgue. At least, that's what Mr. Lynch had insisted upon. Despite the man's testimony, Captain Holzer had nothing on the man, outside of practically admitting to going to the park in order to find a partner for a sexual tryst. Beyond that, he came up empty once again.

Captain Holzer and his detectives had released the man for the time being and offered him some time-honoured advice, such as to never return to that park or any park in his jurisdiction with such intent, nor continue with his behaviour in his city again. And to be sure, the threat was taken seriously, as the look on Mr. Lynch's face clearly expressed. The thin, balding man, his eyes as wide as two hard-boiled eggs, had let the captain and the detectives know that he'd never go back to that park or any park where the stalwart Captain Holzer lived or worked. Such would be the only win for the DeKalb County Police Department this day.

As Mr. Lynch made this promise with a quiver in his voice, the man slowly got up and left the room. He had the fear of God eloquently placed in him, thanks to the kind of advice that only law enforcement could offer such a man. By 2:15 p.m., Captain Holzer released the man and then proceeded to interview the wife of the victim, Mrs. Marsha Prud. And what the woman had to say only justified what the captain had known all along — that people like Nathan Prud and his wife were soulless heathens who looked at life as a sick game; like a cocktail party where the most heinous of lascivious behaviours were the norm, and where decency was an alien and despised concept. The interview had only reinforced the captain's opinions about today's society and why America was falling.

Though what Mrs. Prud had said during the interview hadn't necessarily shocked the captain or his detectives, it was the sheer audacity of the woman's testimony that only added to the befuddlement of the situation, tallying a sense of the perverse and mindless into the mix. Captain Holzer had heard many things in his many decades of career, but her testimony had simply sickened him. Nonetheless, Captain Holzer and detectives Wong and Marino sat as patiently as they could, knowing that the affair at the J. McNeery Forest Preserve was a high-profile case for them.

Each of the men knew that if they fouled this ball, there would be hell to pay from the mayoral staff downtown, not to mention the chance of soiling Captain Holzer's reelection campaign that was coming up in a year's time. Now, they all knew that the entire case depended on what they could decipher about Nathan Prud's wife.

Throughout the course of the hour-and-a-half interview, the police had listened to the drawn-out testimony of a woman with less than noble pursuits. When she divulged her and her late husband's lifestyle, the men weren't just shocked; they were astounded. Detective Marino, however, would later insist that it was, after all, the twenty-first century and that people had become far more enlightened, much like the Hollywood elite in California or the seemingly untouchable politicians in the nation's capital. Captain Holzer didn't share such sentiments, however, even when they were being made in jest.

Being swingers as the Pruds were only made the situation more confusing. That they had an open marriage alone was sickening to the stalwart captain, but that the couple's swing parties could often have as many as twenty to forty people involved, and where the men might be with other men, and the women might be with women, was simply beyond belief to him. It didn't matter that Captain Holzer was a veteran cop; he was honestly sickened by Mrs. Prud's heathenish beliefs, pure and simple.

Toward the end of the interview, Mrs. Prud had mentioned her and her husband's strange involvement with the occult. Specifically, Nathan Prud was a high-ranking official in a kind of devil cult, a Luciferian order devoted to the ramblings of a long-dead Satanist from England's past, specifically, to the notorious persona from the beginning of the last century, one Aleister Crowley — *The Great Beast.*

The cult, as Mrs. Prud had explained it, was loosely associated with 'The Order of Pry Thealemè Ex Mortis,' an unapproved, minor offshoot of one of the original orders dating back to the 1920s, from the temple order known as the 'Ordo Tenebris Lux.' This cult was originally devised by Albertus Thanor Rikus, an Austrian-Hungarian Freemason and cultist, along with a German-American industrialist and inventor named Kort Wilhelm. Mrs. Prud explained that with the realities of Rosicrucianism, the Golden Dawn, alchemy, and magick in general, along with the power and direction of the Freemasons, the cult was born into a minor greatness within the spectrum of the occult world. She beamed with pride.

Now, Captain Holzer just watched in amazement at the woman's enthusiasm for what he had considered bunk and nothing more. But he remained silent.

Mrs. Prud's crooked grin faded now, just as her eyes went glossy. And then, she smiled in protest as she hailed her cult's motto with pride: "Thealemè Ex Mortis! Aritus Nicta-Nuptiae Tu-Ey Aha!" She chimed the esoteric quote with a peculiar zeal that made the captain and his detectives arch back in their chairs.

"What in Sam Hill?" Captain Holzer blurted.

"It means the establishment of Thealemè Ex Mortis as a ritual of love," she continued. "The word is Greek in origin, captain. It means the *Will for Pleasure*. Oh, and yes, you should also know that it's our purpose, far beyond the limits of your ... your Jewish god." Now with a crooked smile on her face, she widened her eyes to offer an expression of superiority. This was followed by an arrogant nod.

Captain Holzer leaned in again and folded his hands together. "Huh ... this is all very interesting, Mrs. Prud, but I—"

"Thealemè Ex Mortis will guide me through this, captain," the foul woman continued, cutting him off in mid-sentence. "Yes ... yes, this too shall pass," she continued, as she wiped the tears away from her eyes and then blew her nose in an old tissue she had wadded up in her purse. She expounded upon the motto's phrase and meaning like a Baptist minister proclaiming his love for Christ, though it had been obvious that there was doubt in her stressed expressions. Nonetheless, she offered her words with the same amount of love a mother would have shown for her child's kindergarten play. The spectacle was simply bizarre.

Now, Captain Holzer found himself with little sympathy for the man lying on the slab at the morgue, as he did for the woman who sat there in front of him gnawing at her Kleenex, wiping her crocodile tears with a dramatic sense of melodramatic exclamation.

This bitch couldn't feel any sense of remorse if she tried to, Captain Holzer thought. *Soulless bitch. Cold as a fish … I wouldn't believe her if she said good morning.*

✠

Now growing incensed, Captain Holzer decided to remain civil with the woman that sat in front of him, where down deep he just wanted to unleash the wrath of God on her. Her lifestyle, her behaviour, and her sick devotion to all things evil were the very things that made his job a living hell on a daily basis. It had made him sick to his stomach.

Remembering his training as a detective over the years, the man knew how to draw out information from any perp, regardless of who they were or what their affiliations were. He was on a mission with this case, a personal mission that wouldn't end until he had answers.

"Mrs. Prud, I do have one more thing to ask you, if you don't mind?" "No … no, not at all," she said, as she blew her nose in the wad of tissue.

Pulling a notepad from the briefcase that lay across his desk, Captain Holzer flipped the pages back until he found the sketch he had made earlier that day at the coroner's office. Now, he held up the notepad with the strange marking on it.

"Have you ever seen this before, ma'am … does this symbol have any meaning to you?" he asked.

"Oh, yes … that's ah, that's a letter from the 'Witches Alphabet.' I don't remember which letter it is, but it's popular with Wiccans and other practitioners of the craft, I know that much," she said. "It's for crafting your *Book of Shadows* and stuff like that … Nat could have told you more about it, of course." She began to cry again and then blew her nose into her now overly-used wad of tissue.

"Book of Shadows … I see," Captain Holzer mumbled. "Did your husband ever have a tattoo or burn mark of this symbol on him … this … this witches' symbol on him?"

"No, he only had one little tattoo on his leg, near his junk … but that was in remembrance of his college friend who died years ago, ya' know … old boyfriend or something like that." She said with a chuckle, followed by another sob. For Captain Holzer and his detectives, it only made her sincerity even more questionable.

Captain Holzer just nodded gently and folded his hands again. "Oh … okay, Mrs. Prud, I think that'll be enough for today," he said. "I appreciate your time, and if there's anything else you might remember or think might be relevant to this case, I'd appreciate hearing from you, alright?"

"Oh, oh yeah, of course … thanks. I know you'll find Nat's killer … eventually. He had enemies."

Mrs. Prud's last comment instantly made Captain Holzer's eyebrows arch. Now, he sat back in his chair and rested his hands on his stomach. "Well now, that's information you should have told me earlier, Mrs. Prud," he said. "Are you saying that you think your husband might have been murdered … by someone he might have known?"

"Well, I, I don't know, not really, I guess … but he did have his share of enemies, ya' know? He was very vocal on his blog pages and when writing for other blogs and stuff like that. He, he was proud of his knowledge of *magick*, and what and who he was affiliated with, ya' know?"

"Please … explain that to me, if you would, Mrs. Prud," Captain Holzer asked, now with a serious but compassionate look on his face. It was a common police tactic he used to draw out information, and it almost always worked on those who liked to prattle on.

"Well, you know … he was a high priest in our Order, and he'd written a lot on the subject too … he, he was an authority on lots of things related to the Order; to the occult in general, ya' know? He was very high up … if, if someone had the nerve to talk about something that he didn't agree with, well, well he'd rip 'em a new one … ya' know what I mean?"

"I see … so you think that he might have had enemies then … an enemy angry enough to kill him, is that right?"

"Well, I don't know … I guess so? You'd have to read his blogs … you'll see that he was always fair, but if he didn't like your writing or a book or artwork, or whatever, he'd go right after you … he was just like that, that's all." She said this with a confused look now taking over her expression as if she were beginning to see through Captain Holzer's obviously manufactured sympathies. Now, a grimace had begun to form on her face.

Now considering that the cadaver in the downtown morgue was a *true-blue scumbag*, as Captain Holzer liked to refer to people who he didn't like, he was now surmising the possibility that the homicide was, in fact, an elaborate murder carried out by someone, or persons, who just didn't like the man's attitude or audacity. He was beginning to consider that it might be an act of revenge, a possibility that could have occurred because of the man's deviant behaviour and possibly because of his attacks on other writers or artists.

"Mrs. Prud, as we discussed earlier, we're all aware of your husband's … ah, shall we say, extra-marital affairs out in those woods?" Captain Holzer said. "And because your husband has had prior arrests for various … various homosexual-related behaviours in those woods, as well as at his university where he taught, I'm leaning on a motive of revenge as the most likely outcome of the day's events."

"Oh, that's old news, and I really don't give a shit about it captain," Mrs. Prud said, now apparently annoyed that that information was even being brought up. She had confided in him and the police detectives about their lifestyle and beliefs, not feeling that there was any pertinent relevance to it. Now, she began stuffing the well-worn tissue in her purse while grabbing a fresh one at the same time. She looked like she was getting ready to storm out of the captain's office.

"Ma'am, can you give us any other information about your husband's affairs?" Captain Holzer continued.

"Oh, what does any of that have to do with anything?" she asked angrily. Her voice had risen a few degrees higher in pitch than before. "I don't know why everyone gets so uptight about it … it's more a way of life that you and people like you automatically think. We have rights, too, and we're not hurting anyone, okay? If somebody killed my Nathan because they have hang-ups or something, then it's your job to get him and not to harass me!"

"Okay, okay, Mrs. Prud," Captain Holzer returned, now holding his hands out to suggest that the now-angry woman calm down. "I'm just trying to put things together in order to find out who could have done this to your husband, that's all ... there's no need to get upset. I thank you again for your time, and please, please remember, if you think of anything else, I'll need to hear from you straight away. This is the only way that my detectives and myself can figure this whole thing out, alright, Mrs. Prud?"

"Oh ... okay, I suppose. It's just that what we did together ... what he did by himself shouldn't have been worth killing him over. We're just more advanced, more enlightened than the rest of the herd. That's what Nat called everyone else, ya' know ... the herd." The woman snorted under her breath and then wiped her tears away with the old, tattered wad of tissue. "We are, after all, more enlightened, and we're proud of our wisdom over the masses. We're proud, captain, and we aren't to be ashamed of it." The woman offered another expression of superiority and quickly flung the strap to her purse over her right shoulder.

"Pride," Captain Holzer repeated. "Pride is something our faith tells us is the very route of evil, Mrs. Prud. It's what got the devil kicked out of heaven, isn't it?"

"That's your hang-up, captain, not ours. You'll see
... you'll *all* see that it's not the meek that will inherit the
earth, but those who know the truth; those who are superior."

"Right, I, I see, Mrs. Prud. When you get a chance,
I'll need to have the addresses of those blog pages, so if you
could call or email them to me or one of the detectives, that
would be very helpful, alright?"

The woman shook her head, got up, and walked out
of the office. She certainly appeared angry about being
questioned in such a manner, but more likely from having her
lifestyle questioned, or why anyone would consider having
sex in a public park would be so wrong or unethical.
Nevertheless, the interview offered enough information for
Captain Holzer to finish his report, along with Dr. Ketchum's
views for the meeting that afternoon.

Detectives Wong and Marino had walked Mrs. Prud
out to her car, where she left, wiping her eyes and nose from
the loss of her husband. She would go home alone to an
empty house, where she could collect herself with a cocktail,
and maybe a little Mary Jane to help cope with her loss, or as
Captain Holzer had suggested to his detectives, that she'd
likely just pick up where she'd left off and return to her sordid
life without so much as a thought. For the three lawmen,
however, they had concluded that the woman was nothing
more than a cold, heartless bitch.

Now perplexed, Captain Holzer just stared at the
woman from his office window. He watched her get into her
car, toss her used tissue to the ground, and then pull out of
the parking lot at a considerable speed. He couldn't

believe people like that could even exist. Once the detectives returned, he just waited for their professional opinions and conjectures.

"Well, what do ya' think, captain?" Detective Wong asked with a smirk on his face. Captain Holzer just shook his head. "Cripes ... that woman's ten pounds of crazy in a five-pound sack," he muttered aloud. He continued to shake his head at the sheerly disgusting beliefs the woman held as important. He knew that this case wouldn't be closed any time soon. He also knew that there were nonetheless enough facts to make sure the top officials understood just how hard his job really was, but more than that, that he and his people were on the case day and night. It would be a bitch of a case, but at least some leeway had been made that day.

By now, both detectives Wong and Marino had finished their reports, placed them in the captain's 'To Do' box on his desk, and left for lunch. They knew they'd be putting in a lot of hours in the next week or so and wanted to get started on it. They also knew that there would likely be an inquest at City Hall, so covering every detail, taking notes and photographs, and conducting interviews would be an overload. They hadn't relished the thought. Moreover, they knew that their captain would be on high alert too, and more likely than not, in a bad mood. This, too, was a matter of form.

Captain Holzer went home that night exhausted and weary. He had a headache that almost prompted him to go to the emergency room. But, a couple of Tylenol P.M.s, sleep, and a firm bed were all he wanted now. He would get his wish. He'd take a hot shower, eat a light supper, and then hit the sheets. Despite his usual habits, however, he would forgo taking his work home with him. Tonight, he would choose rest over tenacity. Tonight, he would sleep the sleep of the dead, though he'd dream of strange things; terrible things.

✠

By Monday morning, Captain Holzer had come to work expecting a typical day. He expected to review the department's logs from the night before, gloss over the incident reports by his field training officers, and the viewpoints regarding new recruits. He'd follow up with the city planners concerning gang activity in the projects and for any progress with the Nathan Prud homicide case. Hopefully, he'd complete his bi-annual mayoral report on the affairs of crime and punishment in DeKalb County on time, and without incident. He expected just another day of paperwork and business as usual, but that wouldn't be the case.

It wasn't even ten in the morning when Captain Holzer's phone buzzed. He was just finishing his third and final cup of coffee when his receptionist alerted him with the number ninety-nine on the phone's digital screen. This was her silent way to tell the captain that he had important guests waiting for him. Thinking it might have been Mrs. Prud returning, hoping that she might have more information about her husband and his activities, he folded the morning's paper and pushed the intercom button down—

"Yes, Jasmine?" Captain Holzer asked sternly.

"Captain, there's two men from the FBI here to see you," the receptionist said.

"Be right there," he returned. A slight look of confusion fell across his face. "Huh … maybe someone told 'em that I was pissed for being kept out of the loop," he quietly muttered. "Now maybe we'll get some answers."

Captain Holzer walked to the front of the office to meet the federal officers in good spirits because he knew he'd finally get a handle on the Prud case. As he approached the front desk, he could see two men; the first was around sixty or so years of age, tall and thin. He had greyish hair and wore a light blue suit with an olive-drab green tie. He noticed that the man's tie was far too wide and far too out of date for any modern federal agent, with a style that defied the current decade, matching something more common forty years ago. It made him appear a bit off. His clothes looked like something men wore in the '70s or '80s, but certainly, nothing that would be accepted today. Regardless of the man's attire, he stood tall and cryptic as he held a dark leather valise. The man barely smiled.

The man standing next to him, however, was shorter but definitely more muscular. He sported a more common suit of the day, and his jet-black hair was slicked back, which gave him a better-than-average appearance of confidence but with just a touch of hoodlum mixed in. This, along with the excessive chewing of gum, had offered a look that suggested the man might have had a rough childhood, but appearances could sometimes be wrong.

Now, as Captain Holzer approached, the young agent ceased his flirting with the receptionist and stood up with even more confidence. Captain Holzer figured he was a cocky sort, but happy all the same to finally get some answers to the bizarre homicide case that had shaken the normally quiet township of DeKalb.

The two agents reached for their identification and flashed their badges. "Good morning, sir," the young agent said.

"Good morning, gentlemen, I'm Jim Holzer," he returned with a smile, and then extended his hand.

"Good morning, captain, I'm Special Agent Martin Le'fadden, Bureau. This is Agent Rovina, my partner on the Nathan Prud Case … I hope we haven't caught you at a bad time?"

"Absolutely not," Captain Holzer replied, "come on back to my office … I've been waiting for the Bureau's take on this from the get-go. Jasmine, I'm in a meeting until I say otherwise, okay?" Captain Holzer barked at the receptionist.

"Yes, sir, I'll hold all calls."

As the two agents took their seats in Captain Holzer's office, Special Agent Le'fadden's cologne had immediately taken residence and in full force. Captain Holzer had recognized the scent as Bay Rum, a cologne that was likely as old as the man's outdated suit. Though Agent Le'fadden had always worn too much of it, it was his signature scent. He had worn it ever since his late wife had bought him a fresh bottle every Christmas. It was her favourite and thus had become a tradition for the man that would likely last the duration of his life. Despite the overpowering scent, Captain Holzer simply ignored it.

"Can I get you some coffee, gentlemen? It's still fresh," Captain Holzer said to the two agents.

"None for me, thank you," Agent Rovina returned with a smile.

"I might have some a little later, captain, but not right at the moment," the elder agent said. Then, he opened his valise and pulled out several papers that were clipped to a manila folder, put on a pair of reading glasses, and then scanned over the documents for a few moments. Then, as if reading from a podium in a class on criminology, he exhaled and prattled off the nature of Nathan Prud's criminal history—

"FBI docket … incident case file, designation PD-nine-ninety-nine-zero-six-dash-forty-five; police report; DeKalb County case number zero-one, seventy-six, regarding murder-homicide … headings are the same in this batch," the elder agent repeated flawlessly. His younger partner, however, had simply watched the police captain quietly and unblinkingly. "The victim's name is Nathan Nicholas Prud," Special Agent Le'fadden continued. "The location of the homicide is listed as the J. McNeery Forest Preserve in DeKalb County, Illinois, three-hundred-and-eighty-one, DeBellamy Road. The exact location is between the front entrance on DeBellamy Road and North First Street, near the west side of the Kishwaukee River, just beyond the nature trail, and approximately twenty-six yards from a wooden board trail … behind a thicket of trees."

"Yes, we're all aware of the details, agent—"

Special Agent Le'fadden ignored the captain and kept reading. "Nathan Nicholas Prud, occupation; formerly, was an assistant professor of English with Nimbus University, also in DeKalb, Illinois. Expertise was twentieth-century British and American linguistics and British literature."

Now looking somewhat confused, Captain Holzer broke in: "I have the entire report here, Agent Le'fadden, if you'd like to look it over," he said.

"No, that won't be necessary, captain, I just have a little more here. I just need to make sure the facts are accurate," he said in a flat tone of voice. He never lifted his gaze from his folder. Leaning slightly over Agent Le'fadden's shoulder, Agent Rovina began to whisper something to his partner.

"Excuse me, sir ... we still have to pick up that information packet from the coroner's office. Would you like me to go over and pick that up?"

"That's a good idea, Vinnie," Agent Le'fadden said. "Go on ahead, and head on over there. Finish up with the medical examiner, and make sure the body is prepped for flight; paperwork, signatures ... the usual. It has to be ready no later than four today. When you're finished, go on and head on over to that diner we saw coming in this morning ... the one off Fourth Street ... the one right up the road. I'll just walk from here, and then we'll go over all of this with something to eat ... sound good?"

"Yes, sir, that'll be fine. Just call me if plans change," the young agent said.

Captain Holzer furrowed his face and then leaned over his desk. "So, you *are* taking the body with you?" he asked.

"Yes, we have orders to transport it to our lab in Quantico."

"I'm still not sure why the FBI is so interested in the Prud homicide, even if it is a little on the strange side," Captain Holzer continued. He decided to see if he could loosen the agent's tongue a bit. "So, agent … I guess you already made contact with the wife?"

"Sure have … she was less than what you'd expect, especially after the death of her husband. But then, her lifestyle is less than typical, wouldn't you say?"

"Oh yeah, I would say so," Captain Holzer snickered. "Just asking, but why would the Bureau want the body … isn't our work efficient enough for a record?"

"Oh, absolutely, but keep in mind, captain, our lab has hundreds of experts and special agents to take a closer look … a very close look at this particular mystery. Besides, I've been ordered to oversee this process, specifically in cross-referencing a new system that can identify certain chemicals and residues that may have been left on the body. It's a new process, and one that's not in the commonplace morgue, and we need to see if there's any connection; any connection at all to Mister Prud and another cadaver we have on ice. So, seeing that our facilities have a reputation as being the top crime labs in the United States, if not the world, we think it's the best choice for Mister Prud's final destination. And we'll release the body as soon as we're finished. We've already notified the wife, so you don't have to worry about that either, captain."

"I guess you have a point there, Agent Le'fadden," Captain Holzer said. "But I'd sure like to hear back from you about all this, though."

"Consider it done, captain."

"THANK YOU!" Captain Holzer spouted in an exuberant tone. "Great Jupiter's balls, between the medical examiner and myself, we're about out of options with this thing. I can't tell you how much we appreciate the gesture, Agent Le'fadden."

"The pleasure's all mine, captain … it's all mine."

✠

Now, as Agent Rovina left the office, Captain Holzer found himself feeling a little incensed. He was trying to figure out why the feds were telling him what he already knew. Despite this, he remained silent, hoping that Agent Le'fadden would eventually spill the beans and shed some light on the whole grisly affair. He just wanted this whole thing to go away, or better yet, to have a logical explanation for it so he could get a decent night's rest again.

"Bear with me, captain, I just want to make sure a few things are secure here," the agent said as he continued to scan the documents. "Prud seems to have had an interesting history; here at the McNeery nature centre… the forest preserve, and several other places in the general vicinity, including at the university where he worked. He's apparently taken a few trips abroad too, specifically to

Thailand and the Philippines … not sure if you're aware of those last details, but we'll fill you in on that later."

"I'd be very interested to hear what you have," Captain Holzer replied."

"He has … he *had*, I should say, a reputation for illicit behaviour; that was sexual in nature and with documented arrest histories. NCIC lists his prior arrests … three counts. The first is a seven-hundred and twenty and a five-eleven-thirty for public indecency that occurred on February third of nineteen-ninety-nine, DeKalb County. And the disposition?"

"Yes, guilty … we're all fully aware of that, agent," the now worrisome police captain said. "But why—"

"He was found guilty and served eighteen months' probation," Special Agent Le'fadden interrupted. "And the current disposition is … expunged, effective May fifteen, two-thousand and two … interesting," he continued. Now, he continued to gaze over the documents with a confused expression. "Hum … curious. He has quite a record, yet with little to no consequence whatsoever. This is strange, wouldn't you say, captain?"

Now looking over his own records, Captain Holzer scrolled down the page on his laptop. "That's right, and it's not the first time he's gotten away with something like that; well, with pretty much everything … zilch regarding serving any time," he said. "This guy must have had a dream team of lawyers."

"That's correct, captain, yet another section eleven-thirty for public indecency on June six, twenty-fourteen, having pled no contest, with all charges dismissed by

September of that year, and one other time. This time, however, the offence is a fifty-one-twenty, which is, is a criminal sexual assault in the State of Illinois, I believe. This charge took place in November, on the fifth of twenty-fifteen; also, in DeKalb County. Disposition is … surprise, surprise … not guilty. Case dropped; dismissed on November … the day after his arrest, in fact. I have that file, and the one from the Illinois State Police, too, if you want to look it over."

"Nope … we've all the info we need on that. This guy was a real piece of work," Captain Holzer said as he continued to read through the case notations of detectives Wong and Marino.

"Indeed … that's one way of putting it," Special Agent Le'fadden returned with a smile. "As for his trips to the Orient, I found his name, along with a dozen or so others from this state who are, or in this case *were*, on the DOJ's watch list. And it seems that our Mister Prud took his sexual escapades to the nth degree, trying his hand at much younger partners … *much* younger partners, if you take my meaning."

Captain Holzer looked up at the agent with a concerned gaze. "My interviews with the wife were confusing … ah, in that they were also into the occult. What about this occult business … is there anything to it?" he asked.

"That's strictly secondary from the issue of the homicide, but officially, I'll just say this, there's much more here than meets the eye." Special Agent Le'fadden said this as ardently as he could, though his answer was still cold and discerning. "There's much more below the surface; we just have to do a little more digging, that's all," he added.

"Prud's wife said they were a part of some cult called, ah … hold on a minute, here … I've got it right here. Yes, and it's called Thh-el, the Thea-lem-ee, ah, ex mortis? Have you heard of that?" Captain Holzer asked, his head now half-tilted and with questioning eyes.

"Sure have … and it's not to be confused with another organization of a similar sounding name … it has nothing to do with the O.T.O., the Ordo Templi Orientis. In fact, I think there were lawsuits back in the seventies, but nothing came of it. The O.T.O. is made up mostly of scholars and intellectuals, and some artists and poets … your basic Bohemian set, I suspect. But the Thealemè Ex Mortis, well, that's another story, and it's not the first time its members have seen notoriety and infamy. There've been plenty of arrests over the years. But I'm not putting too much stock in any of that right at the moment, captain … just need to make sure we have everything else up-to-date; you understand?"

"Oh, I understand, and I don't envy you a bit. Though I have to ask … you know something about our boy in the morgue, I mean, how he was eighty-sixed, right? I'll be damned if I can figure it out, or our coroner for that matter. He's all up in arms over this thing. I guess he doesn't like not having the poop on the details."

"Yes, it's a head-scratcher, that's for sure," Special Agent Le'fadden said. "And I don't mind telling you that with over thirty years with the Bureau, I haven't seen anything quite like this before. I might suspect more than one culprit, perhaps several in order to do what was done to this Mister Prud … perhaps a gang-related event, but that idea doesn't add up either. No, something else happened to him. We just don't know *what* at the moment. As for the occult reference, this is of interest to us as well, and we'll look into it further at a later date. Although there really isn't enough information, either way, regarding there being an active killer cult operating out there, there are, nonetheless, hundreds of cults in operation around the nation, and many of them may very well be deadly."

"A killer cult in DeKalb?" Captain Holzer asked, now somewhat shocked at the suggestion.

"It's a possibility, captain. Case in point, and you'll probably remember the satanic ritual abuse cases of the late eighties and early nineties, but it could be relevant to this case. Do you recall the McMartin preschool case in California and others like that … the Wee Care Nursery in New Jersey or the Fells Acres Daycare case in Massachusetts?"

"Yes, of course," Captain Holzer said, now looking every bit as confused as his friend, Dr. Bob Ketchum, when trying to describe the nature of the death of Nathan Prud. Now, he just sat back and waited for the mystery to unravel.

"Yeah, yeah, I do remember those cases," he continued. "Those were big headlines, but … but nothing came of it, right?"

"Well, the majority of those events took place between eighty-three and eighty-eight," Special Agent Le'fadden continued. "And for the most part, there actually were some spooky characters involved, such as a genuine devil cult that was subsequently operated by a Colonel in the United States Army, no less. But beyond that, the entire 'Satanic Panic,' as that TV show host, Geraldo Rivera, had referred to it, I believe, yielded very little in the way of offering any definite answers, or perpetrators in the alleged sexual molestations, and even cases of ritual execution. Despite the fact that even with the testimony of dozens of children, no factual evidence could be uncovered. And that scare tactic worked on many levels."

"Right, right, I remember that whole thing!" Captain Holzer yelped as if surprised. "It came about from that kid's board game, ah, what was it? 'Dungeons and Monsters,' or something like that, right?"

"Close, captain, but it was called *Dungeons and Dragons*. And no, though tantalizing at the time, it had proven unsubstantial for us, and believe me, we looked very hard at the subject. Hell, even the Senior Special Agent in Charge at the time, Ted Gunderson, was actively researching the whole occult issue, practically right up until his death. So somewhere, regardless that the facts are not found in place, even for federal agents to peruse every now and then, tells us that the answers are simply not available … thus, the mystery remains a mystery."

Captain Holzer shook his head slowly. "Meh … I really hate mysteries, unless I'm watching one on the boob tube," he said. "And even then, I don't like those very much either."

"You're not the only one, my friend," Special Agent Le'fadden returned, this time offering a full smile. This was followed by placing the manila folder back in his valise and standing up quickly. "Now, I really must be getting back, so I'll cut this short. If I have anything else for you, I'll be sure to call you, captain, you have my word on that."

"I'd surely appreciate that agent, but I'd still like at least some answers; something to write down regarding the details of Prud's murder or his killer," Captain Holzer returned. "I don't care if we call it a bear attack, a pack of wild dogs, or Jack the Ripper, so long as a viable answer can appear on the books, and preferably before I end up facing a city inquest the size of Texas!"

Special Agent Le'fadden smiled at this and chuckled for the first time. "I hear ya, captain, and we'll be sure to contact you when we get any *viable* answers once we get them. Until that time, however, I'll keep on this, and notify you if anything else comes up in the meantime."

"Oh yeah, before you go, agent," Captain Holzer blurted. He began flipping through his well-worn notepad until he found the page he was looking for. "Take a look at this ... do you know what this stands for ... I'm told it's, ah, some kind of 'witch writing?'"

Special Agent Le'fadden examined the crude sketch of the strange letter the police captain had jotted down while at the county morgue that morning. "No ... no, I don't think so," he said.

Captain Holzer pulled out his cellphone, brought up the photo app, and opened it. Then he faced the cell to the agent and leaned in so the man could get a better look. It showed a clear image of the strange, burn-like marking on Nathan Prud's body. Now, the look on Agent Le'fadden's face was daunting to say the least, showing part recognition and part annoyance as if he'd have to answer the same questions again.

"I can't say that I have, captain. Interesting though … where did you take that?" Agent Le'fadden asked inquisitively.

"There's a mark on Prud's body, towards his lower back … you'll see it. At first, we thought it might have been caused by being slammed against a tree, or that he had that put there beforehand … but his wife did say that she believed that it was from an alphabet used by witches and such, but I'm not holding on to her ideas too closely at this point."

"Well, I'll look into that as soon as I can," the agent said. "I trust there's also a photo of it in the medical examiner's packet for us?" he asked. The man looked more official than before, as if he had known something and was keeping it secret. At least, this is what Captain Holzer had surmised, despite the fact that Special Agent Le'fadden offered very little, if any, useful information at all. Now, Captain Holzer was beginning to think that the whole meeting with the FBI was just a huge waste of time.

✠

As both men shook hands, Captain Holzer felt compelled to ask one final question. He believed that with a little finesse, he might be able to achieve the information he wanted, lawman to lawman, even though the vibe this federal agent was giving off was anything but a cop's vibe.

He simply couldn't figure the man out, despite his decorum or professionalism.

"Have you, or has the FBI, seen any other cases like this one ... recently? I mean weird cases you can't easily explain?" Captain Holzer asked.

"Hum, that's a loaded question, captain, at least in terms of the word *weird*," Special Agent Le'fadden returned. Then, he turned around and faced the police captain, and smiled as he clasped his hands behind him, almost in military fashion. "Weird ... weird, you say? The Bureau was only mildly interested in flying saucers and things like that for a time, and that was primarily on Hoover's watch ... that was his folly, and for the most part, this stuff was more of the CIA's interest, if at all these days. And ghosts, and goat-suckers, and bigfoot monsters, and the like are more in the arena of that television show back in the nineties."

Captain Holzer smirked and nodded to the comment. "Yeah, I suppose it's all nonsense. But, but you'll have to admit, things have been getting pretty crazy these past few years."

"Yes, such is politics and a breakdown in our social environment, but there's no boogiemen behind it, I assure you, captain. No ... no, captain, weird in my definition is how terrorists can get visas to live in the U.S., get government jobs, and even end up serving as senators and congresswomen without question or proper vetting. No, sir, weird is having open borders with every kind of monster wandering in with absolutely no information about them. Weird is knowing that there are over four hundred genuine terror cells operating in almost every city in the United

States, Canada, Puerto Rico, and on the moon, for all I know, and all without anything being done about it. Weird is having cities taken over by pot-heads and militant anarchists while their mayors and governors sit back and do nothing. Weird, captain, is having drag queens preaching in our churches, and forcing our children to have sex changes with or without the consent of their parents … weird is, well, the concept of weird is something else altogether today, captain, wouldn't you say?"

Captain Holzer just nodded his head. He had agreed with the agent's sentiments. "Yeah, now that you mention it, I guess that is all pretty weird," he muttered.

"Weird is the world we live in on a daily basis, captain, with evil operating right under our noses. What you'll find in the tabloids is far less weird than what takes place on a daily basis, and right out there on our own streets, as I'm sure you can attest."

"Brother, you said it," Captain Holzer muttered aloud.

Now appearing a little agitated, Agent Le'fadden turned and headed for the office door. As he began to walk down the hall, with Captain Holzer right behind him, he continued with his appraisal of the Prud case.

"No, captain, what we have here is something that we'll eventually figure out, in spite of the haziness of the case," he said firmly. "Regardless, we'll figure it out, captain, and I'm sure there'll be no little green men involved in it."

"Well, thanks for clearing that up as best you can, but I'm putting this more in the category of bat-shit crazy if you don't mind," Captain Holzer blurted. This was followed by a soft chuckle. "I guess we both have our work cut out for us, don't we?"

"Yes indeed, and that'll likely be the understatement for at least the next few weeks or longer in my opinion," Agent Le'fadden responded with a chuckle in kind. And as he and the captain reached the front doors of the station, Agent Le'fadden turned to face the captain one last time. "Oh, yes, by the way ... I do have one last question for you, captain."

"Shoot."

"Have you ever heard of anyone by the name of a Bush ... a Patrick Allen Bush? Perhaps Prud's wife had mentioned him to you?"

"No, doesn't ring a bell ... and she never mentioned that name," Captain Holzer said. "Should I have heard of him?"

"No, no, not necessarily ... just a hunch. Thanks again for your time, captain. I'll be sure to keep you apprised of the situation if we get anything on our end."

"That'll be greatly appreciated, Agent Le'fadden, and thanks again for keeping us in the loop."

Now, just as the agent walked out the door, Captain Holzer remained with an expression of being completely confounded. He couldn't help feeling as if he had been taken to the cleaners. Despite this, he knew deep down that the case would remain open until further notice, regardless of the promises by the FBI. He knew there was much more to the case than the FBI was telling him. Call it a cop's intuition, call it years of working in law enforcement, call it what you will — he just knew this whole thing was far from over.

Now, Captain Holzer scratched his mustache and stared out the small window behind Jasmine's desk. He just watched as the federal agent got into his outdated, powder blue Crown Victoria and then nonchalantly drove away.

"Patrick Bush," he mumbled aloud. "Who the hell is Patrick Bush?"

PART II

CHAPTER SEVEN

The Awful Demise of Madam Delevingne

Tuesday, June 30th, 2:23 P.M.

"... Unfortunately, some of our greatest tribulations are the result of our own foolishness and weakness and occur because of our own carelessness or transgression."

— *James E. Faust, American religious leader, lawyer, and politician*

Day One

"She's ain't no beauty, dat's fir sure ... done fell out of da ugly tree and hits every branch on the ways down ... but she's got what we'se need, Rommar. Oh yeah, no doubts bout dat," Hercules Benet said, as he and his sidekick Rommar, also known as Lester Gnaws, gawked at the chalice and athame-dagger that rested in the Hollow Cauldron's storefront window.

The two men were 'initiate elects' with a local occult order and were totally subservient to its ruling mistress, one Madam Tarja Delevingne. Madam Delevingne wasn't just the owner of the store; she was also a witch and the self-proclaimed high priestess of the Order of Pry Thealemè Ex Mortis. She was also the Prime Hierophant with the Order of Magnus Datha, one of the more notable sects of magick in the Southwest and Central United States. In addition to this, she was a spirit communicator, an enchantress of the nether worlds, a paranormal researcher, and a professional ghost hunter who could clear any location of any negative spirit, all for a nominal fee.

Indeed, she was an expert on all things of an occult nature — at least, that's what her sycophantic brood would say of her.

Though the marquee on the window of the Hollow Cauldron had read: 'A Magickal Apothecary for the Enchanted,' the only thing magical or enchanting was her ability to dupe the weak-minded fools of Baytown, Texas.

✠

Lester Lawrence Gnaws had lived in Baytown for the majority of his life and had seen it all, at least, he had thought so. He'd been there before Braeswood Boulevard had been paved and well past the time Hurricane Harvey flooded Pinehurst and Whispering Pines, which had dislocated thousands in the process. Beyond that, the redundancy of working at his father's gas station as a grease monkey had earned him the reputation of being a mediocre mechanic, but mostly as holding the title of village idiot and all-around town lackey.

Lester wasn't the greatest looking man in town either, having a simpleton look, or as his friend, Hercules Benet had described the man as being a greasy cross between a 1980s version of Tom Petty and that skinny dude from the movie *Trainspotting*. Nonetheless, Lester Gnaws knew what he liked, and he liked Madam Tarja Delevingne, warts, bed bug bites, her half-crooked face, and everything else to boot. It was pure love on his part, though she hardly ever acknowledged him.

Hercules 'Herc' Reginald Benet; simply called the 'Fat Man' by the townspeople, wasn't called that just because he was a bit overweight; two hundred pounds overweight, at least, but because he had an uncanny, albeit younger, resemblance to Sidney Greenstreet from the old Bogart films. And regardless that he had a thick southern drawl and had problems pronouncing even the simplest words properly, he thought of himself as wise and beyond Baytown's common folk. He considered himself among the elected few within the world of magick and dark, secret societies, specifically the Baytown order of Magnus Datha.

Herc Benet had moved from Horry County, South Carolina, when he was only nine, but like his father and grandfather before him, Herc was a large-boned man; his appendages, his hands, and feet were lumbering and thick. He was what South Carolinian locals referred to as a 'swamp-slug,' a behemoth of a man who partook in searching out the southern swamps for clams, oysters, and other crustaceans; a common activity in Socastee and the Murrells Inlet area where he spent his childhood. And though Herc never had the chance to grope through the swamp waters as much as his kinfolk had done for close to a century before him, he was nonetheless a swamp-slug through and through.

As each initiate is allowed to choose their ritual or coven names, Herc Benet had decided on one that sounded strong and mysterious. He chose the moniker *Cron*, not because it was a misguided homage to C.J. Cron of the Los

Angeles Angels, as the others had surmised, nor was it taken from Celtic mythology, from the deity *Crom Cruach*, the forgotten god who had governed the ancient Irish plains of Magh Slécht. No, Herc Benet chose the moniker because it reminded him of the unseen god briefly mentioned in the 1982 film, *Conan the Barbarian*. And though he simply changed one letter in the name, Herc had surmised it as being strong and wise. Besides, he loved those movies and thought it would be cool, believing it added mystery to his self-perceived image of strength and greatness.

Because Herc Benet had one of the largest collections of books on the occult and witchcraft in Baytown; mostly from the Llewellyn and Weiser publishing companies, everyone in the Order of Magnus Datha knew that anyone with such a collection of books, especially by those specific publishers must be greatly in-tune with the higher forces of the universe, and most assuredly, must therefore be wise. At least, this is what Herc Benet had believed.

By day, he worked as an underpaid assistant manager at the local Spend-n-Save on the second shift. He was less than polite to his customers and despised black people, yellow people, red people, and any immigrant of any nomenclature. He thought of them as being nothing more than niggers or spics or beaner scum who had invaded and ruined his country, and he was anything but silent on the subject. Herc was a hateful man and often belligerent, but he, like Madam Delevingne, could be magnanimous when underlings showed respect to their worldly wisdom and better judgment. Not only was he a member of the Order of

Magnus Datha and a loyal devotee of Madam Delevingne, his mistress upon high, but he was on the fast track to becoming a member-elect in the coven, and nothing would stop that from happening. This and this alone was the key to any happiness the man could obtain.

✠

Herc and Lester had known each other since the fifth grade and, as such, had been friends ever since. Lester was always the skinny, shy one, to Herc's loud, rotund class clown persona. Together, they had evaded the bullies and an assortment of detractors from the beginning. They trusted each other impeccably, but more than anything, the Order of Magnus Datha had accepted them no matter what. Whether the insults, the humiliation, or all in between, it was all a part of the master plan — Madam Delevingne's master plan.

Now, filled with confidence, the two men had finally decided to enter The Hollow Cauldron, ready to pay tribute to their mistress. And as Herc pulled the door open, Lester quickly looked up at the marquee above the windowpane. It was a habit he had been prone to for the last few years. It made him think of his secret love, the wise and impenetrable Madam Delevingne. Now, Lester mouthed the marquee's credo—

"For whatever ails you, herbs, handmade potions, gifts, and art, all is here for the witch, wizard, or sage in your coven," he mumbled.

The credo always made Herc and Lester feel important. But today, they just wanted the chalice and the dagger; a ceremonial cup to hold the sacramental wine, and the ornate athame with occult carvings on it. They had saved enough money to add the items to the community chest, the supply chest for the Order of Magnus Datha, but they would be able to use it in their own magick workings, so it was well worth it. And as such, tithing was not only expected and appreciated by the cult members, but there was far more than that. They knew it would please Madam Delevingne, and this, they knew, was always the wisest choice.

For what is planned on the night of the thirtieth of the following month shall bring down the town's political leaders who are fighting to stop their gatherings in the public parks, most specifically, the McElroy Park on Craigmont Boulevard. These politically incorrect, Republican nay-saying officials didn't like the fact that only the truly inspired, the chosen few, would practice Magick in their domain. This upset Madam Delevingne, so something had to be done — and something *would* be done.

As such, both men decided then and there that they would get even and stop the plans of the town council and the other bureaucrats stepping in the way of their blessed sect. It was Madam Tarja Delevingne's sect after all, so it was personal. For the angry woman, it was always personal.

Herc tapped his friend on the shoulder, now with a serious expression. "C'mon, Bo, lez go," he said.

"Oh, ah, all right, Herc, but please call me Rommar."

"Yeah, alrighty, all-rites … *Mister Rommar!*"

As the door swung open, the tiny bells that hung above the arches rang from the door's movement. The two men gazed with wide eyes as their mistress looked up to their faces. Implored, and needing to offer devotion to their mistress, they both bowed slightly.

"Good Morrow, Mistress Delevinggg-ge," Herc chimed with just the right amount of honour and subservience, despite his mispronunciations. Lester, keeping his head bowed like a dog before the alpha, waited for permission to speak and pay reverence.

"Come in, gentlemen, such as you are," Madam Delevingne said in a forceful, yet inviting manner. She could be magnanimous too if she desired, even to lowlifes like Benet and Gnaws. They were, in any case, initiates in the Order of Magnus Datha, so pleasantries were kindly afforded, such as they were. The two initiates paid their dues, and they did follow orders, so she could afford to be kind, even to two boobs like Benet and Gnaws.

"Madam Dele-vingn-gee, I greets you fairs, and wit tributes," Herc said.

"Well, I won't stop you, of course," she replied without blinking her eyes. "And for the tenth-thousandth time, Cron, it's pronounced *Dela-veen … Dell-aahh-veen!*"

"Ohs, yeza-ize knows better nows, Madam Dell-ah-veeen, yez ma'amz!" Cron said, now physically shaken by his struggle with the English language.

As Cron was Herc's order name, his secret identity, he felt ingratiated by her acknowledging him the way she did. Lester continued to scan the floor, believing that she could read his mind, actually reaching down into his soul and reading his very thoughts. He feared that she would root him out for what he was, despite desperately wanting to belong. Lester knew he was a dud, *a waste of seed*, as his daddy always said. But he was determined to be recognized, no matter what it would cost — even his life if it came to that.

"And what, pray tell, can I do for you two dignitaries of *The Order* today?" she said with her customary sarcasm.

"We'd like to gits dat most excellent ch-ch-alice and ath-atha-a-amie that yous got in the glass case dare," Herc quipped as he pointed to the glass case. He was trying desperately to sound educated.

"Ah, very good, initiate Cron, and you do mean the athame — *ath-aahh-may*, yes?" she blurted, phonetically spelling out the proper pronunciation for the class dullard. "I do hope you have what it costs, as it's a bit steep, I believe ... for you?"

Still trying hard to sound worldly, Herc responded with his best impression of a southern gentleman — a southern gentleman lawyer, in fact, like the kind of lawyer Andy Griffith had played on television in his later years. And though he tried with all his might, Herc Benet fell short in his attempt, instead, appearing more like a two-bit, Alabama huckster from an old B-movie to that of a sophisticated southern gentleman.

"Yez, Madams, "Ath-tha-may," right you arez ... I've been-ah eying it for a while, Madams, and between I, and Lester ... I, I mean *initiate* Rommar, well, we has enough tribute to best honor thuz order with some to spare, Madams.'"

Thinking that the use of flowery words would help him establish a persona of devotion and expertise, he nonetheless spoke with the desultory semantics typical of the average Arkansas hick or a small-town street vagrant. As such, he almost always received the ever-typical smirk and chuckle from those around him. Despite such dedication, however, it usually only rewarded him with looks of disgust and disdain. Regardless, Tarja Delevingne had enjoyed her dominance over both Benet and Gnaws, but that was largely the extent of her compassion. She was, after all, far greater in significance; far more important than any man would, or could ever be. Certainly, there could be no doubt — she was greater than any mere man.

Gods grant me … I love her, oh great Pan! Lester thought to himself. Now, he bowed his head again in order to divert his eyes from the nasty woman, and had tried desperately to appear noble and strong, but she hadn't even noticed the man.

Now, wrapping up the items in purple tissue paper, along with a modest sprinkling of dried lavender and sage inside to 'bless' the objects d'art, Madam Delevingne took the cash and quickly counted it. Then, looking upward at the fat man, she offered a sideways smile and a raised eyebrow.

"There's eleven dollars and twenty-three cents left … you *could* donate that to the Order, of course … it would be greatly appreciated," she said in her customary tone of authority and wisdom.

"Oh, ah, of course, absolutelys, Madam Delevingn-gee," Herc said, now slightly bowing to his mistress.

"Excellent, Cron, your charity is respected, and ... will be remembered."

"Thank youz, Madams, thank youz! We seez you at the next gather'en, and wit bless'ens!"

At a moment's notice, and with great strength, Lester decided to show his respect and bid his mistress goodbye. "Good, good morrow, Madam ... good morrow," he said while wincing his eyes, and bowing in reverence.

Now, the two men turned toward the door and walked out, fumbling over each other as they did. The image created something not unlike a scene from a Laurel and Hardy skit. And as they exited, the bells above the door made the usual tinkling sound.

"Good morrow ... initiates," Madam Delevingne said coolly, as a smirk silently rose upon her face. When Lester saw this, he managed to face the vile woman one last time as bravely as he could and bowed ever so slightly. He flushed with redness as he caught her smile, and quickly turned away in silence and subservience.

Oh, dear gods above, below, and in the sea and earth, Lester thought. *Grant me favour from Madam ... from Madam Tarja Delevingne ... I beg of thee; I beg of thee!*

✠

Herc and Lester had departed The Hollow Cauldron satisfied, pleased that they had had a good meeting with their mistress, and knowing that they had the implements to best thwart the plans of the hated Baytown council. They were ready to fight now. They would make a sacrifice, if need be, a dog, a cat, or a bird in order to call down the Four Watchtowers of the Spirit Realms; the price for cosmic submission and favour. They would fight to the end if need be. And in three days, in three days on the thirtieth, they would fight for the Order of Magnus Datha — they would fight for their mistress, the great Madam Delevingne.

By 5:52 p.m., Madam Delevingne was finishing sprucing up the store while she talked with her friend Nancy Springwood on the phone. By the time the conversation had ended, it was already going on 7:00 p.m., and it was beginning to get dark. And because there was the threat of a storm brewing in the distance, she opted to quicken her pace. She walked around the store and checked the side door, and then the back door, and then she checked her cellphone for any messages that she might have missed. There were none.

"How about some wine?" she muttered to herself aloud. Thinking she owed herself a treat for making a good profit that day, she went to the small micro-fridge in the back closet and pulled out what was left of a box of Franzia Wine Sunset Blush. She poured what was left of it into a coffee cup and began to sip it. Thinking that she'd answer some questions on the store's website message board, she went to the back room, switched on the small table light, and then began to make herself comfortable in the old swivel chair she had pulled from a garbage dump last year, and then turned on the computer.

Once she logged on to the store's website, she scanned the emails and deleted the assorted spam and other junk mail that typically accumulated. After that, she hit the message board tab and found no new questions or comments on her posts. Remarkably, there were no messages regarding her personal essays on twenty-first- century magick: *Ask a Thealemè Witch*, or even her excellent monologue: *How Eve was Framed: Occult Works from the Witch of Endor to Samantha Stevens.*

There wasn't even a supporting response from her old friend Lee Holloway from Jacksonville, Florida, or from Luciana Sidero of Sacramento, California, or even from her old friend and fellow witch, Marcee Ventura from Pooler, Georgia. Certainly, this was out of the ordinary, but the wise woman vowed to contact them later in the week.

In addition to the strange silence from her friends, there wasn't even a response from her college professor ally from Illinois, Professor Prud. This was particularly distressing because they were ganging up on a so-called Christian writer who had the audacity to publish several essays and religious poetry on one of their favourite websites; *Christian* poetry, no less. He had no right creating, let alone publishing, such drivel, so he was chosen for punishment. This was simply the way of things and must be carried out no matter what.

Even with their blood-letting criticism, which was ripping this guy a new one, her typical fan responses were left blank today. This reality had made the vainglorious woman frown.

That's fucked-up, she thought. *Maybe … maybe they'll post later tonight.*

Madam Delevingne checked the store's blog page too. She wanted to see if anyone had left her love letters, which she had come to expect over the years. But there were no love letters or any such odes or comments there, except for one thing. It was a Biblical verse from the Book of Jeremiah, chapter twenty-seven; verses nine and ten—

Therefore, hearken not ye to your prophets, nor to your diviners, nor to your dreamers, nor to your enchanters, nor to your sorcerers, which speak unto you, saying, Ye shall not serve the king of Babylon … For they prophesy a lie unto you, to remove you far from your land; and that I should drive you out, and ye should perish ….

Now unreservedly unnerved, especially that someone would actually post a Biblical quote on her webpage, Madam Delevingne frowned even more. Surely, everyone knew that her handmade website, *Disuniting the Shroud*, was very clearly designed and made to honour those of the old religion, and not for the Hebrew God, or His cohort of followers. No, it was for pagans — for the enlightened only.

"Don't serve the king of Babylon?" she read aloud. "I'm the queen of Babylon, you asshole. Who wrote this Bible bullshit … son of a bitch! Fuck'en King James too. Let's see … he posted under the name of John Pater … most likely a fake name too. Who the hell's John Pater?"

Now thoroughly pissed off that anyone would have the balls to quote anything even remotely Biblical to her; to a famous pagan witch, and high priestess known all over the internet for her expertise and wisdom was simply too much to bear. Her face was becoming red.

"I've had my share of Bible training in parochial school … for four years straight, no less," she mumbled. "Nobody quotes Scripture to me, you bastard! Now, let's just see where you come from … let's just see where you live, you jerk."

Then, just as she was beginning to check the internet protocol locales using a separate detection site, a comical beeping sound came from her computer, making her look at the screen with a gaze of amazement. There was a message being typed just below the original verse. Madam Delevingne just sat and stared. She was astonished. The message was coming from the same person who sent the first Bible quote; again, from someone named John Pater.

"… *Render therefore to all their dues: tribute to whom tribute is due; custom to whom custom; fear to whom fear; honour to whom honour …*"

Now, thoroughly incensed at the audacity that someone would actually send such a message to her, let alone putting it on her webpage, her obviously *pagan* webpage was crossing way over the line. The fact that some Bible-thumper would remind her of the nature of sin or what was right or wrong didn't just irk her — it made her see red.

"Who the hell do you think you are, asshole?" she typed furiously. "This is my blog page; my subject matter … we don't want your hate speech here!"

Suddenly, the beeping sound echoed again. "Hate speech, madam … really?" the message read as it scrolled across the screen. "I hardly consider the words of the Almighty to be those of hate, madam."

Now thinking that this was a joke from one of her friends, most likely from Joanie Petri from Toledo, she answered as directly as she could. "Madam? Who the hell is this? Is this you Joanie, you dipshit?" she typed.

"No, not Joanie, nor dipshit," the mysterious message continued. "Think of me as a friend who is imploring you to have a change of heart; a change from poor behaviour to that of, shall we say … a more proper form of conduct? To be less cruel to others; less vicious is all I ask. Think of me as a friend, and not as a foe."

"A friend? No dice, shithead, I don't befriend creepers on my blog page; by email, and not in person, especially with Bible thugs like you!" she typed. "Take my advice mystery man, *DON'T FUCK WITH ME!*"

"Oh, heavens, no … I would never fuck with *you*, Madam," the typist continued. Madam Delevingne just squinted at the computer screen as she continued to type her response.

"I can guarantee you a wave of the blackest magick you could ever expect, do you read me asshole!?" she typed.

"Oh dear, I certainly hope not," the mysterious typist wrote. "Perhaps one more; one parting verse before I leave you?"

Now completely outraged at the audaciousness of the Bible-quoting typist, Madam Delevingne's self-perceived coolness had finally expired. "I told you, jerk; I have no interest in your hate speech!" she typed. "… and that means the Book of Job or whatever you're sending me … *STOP … STOP NOW … I WARN YOU!*"

"Oh my, no, no, no, it wasn't the Book of Job, my dear," the mysterious typist wrote. "It is from the Book of Romans, chapter thirteen, verse seven of the King James Version, a genuine sixteen-eleven, Pure Cambridge Edition, in fact."

"I don't care if it's from the fucking *Book of Kells*, dick face, just stop posting on this page! If you don't, there WILL be reprisals, and you will regret it!"

Madam Delevingne was getting angrier by the minute and had decided to block the sender from her computer. She was determined to finish this.

"Cyberbullying," she grunted. She had inwardly surmised that such behaviour was an activity for *her* alone, and especially not for outsiders of the craft, especially for anyone claiming to be a Christian. "Only I can do that," she grunted again. "I'm gonna get this prick where he lives … better yet, I'll expose him for everyone to see … that's it, that's what I'll do!"

Now, Madam Delevingne blocked the sender, and that was that, or so she thought. Because she considered herself to be a better-than-competent computer guru, she began by opening the start menu, selecting the 'run' option, and then the 'command' option. She would begin by testing her own computer's IP configuration, which had been read correctly. Then she made sure her information was safe. It was, so she went to her blog page's administrator section and quickly ran the incoming information, and found the IP address of the mysterious Bible-thumper. The address read: 119.42.70.209.

"Gotcha asshole!" she exclaimed with a smile. "Now, let's see where you live. What the actual fuck … Thailand!?" she exclaimed again, now feeling like a detective for being so smart. She began jotting down the numbers on a notepad when yet another set of numbers started to replace the last one, and then another, and then another. "Seriously, dude? What the fuck is this?" the vile woman belched.

Now, Madam Delevingne began to read out the IP addresses, as one after another would pop up on the screen. From 99.214.62.168, and then 88.19.253.44, a seemingly endless listing of protocol addresses flashed past the woman's eyes. This was followed by a list of locations beginning to scroll across the locator feature on her blog page — London, England; Spain, Portugal, and Ontario, Canada, all within seconds of each other.

"What the, what the hell?" she muttered. Following this, more numbers appeared on the screen— 98.25.231.238 for Columbia, South Carolina; 50.73.157.178 for West Palm Beach, Florida, and then a series of codes from the European Union, including the Netherlands and Switzerland, all flashing across the screen in seconds' time. The numbers on the screen finally stopped at Antarctica, specifically at the McMurdo Station of the United States- occupied Antarctic. "What the fuck!?" she yelled. "How the hell are you … doing this?" She shook her head in disbelief, thinking that someone was playing tricks on her. "That's impossible," she muttered.

Madam Delevingne tried to figure out why her computer was giving so many IP addresses until an expression of understanding finally fell across her face. And just as the epiphany had crossed her mind, the sound of distant thunder echoed throughout the room. She just ignored it, now realizing she had an enemy to take care of. She had a sacrifice to make.

"Oh, wait … oh, oh yeah; you have one of those new router-changers," she quipped, followed by a single grunt that resembled laughter. "You got one of those oscillating systems, huh, like one of those old onion systems … a Nord VPN? Okay, okay, so then you're not the great mystery after all … you're just another sock puppet play'en games." Now, she sat back in her old dumpster chair and giggled to herself. "I'm so on to you, you bastard. Tell ya what I'm gonna do for you, Bible man."

In what took only a few moments to consider, Madam Delevingne had a plan. Having figured out the antics of the mysterious persona she now called the 'Bible-thumper,' she just sat back and looked at the screen. She was thinking about what she was going to write next, knowing that she would use threats and a sampling of her own magick; verses from the *Book of the Law; 777, The Book of Thoth*, and other tidbits from Crowley and his disciples.

Aleister Crowley, yes, indeed, she thought to herself. *Perhaps something from Simon's old Necronomicon or maybe even from the Koran. That'd piss off a Christian,* she thought to herself. Then she began to laugh. Just then, another beep sounded from her computer.

"A sock puppet, Madam?" the message scrolled across her screen. "I think not. A sock puppet, as you say, is like using a photograph or an artist's rendering of someone or something else to represent oneself. Perhaps, something like this?" the typist wrote. A second or two later, a screenshot of just such a false representation had popped up on Madam Delevingne's computer screen. It was one of her own false photos of herself she had designed in Photoshop to head up one of her many online 'fake identities.' This one was from one of her *GoFundMe* ads to raise money for being a victim of bed bugs and homelessness.

Madam Delevingne just stared at the screen now, her eyes transfixed, her left cheek twitching. Even her breathing was becoming erratic. A few seconds after this, another photo popped up; another false photo and fake name from yet another phony *GoFundMe* campaign. This time, it was for flood damage after Hurricane Harvey in 2017. The fake information, such as her name, and that she was mentally ill and in need of special help, was highlighted in bold yellow. The glow from her computer's screen made her facial expression look almost as diabolical as she had wished herself to appear.

Now, Madam Tarja Delevingne knew what was best for the Bible-thumper, but at that moment, she had remembered that she hadn't *typed* anything; she never typed the word 'sock puppet' anywhere. She remembered that she had only spoken those words aloud. This had made the woman let her mouth fall open where her normal smirk-riddled face had once occupied. Now, her red, glossy eyes were as wide as the opening of her coffee cup — and as red as the wine within it.

"What the fuck?" she burbled to herself. "That's, that's impossible …."

Remembering that she has a speech-recognition program working on her system, as well as a camera attached to her computer, it all began to make sense to her. Thinking that this guy had somehow patched into her network, and was watching her, and listening to her talk to herself, she felt that had to be the answer. In an instant, the mighty witch of Magnus Datha had felt weak and powerless
— she felt naked.

Madam Delevingne, being of exceptional wit, far more than some dude on the internet, had quickly reached into her desk drawer and pulled out a piece of masking tape, ripped off a small portion of it, and quickly placed it over the computer's built-in camera aperture.

Then she opened her desktop icon, went to her computer settings, and quickly disabled the speech program so that her intruder would lose his sight and sound once and for all. She'd figure out how he did it later and get even with him another day. Now, she just wanted information so she could exact her revenge on the Bible-thumper.

"Okay, you son of a bitch," she said aloud. "You want to play with me? No problem, I'll play … I'll play! The Bible-thumper thinks he's smart … but I'm smarter!"

✠

Down deep, Madam Delevingne knew the Bible-thumping intruder was one of those born-again Christians who attacked pagans minding their own business; attacking their websites, and or disrupting her people from the natural ways of the Paganus path. She knew they were all just a bunch of fascists who always kept her people down.

"God damned Republicans," she sighed, as she punched in codes and commands on her computer's console. "You fucked Hillary … you constantly made fun of our Biden and Harris, and you totally screwed over the whole Democratic Party; took away our freedoms, you bastards. And then you lost everything, right on down to your fucking Nazi party … and now you're aiming at us?!"

With lightning speed, she typed in one last code and opened and closed programs, reset passwords, and rechecked connections, all while sporting a facial expression that clearly stated her resolve and her anger equally.

"Not this time … no sir, not to us … not to me," she burbled. This was intermixed with what sounded like a warped laugh. And after a moment of silence, with nothing scrolling across her monitor, the mysterious writer returned—

"Well, I really must get going, Madam Delevingne, oh High Priestess of Magnus Datha. I do hope I haven't distressed you too much. Regardless, it is within my best interest, and *yours,* to get you back on track, so to speak. That is to say, that you reconsider being so cruel to others, online or otherwise. You must return to Jesus … Son of the one true God."

"What the fuck!?" the vile woman screamed. "I just blocked you, you bastard … how … how do you know my coven's name?"

Madam Delevingne, her senses now spinning, began to check her website's incoming information again, and found that the IP addresses were once again rifling from location to location just as before. This time, however, the sender's name read 'Jacob Wells.'

"Oh, we've gotta a smart egg here," she muttered. "So be it. I'll show you how cruel I can be asshole, and you'll see it manifest right before you." Now filled with rage, she began typing to Jacob Wells. "My dear, Mister Wells, or Mister Pater, makes no difference who you say you are, I'm not alone, and I know who you are!" She kept typing; her eyes now wide and reddened. "You'll be sorry for fucking with us!"

Madam Delevingne had had enough, and now was the time for befriending those things that could pay her enemies for their deeds. Understanding the *Book of the Law* and of the articles of *Goetia*, as well as the articles of the *Liber B vel Magi*, she had instantly recalled the teachings of Crowley with considerable ease. She began reading aloud as she typed a reply to the mysterious writer:

"For the curse speaks of his grade is that he must speak Truth, that Falsehood thereof may enslave the souls of men," she typed furiously. "And woe also be unto him that refuseth the curse of the grade of a Magus and the burden of the attainment thereof! Do what thou wilt shall be the whole of the law,' *SO MOTE IT BE!*'"

A few seconds had passed, and Madam Delevingne waited and watched as the mysterious intruder finally replied to the quotation.

"Ah, yes," the mysterious writer typed, "Mr. Crowley, of course. Perhaps I understand more than you think. What was it that Aristophanes had once quoted? *Wise men learn many things from their enemies?* Yes, I believe that's the proper quote, don't you think, Madam? And to be sure, to be well warned with what comes from you shall return in kind, and with fire and wind and aught raging storm. Such shall arise from all the dimensions of the hell you so worship; that indeed, what the Order of Pry Thealemè Ex Mortis doth worship ... such shall come to you all, should you not alter the course of your ways, and posthaste."

As the words scrolled across her computer's screen, Madam Delevingne just read them as she sat numb. She couldn't help feeling that she knew this person somehow. She surmised that it was one of the people she had been razzing online; people who had done their research. After all, they knew the proper name of her cult and her coven's name. Because these things were relatively secret, whoever was taunting her must have known her. Though there were at least a dozen or more such people she could think of, she felt confident that she could find the culprit. But, just in case she couldn't, she'd call on her own people to help her. She knew she'd get this guy, whoever he was.

The typist continued as another sentence scrolled across her computer's screen. "Remember, Madam, that such cannot be dispelled by the simple chanting of a demonically deranged mind. So, I will leave you with this one, final plea: Turn back to God before it's too late. I offer this unto you … not in my best interests, but in yours. I beseech thee to take heed my warning, for once it comes, it cannot be stopped. Like a fever, like a virus, it must run its course. You will either live or you will perish, Madam Delevingne, or should I call you … *Juliana?*"

In the few seconds it took her to read the message and then re-read it again, Madam Delevingne's face took on a ruddy-red hue, with her eyes bugging out of her skull, almost to the point of appearing comical. And then there was the slight distortion of her face, which had made her look truly evil.

Few had known that the woman's general appearance of distortion originated from a childhood condition, having been caused by a bout of Bell's palsy when she was seventeen; a disease that should have left her face normal after a short period of time. Despite this, the disease had somehow remained, having enlarged the lymph glands of her face permanently. Even today, the vile woman couldn't help appearing like some horrible Picasso. It gave her face an unbalanced look — the look of a sinister soul.

Now, the sarcastic nature and the self-assuredness she always commanded had departed. She was angry beyond comprehension; beyond reason. Madam Delevingne's entire body began to quake with rage.

"*YOU FUCKING SON OF A BITCH!*" she typed as fast as she could. "*YOU'RE STALKING ME? LISTEN TO ME WELL, BIBLE MAN! YOU DON'T KNOW*

WHO YOU ARE FUCKING WITH! I WILL DESTROY YOU!" she typed, pounding the keys so hard that the computer's keyboard bounced up and down on the flimsy table. "*I AND MY COVEN WILL DESTROY YOU AND ALL THAT YOU LOVE!*"

After a few moments of pause, Madam Delevingne sat and stared at the screen, waiting for a response; waiting for the next salvo of attacks to commence. She breathed heavily, almost panting in the heat of her rage and madness, and her heart pounded loudly, so loud in fact, that it could almost be heard as her chest would ebb and tide — up and down — up and down.

"Very well, Madam, I will respect your choice," the mysterious typist wrote. "I have tried to implore upon the innocence in you, but I can see that the little girl you once embraced has left you altogether. I will, however, give you one last chance. One last chance to turn, and return to whence you have come … back to the childhood you might recall … before such crimes were plied unto you. Leave this hate at the feet of our Lord, and repent. There is no hope otherwise. Please, I beseech thee."

Several moments had passed, and Madam Delevingne just watched the screen. She couldn't understand how anyone could have known about her molestations as a child. She wondered if the typist had actually known or if he was just making a generalized assumption.

Now, with her head still spinning from the intrusion, she drank what was left of her wine with a quick gulp and continued to watch. She just watched the screen, thinking that she could bring the identity of the strange writer to light. She waited; waited and contemplated on her revenge. Her face a dull red, her eyes still bulging from their sockets, and her hands trembling in wait. She trembled with a silent rage of the insane. Then, after a few moments, the mysterious writer returned with one final note.

"Oderint dum metuant. Sic semper evello mortem tyrannis ... et in tribus diebus ... luna incidit tribus diebus ... Evocatio obscuram noctem, ita ruinas ...."

After trying to read the strange words, Madam Delevingne decided not to write back. Instead, she highlighted the foreign words, which she thought were either Latin or Spanish, and then copied them and then pasted them into her computer's notepad. Then, she jotted them down in her little pocket notebook. This was followed by checking the administrator section again in order to jot down the last numbers of the IP address, and then she would wait for another response. She waited while mentally planning to meet with her allies the following day.

Now, she began to recall her allies, all of whom were far better with technical things than she was, and would find out who this guy was, where he lived, and what his name was. She'd find every spec of information she could get about the mysterious man or woman behind the quotes. One way or another, she would find out. One way or another, she would have her revenge. The goal now was vengeance, pure and simple. She would ruin the mysterious typist; this Bible-quoting attacker in any way she could.

Madam Delevingne knew that she could do this, and that was, after all, the end game to anyone who challenged or threatened her.

"So mote it be," she muttered, now far more subdued, far more peaceful of mind than before. "I'll have my day, my friend; my vengeance upon you … I *will* destroy you."

✠

Madam Delevingne had had enough of cyber jerks for one night, thinking she'd deal with it later on the next black moon; the dark of the moon, which was to be in three days. In three days, she would have the Order of Pry Thealemè Ex Mortis concentrate on the mysterious attacker, finding his spirit's location, and then send him something very special — something very special indeed.

"But that's not all, my friend," she mumbled. "I'm going to see that the Order of Pry Thealemè … the daughters of the Ordo Tenebris Lux seek you out, and banish your spirit; your soul, oh yes … I will kill you one way or another, you sonofabitch."

Madam Delevingne considered the timing of the approaching black moon, which was an event only recently predicted by astronomers and meteorologists a month before. And there could be no doubt that this astronomical oddity had presented itself at the most opportune time imaginable. Because such events like *Blue Moons* and *Red Moons*, as well as the darker aspects of those lunar phases, are not only rare but completely out of season, made her consider the magical significance of such timing. She considered the possibility of gaining great power from destroying a Christian, especially an arrogant, apostle want-a-be Christian like the mysterious Bible-thumper who had plagued her that evening.

Black moons only happen in February, she thought. *This shit isn't happening now without a very good reason.*

Now, as if a portent of doom, a low rumble of thunder could be heard circling the distant mountains. As it did, the evil woman simply smiled at the thundering echoes.

"Yeah, now's a perfect time … fuck yes, it is," she muttered aloud. Now grinning happily; her eyes took on a slit of glossy redness that offered a look of sinister joy. Now, she was formulating a plan.

✠

As the hour was getting late, Madam Delevingne got up, turned off the computer, and waited for the screen to go black. Then she turned the small table lamp off, rendering the little back room as dark as her soul. She had never been this angry before, at least not in a very long time. She would get her revenge one way or another, no matter what, this she knew without any doubt. She turned off the lights in the main building, leaving only the soft red glow of the wall clock above her. Now, the red neon light that surrounded the clock had lit the entire room with an eerie red hue as if the whole room was ablaze. Once again, the sound of distant thunder echoed throughout the room, and once again, it caused the woman to smile wickedly.

As the hour was getting late, Madam Delevingne left her makeshift office and looked around the store, behind the counters, towards the back closet, and in the little storage room just off the little kitchenette. She just couldn't help having the feeling that she was being watched. She looked around, and out the windows down the street, which afforded her a clear view now that the inside lights were off, but there was nothing out of the ordinary as far as she could see. All seemed calm and quiet, save that of the low, guttural thunder echoing in the distance.

Though there were a few people walking about the sidewalks, with an occasional car passing by, the dark of the night had quickly taken over the landscape. This, and the soft rumble of thunder, as well as the subtle, though obvious bursts of lightning dancing in the distant skies, its mauve tint gently offering a soft glow in the black night, had created an ominous feeling that could not be ignored, not even the rage-filled Madam Tarja Delevingne. Even she had a cold feeling of apprehension.

Regardless of her feelings of dread, the unpleasant woman took a portion of the contents from the cash register and counted it. She took six twenty-dollar bills and a ten-spot and then returned the rest to the drawer for change for the next workday. She made the bulk of the cash from Herc Benet and Lester Gnaws earlier that day. The rest came from selling a few candles and bottles of her 'enchanted' oils and potions, a guaranteed money maker from the town's lost souls; the witches and warlocks that scurried beneath Baytown's underbelly.

In truth, the liquids were nothing more than peanut oil and some synthetic aroma therapy knock-offs she'd bought at the craft store on the east side of town. This blend, along with some tiny seashells or maybe some dried herbs mixed in, and then poured into some fancy bottles, could sell for fifteen to twenty dollars for a half-ounce. It was a time-honoured ruse that the locals had always bought.

With the scent of incense burning, a few well-placed candles, and the soft sounds of new-age music wafting through the air, the rubes were always willing to dole out their hard-earned cash. Without a doubt, Madam Delevingne was an expert at tweaking Baytown's weak-minded fools. She was brilliant at it.

Idiots, she thought to herself, *simple idiots for big money. Shit, there'll always be enough morons to count on ... brainless, new age-believing morons.*

Now, she laughed loudly as she walked about the little store again, and just as she was about the turn the corner back into the kitchenette, she had, for the briefest moments, thought she saw a dark shape standing just outside the furthest window, just beyond its westernmost frame. For the briefest moments, she thought the black shape's eyes had glistened just enough to betray its hiding place. Feeling a sharp chill flashing down her back, she stopped and stared, but the image was gone as if it had never been there in the first place.

"Bullshit," she muttered slowly. Then she walked back into the little kitchenette, turned off the light, and then gathered her things, stuffed them into her extra-large, purse-like bag, and went for the door. Now, she laughed as she took one last look at the now dark and empty window. "I ain't buying it," she muttered again. "I ain't buying my own line a crap."

✠

Before she walked out the front door, Madam Delevingne took the piece of paper out of her pocket, the one with the IP addresses and the cryptic words on it. Whether French, Latin, or Spanish, she didn't know for sure, but she knew she'd find out.

Now, she looked at the words for a few minutes, trying to decipher as best she could, but wasn't able to get anything even remotely English-sounding from the words, except for maybe the word *tyrannis*, which she figured might have meant 'tyrant.' She decided to check her cellphone.

"Oderint dum metuant – Sic semper evello mortem tyrannis," she said into her phone.

"Oriental; Asian style dim-sum soup," the phone's speaker responded ... "A type of meat-stuffed dumpling, usually pork, and soup made with a broth and sometimes vegetables, along with herbs and spices to make a popular Chinese dish—"

"No, no, you, asshole!" she shouted into the phone.

"I cannot find that topic, please repeat the word," the cellphone echoed back. Now sitting on the chair near the front door, she decided to type in the words individually, under the translate icon, but she couldn't find an answer to the question. And then she remembered that Google had a translation page. "Of course," she muttered.

Now, the angry woman opened the app on her cellphone's screen and held it close to her mouth. "Let's try Latin to English first," she muttered to herself. "Oderint dum metuant ... Let them hate so long as they fear, and Sic semper evello mortem ... and thus always ... death to tyrants?" she read aloud. She continued to type the words individually, with the meanings popping up on the cellphone's screen one by one.

Once she had the information, she jotted the answers down as they appeared.

"Who sent this shit?" she mumbled to herself. "Is he someone I know? Of course, he has to be ... but how does he know information privy only to coven members, and in both my orders? How else could he know my coven's name ... not to mention my real name? It's someone I know ... has to be."

She looked around the store, and out the now dark windows again to see if anyone was out there. The streets were dark, only lightly lit by the dull street lamps.

"Luna incidit tribus diebus," she burbled into the cellphone. "The moon to fall? The moon falls in three days? And et in tribus diebus ... three; in three days." She stared at the screen with a grimace. "In three days, huh?" she said aloud. "What a coincidence, Bible-man ... in three days you'll know me, and my coven, oh yes. "Now ... this last part ... let's see what that means," she continued. "Evocatio obscuram noctem ... ita runinas!" She had to squint to read the meaning of the translation. "A dark night's ... to summon ... a dark night's summoning ... thus to ruin! What the fuck is this shit?" she belched again.

Now, Madam Delevingne continued to smile at her own ingenuity as she jotted down the translations. "You're gonna get so much hell you'll wish you were never born." She swiped another app on her phone and began to look up Herc Benet in her directory. Ever so slightly, she giggled in anticipation.

"So, our friend likes to use Latin to add to his mysterious persona ... okay, that's fine and dandy," she muttered, now in her typical arrogant manner. As she pressed the number for Herc Benet, she looked around the room again. She just knew she was being watched, but from where she couldn't be sure. "Maybe that son of a bitch is here in Baytown ... someone I know around here," she mumbled. "No matter. I'll find out, you can bet your ass on that."

"Yell-o," Herc's loud voice boomed through her cellphone.

"Initiate Cron ... Madam Delevingne here ... now, listen! I need you and Rommar to meet with me here tomorrow afternoon, here at the Cauldron ... no later than three," she exclaimed in her most authoritative voice.

"Oh, ah, of course, Madam Dele-vingg-nee, I'ze be theres, no problem ... I'ze take a eurlie lunch, and be there bout two or so, al-alrights?"

"Very good, Cron ... don't worry about Rommar if he can't make it, but you can inform him anyway ... I've a feeling he'll make it though."

"Absolutelies, Madams, absolutelies ... iz dare, iz dare a problems, Madams?"

"Oh yes, there's a problem alright, and I will be requiring magical help from all sides to end a certain gentleman … a hacker on the store's website who has gotten far too close to me, and to the Order, so revenge is now required," she said, now with the most dreadful overtones in her voice.

"I, I seez, Madams. Of course, and we'ze do our best … tis dis to be done on the *black moons*, Madams?"

"Naturally it is, Cron, and I don't want you or the others missing anything on this … I want the entire Order there at the park, at the peak of the witching hour, understand?"

"Oh, Great Pans, yes! I'ze makes shore of its, hells yeaz … I'ze call Rommar directly and let 'em knows youz orders, Madams!"

"Excellent, Cron … I'll be expecting you around two tomorrow … that's TWO in the AFTERNOON, CRON … TOMORROW!"

Madam Delevingne disconnected the call, denying Herc Benet the courtesy of a goodbye. It was the right thing to do, especially when she needed to keep her underlings in line, and of course, to instill the feeling of dominance and fear over them. She knew that her voice of command within and outside of the Order's dealings was necessary, especially to insignificant fools like Benet and Gnaws. Nonetheless, she knew they served a purpose; a purpose that would be realized on the night of the black moon. And with that, she felt she had had enough of the day, her anger subsiding to a dull feeling of power and the desire for revenge.

Now, she decided to get something to eat and then head home. Madam Delevingne grabbed her bag, tossed her cellphone into it, and then walked out of the building. A subtle, twisted smile took over her expression now. And as she locked the front doors of the Hollow Cauldron, a flash of lightning lit overhead, causing her to jump ever so slightly. She mumbled obscenities as she made her way to her 2007 Suzuki Forenza, which was parked on the other side of the building. She felt she was being watched.

Though the street appeared vacant, she just couldn't help feeling someone was next to her. Nevertheless, when she looked at her watch, she grunted when realizing that it was already going on 9:45 p.m. This amazed her, especially as so much time had passed. She knew that something was different; that something wasn't right. She could feel it in the air; in the way the air felt around her as if a storm was fast approaching — something just wasn't right.

CHAPTER EIGHT

Wednesday, July 1st, 9:58 P.M.

"So glistered the dire Snake, and into fraud led Eve, our credulous mother, to the Tree of Prohibition, root of all our woe."
—— *Paradise Lost, (Book IX, 641–646) John Milton, 1667*

Once Madam Delevingne left the Hollow Cauldron, she decided to head over to Denny's for something to eat. There, she would research the IP addresses again from her cellphone, and hopefully, find something that might match the Bible-thumper to someone she knew. She wanted to know — she needed to know.

She pulled off the East Freeway Service Road to the little plaza where the restaurant was. She figured she'd eat, find out who her new enemy was, and then fill up at the Conoco gas station across the street afterwards.

"Thanks for the grub 'n gas, *Crum* and *Romeo*," she burbled to herself, giggling in between her words. She pulled in and parked, now with a big smile on her face. Feeling superior, she knew full well she was going to nail this guy; this Bible-spouting invader who had the audacity to not only question her faith but issue downright threats to her and her ways of life. "I'll give you one more chance to return to Jesus? shit," she muttered. "I won't give you another chance, you bastard."

While she waited for her *Moons Over My Hammy*, she scrolled through the white pages app to find people she might have known in those locations where they had originated from. Knowing that even though there were dozens of addresses rifling from one name to another, one of them could have been the actual locale, minus those in Europe or in Thailand and Antarctica, of course. She found one that might be a match. The first was Rebecca 'Becky' Smithson from Terre Haute, but she was almost seventy years old now, at least in her late sixties, that was for sure. She was a witch, yes, but they were somewhat friends, at least she had remembered it that way.

Did we have a fight ... can't remember, she thought.

As she continued to scan her cellphone, she remembered Sheila Vose, another Wiccan acquaintance of hers, a *Stregheria* from Orlando, Florida. She liked to use an alias on the internet, like Cavallo, Vaux, or sometimes, she even used the name Kathleen Hyacinth, a persona she stole from an old British comedy show. And then there were the more comical monikers, such as Lady Brisbane and Mistress Merlin, and hokey personas like that. She was an angry woman, but mostly harmless.

"Crazy cat-lady ... yeah, she's a nasty one, that's for sure," Madam Delevingne mumbled to herself. "But we're still friends ... aren't we?"

As she continued to look through the websites that had her name, she found another listing. This time in the Orange County Obituaries, the one that read—

"Vose, Sheila, died Friday, March the seventeenth ... holy shit," she said a bit louder this time. "Damn, the old witch is dead ... I'll have to look into this later." Now, a worried look had fallen over her face. She was beginning to suspect that maybe there was a connection between the online Bible-thumper and her friends, but had quickly dismissed that idea. Her friends, much like herself, would have taken care of the hatemonger and fast. Now, she realized that no one would be that crazy, crazy enough to take shots at people like them. Nobody would be that stupid.

Just as her *Moons Over My Hammy* and seasoned fries arrived, she remembered Vic Deslaurier from New Orleans, Louisiana. Deslaurier had belonged to 'Le Temple du Séraphin déchu,' a French-based cult that specialized in ransacking churches, primarily Catholic churches. He had been its key organizer and a man who took great pleasure in the destruction of church property. Even by Madam Delevingne's own admission, the man was a monster.

"Now there's a prick," she mumbled, and then quickly began looking him up. It didn't take long to find a listing of addresses. Then she checked the *Been Verified* site, for which she had had a subscription for the last two years. She felt it was worth it, especially when she needed valuable information on others, specifically, her enemies.

Almost as soon as she typed in the name Victor Michael Deslaurier, she quickly received a response—

"Forty-four years old …blah-blah-blah … deceased, two-thousand-twenty-four? What the fuck, deceased?" She mumbled even louder, loud enough to receive scornful looks from the other tables. "Huh … guess it's not you either, then. Ah … who fucking cares? You were a prick anyway … not sorry a bit."

Despite Madam Delevingne's flippancy at the deaths of her acquaintances, however, she was concerned that they might have been connected somehow; that maybe the mysterious Bible-quoting antagonist was somehow involved with their deaths. For the briefest of moments, she considered the idea that her friends had dealt with the mysterious Bible-thumper, and he had got to them, maybe even had killed them — maybe.

"Bullshit," she mumbled in exaggerated protest, quickly denying any such possibility that the scripture-touting cyberbully had killed her friends. "It's just some asshole messing with me," she continued to burble. "Yeah, that's all that is. When we get 'em, he'll be sorry … you can count on that, Bible-man."

✠

By the time she finished eating, she had completed most of her IP address research. Next, she checked The Hollow Cauldron's website again and then checked her emails. There were no messages since she had left the store.

"Guess you lost your nerve, prick," she burbled. "Makes no difference to me, you're still mine … all mine."

After finishing her *Moons Over My Hammy* and fries, a side-order of Zesty Nachos, and a hot fudge sundae with extra sauce, not to mention four and a half glasses of sweet iced tea, she got up and ambled to the restroom. She did her business, checked her makeup and what was left of her teeth, and then returned to her table. Reading the check, she thought $24.84 was far too much. And it didn't matter how much she enjoyed the meal; she left a dollar tip as a protest. Now, she strolled leisurely back to her car, bloated and feeling ever-so cocky about her new enemy. She felt triumphant in knowing she'd ruin the man, whoever he was.

I'm gonna nail that asshole ... Yessiree, Bob, I surely shall ... by the goddess, I promise that she thought. A greasy smile now draped over her lopsided face.

As she drove the two hundred yards to the gas station, she pulled into aisle eight and went inside the store to pay. As she reached the front door, she felt a cold draft come over her, accompanied by a sharp pain in her stomach. She immediately thought it must have been the food, most likely the nachos.

They were too spicy, and too goddamn salty anyway, she thought. *Fucking jalapenos.*

As she stood in line, she began feeling hot; hot enough to sweat, with her perspiration now falling off her brow. She'd continue to wipe off the sweat with the sleeve of her shirt, but the warm liquid just kept exuding. In seconds, she began feeling feverish, and for a moment, almost nauseous. Now, she crossed her arms around herself when yet another chill fell over her.

"Jesus, it's freezing in here," she muttered. She looked at her cellphone for a time. It read: 12:03 a.m. Central Time Zone. "The Witching Hour, she muttered with a smile. "Perfect time to call the devil. Yeah, he'll do my bidding ... guaranteed." The vile woman just smiled. She knew what she was going to do now; formulating a plan to take down the Bible-thumper. She would have her revenge. In the name of Satan, and all the goddesses, she would have her revenge — an unholy revenge.

✠

Day Two

After she filled her car up using some of the money she had made from Benet and Gnaws, Madam Delevingne found herself giggling. She had felt a little better now, the chills and sweats having passed. In addition to that, it had been the thought of making a sixty-five-dollar sale from a resin and die-cast metal knife that morning, especially when she had paid exactly nineteen dollars and seventy-five cents for it online. She smirked at the knowledge of swindling the two boobs; Benet and Gnaws with such precision. She smiled, despite feeling a little sickish. Having that knowledge offered her a now accustomed sense of accomplishment and pride.

Now, the vile woman believed that she was truly a gift to feminism and that any man, at best, was nothing more than a secondary tool for work or baby-making. She was filled with confidence, yet she still couldn't get the feeling out of her head that she was being watched; spied upon by someone hiding somewhere. Just who it was, who *they* might be, is what was making her nervous, certainly not some Biblical verses about a God she didn't even believe in.

Just after entertaining her knowledge of self-superiority, she found herself feeling cold again, and she was sweating, too. She felt her body shake in order to keep warm and sweat to keep cool at the same time.

Maybe I'm getting the flu, she thought. *Yeah … guess that's what it is … fuck me!*

As she began driving past the Southwest Shipyards and then down Decker Drive, past the scrap metal yards, she gazed into the rearview mirror to check her face. As she did, she noticed what appeared to be a shadow-shifting, moving, sitting behind her. She saw what appeared to be tiny yellow lights peering at her; pinholes of sharp light from within a mass of darkness. The outline, or *whatever* it was, couldn't have been a man, but a form that had a basic human shape; a mist-like, misshapen blob that practically filled the mirror's circumference. And for the briefest of moments, she had recalled the dark shape that stood outside the store window of The Hollow Cauldron and thought that maybe, just maybe, whoever it was had somehow gotten in her car, and in the back seat.

The Bible-thumper! she thought to herself, now slowing down, trying to keep her eyes on the road and on the little mirror at the same time. *It can't be; it just can't be!*

Madam Delevingne, now understandably startled, had become so completely horror-struck at the misty image, an image that looked as if it were about to overtake her, that she slammed on the brakes. She had done this so forcibly that it had jolted her car so hard that its back end had lifted up at least a foot, with the vehicle finally coming to a screeching and sudden halt.

"What the fuck!" she screamed. Now, Madam Delevingne, the typically unfaltering femme fatale, had jumped out of the car with such veracity that she fell to the gravel shoulder and rolled down the small bank and into a muddy puddle. Just as quickly, she jumped up as fast as a martial artist in the heat of combat, having moved as she had never moved before. Then, her body had arched and jumped off the ground, almost as if her very life had depended on it.

As she stood there, now covered in mud, she stared into the foggy windows of her car. She saw nothing, absolutely nothing. As she approached the rear passenger section of the car, still shaking from the fright, she walked towards the rear window, slowly, ever-so-slowly, and leaned forward in order to get a better look inside. She peered down into the well behind the driver's seat but only found an assortment of paper cups from McDonald's and Hardees and the many balled-up Kleenex tissues from blowing her nose over the past year. Everything was as it should be.

Now, the soft light from the streetlamps had offered just enough of a glow to see within, but there wasn't anyone there. There wasn't a mysterious person or stowaway hiding anywhere in the car. It wasn't the Bible-thumper, who more likely than not, it was someone she knew, and who had most likely lived in another state. There was nothing there — absolutely nothing.

Still startled, Madam Delevingne slowly walked around her car, half-heartedly thinking that someone might have jumped out when she did; that *he* might be hiding behind the car on the other side. There was no one there, of course, not a soul. Nor was there evidence that anyone had been; anyone who might have run off when she tumbled into the muddy ditch. She just stood there, dumbfounded and confused.

Now relaxing a bit, she exhaled and flatulated loudly; a fart loud enough to alert an elderly black man who was riding his bicycle on the other side of the road. The old man just stared for a moment or two, as if his whole world had been shaken by the event. He even stopped peddling and put on the brakes for a moment, and just stared at the woman with sheer amazement. Then, he began laughing hysterically as he peddled away, and down the old gravel road.

"Damn, bee—otchh … hee—hee—heeee," the old black man laughed; his laughter echoing as he rode away, and then out of sight.

"Yeah, fuck you too … dumb nigger," she burbled under her breath.

Feeling slightly dumb herself, Madam Delevingne figured the whole thing was just an illusion, a trick of the light. She figured she had worked herself up over the mysterious Bible-thumper; the jerk that had the audacity to leave those hateful verses on her website — The Hollow Cauldron's website. She just shook her head and then got back into her car, took another look behind her seat and around the floor one last time. Now feeling a little stupid, she just shook her head and snickered at her own ignorance, as if someone could have actually hidden there in the first place. Unnerved, but understandably cautious, she started her car and proceeded for home.

"Well, I'm either losing my mind, or it's the greasy food," she said aloud.

As she approached her neighbourhood, she remembered that Oakland Street was blocked due to construction work on the roads there, so she'd have to go down to Maple Street, and then down Burnett Street in order to get back onto Oakland on the other end. She did and found that the already scarce number of street lamps were only half-lit, minus the soft glow of the blinking yellow construction lights. They eerily blinked, on — and — off — on — and — off.

✠

The street was dark, darker than usual. Even the trees that huddled in patches near the road seemed darker, too, and especially the tree line in the distance. The whole scene was spooky, even for Madam Delevingne, who, as the entire city of Baytown had known, was *the* top psychic and dispeller of negative spirits, whatever and wherever they might be. Nevertheless, she was spooked, and with the already cold chills running down her spine getting colder by the minute, she found herself actually being afraid.

Now feeling a chill, she looked in the rearview mirror to check the back seat again. This time, only the shadows from the fleeting lamplights crossed over her back seat, and then once again, an illusion of a misty shape began to appear sitting directly behind her.

"Fuuuccckk you … not this time!" she blurted out to herself. She laughed and then pulled up to her driveway and parked her car closest to the garage door. When she got out, she just stood by the open car door for a few moments. She waited to look around the place, checking her surroundings, but she just couldn't help feeling that she was being watched. Quickly, she shook her head and slammed the door, locked it, and then slowly made her way to the side door of the garage, while at the same time watching the wooded thickets that lined the old home and the pathway leading to the side door. She just could not shake the feeling that someone was out there, watching her from the darkness.

In a hurry to get inside, she scanned her surroundings again as she entered the garage apartment, quickly slamming the door shut as she did. She rented the space from old Arnold 'Arnie' Hammond, a retired dock worker from the shipyard. It was cheap enough, and was close to work, so she was content enough to stay, even when having to do *extra* things in order to stay there. She told herself it was worth it, that someday she'd have her own place, but that was a lie she made herself believe. In truth, she knew she'd always live there.

Upon entering, she looked around as she switched on the overhead light. All seemed normal; the typical mess, with shoes and underwear and bras lying about. There was stack upon stack of books piled high around the little makeshift domicile, including a more recent *Witches' Spell-A- Day Almanac* on the top, and of course, one of Llewellyn's *Woodland Faeries* calendars tacked to the wall. This helped in relieving her tension a little. She began to feel at ease, at least a little.

Madam Delevingne was happy with her collections, knowing that the majority of it all came from idiots like Benet and Gnaws, or the multitude of Baytown's moronic, new-age masses. Her little garage apartment was rife with such junk, an assortment of weird knick-knacks, and useless paraphernalia. From plaster dragons, gnomes, and faeries of every colour and shape, to medieval and renaissance-like clothing that hung on nails across the walls of the converted garage, all creating a look of someone who delved deeply within the realms of fantasy, the place had looked like a nerd's paradise. It looked like a mix between a *Game of Thrones* prop room and a *Twilight* convention gone horribly awry. But then again, she was a sorceress, after all, a psychic witch with occult powers, so such trappings were to be expected.

Madam Delevingne had lived in the little garage apartment practically for free, minus that of a few favours now and then when the old coot needed his manhood relieved — when he could get it up, anyway. She had the run of the kitchen, and she had her own bathroom in the main house downstairs, but tonight, she just wanted to lock the door, turn on the boob tube and watch something on the Syfy Channel. She just wanted to relax, calm down, and get some sleep. Getting the thoughts of the Bible-thumper out of her head, at least for the time being was her only mission tonight.

Now, as she flipped through the channels from one infomercial to another, she finally came upon the Syfy Channel. This was followed by one of her customary looks of disdain.

"Reruns of Ghost Hunters ... nice, just nice," she blurted. "Oh, what the hell ... I could have done a million times better than these dumbass plumbers ... bunch of fucking hacks," she blurted again. "But ... I suppose it's better than nothing."

She went to her micro-fridge and pulled out a Shasta soda, *California Dreamin' Orange creamsicle, yeah, that's it*, she thought, and then sat down on her old fold-out couch. She flatulated again, just as loudly and as obnoxiously as before, but this time it was muted by the old, soot-covered cushions of the couch.

"A fart's, a fart, but damn that was the worst one yet," she muttered. She giggled and then flatulated again, now laughing aloud at the rancid scent that went with it. For a moment, she had found herself unnaturally happy; happy that she'd be getting revenge, happy that she and her cohorts would be taking down an uppity Christian, the new enemy of a new, enlightened United States. Finally, she was getting respect, as were all those who had taken to the wise paths of the pagan ways of life, for those who had hated and denied the Jewish God.

✠

Madam Delevingne fell asleep just as the Ghost Hunters' marathon was going into its eighth hour, just as Jason Hawes and Steve Gonsalves were beginning to give the 'Big Reveal' of a supposed haunting in some brewery in Colorado. She fell into a deep sleep. Now, she tossed and turned as the deep, yet restless sleep had created a series of weird and troubling dreams. From 2:56 a.m. to 6:37 a.m., she slept in a state of nightmares and night sweats as she tossed and jolted on her old, dirty couch. Now, only the shadows of her sins could be seen in her mind's eye. She was terrified.

Her dreams were filled with images of devils and daemons racing after her, and by her side, as she ran down a seemingly endless path, down treacherous hills on some strange mountaintop. She knew it was her because she could see her image running by what appeared to be sheets of ice that were like mirrors; mirrors that had reflected her image as she ran. She knew she was in some forest too because she could see that the sheets of ice were covering trees. When she looked closer, she could even see an older version of Murfreesboro, Tennessee in the distance, the small town where she had once lived — back when she was learning of witchcraft, the magical arts, and the path of the Ordo Tenebris Lux and the teachings of Pry Thealemè Ex Mortis. This is when she began her life as a witch and her worship of Lucifer.

In what might be considered very Goya-like in meaning, such as one might find in his art, there could be little doubt that her guilt was catching up with her. And though all of this might be surmised from a Freudian perspective or even that of Fyodor Dostoevsky's nightmarish visions as found in his *Manuscript of Demons*, Madam Delevingne wasn't simply afraid now, she was thoroughly terrified.

Her dreams, so lifelike, so real, had made her feel as though the demonic-looking things that were chasing her weren't just trying to pursue her, but that they hated her with all their might; with all their will. They were of many shapes and sizes; some as large as houses, while others as small as domestic cats. Some were a mass of tentacles or tendrils, some masses of iridescent flesh, though all of them came with razor-sharp teeth and eyes that glowed like fire, like burning embers of some otherworldly hue. They made sounds like chittering or like teeth chattering, and the smacking of spit-soaked mouths, all gaping and gnashing.

The demons, she deduced, were mad at her, seeking revenge, just as she had sought revenge on so many others she didn't like or were jealous of — just as she sought revenge on the mysterious Bible-thumper who dared to quote scripture to her.

"Venn—ven—geance ... is mine!" she screamed in her sleep. "Revenge! I, I ... I'll get you! I'll get you FUCKER!" She awoke with a scream and jolted upward as fast as lightning, as if being shocked awake. Now, she threw the heavy wool blanket off her body as she coughed loudly. It was as soaked as her body was. She immediately figured that this was the cause of her bad dreams and night sweats, figuring that it was just a bad dream, and nothing more. Secretly, though, she worried that something might be medically wrong with her, thinking that she might have contracted food poisoning or worse.

After a few moments, the angry woman tried to get back to sleep, but she only tossed and turned. She felt paranoid, too, as if someone was in the room with her, as if someone had somehow gotten into her converted garage-turned-bedroom. The only place where she could feel safe now felt like it had been invaded by some unseen force. The whole place just felt wrong to her, as if she were in another room, as if in the wrong house. Now, she began to feel nervous, as if someone was following her.

As she sat up again, Madam Delevingne focused her gaze on the television for a few moments and then turned down the volume to its lowest setting. *Battlestar Galactica* was playing now. The now antiquated space opera from the 1970s was tolerable to her, and she watched a little of that. She wiped the sweat off her face and neck with her blanket and then held her stomach because it ached a little. It hurt down deep, having a hollow feeling, like the ones you get when you find out someone you loved has died, or when the doctor gives you bad news. It was an empty feeling.

Madam Delevingne was afraid, but afraid of what, she couldn't figure out. Now, she sat on her couch and looked around the room, gazing upon the many knick- knacks she had acquired over the many years, mostly stolen from occult stores or from her friends and the occasional lover. *Male, female, whatever*, she thought, *they all deserved it*. She felt they all owed her something, no matter who it was. They *all* owed her something.

As the television program had turned to a commercial for some feminine hygiene product, Madam Delevingne noticed a slight movement towards the front of her little garage apartment. She stared at the heavy curtains that covered the garage door and determined that there wasn't anything there. For a moment, though, she thought it might be rats or mice scurrying about, but no, there was nothing there. She loved the heavy curtain-like tapestries and had always worried about rodents getting to them, knowing full well that Arnie had had a rodent problem before. She always worried that rats would have loved chewing on those heavy fabric tapestries that she had hung over the garage door, and had checked them periodically to make sure they hadn't become a rat's midnight snack.

Madam Delevingne, now feeling sickish, had reminisced of days gone by. She remembered having put the tapestries there to give the place a homey feel, even though the smell of gasoline and grease from Arnie's workshop days had still permeated the place years later. In an instant, she recalled her childhood but had quickly discarded the thought, returning her gaze to the beautiful, though out-of- place tapestries. And as for the makeshift domicile she now called home, that was the only place she could afford; the best she could do. It was cramped, filthy, and either too hot or too cold — but it was hers.

"There'll always be idiots like Benet and Gnaws," she burbled arrogantly. "I'll get out of this shithole sooner or later."

✠

While she lounged on the couch, listening to Captain Apollo and Lieutenant Boomer talking about some aliens or robots or something like that, she began to finally relax a bit, easing back into the softness of the now sweat-soaked couch's extra-damp cushions. She was just beginning to fall back into a daze, a kind of elevated state of sleep, like a twilight sleep. And then she saw something move. From the corner of her eyes, she thought she saw something fidget. She thought she saw the curtains move. The heavy tapestry curtains seemed to move just a little, almost as if someone was standing behind them. They had shifted a little, as if someone was slowly pacing back there, back and forth — back — and — forth.

Now seeing this directly, her eyes opened wide, Madam Delevingne jolted out of her daze and stood up as if being electrically shocked again. In a second, she quickly picked up a heavy glass ashtray that sat on her nightstand and lifted it up as if to throw it at the hidden assailant, whoever it was, standing behind those curtains. She remembered the curtains were given to her by her mother before she died. She also remembered that they were affixed tightly against the garage door, and were tacked solid, being tightly flush with the garage door, so nothing could have hidden behind them. It would have been impossible.

Regardless of such simple logic, however, any reasoning that should have eased her mind had escaped her. Now, Madam Delevingne felt an overwhelming sense of fear intermixed with anger running through her mind.

"Who's ... who's there?" she softly murmured.

Now feeling bold, and armed with her ashtray, she walked to the other side of the television stand where one of her cheap daggers had hung on the wall by two nails. It was just like the one she had sold to Benet and Gnaws. She picked it up with murderous intent in mind; placed the ashtray firmly under her left arm for a moment, and unsheathed the dagger, then tossed the metal scabbard to the ground. It made a hard, metallic-sounding thud as it hit the carpet-covered, concrete floor. Now, she just stood there waiting for someone to pop out. She trembled.

Madam Delevingne had decided to challenge the unseen intruder. "Hey ... come out ... *COME OUT*

NOW!" she bellowed at the top of her lungs. She didn't care about waking old Arnie Hammond, even if he was home.

He's as deaf as a rock, and his room is way upstairs … at the furthest fuck'en end of the house, she thought. *He wouldn't be able to hear a damn thing, not even if I was getting murdered down here!*

No answer came from behind the curtains, so she waited a few seconds more and again yelled out to the unseen intruder. "*WHO'S BACK THERE? YOU COME OUT RIGHT NOW!*" she screamed. There was no answer; nothing, not a peep or any movement at all.

There was only silence. And after a few seconds of standing there as still as a statue, she slowly approached the curtains, with her dagger outstretched as far as her arm could go. She slowly walked forward, the ashtray, now in her left hand, had been raised high above her head, and poised to come down on whoever's head might rush out, while her dagger was poised for the kill. She believed she could kill someone now. She at least knew that much for sure.

✠

Madam Delevingne trembled as she approached the tapestry curtains — four feet, three feet, and then two feet away. Now, she knew she had to either drop the ashtray or the dagger in order to draw back part of the tapestry, and it sure as hell wasn't going to be the dagger. As such, she decided that if she tossed the ashtray towards the far side of the curtains, away from her, that whoever was behind them would most likely jump out and attack over there. Now, she raised her dagger in the stereotypical slasher movie stance, and then quickly tossed the ashtray to the furthest side of the room. The glass made a loud cracking sound as it shattered on the floor, splitting down the middle as it did. She watched closely as it spun for a second or so until finally coming to a standstill, but nothing happened; nothing at all.

Now enjoying a moment of relief, having realized once again that the curtains were far too close to the garage door to ever move, and that no one could have hidden behind them, she quickly began to feel stupid. But that was an emotion she wouldn't favour for long. Despite having applied at least some common sense to the whole affair, she had nonetheless half-expected someone to jump out but had once again realized that there was no way for anyone to hide behind those curtains, largely because they had rested no more than an inch or two from the garage door, making it simply impossible for anyone to be there unless they're only an inch-wide themselves.

Madam Delevingne had realized the obvious now and let her hand slowly fall by her side, with her dagger resting limply between her fingers. For the moment, she felt safe, but that feeling wouldn't last for long. Now taking a deep breath, and then letting out a sigh, Madam Delevingne pulled back the curtain from her side of the room, pulling out the tacks as she did, and then the curtains out as far as she could make them go. Naturally, there wasn't anything there. There was only a mould-covered garage door and a few tacks on the floor. Almost immediately, she had reassumed her former emotion, though secretly, she felt like a complete idiot.

She remembered that the garage door itself wasn't only glued to the flooring, along with metal brackets riveting it to the concrete, but that there was also a two-foot-high wall built against the door on the outside, too. It was simply impossible for anyone to get through there. Old Arnie Hammond put the walls there and sealed them with heavy construction-grade glue in order to keep floodwaters out whenever hurricane season came around.

In an instant, she remembered that the garage door could not go up or down again because it was bolted and sealed. In addition to that, the motor and chain to operate the door had been removed around that time, too, so the garage could be rented as a living space without having it look like a garage. She realized that that room was never going to be a garage again because he had a massive old barn behind his home just for that purpose.

"Get a hold of yourself," she mumbled loudly. She knew all this before, and she didn't believe in all the crap she peddled to others, not really. She was smarter than that. "No online creep is gonna win over me," she told herself. "I'm not gonna fall for your cheap, trick words or Christian curses on me, asshole, I'll never allow that."

Madam Delevingne, the grand witch of Magnus Datha, the sage woman of the Paganus tribes, had known her strength. She knew she was wiser, and stronger than the Bible-thumper, but for some reason she wasn't believing it, especially now. And as a low rumble of thunder sounded overhead, she had an epiphany. "Yes," she hissed. "It *is* that fucking Bible-thumper. Shit, either that or I'm going out of my mind; losing my goddamn mind."

✠

Madam Delevingne returned to her couch and turned the volume up on the TV. An episode of *Farscape* had just come on, which was good because that was always one of her favourite shows. She had always thought that Claudia Black's character was cool, and she believed that they were very much alike. She believed that they were both bold ass- kickers and smokin' hot, and that they were completely able to kick ass. Now, she knew she'd find out who that Bible- thumping bastard is, and finish him for good. She knew full well that she'd not only be victorious but that taking down a follower of Christ would be the feather in her cap, for women everywhere, for those on the pagan path.

Thunder slowly rolled above her, like a slow drumroll, as she reached into the night table drawer to pull out a pack of West Virginia Slim 100s. She had been trying to quit, but had figured now was a good time for a smoke.

"Vagina-Slimes," she muttered with a giggle. In an instant, she had recalled that that was the nickname for those cigarettes back in Catholic school; back when she ruled the roost, back when she and her lackeys had terrorized the nuns without shame. Now, a half-smile fell across her face at the thought, and then she sat back into the soft, though worse-for-wear, couch. "I need one of these bad girls more than anything right now," she murmured.

She took a cigarette from the pack, lit it, and then sat back to take in a long drag of smoke into her lungs. Then she reached into the same drawer and pulled out a bottle of sleeping tablets. She figured the little purple no- name tablets she bought at Walmart a few weeks ago would be the answer to her problems.

"These should do the trick," she muttered. "Dip-hen-hydra-a-mine … fifty-milligrams … perfect.

She shook the bottle until three tablets fell out and then tossed them into her mouth. She chewed them up until they were a creamy paste, and then swallowed them. Now, she just sat there for a few moments and just stared at the garage door as she inhaled the cigarette's fumes. She tried to figure out how the curtains had moved, especially when there wasn't any fan on, and the small box air conditioner that was affixed to the window wasn't strong enough to blow the curtains. None of it made any sense to her, but she knew she'd figure it out.

"I'd think it was a ghost, but I don't want to drink my own Kool-Aid," she muttered. "Don't want-ah buy my own line of shit … that's for the rubes." She giggled as she took another drag. Her stomach was acting up again, churning as though she'd have to vomit or worse. And there were cramps too, but she knew it couldn't be her period, not yet, anyway. Begrudgingly, she got up and headed for the bathroom in the main house and sat on the toilet. She left the door open, not caring if old Arnie would walk in or not. She had to go, and that was that. In a second, a burst of explosive diarrhoea had made its presence known with a loud, unmistakable sound of one's gullet being forcefully purged.

"For fuck's sake ... what the hell!" she bellowed loudly. "It was that damn food; it has to be!"

Madam Delevingne, now hunched and holding her stomach, now believed that she might have had food poisoning after all. She just sat there, waiting for last night's sandwich and nachos to get out of her system. Between the horrible sounds of gassy explosions and liquid being forced out of a frayed hose had only gotten worse with the rancid odour that quickly followed. Nonetheless, she began to feel a little better than before. Now, she contemplated on the weird dilemma the night before, the frightening shape she saw in the backseat of her car, twice, no less, and of course, the slightly fluttering curtains in her room. Not entertaining the possibility that it could have been an actual paranormal event, she surmised that the curtains were far too heavy for any movement to take place behind them, let alone for anyone to fit behind. None of it made any sense.

That'd be impossible, she thought. *No ... I call bullshit. It just couldn't happen.*

In seconds, she remembered the night when she helped her mother carry those curtains into their old home a decade or so ago, just after her mother snatched them from the old MacLarsen-Ward Museum; back when they lived in Beaumont, way back when her mother worked as a docent there. She remembered that they must have weighed at least a hundred and fifty pounds when folded and carried together. The curtains, being made of a thick, tapestry-like cloth, added an almost unbelievable weight to them, so no amount of air other than a hurricane could have shifted them in a small room like her garage apartment, not without the aid of something else.

To move them really would take a hurricane, she thought. *No fucking way.*

Now giggling again, Madam Delevingne began to reminisce. "Mama was a much better thief than ever I was … yes, she was … oh, great goddess, I miss the old gal," she mumbled to herself, followed by an audible chuckle. With her stomach feeling somewhat normal again, and the horror show which was her diarrhoea event of the century was finally over, she got up, flushed, and returned to her comfy, though nonetheless sweaty couch where she could catch her breath and regain her strength for the coming day; the day where she'd figure out who the mysterious Bible- thumper was, and how best to deal with him.

Her thoughts had, in that moment, altered from fear to anger in a matter of seconds. She imagined what she and her mother would have done by now; what they would have done together to get even with this Bible-toting abuser, this attacker upon the chosen and the wise.

We'd rip this guy a new one, she thought, now with a greasy smile taking over her expression. *Yeah, we'd fix his wagon quick-like … and it would hurt, you bastard.*

Now, sitting back on the couch, she thought about her revenge on the unknown harasser for a minute or so before lighting another cigarette. She watched the television for a few minutes more, and then flipped back to the SyFy Channel, then snubbed out what was left of her smoke. She giggled as she lifted her left leg off the couch and flatulated once again. This ended with yet another series of giggles and laughter. Now, feeling at least a little better, she watched a bit of *Farscape* and lay down on the sweat-soaked couch. She decided she'd get some sleep.

By hell or by high water, I'll get you, you sonofabitch, she thought. *Oh yeah, I'm gonna get you … you can count on that!*

Thunder rumbled loudly, just as her little desk light flickered three times; just as the old, battered television blinked off, and then miraculously turned back on. Now, the volume was lower, which was good because some annoying infomercial had taken the place of the space opera she had been watching. It didn't matter anyway. She was just beginning to doze off into yet another deep sleep. And right before drifting away, she turned her cellphone off and rolled over on her side. Her stomach began to bother her again, just a little, but she'd sleep anyway. She would sleep deeply, yet again, restlessly. And once again, she'd be plagued by dreams — those horrible, oh-so-horrible dreams.

CHAPTER NINE

Thursday, July 2nd, 1:23 P.M.

"… The philosophies of one age have become the absurdities of the next, and the foolishness of yesterday has become the wisdom of tomorrow."

— *Sir William Osler, 1st Baronet, Canadian physician*

Day Three

Madam Delevingne awoke to the theme music of *Wizard Wars*. The Syfy Channel was running old episodes that day, and the gaudy music of the last generation had announced the passing of another heated night. She felt better now than she had just a few hours before. She had had horrible nightmares again, mostly of being chased by monsters or demons, but she'd always get away from them. In her dreams, she could jump, or more seemingly, float up as far as she wanted in order to escape the monsters. She could float as high as a telephone pole, and then just hang off the top of it, as if she were in a swimming pool as if holding onto the side of that pool, while looking down into the murky depths below with those razor-sharp teeth-gnashing, and those blazing, yellow eyes just staring at her.

The monsters, all of which were distant and fuzzy-looking to the eye, couldn't get her from her imagined safe place. She felt secure there, but still, somehow, she just knew something was hunting her — taunting her, even in her dreams.

✠

Madam Delevingne was fully awake now and felt superior again. She was certain of her self-aware understanding, realizing that she was above others, completely confident of her place of surpassing any idiot man in intellect and knowledge, and especially that of the most arcane, the most secret. Now, Madam Tarja Delevingne could add scaring off monsters of the nightmare world to her occult credentials. Now, her wisdom and self-assuredness had returned. She was ready for the overly proud Bible-thumper and knew she'd have her revenge.

I win again, she thought as a subtle smile rose on her face. *I'll always win.*

Sitting up and propped against the extra soft cushions and pillows that lined the couch, she just watched the TV and shook her head at the stupidity of modern television shows.

"Not more of this damn reality shit," she mumbled as she looked around the room and tried to cerebrally re-examine the reasoning for the moving curtains and the uncanny feeling of being watched. She tried to figure out why she was scared in the first place, which was an emotion that was more uncommon to her than to other people. Nonetheless, she tried to understand why the messages she'd received from some Bible-toting, internet whack-job could have scared her so much. None of that should have angered her so; none of it. She had life by the balls, and no one, especially an insignificant man, would ever, could ever get the better of Madam Tarja Delevingne, the High Priestess of the Order of Magnus Datha.

"I'd dealt with people like you before," she muttered to herself as she stared at the television. "Oh yeah, I'll put you in your place … just like the street preachers, the holier-than-thou jack-offs that actually think they communed with some Hebrew God of some sort as if they were Moses from that old '50s flick." She slowly wagged her head in disgust. She had been inspired at an early age, understanding what the rest of the common herd could never understand. She didn't believe in all that Bible nonsense despite her Catholic upbringing. Her god was a goddess; the goddess Diana, goddess of the hunt, and of course, *his* majesty, the outcast seraph of the Old Testament. *He*, being of great power and wisdom and light, Lucifer, the male counterpart to the intellect and circumference of her greatness over others.

Madam Tarja Delevingne was back. Now, she was certain that she had made possible the direct link between her and the netherworlds of wisdom and power, where only those infused with the wisdom of the old religion could venture. She believed she was among the highest in the eyes of the goddess; the goddess's favour, like that of Baubo, of Persephone, and of Demeter's favour, in the favour of Eris, mother of chaos, and in Hecate's favour, as in Diana's favour. And of the most select, was in *his* favour — her master, Lord Lucifer, the bearer of light and mirth.

Now, Madam Delevingne smiled. She figured that perhaps she would be admitted to the holiest realms, where she would perfect her wisdom and become a goddess herself. In her best judgment, she believed that she would be allowed entrance into the most clandestine of realms, likely as her favourite psychic, Sylvia Browne would have referred to as the 'Library,' or the 'Hall of Records,' where she and those like her would learn of the most sacred without the impediment of man's so-called intellect, where she would intervene or stifle the naysaying of such undeserving ilk.

✠

Madam Delevingne nodded and smiled as she watched the ridiculous garbage that was now being exhibited on her old Sylvania television. She just shook her head in disbelief at the spectacle. On the screen were a somewhat popular magician and his straight-man sidekick, a short man who never spoke, but made funny expressions to his much larger, far more obnoxious partner. The magician was an outspoken atheist, so Madam Delevingne was *okay* with that much, though today, she couldn't stomach the loud and arrogant man. Today, she just couldn't tolerate the insolent fool.

"Ugh, not this asshole again," she burbled. "Not so early in the morning … not this phony street juggler again. Not this early. Oh, great goddess, help me," she continued to exclaim while she yawned. "He is, without a doubt, the biggest moron in the universe, hands down. Thee biggest!" Now fumbling with the TV remote, she began her customary habit of channel surfing until she found just the right station, and then dropped it to the couch.

"Big, lumbering schmuck with his little mute toady," she burbled again, just as the acidic comedian and his sidekick faded off the screen for the last time. Madam Delevingne got up and headed into the main section of the house, and then off to the kitchen to make some much- needed coffee.

Old Arnie Hammond had left for the day, as usual. He made a habit of eating most of his meals at the Waffle House across town, off I-10. He didn't like to cook, and at sixty-seven years old, he didn't have to. This was good because she liked the run of the place without someone watching over her every minute, or having to feel obligated to give the old fart a blowjob when he wanted one; sixty-seven years old or not.

Once in the kitchen, she began preparing a paper filter with some of the generic brand coffee that Arnie had bought down at Big Joe's Smart Shop Grocery. She filled the tank with water and turned on the Mr. Coffee. It began to drip and hiss, emitting the now predictable rancid odour of grade-F coffee, like a toilet full of shit being boiled into a brew. But it was, after all, caffeine, and she needed that right now.

As she leaned against the ageing and tattered linoleum counter, she waited impatiently for her morning cup of joe. And, impatient as usual, she pulled the pot off the burner and dipped her coffee mug under the dripping spigot to fill her mug. She returned the pot, but not fast enough to prevent some of the hot coffee from splashing on the burner, which naturally shot the hot liquid on her hand, causing her to jerk the pot in her other hand, and towards herself. This, of course, had splashed some of it on her stomach and chest.

"Mother fucker!" she screamed, "Ah ... goddamn it! You fucking asshole!"

Believing that the coffee pot was responsible and not her own impatience, she slammed the coffee pot back on the burner while continuing to mumble obscenities towards Mr. Coffee. Then, she walked out of the kitchen and back to her converted garage apartment. She figured she would drink her coffee and get down to the Hollow Cauldron before 3:00 p.m., and pick up something from McDonald's or Hardee's on the way. She figured it was her store, thanks to big-hearted morons and Baytown's own, homegrown New Age idiots. She was the boss, after all, and she made the rules, so being late was her privilege.

"I can open any time I fucking want to," she mumbled. "So, if they don't like it, they can kiss my lily- white ass."

Madam Delevingne turned off the television and checked her image in the full-length mirror that hung on the door that led to the kitchen. She discovered she was wearing the same clothes from yesterday, so she began scrounging around a pile of clothes that were bunched up next to her nightstand. She found a brownish-coloured blouse on top that was less dirty and less sweaty than the others beneath it. Though it did have a ketchup stain on the midsection, she didn't care.

"Fuck it," she said aloud, and then quickly put it on. She figured her blue jeans were fine and slipped on her purple jelly sandals, which she had recently purchased downtown. She decided she'd slum it that day because she'd felt like shit all day yesterday and that night. Plus, she had to put up with a mysterious, Bible-thumping attacker, too, so she'd slum it today. Besides, whoever that Bible-thumping asshole was, she had no doubt whatsoever that he or she would get what's coming to them, so it was all well worth it.

Snickering, Madam Delevingne unlocked the side door and walked out. The first thing she looked at was the trash cans, both of which needed dragging to the front driveway for pick-up the following day.

"That's your job, Arnie," she grumbled bitterly. Then, as she looked out at the street, her eyes quickly turned upward towards the sky; a sky that was as yellow as a canary, only duller, and hazier than any sky she'd ever seen. "What the fuck is this shit?" she muttered loudly. "I've never seen anything like this before ... seriously, what the fuck?"

Now thoroughly freaked out, she went back inside and looked around the television, and then looked on the floor for the remote. Finally, finding it a few minutes later, a process that was accompanied by curses and swearing, and a plethora of other tidbits of nasty verbiage, she turned the TV on.

The remote was lodged halfway under the couch, likely ending up there during her tumultuous affair the night before and most of the morning before she finally got to sleep. Regardless, she clicked the remote and scanned each program until she came upon the Weather Channel. They were only covering some kind of tropical depression in the south, somewhere near Jacksonville, Florida, so she kept scanning until she found Channel 26 out of Houston. There was video footage of the same yellow sky, with some of the most bizarre clouds she'd ever seen.

The broadcast was being filmed live because of the strange colour of the day's sky, and because of the overall weird weather churning in the atmosphere. There were two men talking to each other about it, one man, Dr. Preston Prendergast, Houston's chief meteorologist, and a guest of the Baytown station, was explaining certain aspects of the weather to a curious population. Next to him stood a young man who had taken the reins from Jim Siebert, the former weatherman, when he retired a few years before. He was helping the elder meteorologist with the task of figuring out the odd-looking sky that day. Now, the younger man, whom she recognized as Mike Reardon, the new weekday weather reporter, was conversing about the strange weather. They were trying to explain what was going on for the otherwise ignorant populace of East Texas.

Now, Dr. Prendergast smiled assuredly as he pointed at a large mass of churning clouds on an animated screen. "Well, as you can see, Mike, these fluffy cloud formations, also known as Mammatus clouds, appear like pulsating nodules, like little balls of fluff hanging down from a larger mass of blanketing clouds, right here," he said, as he pointed to the weird formations with what looked like a laser pointer. "They're typically associated with what we refer to as anvil clouds," he continued, "which occur when severe thunderstorms are about to form or while forming … or when one is approaching. It's not the rarest type of cloud cover by any means, but they're certainly not that common either … and certainly not like this," he said.

Mike Reardon nodded in agreement. "They jut out from the underbellies of cumulonimbus clouds, too, don't they, Preston?" he asked.

"That's right Mike, and as you can see here, this great, big anvil-shaped cloud that reaches way up as far as you can see; right here … this is basically a giant churning air mass that can create such phenomena, though they can certainly form under other cloud masses too, including what we call stratocumulus, altostratus, and altocumulus clouds, and of course, cirrus clouds as well." The older weatherman continued to explain to the cameras as if teaching a beginner class in meteorology.

Mike Reardon simply turned to the camera and smiled, and then offered a slight chuckle to the elder weatherman's explanation. "Wow, those are some pretty big words, Preston. And what do we have in store for the rest of the day? Any insight on what to—"

"Oh, shut the fuck up!" Madam Delevingne belched arrogantly. She didn't want to be lectured, she just wanted answers. Now, just as the two men continued to describe the strange cloud formations, she found herself becoming even more anxious. "What about the colour of the sky, you assholes!" she belched again. Reluctantly, the vile woman turned up the volume and sat back on the grimy couch, just as Dr. Prendergast continued.

"… Again, as for the tint of the sky, well, that can happen for many reasons too," the elder weatherman continued. "This might include a massive bright flare-up occurring nearby, like a forest fire, but our 'Eye in the Sky Chopper' reports no such fires, thankfully. And we would have been alerted by fire-watch services in any event. But what we do know; what science tells us for sure … well, what is certain is that molecules; basic air molecules can actually pick up colours and hues, in this case, it's likely being illuminated by the sun, along with various dust and soot particles that exist everywhere in our atmosphere. In fact, this is most likely a mixture of volcanic ash in the atmosphere and the sun's rays to give off the flare effect we're seeing right now."

The younger weatherman nodded again in agreement. "There's volcanic activity going on in the South Pacific right now, isn't there, Preston?" he asked.

"That's correct, Mike, but we can also see such effects from approaching thunderstorms and after such storms as well, typically during late-day T-storms. But as this is not the case, this all can seem a little strange, especially since this all began early this morning."

"That's right, Preston," the younger man blurted. "We began getting calls from concerned citizens about the strange colour of today's sunrise … people were concerned that there might have been a fire, as you suggested as a possibility, and for sure, there were a lot of panicked people out there."

The elder weatherman returned a chuckle to the comment. "Well, I'm sure this will blow over before tomorrow morning, as the winds are picking up a little this week, but in the meantime, radar promises a clear day ahead, with temperatures topping off at just around ninety-one degrees, and with the humidity index, it should feel more like ninety-five to ninety-eight degrees. But more importantly, there's no rain in the forecast."

✠

As Madam Delevingne got up and turned off the television, she could still see the odd, yellow colouring seeping through the side vents of the small air conditioner. It looked as if someone was shining a bright yellow light through the cracks, as if someone was toying with her, harassing her.

When she opened the door, the light was even more intense, bright enough, in fact, to make her squint and shield her eyes with her hand. Now, she went outside and walked down the path to where the driveway met the road. When she gazed up, she could see that the sky was churning, with the weird nodules oddly swaying, just as the older weatherman had put it. They were hanging down like the udders of a cow, swaying to and fro, as if they were somehow alive. The image was completely bizarre. Regardless, the weathermen promised that the day would clear up and return to a customary blue sky with no rain. They would be wrong, of course.

The weathermen, with all their technical know-how and scientific gadgetry, could not properly detect any concrete reasoning for the yellow day. And it was true that people from all over Harris County were calling in about the strange skies, even as far as Beach City and Mount Belvieu. The sun would not be made out that day, only its intense light setting the scene like some sick, surreal painting.

By 2:45 p.m., Madam Delevingne was rushing to get to work. She figured she'd forgo McDonald's today and just order a pizza when she got to the Hollow Cauldron. And then she remembered she had to meet Benet and Gnaws by 3:00 p.m., so she quickened her pace. In haste, she drove off, thinking that the whole affair the night before, her upset stomach, the diarrhea, and the nightmares were just an aftereffect of eating spicy or undercooked food. She was sure of herself again and confident, as per norm. And with that, her lust for revenge was once again in full force. She was ready for a fight.

Madam Delevingne checked her cellphone for any messages and then checked the store's website for any posts, but there were none — nothing at all, not even from the mysterious, and yet-to-be-identified Bible-thumper.

"Makes no difference," she muttered. "I'm not done with you yet, Bible man … not by a long shot." Her eyes squinting through the strange glare of the day, she looked up and ambled to her car. As she drove down the road, she watched as a spattering of people gathered to gaze at the weird sky. The weird, yellowish nodules swayed like blunt tentacles reaching down for her, but her anger had retarded her glances upward. "No," she grumbled. "I'm nowhere near done with you."

✠

By the time Madam Delevingne arrived at the store, her two initiates were waiting outside. Herc Benet was eating a double-decker burrito the size of a kitchen table placemat, rolled up with gooey sauces and what looked like greens mixed in. The greyish-green glop oozed from one end, with a good portion of that dribbling down his white, button-down shirt. Without a doubt, the image seemed typical of the nasty high priestess.

Lester Gnaws, seemingly oblivious to the world around him, was kneeling against the wall of the building, with his knees pressed up against his chest. He was smoking on a device that looked like some kind of asthma breathing apparatus, but when it let out huge plumes of a white, smoke-like mist, it became obvious that it was one of the more expensive vapour cigarette devices. It filled the circumference where the two men were camping out in wait for their mistress.

Lester wooed over the idea that Madam Delevingne had noticed him, and more than that, wanted him as much as he wanted her. He was in his own world now, dreaming about the vile woman and how it would be if they were an item; if they were lovers. He knew that she dated men sometimes, even women too, which he thought was cool, now imagining how he'd love to be mixed up in that; that he'd rise through the ranks of the Order, even surpassing his lifelong friend, Herc Benet, for supremacy.

If only, he thought.

By the time Madam Delevingne was getting out of her car, Benet had finished his massive burrito and was now wiping his hands on his pants, a ne'er-do-well behaviour that was far too commonplace for the fat man. It was the custom after eating, and Benet didn't care if anyone was watching. Now, as Herc began his trek to meet their mistress, Lester had quickly gotten up off the ground and began to walk behind his friend. He just looked at the ground as he did, his hands firmly tucked in his pants pockets. He had returned to his gait of subservience, just as Madam Delevingne would have wanted it.

"Here she be," Herc said cautiously. "Let's go, Bo, fir she gits mad."

Madam Delevingne got out of her car, carrying a backpack-like purse under one arm and a bag of candy corn she had just found on the floorboard as she was leaving the car. She looked mad, really pissed off at something, just as the two men had surmised. And as she walked purposely toward the front door, her car's horn began beeping repeatedly. The after-market car alarm sounded with its lights flashing on-and-off-on-and-off.

"What the fuck!" she screamed. Quickly, she began scrounging through her handbag to find the keys that she had just tossed in. She continued to mumble obscenities as she did, and then dropped her bag of candy corn in the process. "Fuck!" she shrieked again. Now finding the keys, she began hitting the button again, and again, until the car's alarm finally ceased its maddening racket.

"Haz you evers seen the likes of a yella skies be- foes, Madams!?" Benet shouted to Madam Delevingne. "No sirz, I'zea tellin-ya, neva-foe seen such a sky like dis!"

Now appearing angrier than before, Madam Delevingne just stared at the two men as she walked toward them. "Well, better late than never!" she barked at Benet and Gnaws, almost as if they were the ones who were running late.

"Let's go!" she bellowed. "I'm gonna need some footwork regarding a new enemy we've procured ... and we're gonna knock this asshole for a loop, understand?"

"Oh ... ah course, Madam Dele-a-ving-nee, whatever youz wants," Herc said. "What can wez do?"

As Madam Delevingne unlocked the front door of The Hollow Cauldron, and then rushed in with a huff, and then practically letting the door slam in Benet and Gnaws' faces as she did, she would conclude by bellowing out one final, though nonetheless all-too-common set of commands to hurry, or else. Now, it only took seconds for the two men to jolt, immediately fumbling over her loud commands in the process. As such, the two initiates tripped and fumbled over each other as they tried to obey their leader. It had created a scene right out of a Laurel and Hardy skit.

Heading back to the little office at the rear of the store, Madam Delevingne turned on the small desk lamp and then the computer. She sat down in the old chair she'd picked from the garbage heap with an audible plop, and waited while the computer started. Now, she just stared at the computer, and then back at Benet and Gnaws, her loyal, if not a bit stupid, initiates of the Order of Magnus Datha.

"Cron and Rommar ... ye shall always be," she said to them with a cryptic tone. "And ye shall always be faithful ... *yes?*"

"Yes, Madam ... faithful!" the two men said in unison as if well-programmed robots. "Good! We've a lot ahead of us, so I expect your total cooperation ... tonight!"

She looked at the two men with a face of pure rage; with her features a dull red, and her eyes wide and angry.

She just stared at both men with a questioning gaze, almost as if she were about the yell at them for something they did. Madam Delevingne was clearly pissed off at something, but the two men couldn't figure out by what, or why.

"Cron, I want you to read this ... this ... this hateful piece of shit I got yesterday," she asked. "Just read it completely, and then tell me if you know who this is ... I don't care if you do, or if he or she is a friend, I just want the truth ... understand?"

"Yez, right, of course, Madam, whatever you sez," Cron replied as helplessly as he could make himself sound; his southern drawl making him sound hopelessly stupid.

Madam Delevingne got up and pointed to the chair, for Cron to sit in. He did, and immediately began reading aloud—

"Therefore, hearken not yee to your pro-phets ... nor to your di-vin-ers, nor to yourz dree — dreamers, nor to your en-chanters ... ah, nor to your sorcerers, which speak unto youz, saying, ye shall not serve, ah ... da kingz of Baby-a-lon—"

"Well? Do you recognize any of that, Cron ... do you know anyone who uses Bible quotes?" Madam Delevingne asked impatiently. "Who do you know spouts religious shit like that?"

"No, Madams ... I, I'za don't, I'za know no ones who talk like dat!"

"Keep reading then, and let me know if you do ... no matter whom you think it is; you *WILL* tell me!"

Cron read on, shaking his head as he did. Either in confusion of the Middle English wording, or that he truly didn't know who the author was, he looked as if he were taking an entrance exam for Mensa. The sweat now rolling down his forehead and cheeks, his mouth in the shape of wonderment, he just stared at the screen and mouthed the words as best he could. The man looked as if he would have a stroke at any moment.

✠

As Madam Delevingne watched his sweaty brow, the fluids dripping down his face, and onto his stained shirt and lap, she stared amazed at his giant belly that jutted at least a foot-and-a-half from his beltline. Now, she slowly shook her head in disgust.

He looks like a heart attack waiting to happen, she thought to herself. *Jesus, what a slob … no wonder everyone calls him the Fat Man, the dumb lummox … what-ah disgusting pig.* She continued to shake her head with a mixture of repulsion and pity. Then, she gazed over to Rommar, who had quickly lowered his head towards the ground in nervous respect.

Romeo, she thought. *This sap would step in front of a speeding train for me. Well … at least there's that in his favour … poor dumbass.*

Now with a subtle smile rising across her face. Madam Delevingne resembled a female version of the Grinch who stole Christmas. She looked back toward the computer, her face immediately returning to one of anger. "Well, Cron … do you know who it is?!" she barked again.

"No, Madams, I ain't any idea'z … do youse spect tis one of us … from our Orderz, dat is?"

"I don't know Cron, but I'm gonna find out … and when I do, all hell's gonna break loose, I promise that … therefore, Cron, you, and Rommar will contact the others, and have them meet me at the preserve; at the front gates no later than eleven o'clock tonight … *NO LATER THAN ELEVEN, UNDERSTAND!*"

"YEZ, yez, of course, Madams, I … I'za start call'in dems right nows!" Cron responded, now finding himself somewhat terrified at Madam Delevingne's rage. Now in a subtle state of shock, he wiped the sweat from his brow and panted heavily.

"Rommar!" she barked. She just stared at Lester Gnaws with a murderous look.

"Yes, Madam, ah, ah, YES?"

"I want you to go to Grizzela's mobile home and tell her directly! She doesn't have a car, and you'll need to drive her, understand?"

"Yes, Madam, I'll go right now and tell 'er … ah, I'll wait until she's ready to go … okay?"

"No, you idiot, it's only four o'clock or so, way too early. Go to your homes and get ready … make sure you have your cloaks, full regalia, and whatnot. Get candles and incense, if you have them, and incense bowls, and your athames too, everything to prepare for the ritual … a full-fledged ritual. Don't forget anything!" she commanded. "It's a *Black Moon* tonight, and we're not going to miss this, not by a long shot, understand?!"

"Yez, Madams, wez-a go'en!" Cron bellowed fearfully. Lester followed close on his heels; his head bowed in subservience again. He was almost rubbing against Cron's massive backside as they hurried out the door. The scene was both comical and pathetic, but the cruel woman knew she could count on them. Now, ever so slightly, a crooked smile rose upon her twisted face.

"Rommar … you stay a minute," Madam Delevingne said impatiently, and somewhat seductively.

As Cron lumbered as best he could away, and outside of The Hollow Cauldron, he got into his 2015 Dodge Grand Caravan. Once seated, he began flipping through his cellphone's address book, scrolling down the list of names of all the members of the Order of Magnus Datha. He sat as far back as the car seat would go; his giant gullet pushing up against the steering wheel, though the fit remained tight. Certainly, his nickname 'Fat Man' had fit the image of the man with crystal clarity. Now, by hook or by crook, he was going to follow Madam Delevingne's orders to the letter. He simply had to.

Everyone knew Herc Benet was a slob, not just because he dressed like a slob, or that most of the time a good portion of whatever he was eating usually ended up on his shirt and pants as if he had some kind of palsy and couldn't put his food in his mouth properly, he was just a gross, fat slob. Without a doubt, his entire persona echoed a man who just didn't care about himself. He was indeed a slob. Nonetheless, slob or not, Herc Benet was obedient and loyal to Madam Delevingne, and to a fault. And it was this fact that saved him from being banned from the coven altogether.

Although Madam Delevingne had realized that regardless of Herc Benet's grossness, or that the man was an adult man-child who could barely pronounce simple words and sentences in an intelligible manner, let alone correctly, he was loyal, just as his sidekick, Lester Gnaws. And there was no doubt that she had owned both of them, a fact that they had accepted graciously. This fact would always be advantageous for both parties — the mistress and the servant.

Now, as Herc Benet began his task, Madam Delevingne continued to instruct Rommar on the finer things of being her servant. She knew full well that he was infatuated with her and had decided to use that fact to the hilt. This she did without a thought or hesitation. But more than that, she figured she could have a slave all her own; a slave that would be subservient to a fault, a slave that won't question her commands or her very wishes.

Do As Thou Wilt, she thought. *Might as well take it all while the takings' good ... yes, and this dipshit's ripe for it ... everything and everyone should be mine; is mine, just as it should be.*

"Rommar ... you have the unique chance to move up in the ranks," she said seductively. "From initiate to member-elect, you have a chance to make some progress."

"I ... I do?" he asked, now looking at her with puppy dog eyes.

"Yes ... and if you play your cards right, my loyal friend, you'll end up my personal attendant." She said this with a look of promise and with just a hint of sexual prowess. "So, here's what we'll need to do ... you and I are going to work together in the next few weeks, maybe months or more. I'm planning a campaign to make some money for both the Order and the Cauldron, okay?"

"That sounds great, Madam … I'll do whatever you want, of course!"

"Excellent … I knew I could count on you, Rommar," she said, now with a grin that exposed her greyish-yellow teeth. We'll start tomorrow night after we've had a nice long rest after the ritual, and I suspect it's going to take a lot out of us, okay?"

"Yes, Madam, I understand."

"Excellent! You'll need to take some photos of me next week at a deserted house over on Tenth Avenue, the big two-story dump, you know the one?"

"Oh yeah, the one with the burned-out roof on the back … that one, right?"

"That's the one. It's full of really shitty furniture too, where you'll take a few shots of me there, and near the burnt-out kitchen … I just need you to take a few photos on my digital camera for this campaign I'm going to launch, understand?"

"Sure, whatever you want, Madam," Lester returned, just as a slight smile began to rise on his face.

"Excellent, Rommar, excellent. Between you and me, and the lamppost, it's going to be for a *GoFundMe* page, which has always been profitable for the Order, and now … and now for The Hollow Cauldron too, and perhaps, if all goes well, enough left over for you too … do you read me, Rommar?"

"Oh, hell yes, Madam, I do, and thanks; thank you for thinking of me … I'll do whatever, *WHATEVER* you want of me," he said with a notable echo of will and excitement.

"Excellent, Rommar … excellent. Right now, I just want this Bible-toting asshole to get what he deserves, and once I have the testimonies of each of our members as to how we set the curse upon him, he'll realize just how real magick is."

Lester offered a confused look and then managed to lock eyes with the vile woman. "Um, who, who do you think it might be, Madam?" he asked sheepishly.

"I don't know, Rommar, but once I post our dealings on my blog page, he'll no doubt read it and … and that's all we'll need, my loyal servant," Madam Delevingne chimed proudly. "This is, after all, how magick works. We curse him, and he shits himself. He'll actually create his own hell, Rommar, right here on earth. It's a win-win scenario, my friend, and we're gonna pull it off perfectly."

"I don't doubt that a bit, Madam!"

"Good, very good, Rommar … I have the feeling that this shall work exceedingly well for both of us. Perhaps your example of good judgment shall inspire the others."

"Yes, ma'am … I'll do it! I'll do anything!"

✠

Madam Delevingne was pleased with her initiate's promise of compliance and with his obvious zeal in doing so. She considered the possibility of there even being more to this new alliance. Having gazed at Rommar for a few moments, considering his body, being a million-and-one times more appealing than his fat sidekick, Herk Benet, she figured that not only would she make a shit-load of cash through yet another bogus *GoFundMe* campaign online; a system that had made her thousands, literally thousands of dollars from well-meaning idiots from all over the nation, but also, that she could get laid once in a while too.

Now inspired, Madam Delevingne considered the prospects. First, she'd carry out her mission in routing out and destroying that secretive, name-changing Bible-thumper … this was job one. This, along with notifying her primary order, the Order of Pry Thealemè Ex Mortis, would be job two. She knew full well that they would be assembling for the important Black Moon event and knew that with their help, they would only intensify the ritual. As she was a high priestess with both the Order of Magnus Datha and the Order of Pry Thealemè Ex Mortis, she knew she'd receive the answers by way of magick. And she knew that such an allegiance would only cement the act of finding and destroying the mysterious Bible-thumper.

Secondly, her new *GoFundMe* campaign would be carried out, as of that day, by her new compatriot, who would also double as her on-call sex tool. She felt that things just couldn't go wrong now. She gazed at her new acquisition, Rommar, and smiled. The thing to do now, she surmised, was just to keep that machine well-oiled and in perfect working order.

Shit-loads of cash, she thought. *Shit-loads*. Now, she giggled as a smile slowly draped across her slanted, misshapen face. And what would be a religious experience for Lester Gnaws, an experience that would cement his devotion and love for his mistress, Madam Delevingne, took it upon herself to gently reach out and cup the man's testicles. She did this seductively, and ever-so-gently with her left hand. She caressed them softly as she stared into his eyes, with what she considered to be a result of her knowledge of magick and her obvious power over the poor fool.

Lester stared back into her grayish-green eyes with an uncontrollable urge to embrace her and start kissing the object of his most profound love — but he waited in subservience.

As she continued to fondle his testicles, rubbing upwards and downwards on his now-growing shaft, he finally lunged towards her and began kissing her voraciously. Even Madam Delevingne was impressed, contributing to the impromptu make-out session by thrusting her tongue down his throat. They continued to do this for close to ten minutes until she had become completely moist. Lester had grunted as he groped her breasts until finally, he had an orgasmic reaction in his pants. Now, she could feel the heat emitting from his crotch; a heat that equaled her own. And in that moment, she had realized that she had enjoyed it as much as Lester had, but knew it was time to break the session off, at least for the present time.

The two continued in their embrace until Madam Delevingne, remembering her position, recalled her attention to who was the mistress and who was the servant. She pushed her lover away with one hand; her head bowed, and her chest rising and falling in a near-breathless state. Lester just stared with a lover's gape, his mouth slack-jawed and panting like a dog that had just finished mounting a bitch in the street. And she had noticed that the front of his pants was visibly wet with semen. Now, the two were spent, though an unequal bond was formed — a bond forged in lust and wickedness.

"Okay, okay, Lester," she panted, as her arm was now bracing his chest away from her. It was the first time she had ever called him by his Christian name … his *former* Christian name. "We're, we're done with that for now, okay? I, I, still need you to complete your mission … for tonight. Do you understand?"

"Yeh … yes, yes, Madam, yes," Lester panted in response. "I under-understand."

Madam Delevingne knew without a doubt that she had owned Lester Gnaws, her now lifelong servant. "Rommar, soon-to-become *Member Elect, Rommar*.

"Excellent … very good," she said as she leveled off into normal breathing. "Now … I need you to inform Grizzela of our plans tonight. Make sure she knows what to bring, no matter how much she might bitch and complain, make sure she's ready to go, and more importantly, that *EVERYONE* is there just before eleven tonight … no later than eleven, understand?"

"Yes, I understand, my mistress …."

"Very good, Rommar. Tonight, the stars are right, and the moon is in its perfect phase. We're gonna nail this asshole, so everyone needs to take part in the ritual. You understand the importance of this, don't you?"

"Ah, yes, yes, of course. We'll take care of this guy, you can count on that, Madam, you can count on it!"

"Excellent! Now go; make sure everything goes as planned."

✠

Lester Gnaws was a new man, not just Rommar the initiate, not just the soon-to-be Rommar the Member Elect, but Madam Delevingne's personal attendant — Madam Delevingne's lover. He was elated like he had never been before. For the first time in his life, he felt that a true sense of meaning was being poured into him. He felt exuberant, finding himself daydreaming of their future together in clumps of images. He dreamt of a romance between them. He dreamt of them being lovers, and ruling *The Order* together — he dreamt.

By 6:38 p.m., Lester Gnaws had finally walked out of the Hollow Cauldron's front door. Madam Delevingne, however, just sat in her old chair and tried to catch her breath and her wits. Feeling overwhelmed that she was able to get so excited over the likes of Lester Gnaws was astounding to her, yet at the same time, she was thrilled, even if secretly. As she was finally beginning to relax, she checked her cellphone for any messages. There was one text from Herc Benet, which read—

I got most of the members. Now working on the rest- will call later- Cron. "Good job fat ass," she muttered. "Now … onto other things."

As she scrolled through her phone's index, she quickly found who she was looking for. Now, a smile rose on her sweaty face, followed by a joyful grunt.

"Ah, there you are, my dear ... Maybelle Riclou, great Mithrus of Sin, and second in command of the highest Order," she mumbled. "A genuine Hierophant, and eighth-degree Magus of Light of the Second Triad ... you're just what we need." She said this as if reading from a roster of war heroes, or from a list of all-star NFL champions. "She's as deadly as a rattlesnake, and she knows magick like the Pope knows a prayer," she continued to mumble. "She'll find you Bible-man ... and when she does, you'll be so sorry... you'll wish you had died long ago before you ever met us."

Now with a face of pure, tyrannical rage, and with a large, yellow, toothy grin, she sat back in her old, garbage dump chair and prepared to reconnect with her mistress, the grandest of all. She smiled with evil delight.

✠

Maybelle Desdemona Riclou, better known as 'Mithrus' amongst the *Guild of Tamar*,' a guild which is directly associated with the *Black Nub-En-Set Lodge* in Dayton, Ohio, and the *Silver Twilight Oasis* in Drexel, is one of the most recognized personalities in the occult world.

Though few hard facts were found on Riclou before her dealings with the Order of Pry Thealemè Ex Mortis, there had always been rumors of her nefarious beginnings. What is for sure is that before she devoted her life explicitly to the mystery schools of Thealemè and Satanism, she was once a young member of *The Children of God*, the hippie generation's Christ-inspired love cult of the 1960s. She was a member of the group's *Teens for Christ Crusade* out of Huntington Beach, California, from 1967 to 1969, and was said to have been a personal confidant and lover of David Bernard Goldberg, the group's leader. The infamous conman and religious paedophile who went by such self- chosen epithets as 'King Moses' and 'The Godhead' had made the young Maybelle Riclou a cherished extension of the cult. Indeed, she was as ruthless and as wicked as he was salacious and crooked.

From the 1970s, rumors had spread that Riclou and others had recruited children, mostly little girls, to be the 'lovers' of Goldberg and his cohorts, and that she herself enjoyed the idea of using Christianity as a staging platform to not only recruit for other, less noble causes, but that she saw money in her future as a result. This was a philosophy she has successfully used throughout her forty-five-year career.

With the *Children of God* cult waning by the mid-1970s, she began to operate her own, fledgling group called *The Regulate of the Unseen*, a group of self-imagined intellectuals designed for the research and authentication of the esoteric. Riclou believed that there were more than the teachings of Christ to the truth of the universe. Thus began a life towards the opposition of Christ and His works, and for the glory of her own, self-perceived greatness.

During this time, she was known to attend many meetings and weekend flings with one Howard Stanton 'Anton' Levey. Levey's teachings obviously swayed his new pupil, further enticing her to follow the methods of LaVeyan Satanism later in life. There, she met a young

LaVey devotee named Andrew Nikolaos, an inspiring psychology student at the City College of San Francisco. The affair would grow while they both formed their own cult order known as the *Guild of Tamar,*' and adopted the title 'Mithrus' as her personalized ode to the Roman sun god of the second and third centuries. Andrew Nikolaos, ever the devoted acolyte-turned-cult leader, had chosen the cryptic moniker of 'Zilranar Pathos' as an ode to an obscure Greek prophet of the second century. They had become a power couple of debauchery and wickedness.

Riclou and Nikolaos would later relocate to Montebello, in Los Angeles County, where they built on the *LaVeyan* concept of philosophy. Soon thereafter, they would begin training students in a similar fashion, but with a more feminine aspect to the daemonic teachings. Here, they would concentrate on the goddess in ritual, though having been directly derivative from Aleister Crowley's teachings. They had kept his philosophies as true-to-form in order to fight what Riclou had considered the everlasting and numbing ramblings of what she referred to as the 'pointless drivel of a dead carpenter.'

Among her students were many influential people, including actors, actresses, comedians, and those in the music industry, as well as political leaders, educators, and others in hidden power. Maybelle Riclou and Andrew Nikolaos became superstars seemingly overnight.

On November 1st, 2001, Maybelle Riclou inherited more than a half-million dollars when her mother died of a subarachnoid haemorrhaging brain aneurysm. She and her lover promptly moved from their three-bedroom apartment in California to her mother's eight-bedroom Victorian home in Dayton, Ohio. By February the following year, she and her lover purchased a new age store, which they called 'The Lessening Veil' in the nearby neighborhood of Drexel. The little shop also served as a conference center for the newly founded Silver Twilight Oasis.

Now, as the Black Nub-En-Set Lodge's member list began to grow, so did its revenue. And as members of the Order of Pry Thealemè Ex Mortis, the devil coven that stylized itself after the original Ordo Tenebris Lux, had practically become a household name. And though their goals were lofty and great, they had plans to keep, and enemies to crush. Certainly, there could be no doubt now. The couple's tenure of evil was just beginning.

✠

In 2005, Maybelle Riclou and Andrew Nikolaos single-handedly fought the Ohio Board of Regents and the State Board of Education in allowing Satanists to form in public schools, while at the same time, outlawing Christian prayer in those same schools. Their group considered the teachings of Christianity to be 'hate speech' against them and directly detrimental. Riclou and Nikolaos' lawyers had won the case, and from that date onward, Ohio was ordered to allow Satanists to not only form clubs and organizations in schools across the state, but they had arranged this a decade before it would become a popular agenda with other groups, like *The Satanic Temple Detroit*; long before Satanism was the foundation of the music industry, and long before the Hollywood elite would publicly proclaim their love for the Dark Lord. They were the heroes for free speech, feminism, and Transexual rights. They had become the defenders of the plight of the social justice warrior, becoming an inspiration for devil worshipers worldwide — they were and remain the relentless icons of evil.

In 2009, Riclou amicably separated from Andrew Nikolaos, and he departed for California to teach parapsychology at a local community college, while Riclou took the grandest of oaths and became an eighth-degree magus and a Grand Hierophant of Sex Magick. Andrew Nikolaos had inspired a nation to hunt for ghosts and abandon reason behind a lecture podium, while Maybelle Riclou would organize magick orgies designed for all participants of her Order, including children and animals. It was an age of criminal perversion.

During these years, Riclou had openly supported child and adult sexual relations, just as her idol and model had done before her, as Aleister Crowley had done a century before. She had never been silent on the subject, becoming a frequent guest speaker at numerous LGBTQ and NAMBLA meetings throughout the West Coast. During this time, Riclou would *accumulate* close to twenty thousand dollars for the 2016 Democratic Convention and is said to have been a close, personal friend of the Democratic Presidential Candidate and her faction. She did this again for the 2020 elections, having been a personal friend of the most influential leaders of that party and its cohorts.

In the years following, Riclou had been invited to many ceremonial gatherings, namely under the hosting of a so-called performance artist named Mistress Narinas Kambrovic. She had also been a frequent guest of the many nefarious associates of these political powerhouses, a fact that only made her greater in strength. Without a doubt, Maybelle Riclou had remained well-connected in areas of politics and legal reform, beyond her Hollywood connections. She was as smooth as the skin of a baby and as poisonous as a viper.

Despite her greatness within the realms of the Order of Pry Thealemè Ex Mortis, for the chosen few, the very few, however, Maybelle Riclou would allow the title of *Kith* to be applied to that of her official title of Grand Hierophant. This she allowed as a sign of appreciation to the devotion that was given, but this was a rare honour indeed. Madam Delevingne was allowed just such an honor; an honor that was held with the highest amount of love and regard.

Now, Madam Delevingne knew that Maybelle Desdemona Riclou was the person to call, and quickly began searching for her contact information. She found Riclou's email address and started typing while smiling and whispering to herself with heated glee.

"Oh, yes, Bible man, you have no idea what's waiting for you," she muttered. "You have no idea who my mistress is, but you'll soon find out. Now is the time for daemons to be befriended … once again. Now is the time for war. Now it's time for unholy revenge."

✠

By the time Lester Gnaws had left the building and Madam Delevingne had finished emailing Maybelle Riclou copies of the Biblical rants she had received, along with her intentions, it was already going on 6:20 p.m. She figured it was getting too late and needed to know how Herc Benet was doing rounding up the others, so she phoned him as she surfed through her webpage's message centre. She was distressed to find it empty. There wasn't even the customary array of compliments and love letters, a fact that left her somewhat flat, and wondering if the store's website had been working properly. Finally, Herc Benet answered his cell.

"Yez, Madams, I'ze here … just driv'en, dats all," he said in a stressed manner.

"What's the deal Cron? What's the story with the other members?" she asked impatiently.

"I'z gots alls of ums, sept Grezzell-ia, and dat boy Brian from the other side of townz. Da rest on dey way, dough."

"'Grizzela,' Cron, it's pronounced *Grizz-ell-ah*," Madam Delevingne barked. "And yes, I know … Rommar is off to get her right now. And what about the rest, what about *Kid'en'el*, what about him? Why can't he come?"

"Right … dey all cum'en, no problem … sept, I tink *Kid-and-ell* … he in sum kinda trouble at hiz house," Cron responded in a sheepish manner. "Sumpin goen on dare, so I don't tink he ain't be cum'in, dats all … oh, and, ah, and den Madam Kras-a-kraz-a-mola ain't cum'in ether, dats what she told me … sorry bout dats!"

"Yes, I figured that for myself, Cron … and it's *Kras Mala*. She's in her eighties, after all, so I didn't expect her anyway," she grunted back. "As for *Kid'en'el* and *Kras Mala*, we can do without them at the site. I want you to call them and have them begin their meditations exactly at midnight. It'll work."

"Yez, Madams, youz knows best!"

"Okay, Cron, get home and get ready … *AND DON'T BE LATE!*" she barked again. "*MEET US AT THE FRONT GATES, GOT IT!?*"

"YEZ, MADAMS!" he resounded quickly, like a buck private in the army responding to his drill sergeant.

By the time Cron had finished calling Kras Mala about the need for their prayers that night and then texting Kid'en'el to do the same, it was just going on 6:58 p.m., just as Madam Delevingne began calling Rommar to make sure all was going as planned. He had informed her that he had Grizzela with him and that they were going to get something to eat before going to the park.

Madam Delevingne couldn't help but smile now. Everything was finally coming together, and the thought of defeating some uppity Christian made her giddy with perverse delight. Now, having been assured that the others would remember to bring all the proper materials for the night's ritual, which they promised they would do, the plan was set, and the mission ready.

As she hung up with Rommar, she immediately received a text. It was from Maybelle Riclou. The text simply said 'call me,' along with her direct number.

"Blessed be," Madam Delevingne mumbled, now with a sinister, yet pleased expression on her crooked face. Again, she resembled the *Grinch* from that children's book she had so loved as a child. "Blessed be, *Mithrus*, Blessed be."

✠

Madam Delevingne sat back in her rickety, old garbage-dump chair and began to call Maybelle Riclou. The woman answered just after the second ring, something Madam Delevingne hadn't expected. Riclou always made her subordinates wait; a habit that made the vile woman evermore worshiped by her underlings, placing just the right amount of mystery to her dark persona, leveled off with just the right amount of fear.

"Yes," a low and brusque voice responded.

"Ninety-three, oh, Grand Hierophant, my *Kith*," Madam Delevingne offered. She always started a conversation with the word ninety-three, the magical number to equate the code originated by the Orders of Thelema, though the original sect of Aleister Crowley had nothing to do with the Order of Pry Thealemè Ex Mortis. The use of the numeral greeting had nonetheless meant the cosmic love of their gods, despite the fact it was just another stolen aspect from another occult order.

"Oh, Grand Hierophant, my *Kith* ... this is Madam Delevingne," she said again, now echoing a similar subservient tone, not unlike that of Benet or Gnaws. It was a tone of respect, like that of a Catholic altar boy meeting the Pope for the first time. It held the tone of fear.

"Ninety-three, Madam Delevingne," the stoic woman replied. "Now, what is this about? Who is this person *we're* now interested in?"

"We have no idea, my Kith, just that he knows far too much; our names, and my name specifically, but he knows something about *all* of us ... I can't explain exactly what it is, but I ... and others believe he, or she, perhaps, maybe a part of us. He ... he threatened me personally, and he used hate speech against us; against the Order! This guy has way too much information. In truth, my Kith, I want this person rooted out and destroyed ... not just for my sake, of course, but for the sake of the Order."

"I see ... very well, Delevingne, for the sake of the Order, and in our protection, I shall devote a part of tonight's assembly for this purpose. Hum ... I must say, Delevingne, this all seems rather opportune, as the dark of the moon approaches this evening, and our gathering being assigned all the same ... seems kismet, does it not?"

"Yes, my Kith, it does indeed," Madam Delevingne said, now in a loving manner, like that of a child to her mother.

"So mote it be, Madam Delevingne."

"SO MOTE IT BE, my Kith; my Kin!"

"Then, to mystery supreme, and to the aesthetic, formless spawn we praise! To the archaic realms, we shall obey the whole of our path … do as we shall do … this is the law of our path!" the Grand Hierophant retorted, now with cryptic esteem found in only the most supreme of the elect. "And with the highest purpose in securing our rights," she continued, "that of the sacred and of her and his achievement in the blackest of night, the wisdom, the knowledge, and the rage through the arcane, the wise, and the sinner alike, on the foundation of Dark Sisterhood … and on the Unholy Swain Brotherhood, we shall be supreme!"

Now, Madam Delevingne recited the Order's anthem, their credo of supremacy to her beloved mistress. She understood that the power of her mistress was beyond simple explanation; that Madam Riclou, the Grand Hierophant of all things arcane, was aware of the realities of all aspects of the universe. She was to Madam Delevingne, and in no uncertain terms, a messiah-like persona worthy of praise and love. Second, only to Lucifer himself, she had so given her love that all that is wise enough to praise her shall be blessed, and Madam Delevingne knew it. She felt ingratiated to serve her, obey her, and love her.

"Very well, Madam Delevingne," Maybelle Riclou chimed with an echo of superiority. "The Order, this, the first of the great, *Old Æon Sects* shall respond to your favour; to Our favour … this man, this woman, the traitor that slithers upon our path shall pay … tonight, we shall reside at Midnight, exactly. We shall share the hour together, in the name of revenge … in the name of hate we shall learn of this enemy, and we shall defeat this enemy … So Mote It Be?"

"So Mote it Be! My Kith; my Kin, oh Grand Hierophant!" Madam Delevingne said this with tears of joy welling in her eyes. Now, her body trembled with exuberance and lust for revenge, and had echoed this feeling through her innermost voice, which was apparent to Maybelle Riclou. It was the way Madam Delevingne's voice trembled when she spoke those words that made it clear that not only subservience was assured, but that love was there too.

"Hail Satan … Hail Lucifer?" Maybelle Riclou asked.

"Hail Satan, Grand Hierophant, Hail Lucifer!"

CHAPTER TEN

By the time Madam Delevingne had offered her final farewells to Maybelle Riclou, having realized the length of their phone conversation, she gazed briefly at the hour on her cell. It was already going on 7:45 p.m., so she knew she'd have to hurry in order to get to the park on time. Plus, she had to dig through a mountain of clothes and useless paraphernalia to find her regalia, a fact that she knew would probably take at least half an hour to find. She had to hurry.

Madam Delevingne made haste as she packed her things, stuffing her backpack-like purse with candles and incense, while she rummaged from the underside of her display counters to find other essential occult knick-knacks. Black candles, white candles, red candles, and small votive candles of every colour. She found a small altar table and a folded square of black linen dressing to be placed on top of it. Then, getting on her hands and knees, she pulled out a large, black, and red wooden chest that was kept hidden under the largest display table at the rear of the store. She opened it to find her own special collection of Bolines and Athames, as well as her finest collection of ceremonial knives that she only used on high holidays and on various Sabbaths, even impromptu Sabbaths like the one she was to partake in that night.

Now kneeling on the floor, she pulled out a smaller chest from within the larger one and placed it on the floor. Though small, the ornately designed box was filled with tiny cloth bags, all tied with string and yarn of various colours.

Some were filled with the hard resin of incense, some with powdered incense. There was Dragon's Blood, Devil's Foot, and camphor. There was also an array of herbs, some quite deadly, though all used for the blackest of rituals. Here, she had dried samples of Cruel Man of the Woods, Henbane, Wormwood, and Knot Weed.

There was Asafoetida and Balmony in black bags, Betel Nut, Bladderwrack, and Blood Root in yellow bags, and then there was Snakeweed, Belladonna, and Mistletoe in green bags. In the grey ones, there was Monkshood, Wolfsbane, and Dogbane, all tied with tiny, white tags. And written on each tag were strange words like: 'Aconitum' and 'Apocynum cannabinum' in red letters, while still others had the words like 'Conium maculatum' and 'Hyoscyamus niger' written in green ink.

Throughout her collection of the stale herbs and spices, and knowing not what the strange words had meant, she knew all the same that each was as poisonous as herself, and just and worthy of the blackest of magick.

✠

Next to her collection of herbs were small glass vials, all filled with the satanic diablerie that only people like Madam Delevingne would have owned; all that glistened in a dull and diseased manner. With graveyard dirt, toenails and fingernails, swatches of hair, both from the scalp and the pubic regions, from whom no one knew, had all lingered in the little green glass bottles like a collection of cancerous neoplasm. There were ones with untitled liquids too, items that only the vile woman had known. Among the most profane were urine, spittle, tears, and semen mixed with oils, with others containing samples of human blood, animal blood, and excrement of unknown origin. Indeed, it was a collection worthy only of a true dabbler in the black arts.

Now feeling rushed, she grabbed the small box and shoved it in her handbag. Then she raced to the tiny broom closet and began rummaging through an old FedEx box that lay hidden under a mound of rags and crumpled-up paper bags from Kroger's Grocery. There she found the last shipment she had received from *The Occult Goods and Bads' Outlet*, an online occult retailer out of San Francisco.

There was a collection of magick-related nonsense she had bought for pennies on the dollar that she would sell for top profit, but among the cheap garbage had existed items that the evil woman had cherished, and it was these items she coveted now. Madam Delevingne was, after all, smarter than the mundane herd, so such business practices were not only advantageous for the Hollow Cauldron but a testament to her superior wisdom.

"Yeesss," she hissed. "I was saving this shit for the boneheads in town; for the unlimited rubes in old Baytown … but today … tonight … in the coming hour; I need you more right now."

Of the cheap items, she pulled out a bottle of *Black's Banishing Oil* and a small bag of black salt, both she would use to quickly lay down as a barrier around their magick circle once all were assembled at the park. She believed this would stop any attack, even the mysterious Bible-thumper, should he actually be in the area that night. Finally, she found what she was looking for: a resin and tin Baphomet goblet she had bought on sale at the Hot Topic while visiting the Deerbrook Mall last week. It was wrapped in an old black hoodie and was complete with an inverted pentagram and a goat's head at its centre.

"Fucking awesome," she burbled, intermixed with a giggle. "I love Hot Topic … a testament to freethinking if there ever was." She laughed again and then stuffed the thing in her bag.

Madam Delevingne realized that the resin-cast goblet, hand-carved with Celtic artwork and knots, the ever- lasting goat's head and inverted pentacles all around it, all elaborately set with faux rubies, would make the ritual complete. She considered using another one, a cheaper one, but she quickly realized that she could just wash it out and sell it anyway.

Finally, having gathered the wicked goods in a pile, she began stuffing them within the old cloth sack. But there was one more item, the *Carcanet of Spite*, a crudely made, though nonetheless priceless necklace she only wore on high pagan holidays, and especially for any ritual involving revenge or death. This, she kept in a small black box hidden beneath the long glass display case in the main showroom. She had kept it there because she didn't trust her living space or the old man she lived with. The necklace was sacred to her, for its history is as black as the woman's very soul.

"It's all good," she muttered. "This … this will bring the end to that fucking Bible-toting sonofabitch!"

Now standing up again, she walked into the back of the shop and checked the back door, and turned off the lights. Then, she checked her cellphone for any last-minute texts or messages, but there were none. She then checked the store's website as she hurried to get out the front door. And knowing that time was of the essence, she picked up her pace.

"Fuck!" she bellowed. "Fucking, almost nine o'clock … gotta get outta here now … shit, shit, shit!"

Now, slapping her hand against the light switch of the front door to turn them off, she raced out and slammed the door shut. As she began to turn the key to lock them, the entire building shook for a second or two, followed by all the lights flickering on and off by themselves, if only for a second. The lights did this three times in succession — on — and — off — on — and — off — on — and — off.

Madam Delevingne just stared at the room, trying to figure out why the lights did that, but she didn't care now. She had bigger fish to fry.

As Madam Delevingne was getting into her old Suzuki, she watched as the street lamps that lined the sidewalks all went out at once, making the entire street as black as any rural dirt road at midnight. Her eyes were wide now, and as she looked around, almost in a frantic sort of way, she quickly slammed the car door shut, locked it, and fumbled to find the ignition with her key. In an instant, she remembered the misty black shape she saw the other night in her rearview mirror, the glowing yellow eyes, and the feeling of total dread. Quickly, she turned around to look into the rear foot well on the backseat, only to find a collection of paper cups and soda cans, and four or five tampons that had spilled out of her backpack. And then there was the wad after wad of crumpled-up tissue from blowing her nose. But there was nothing else there.

As she turned the key, she found her car's engine wouldn't turn over. Now, the dash lights flickered as she turned the key, and then again and again, but the car just wouldn't turn over. In that space of time, the ill-tempered woman found herself filled with fear; a fear she couldn't explain. She felt paralyzed as she stared out the passenger window, and then out of the driver's side window, and then out the rear window. She saw nothing out of the ordinary. Just blackness.

For a moment, Madam Delevingne felt cold, and then it became frigid inside the old car. In seconds, she began to see her breath in front of her. She immediately noticed the darkness outside of her car, and all around the alley-like parking lot next to the building seemed darker than it had just a few moments before. It became so dark, in fact, that she couldn't even see the details in the brick wall ahead of her. Instead, everything looked like a dull, grey, and blackish blur, and for the briefest moment, she thought she had seen the shape of a large man; a large man as black as pitch, save that of two glistening eyes, staring down on her like a snake preparing to strike.

"Who, who the fuck … who the fuck is that!" she shrieked. Now terrified, she just stared ahead while turning the key again and again. No matter what, the ignition was dead, not even the dash lights had flickered now. Madam Delevingne wasn't just scared; she could feel the tiny hairs on the back of her neck begin to stand straight. And then, as quickly as it had begun, the intense darkness that had enveloped her surroundings like a thick blanket being draped over her world had returned to a normal vision of the night, like that of any typical night in Baytown, Texas.

After a few moments, a low rumble of thunder could be heard in the distance, and then the car started. This time, however, it started without her even turning the key. The headlights had turned on by themselves, and then the car's radio began blasting out a familiar tune. Now, *Bad Moon Rising* by Creedence Clearwater Revival began blaring through the crackling speakers. The antiquated tune had a weird resonance to it, as the interior lights flickered in protest.

Madam Delevingne just sat there trembling, with her mouth now hanging open as if in a state of shock. And then, all the streetlights had gone on at once. And though the light was long in achieving its former strength, this prompted Madam Delevingne to hold up her hands; her fingers outstretched in a question-like manner, with her mouth and eyes even wider than before. She had the look of an animal that was cornered, like an animal that was being observed by a hungry predator that was about to strike. Despite this, she put the car in reverse and backed out of the parking lot with a jolt, giving little consideration to anyone who might have been walking on the sidewalk behind her. She didn't care; she just wanted to get out of there and get home as fast as she could. Nothing else mattered to her now.

Quick like, the now frightened woman raced down the almost deserted street. As she did, she gazed at the rearview mirror to observe the dimly lit streetlights slowly getting brighter and brighter as she drove away.

"Well, that was fucking weird," she blurted. "Must-ah … must have been some kind of an electrical glitch or short or something … weird."

Madam Delevingne tried desperately to explain away the strange occurrence, the blacker-than-black darkness, the flickering lights, and the shape of a man that was almost as dark as the night had become, but she simply couldn't. Now, the typically self-assured woman had no answers and had remained silent as she drove down the street and into the underpass that led to I-10 with little hindrance. She tried to reestablish herself and back to her former greatness, but she just couldn't get the image out of her head.

Now, she could only contemplate how dark it was back at the Hollow Cauldron, and why it could have done that. Immediately, she remembered the odd, yellow sky that morning and the weird shape of the mist or shadows that formed in the back seat of her car the night before. She was beginning to question her sanity, but just as quickly had regained her place in the universe, which was, of course, one of superiority.

"I know what I saw, goddamn it," she belched out. "What, I don't know … but something's going on … something."

As she approached her neighborhood, remembering that Oakland Street was still littered with trucks and bulldozers, she turned down Maple and onto Burnett Street, and then got back on Oakland. And again, the already limited streetlights were half off, minus the eerie soft yellow glow of the construction lights that continued to blink on — and — off — on — and — off — on — and — off.

Just before reaching the innermost set of construction barricades, which was no more than a hundred yards from her garage apartment, her old Suzuki began to choke and sputter, creating a gurgling sound she had never heard before. The car continued to spit and sputter, and then it backfired, creating a huge blackish-grey plume of smoke. Then, the car died right before reaching the first house on the street. The house had belonged to Joyce and Dmitri Cusack, a retired oral surgeon and his homemaker wife. Their home was a large, two-story structure that resembled a 'Little House on the Prairie' design. The entire section of that community was sparse at best, offering a lot of privacy for people wanting to be left alone, which was good, but it was also bad when one needed to feel secure.

Because that area of Baytown has always been somewhat rural in the first place, street lights weren't a priority for the homeowner's association in the four communities that it covered. Their philosophy was 'If you want to live in the boondocks, then you'll live as if you belonged in the boondocks.' Certainly, such a philosophy was well suited to people like old Arnie Hammond, who was already a recluse long before moving there in 1983. The only other people she knew on that street were Joyce

Cusack, the retired fifth-grade school teacher from Milwaukee, and, of course, her husband, the retired dentist, whom she only met once. And that was okay, too, because Dmitri Cusack was far too self-assured of himself. Madam Delevingne didn't like self-assured men. She preferred them weak and subservient, and who knew their places. Nonetheless, the Cusacks were quiet and they minded their own business. So much the better.

✠

As she sat in her car, Madam Delevingne surveyed the land as much as she could see. The Cusack house was dark, and the whole area across the street from them was nothing more than a quarter-mile or so of vacant fields, with a spattering of Australian Pines and masses of native shrubbery. Arnie's house was still about a football field's length from the Cusack house, and the only light at all had come from the dull yellow flashes of the construction barricade lights.

"Fuck'en H.O.A.," she bellowed. With her car door open, she turned the ignition again, and again, but still no life. She figured it had to either be the battery or the alternator because there wasn't as much of a flicker from the dashboard. "You've gotta be fucking kidding me!" she bellowed again.

In one last-ditch effort to start the car, she turned the key one last time. She pumped the gas with her foot as she grunted and cursed at the car. Then, as if by magic, the dashboard warning lights had lit up, and a moment later, the lights began going out again. In a matter of seconds, the transmission light, the battery light, the oil light, the temperature warning light, and the brake light all went out, leaving the dashboard as dark as the cover of night. A moment after that, the overhead cab light went out too, leaving everything that gave her at least a little comfort and security, a little piece of mind to be lost to the night — a night that was now filled with strange sounds and even stranger weather.

Madam Delevingne found herself frightened as she had never been before. She felt she was being watched. Now checking her cellphone for the exact time, she saw that it was now going on 9:25 p.m. She had to hurry, for even though the Baytown Nature Center was only a few miles away, she still had to find her robes and sash, and then she had to prepare too; wash and anoint herself, and then apply her tribal face paint, a process she felt was accustomed to the ancient Celts and Druids. She was a high priestess, after all, and it was her obligation to ensure the proper dress and command over her underlings.

Knowing this and wanting to get a move on, she turned on the light on her cellphone and aimed it at the road ahead of her. The rocky gravel of the road was now somewhat lit, in addition to the amber flashes of the construction barricade lights, but everything took on a surreal look that couldn't be ignored, offering imagined glimpses of things that just couldn't have been real. She at least realized that much. Despite her logic, she couldn't help thinking that she saw faces, arms, and even gigantic eyeballs and teeth that glimmered from the darkness.

Irrational bullshit, she thought. *I'm not gonna fall for it again.*

If the lighting wasn't strange enough, then the low rumble of thunder that echoed in the distance only added to the rather creepy circumference of her surroundings. The shapes that she quickly surmised as being a part of her overly stressed imagination didn't help either. She needed to get to the park and complete her end of the bargain; the bargain she had arranged with none other than Maybelle Riclou herself. She surmised that the concept of 'stress' was not logical, especially if planning to fail the Grand Hierophant. This she couldn't allow.

Now with heightened senses, Madam Delevingne continued to walk as gingerly as she could, stepping over the larger, jagged rocks that could do some real damage. Regardless, she still had to fight to maintain balance with every other step. This made her efforts to appear both humorous and redundant, but it was the fear on her face that proved her vulnerability. Then, another round of low, ominous thunder sounded in the distance, and as soon as she looked toward the now oddly-coloured sky, her cellphone light flashed, flickered, and then went out altogether.

"Now what ... what the fuck?" she blurted. "Jesus, you've gotta be fuck'en kidding me!"

Madam Delevingne shook her cellphone for a few seconds, but there was no help in re-establishing the light. She continued to shake it, thinking that the battery was loose, hoping it would just come back on, but no luck. Now, she looked around her surroundings, squinting as hard as she could in order to see, but it was just too dark. Even the sickly yellow barricade lights seemed to be fading. And though the majority of the lighting had come from her cellphone, the ground was just a black and grey mass of nothingness, with only the silhouettes of the construction equipment forming bizarre shapes in front and all around her. Now, only those dark shapes that danced and flittered about had taken over her senses.

"No ... no fucking way," she muttered quietly. Now, she squatted down low again and tried desperately to focus on what was ahead of her and around her. Nothing. "Hey!" she shouted. "Who ... who's out there?!" There was only silence as those shapes of every size continued to jump and hop about like so many nightmares. Now, she could feel the tiny hairs on her neck bristle and stand erect. She trembled.

When Madam Delevingne looked up, she noticed that the dull, yellowish sky that had dominated the day, with its swaying, udder-like clouds waving at the world below had now taken on a bloody red hue, like the kind of sky one might see when the lights from a massive city glowed from a vast distance. The clouds were different, too, more like a gigantic, low-lying blanket covering all of Baytown. This was accented by an eerie glow illuminating from behind the cloud cover, as if from some alien source lighting it. Oddly, the night sky had taken on an abstract look that was as astounding as it was startling. It was unnatural.

As Madam Delevingne walked slowly over the jutting rocks and gravel, she figured that maybe it was best that her car hadn't driven over it anyway, thinking for sure that a flat tire would have been the end result. Her primary concern now was to get to the house and get ready, but driving her car was obviously out of the question. She'd have to call her new swain, her new boy-toy, to get a ride.

A perfect breaking-in session if ever there was, she thought, just as a slight grin began to wash over her face. *Come and get me, Romeo, and don't worry, sweetheart, I'll give you the first of your slave orders just as soon as I get home.* She laughed heartily at this thought, thinking that doing so might relieve her tension, but it didn't help. Now, in spite of her typical confidence, she only felt fear — an unnatural, and almost debilitating fear.

✠

As the cover of darkness was all too daunting, despite the construction barricade lights, which were still technically working, the light they were putting out was flimsy at best. They were no better than a nightlight now. Madam Delevingne, in all her wisdom, had figured that the batteries must have been dying. In order to calm her nerves, she considered the reasoning for going to the Baytown Nature Center Preserve instead of the Order's usual haunt at McElroy Park. She considered it the better plan because the last thing they needed tonight was to be hassled by the cops, especially as everyone would be dressed in full regalia and obviously, working magick too. Such a sight would have made the cops even more jumpy than usual.

No, she thought, *the cops would shit themselves if they saw us like that, and we'd get busted for nothing ... best to stay under the cover of darkness, deep within the woods tonight, and under the safety of the trees … under the radar.*

As she approached the opposite end of the Cusack house, Madam Delevingne could see that there were about fifty yards of open space and field before reaching old Arnie Hammond's place. That area was surrounded by thick clumps of trees and bushes, just as the back fields were, and with no working streetlights there, the entire area was as black as pitch.

Without a doubt, that area was intimidating during the daylight hours, but at night, it was so dark that you couldn't even tell if there were trees there at all. It was just a wall of darkness.

"May the goddess be praised … may the Dark Lord be praised!" she said aloud; loud enough to alert anyone who might have been out there in the night with her. "It's a good thing I'm armed!" she bellowed again as if to reassure herself with the false threat, just in case someone actually was out there with her. Instead of being comforted, however, Madam Delevingne was treated with a flash of blinding lightning and a deafening clap of thunder. The thunder and lightning seemingly came out of nowhere, making her jump, and then to crouch to the ground as if her life depended on it. Her eyes were as wide as silver dollars.

A moment later, she began to feel hot and humid, which wasn't totally out of place, as it was in the height of summer after all. But the wave of heat that blew over her was like a draft from a huge fire, or as if she were standing next to a massive furnace that forced out blasts of heat. The only thing missing, she surmised, was the licking fire in order to make such heat. More than that, there was an odd scent in the air, too, a scent she had recognized from somewhere before, but just couldn't remember.

Now, Madam Delevingne, the wise sage woman, had felt a shrill of fear pass through her body as if something had touched her in the night. She could only stand still now, shaken by the fear of the unknown. And the strange scent, this had scared her the most.

It's almost like the burning of camphor or sulfur, she thought. *I know it … it's horrible … but from where?*

✠

Madam Delevingne knew what burning camphor smelled like, having burned it in banishing rituals and spells before, but this was too strong, somewhat like spent fireworks, or like what you'd smell after a Fourth of July celebration, but it was rancid too, like that of rotten eggs or decaying meat or both. In addition to this, the strange night sky seemed to be getting darker and darker in a matter of seconds. Now, the sky had turned from a sickly blood-red hue to a dark, almost greenish-grey, and then almost completely black again.

In addition to the visual strangeness, the trees and bushes began to take on a life of their own, as they seemingly appeared to sway back and forth, while making an almost lyrical rustling sound, like trees being blown on a windy, autumn night, only with a strange, soft melody in the distance. Now, the foul-smelling winds that wafted past her earlier seemed to be a one-time thing, as the atmosphere quickly became still and hot around her. Strangely, the trees still appeared to be swaying in the breezeless night.

"It's hot as hell out here," she muttered. "Shit ... and as black as a raccoon's asshole." And as the trees continued to sway back and forth, now appearing to move more violently, she had to squint harder in order to watch nature's unusual behaviour. As she did, finally getting a focus on the tops of the trees, all had shaken violently, and most unnaturally. It was as if some big hand was straddling the tree trunks, forcing pinecones or twigs to fall to the earth below, thus forcing the typically angry and self- possessed woman to stand still and silent.

Now, she could only watch in a state of muted dread. This continued for no more than two minutes, and then it simply stopped. The trees had come to a halt with a sudden jolt, followed by an unsettling silence.

"What the fuck is ... what, wh-aah," she muttered under her breath. For as soon as the trees stopped moving, as they stopped shaking, towards the top part of the trees, she could see several golf ball-sized flashes of light. They could be seen through what could only have been the branches of the trees, as many pairs of eyes, like cat's eyes, had stared angrily down upon her. Those piercing yellow eyes, blinking — blinking — blinking.

A second or two after this, another set of strange, yellowish flashes were seen slowly descending those branches, and then the trunks of those trees. And then another, and another, and another. The trees, which were as still as statues only moments ago, were again taking on a life of their own, as if forty or so cats that had taken nest in the trees were alerted by her presence below, and were coming after her.

Madam Delevingne just stood there, watching the bizarre sight as the feline-like eyes blinked and glistened within the black silhouettes. She remembered something, something like this before. She remembered something, but she couldn't put her finger on it. However, it only took a few seconds to recall the nightmare she had had earlier that morning, the night before, before going to The Hollow Cauldron. She remembered the yellow-eyed demons chasing her on some surreal landscape, being chased by monsters of every size and shape. In seconds, she remembered the glowing eyes and the razor-sharp teeth, all gnashing and chomping as they chased her. She remembered the intense fear that followed.

Now feeling the hairs prickling up on the back of her neck, and even the bristly, not-so-lady-like hairs standing under her chin, her whole body began to tremble. The hot sweat that ran down her face had turned to a cold, greasy liquid, a liquid that stung her eyes as she stared at the now terrifying, dreamlike vision before her. In what should have been dismissed as a nightmare, however, an aftereffect of spicy food and a pissed-off demeanor had become reality. She watched as the flashing eyes blinked, and then got thinner at the corners, as if the heads that held those eyes were looking about, from left to right — right — to — left.

Slowly, one by one, those eyes crept down the trunks of those now motionless trees and onto the ground below. The glowing eyes had become a sea of unearthly, ground-level stars that slowly moved toward her; ever so slowly.

Madam Delevingne just watched as those eyes, those horrible, yellow, glistening eyes, slowly approached her through the blackness of her surroundings. Now, as if creeping as low to the ground as any animal might creep, the seemingly formless things approached closer and closer. But now, the eyes didn't blink; they just stared with a pang of hunger, as if lions preparing to leap upon an unsuspecting prey. Now looking quickly behind her, Madam Delevingne saw the porch lights on the walls that arched the garage door at Arnie Hammond's house. It seemed far to her, maybe another hundred yards, but she knew that couldn't be right. She knew she was only forty or so feet away.

I, I CAN MAKE THIS, she thought, and from some unseen force within her, she began to run; she ran like never before.

As she ran as fast as she could, panting like a dog in heat, she looked behind her again to see if the eyes were still there. They were only now keeping pace with her as if toying with her like a wolf would when taunting its forthcoming meal. The sound of her feet on the rubble and gravel of the torn-up road had made a loud crunching sound that was almost as loud as her panting—

"*GET … GET AWAY FROM ME!*" she screamed. "*GET THE FUCK A-AH-AWAY FROM MEEEE!*"

Now keeping her eyes on the porch lights, she grabbed for her car keys, fumbling for the keys to her garage-apartment door. She clenched them tightly within her palm, quickly surmising that whatever these things were, cats or dogs or coyotes, whatever they were, they would surely turn away when she neared the garage lights, so she kept running. She ran and panted so hard that she could feel her heart pounding in her chest — she thought she'd die right there on the spot, but she kept on going.

In a second of clarity, she remembered, or perhaps it was a moment of déjà vu, but the entire scene, the glowing eyes, the landscape, and her feelings in their entirety were exactly like the dream she had had. Madam Delevingne was experiencing the nightmare she had had the night before.

As she looked back again, just before reaching the edge of the grass that led to the side door of the garage, the yellowish-amber eyes appeared to be standing still as if crouching low to the ground, as if having given up the pursuit. But that didn't slow her running. She continued on to the house, which appeared to be closer to her now. Within a second or two, she was at the side door of her garage apartment, its low-watt, yellow bulb aglow, making her door look like something from one of her favourite mystery novels, or like her surreal dreams; cloudy, hazy, and just plain bizarre.

It only took seconds for Madam Delevingne to pry the clump of keys out of her hand, which had been so tightly gripped that there was a bloody indentation in her palm. She fumbled, looking behind her until she finally located the longest key, the key to the side door deadbolt. She inserted it, practically with a skill that amazed even her, and then turned it. And to be sure, she opened the door faster than any door had ever been opened. And just before she would slam the door shut, she looked back one more time. In that second or two, she could only see the bushes that lined the little pathway to the side door. They, too, began to shake and rattle, now with tiny yellow eyes peering through the leaves.

In a tremendous huff, the visual revelation had prompted her to slam the door shut behind her. She quickly locked the deadbolt and then the turn-lock on the doorknob until it could move no further. Now, she continued to pant excessively as she held on to the doorknob tightly, thinking that doing so would help keep someone from entering, just in case whoever or whatever was chasing her would try to get in.

Madam Delevingne wasn't ready to relax by any means, even though she was beginning to breathe a little more calmly now. She was a little less terrified because she knew cats and dogs couldn't open doors. Nevertheless, she continued to hold on to the doorknob tightly, believing that she'd feel something; that it would move in her hand if someone tried to get in. At the same time, she began to explain away the entire affair as if it were just a matter of circumstance. She told herself that all of it was a mixture of having had food poisoning the night before and being harassed by the mysterious Bible-thumper.

Now, forgoing any supernatural cause for the strange events, Madam Delevingne was almost certain that it was nothing more than a trick of the light. And that was what was following her was nothing more than a bunch of stray cats or dogs. But this idea didn't last for long, quickly returning to the reality of what she was witnessing firsthand. She did see something in those trees that shook violently, as well as those weird lights peering through those damned bushes only inches away from her, just minutes earlier. Though she couldn't explain it, she knew that what she had experienced was real. Now, she just stood behind the door and pushed on it, while at the same time, holding the doorknob tightly in her sweaty hands. Her eyes unblinking, she whimpered as silently as she could.

No matter what, she knew there was something chasing her out there — something beyond reason.

✠

"*FUCK YOU!*" she finally bellowed in defiance. "Fucking … *ASS* … *ASSHOLES!* Whatever the fuck you are! I don't care what you are, rabid cats or whatever … sons of bitches!" she continued to belch out in a fit of rage. Madam Delevingne just didn't know what the things could have been, but surely, she surmised, it had to be purely natural. It just had to be.

"Yeah, cats, that's all they were … just cats in the trees, and they were coming down for food … of course," she said to herself, now feeling slightly better about the ordeal. She surmised that she was just frightened after all and that she had a lot on her mind, especially with the ritual close at hand.

Now beginning to calm herself, at least a little, Madam Delevingne's breath had begun to taper off. She sighed, just as her panting finally began to return to normal breathing. "And let's not forget that Bible-thumping asshole," she burbled. "That's the biggest thing that needs fixing right now." The very thought of her renewed anger had made her nod and smile. It had made no difference that the mysterious scripture-slinging typist had stopped messaging her, and had stopped sending nasty Bible quotes, she was still pissed off over it all. As she thought about it, she gripped the doorknob even tighter. She felt herself getting angry again; her face getting redder by the second.

"You fucked-up, guy," she mumbled a bit louder. A baleful smile rose on her face now, just as she let go of the doorknob. Now, it only took a matter of moments to realize that what she had experienced might have been due to the fact that she was stressed by the as yet unknown cyber attacker, the Bible-thumper who had terrorized her in her own space, and against her will. This person, whoever he or she was, had threatened her very life with his hateful words. And the very thought of it had once again propelled her into a state of rage.

Despite her growing anger and the intermittent fear that flushed through her, she knew that the ritual that would soon take place would work. She believed now, regardless of her shaky philosophies concerning the occult and the hidden powers it supposedly holds. She understood now. She realized that the combined ritual overseen by her mistress, Maybelle Riclou, would bring satisfaction and peace of mind. She knew she would have her revenge.

Madam Delevingne smiled ever so sinisterly. "You made the mistake of messing with us," she burbled. "But my turn is coming soon … very, very soon, Bible-man. Tonight … tonight you'll pay."

✠

Now looking around her domicile, looking for a weapon of any kind, she remembered the cheap dagger she had dropped near the heavy curtains; the curtains where she had thought someone was hiding behind that early morning. She just wanted something to hold on to, to pacify her until she would get a hold of herself. She figured that her car was down for the count, so she'd wait a few minutes to collect herself and then call Lester Gnaws to pick her up. She figured it was only a little after ten, and that the park was only three or four miles from her place. She figured she still had time.

Madam Delevingne pondered how she could have possibly thought that someone could have been hiding behind the curtains. This made her smile. And as she was in the process of dismissing such an erroneous idea, she spotted the two pieces of her ashtray on the floor ahead of her and bent down to pick them up.

"No, not this time," she muttered, as she grabbed for the broken shards of green glass. Then, she proceeded to walk over to where she had tossed the dagger. "Okay, okay … just get a hold of yourself so I can get the fuck outta here," she mumbled under her breath. She laughed quietly, but she *did* laugh.

As she approached the knife, she had for an instant, if just for an instant, considered that someone *was* actually behind those heavy curtains. She laughed to herself and quickly shrugged that nonsense off. And as she reached down to pick up the die-cast metal dagger, she placed one hand on the curtain-shrouded garage door to reassure her balance, as well as to prove once and for all that no one could be there in the first place; feeling around it to authenticate the fact that a garage door was the only thing behind the curtain. And just as she bent down and placed her fingers on the handle of the knife—

BOOM-BOOM-BOOM!

A crescendo of booming sounds sounded as soon as she touched the pommel of the dagger, forcing the vile woman to topple over and crash against the garage door. And as the loud booming crashed and vibrated from the other side of the door, Madam Delevingne could only stare at the now shuddering door with widened eyes and an open mouth. Someone was pounding on it with all their might.

BOOM-BOOM-BOOM! BOOM-BOOM-BOOM!

Again and again, the thunderous pounding rang throughout her tiny garage apartment. The almost deafening booming on the garage door was so loud and so powerful that the entire garage door shook and jolted, almost out of its cemented foundation. It had actually caused the heavy curtains to bounce off the door's face. Madam Delevingne was so startled by the shock of the pounding clamor that when she tried to recover and get to her feet, she had jolted backward and fallen over the crate-like box that served as a coffee table. She landed halfway on the couch and halfway on the floor, slamming her head against the armrest as she did. This had caused some of her knick-knacks to topple off the television set with a crash. Even the poster of a pixie sitting on a red and white-spotted mushroom had fallen to the floor.

"*WHAT THE FUCK! WHO THE FUCK IS THAT?!*" she screamed.

BOOM-BOOM-BOOM! BOOM-BOOM-BOOM!

Madam Delevingne was stunned, more at that moment than ever before. But she was also angry, far too angry to ever let such an infraction be forgotten or ever forgiven. She knew that someone was playing with her now. Her first thoughts had pointed to someone that she knew, like her ex, Roddy Clinson. They had left on fairly awful terms only a few months ago, and he was really pissed off at her.

BOOM-BOOM-BOOM! BOOM-BOOM-BOOM!

Another round of pounding sounded from the other side of the garage door, this time louder and deeper sounding than before. And no more than a second or two after that, she began to hear a light tapping on the small window near the side door. Now, the window that held the small box air conditioner had begun to shake.

TAP-TAP-TAP-TAP-TAP!

"Who ... *WHO IS THAT!*" she yelped. "*WHO ARE YOU?!* The tapping continued to sound from the window, this time much louder and much deeper. The little box air conditioner began to wiggle and creak as if someone was trying to pull it out of its frame. *TAP-TAP-TAP-TAP- TAP*, the tapping sound rang again, now with less voracity than before. She could hear the glass making a splintering sound as if it would shatter at any moment — and then it stopped.

Madam Delevingne had considered the possibilities, for which there were many. She had her admirers; that went without saying, but if truth be told, she had an unhealthy assortment of sycophantic followers too. From want-a-be-witches to the typical superstitious lot that actually believed her bullshit and bought the junk she peddled at the Hollow Cauldron, she had been honored in her own right, but she was also coveted by a few weirdos. Indeed, there were hundreds of anonymous fools who followed her blog pages, self-absorbed exposés, and those who gave exorbitant amounts of money to her bogus charities. It was business after all.

Madam Delevingne was, for some, worthy of worship. She knew this and immediately consigned her followers in order. Whether Kras Mala or Grizzela, her most favoured, right on down to her underlings, she knew she had owned each of them. They would never disobey or betray her; this she was certain of. For the foolish few who bought her magical shtick, they would never learn the truth. Yet, there were others who knew her up close and personal, those rare few who actually knew who and what she was. She was a fraud.

✠

Madam Delevingne realized that Baytown and nearby Houston had a good share of mystic and new-age shops. Stores like The Spiral Circle Books & Gifts in Houston or The Red Moon Occult Shoppe out by the technical college were all obligated to be punished by her from time to time. Whether by her online personas, or her website's blog page, which she referred to as her 'seek and destroy platform,' Madam Delevingne could be a real bitch. But it was her highly enlightened website, *Disuniting the Shroud,* that served as her personal temple of wisdom — it was her most prized possession.

Now panting excessively, Madam Delevingne stood halfway between the side door and her old couch. She pushed against the door with all her weight while using her leg to brace the floor. And despite the anger brewing within her, she huffed and wheezed with a mixture of fear and rage.

"So … it's a plot to get even with me, is it?" she asked herself in a shaky voice. "Okay … games on, bitch!"

She turned to look at the tapestry-covered garage door, then turned back to visually inspect the small window by the side door. The tapping had been reduced to a series of barely audible clicks. She had figured that it had to be someone she knew; someone she had pissed off. She admitted that she wasn't alone in any guilt, certainly not. She frequently hosted 'Rag Parties,' as she referred to them, and would team up with other occult experts to rip her enemy's new assholes. Such an honor was reserved for those who had the audacity to insert their opinions, and goddess-help- them, question her faith.

As *Disuniting the Shroud* hosted many of these so-called rag parties, or, from a lesser description, down-and-out character assassinations, Madam Delevingne never fathomed what those sour grapes might turn into down the line. She believed that her rag parties were done for their own good and that, after time, her victims would come to their senses and end up loyal followers of the craft. After all, her website was designed specifically to root out the chaff from the wheat; the neophyte from the sage. She always told herself that it was more of a service than an attack, but she knew that was a lie. Nevertheless, should the offender be polite, if he begged for forgiveness for his or her indiscretions and mistakes, or lack of knowledge, then perhaps forgiveness could be rendered. But this was rare, indeed.

Madam Delevingne had considered her followers. Those select few who supported her efforts with her online character assassinations, her 'Big Guns,' as she referred to them. They would always help in hammering the last of the nails in her victim's coffin. They were all professionals in the craft, despite any particular discipline. Of those in her occult community, those who had equally potent passions in issuing much-needed realignments to her enemies, there were many. She knew them — she knew *all* of them.

Of the best, there was Jean Pierre Baptiste, a world-class Vodou master from New Orleans. She would team up with him when she needed a little assistance in such matters where the Haitian and African arts were called for. And then there were other notables of the Order of Pry Thealemè Ex Mortis, as well as those from straightforward satanic cults. From Illinois, there were Professors Prud and Dunn, and then there were occult scholars like Toussaint, Horst, and Frigmann to consider. They were from Indiana. Others, like Nikolaos from California and Roman from Florida, had been the most successful in their crafts, but they had been gracious to her. Certainly, Madam Delevingne was well-armed with professional backup. She even had an assortment of witches and sex magick practitioners like Kavas, Kunzie, and Davis on her side, with there being dozens upon dozens more. Madam Delevingne was as admired as she was feared, as she was hated.

Regardless of her friends or foes, the events taking place that night had railed her into a sense of fear that she had never experienced before. Madam Delevingne was scared for her life that night, thinking that whoever was out there pounding on the garage door and walls, or who was tapping on the window, was there to hurt her or worse. That night, she was scared like she had never been before.

CHAPTER ELEVEN

Madam Delevingne waited and watched the little air conditioner to see if it wiggled again. She listened intently for the tapping sound to return.

"Maybe it's … it's Roddy," she whispered to herself. "Maybe he finally figured it out … that I was the one who stole his mother's fucking wedding ring," she sighed loudly. "They were close … or, or maybe it's that Joanne Clark from The Spiral Circle … I have been ripping on her all this year. Shit, it's just a blog page for Christ's sake! Maybe she figured it out … maybe she figured out one of my aliases or something? Nah, no, no fucking way … she's not that smart, not enough to figure *that* out! I covered my tracks. Wait, ah … maybe, maybe it's that bastard, that son-of-a- bitch Bible-thumper … that crazy religious fucker."

Madam Delevingne's facial expression had changed from one of being terrified to one of pure, heated rage. "*YOU … YOU HAVE … HAVE THE AUDACITY TO CHALLENGE ME!?*" she squealed. "*YOU HAVE THE BALLS TO CHALLENGE ME AT MY FUCKING HOME!?*"

Now, she just stood there a moment, as if waiting for a response. In an instant, she was as angry as she was the day she received those hateful responses from her as- yet-unknown online assailant. Her eyes were getting larger, her skin redder, and the veins in her neck and forehead were now more pronounced, and it didn't take long for the woman to be filled with an unnatural fury all over again.

As the vile woman sat in place, sitting halfway on the couch and kneeling on the floor, she held the makeshift coffee table as if she were hanging on for dear life. Then, she began to hear what sounded like rustling sounds or movement outside. It sounded like the sound of rats scurrying in the walls. And then, from above her, she began hearing something moving, like shuffling on her ceiling, as if someone was shuffling their feet or moving boxes around on the second floor. At the same time, she started to hear what could only be the sound of whispering.

The whispers, as she had finally concluded, were not coming from one or two people, but from lots of people. And though she couldn't make out the words, the sounds were definitely human, or something that sounded human. Now, the powerful and wise Madam Delevingne tried desperately to understand the weird words—

"… *Quid agis-quid-agis-quid-agis-vadis, Julianae-quo vadis*, the words echoed from the darkness. She listened intently to the strange words, but she couldn't decipher them. Regardless, those whispers echoed again and again from the darkness. *Julianae … Quod pertinet ut animam tuam-Julianae-quo vadis Julianae-quo vadis … Julianae?*"

The whispered voices repeated over and over again all around her and in her head. Madam Delevingne just sat in place and listened as the unearthly voices rattled on in words she couldn't understand. Then, she got up and walked as close to the garage door as she could, and then put her ear close to it. After a few moments, she slowly approached the side door to do the same. She tried to hear if these almost inaudible sounds were coming from outside or from inside the house. She tiptoed to where the little air conditioner was and leaned in to see if someone was outside the side door, hoping that it was just an elaborate trick someone was playing on her.

Maybe it's, it's … it's just some of my friends? She thought to herself. *No. Nobody's that stupid … nobody would do that … not to me!*

Madam Delevingne knew that old Arnie wasn't home. The house was dark, and there were no lights on at all in the main room, the family room, or the kitchen, and she remembered she didn't see any lights on when she ran from the road. Plus, his old truck was gone too. She knew that he really didn't have many friends, not really, but he'd never let anyone borrow that old, broken-down truck of his. *Maybe, maybe,* she thought. *Maybe it's …*

✠

"… *Quid agis-quid agis-quid agis-quid agis-quo vadis Julianae-quo vadis Julianae-quo vadis,* the strange whispers echoed again. The voices would continue, again, and again, and again, repeating the strange words over and over, as if taunting the now totally unnerved woman. Finally, the eerie words had stopped. This was followed by the slightest rumble of distant thunder, as if a storm was taking place in the next county. Now, a cold chill ran down Madam Delevingne's back.

In an instant, the low mutterings and whispers ceased, only to be replaced by dull shuffling sounds that vibrated above her. Seconds after this, the meandering sounds above her had turned into thunderous footfalls. The heavy-footed sounds had turned into what could only have been running or shambling, as if a very large man or men were running from the second-floor window to that room's door, and then onto the foyer, and then running down the hallway in the other direction, towards the staircase. Now, in a state of shock, she remained perfectly still. She trembled; her eyes as wide as they could be.

Terrified, she could hear the footfalls echoing less and less, minus the sound of a heavy thud that came from the wall as if some huge brute had slammed into it as he was trying to make a turn to run down the stairs. Here too, the footfalls echoed loudly, shaking the walls as they boomed; booming loud enough to know that someone was sprinting down the stairs — the stairs that led right to the kitchen — the kitchen that led right to the front door to the garage — the door that led right to her room.

BOOM-BOOM-BOOM! BOOM-BOOM-BOOM!

Madam Delevingne's eyes and mouth competed for which could become the largest at the sound of the thundering pounding that rang out on her bedroom door. Though she was still lingering by the side door, having checked and double-checked the deadbolt and the lock on the doorknob, she quickly jolted upward like an athlete in order to secure the other door that led to the kitchen. And in less than a second, she had landed on her knees as she reached the door, grabbed the doorknob as fast as she could, and fumbled at the turn-lock to make sure it was secure. It was just as she had left it, but before she could remove her hand, she felt the doorknob become icy cold and then begin to wiggle in her palm. Someone was there, trying to get in. And then, she heard ever-so-slight whispers from behind the door.

"*NOS AUTEM VENIO AD TE — NOS AUTEM VENIO AD TE!*" a muffled, yet just loud enough set of strange words echoed from beyond the door. The voice was deep and gruff, having sounded more guttural than human. And Madam Delevingne, now fully terrified, had held the doorknob as tightly as she could.

"*NOS AUTEM VENIO AD TE VENIO TIBI,*" the weird voice continued, "*QUOD PERTINET UT ANIMAM TAUM … PERTINET UT ANIMAM TAUM!*"

Though the whispers began quietly, they had become brusque grunts, like that of an alligator or a crocodile attempting to speak. The words were of broken Latin but were filled with a hatred that was unmistakable. As Madam Delevingne's hand now gripped the doorknob as tightly as she could squeeze, it continued to turn, and as far as it could go, making a clicking sound when it stopped in either direction. And then it turned ever-so-slowly three times in a row as if to taunt her, and then it stopped. A second later, the overhead lights flickered a few times and then went out. The room had become as black as tarpaper. As the doorknob was now far too cold to keep holding, she let it go with a hiss.

"WHO ARE YOU!" she screamed at the top of her voice. *"LEAVE ME ALONE!"*

"NOS AUTEM VENIO AD TE VENIO TIBI," the loud whispers continued. *"NOS AUTEM VENIO AD TE VENIO TIBI ... QUOD PERTINET UT ANIMAM TAUM!"*

✠

Now sitting on the floor, she trembled as she held and rubbed her almost frost-bitten hand. A second after this, the overhead light, a standard two-bulb fluorescent light, began to hum and slowly come back to a soft luminescence. Though it was dim, too dim to read by or see clearly enough to do anything without falling over something, she could see the layout of the tiny garage-apartment. Now, she slowly stood up. The lights flickered ever-so-gently, adding to the already disturbing atmosphere her surroundings had taken on. She could, however, see just enough to pull out her cellphone and check if it was working again. It was now offering her the chance to call for help.

Madam Delevingne quickly retrieved her cellphone and punched 911. Instead of ringing, a *bloop—bloop—bloop* sound echoed. It was the customary sound of being disconnected. Now, she could only stare at the phone as it went dark. She tapped it again to make sure the battery was still good and if it had enough bars to make or receive a call. All the bars were lit, and the phone was fully charged, so she punched 911 again. Once again, the call ended with the now customary blooping sound. She looked around and touched the doorknob again, which was now at room temperature. She just stared at it, wide-eyed and in shock.

"I, I don't get this!" she said, as she began scrolling down her contact list, while periodically looking at the door to see if the doorknob was turning. Then, she punched in Lester Gnaws' number on speed dial. "Answer your cell dumbass … c'mon dude, answer your fuck'en phone!"

"Hell-o … Madam—?" a shaky voice echoed from her receiver.

"Lester … Rommar! You need to get over here fast and pick me up!" she screamed into her phone.

"Okay, okay … whhhaa … what's go'en on?"

"There's … there's somebody in my house, I, I think!"

"Okay! Okay, I, I'll call the cops! Just, ah, just give me a—"

"Wait, wait!" Madam Delevingne belched, cutting off the love-starved man from completing his idea. "Just, just wait a minute, Lester!" In the time it took to place her ear to the door again, in time to hear only silence on the other side, she had come to the conclusion that if the police were to arrive, they would scour the place with their fine- tooth combs, and maybe they'd find someone in the home. Yes, there was that possibility — *but* that while they searched through her room and through her things, the police might just find all the stuff she had stolen from all those Baytown churches over the years, too, and that was simply not allowed. Besides, there was still a strong chance that one of her friends was playing a trick on her, so it may all be for nothing.

Now, the vile woman had decided to wait until Lester Gnaws arrived. Then, and only then, would they find out the truth together.

"Ah, Madam … Madam Delevingne? Do you, do you want me—"

"Never mind that now," the woman grunted. "No, I think, I think it's okay, Lester … Rommar. Where, where are you now?"

"I'm at the park, everyone's here … we're waiting for you … we're ready to go."

"Get over here now, Rommar, you need to pick me up … my car's dead … do you remember how to get here … my address?"

"Yeah, sure, of course!"

"*NOW, ROMMAR, GET OVER HERE NOW!*"

"I'm on my way now, Madam … I, I'm come'en right now!"

As Lester Gnaws disconnected the call, Madam Delevingne felt somewhat secure, somewhat safe, even if it was just for a moment. And then she considered calling the police anyway. She still needed to tell someone that an intruder or intruders were in the house. Besides, she could just as easily hide all the things she and the others had stolen; hide them in one of Arnie's old trunks in the living room. They wouldn't search there, why would they? And then the epiphany hit her like a ton of bricks — she'd have to actually go into the damned Livingroom in order to get to those trunks, and whatever was pounding on her bedroom door was obviously in there too, so that was a no- go. Now, she quickly surmised the logic and threat of it all and tried the police again, only now, she would receive the now customary *Bloop—bloop—bloop* sound.

"What the fuck?!" she bellowed. "How can my phone not dial nine-one-one?" she bellowed again. She figured that there was something wrong with her settings, so she decided to call Rommar again and have him call the cops for her. She redialed his number, but instead of hearing his much-desired voice, she again only received the sound of being disconnected. "*SON OF A BITCH!*" she screamed. She gazed at her cellphone and attempted to redial his number again, just as the phone's logo appeared on the screen. The words *Goodbye* scrolled by, and then it shut down.

Madam Delevingne just stared at the phone. Her body tingled with fear, as if having been lightly electrocuted, like touching a live wire within a toaster, like when poking and prodding for a piece of toast that got lodged inside. Then, ever so lightly, the door ahead of her, and even the walls all around her, began to shimmer, as if a dozen semitrailers were circling the house, only to stop a few seconds later.

"What the ... what the fuck?" she asked herself, now in a tone suggesting that the whole event had either been supernatural in nature or that whoever was playing these tricks had been very good at it, and extremely savvy in electronic manipulation. Now, she looked back at her cellphone and lightly shook it. The damned thing was still dark. "How's that even possible ... I, I had a full charge!" she mumbled. She restarted her cellphone three times in a row, but every time she did, the same thing happened, *bloop— bloop—bloop*, and then the words *Good Bye* would scroll across the screen, only to go dark, and its battery drained each and every time.

Now thoroughly enraged at the cellphone's odd behaviour, she put it in her back pocket and checked the doorknob again, and then hobbled over to the side door and checked that doorknob. They were secure, and both were at normal room temperature again, and both were still locked. Madam Delevingne just stood in the now quiet garage apartment for a moment and looked around the place to make sure it was still secure. And then she remembered her dagger, the cheap athame knock-off that rested on the floor. She picked it up and held it tightly in her right hand.

I'll fucking kill anyone now … bust through that door, and I'll stab you dead you son-of-a-bitch, she thought. She was still frightened, but angry too. She had had enough, and if it were someone trying to harm her, someone she hadn't known, then she knew she'd kill — she wanted to kill.

As she looked around, checking every corner of the room, every nook, and cranny of her little, run-down excuse of a dwelling, her cellphone vibrated in her back pocket. This had made her jump as if being electrocuted, but she had immediately pulled the phone from her pocket and watched as it began to turn on again, first showing the logo, and then the word *Hello*. After her screen had come to life, she saw that there was one text message waiting to be read. Now enraged all over again, she grunted in anticipation and then opened it.

Evil events from evil causes spring — Aristophanes, it read.

"What the fuck … Lester?" she asked herself. "Evil events … and who the fuck is Arist-astro-phan-ees?" As soon as she muttered that question, her cellphone once again began shutting down; once again showing the cell's logo and the words *Good Bye*. In less than a minute after that, her phone started up again, vibrated, and then lit up with the customary word: *Hello* running across the screen. And once again, a text message was waiting to be read. She opened it.

"In flaming fire taking vengeance on them that know not God, and that obey not the gospel of our Lord Jesus Christ: Who shall be punished with everlasting destruction from the presence of the Lord, and from the glory of His power."

— *II Thessalonians I: VIII-IX*

✠

Madam Delevingne felt a flush of blood run through her face and hands now. She wasn't scared, she was rage-filled, seeing nothing but red. Her eyes were as red and as bulging as two ripe tomatoes, just as they were when she had first read the impudent Biblical quotes from her yet unknown online attacker. The veins in her neck and forehead were now visible and protruding. Now, she had the uncanny appearance of someone getting ready to explode.

She tilted her head back as she gripped her cellphone and screamed. "You … you fuck … *YOU … YOU FUCKING SON OF A BITCH, I'LL FUCKING KILL YOU!*" She believed that she could kill someone now.

No, she *knew* she could kill this person, the vicious Bible-quoting asshole without any moral compunction.

✠

Madam Delevingne believed she had an unlikely epiphany; the foreknowledge of the arcane, the esoteric, and all things of a preternatural nature. She knew the message on her cellphone had come from the Bible-thumper, and that it was he that was causing all the seemingly weird events that had happened to her that night. Somehow, somewhere, her mysterious enemy was responsible for all of it. She didn't know how, and she couldn't explain it, but she knew — she just knew.

Just as she turned to check the door to the kitchen again, the unmistakable sound of a car horn blared outside. This startled her, too, because she couldn't tell if it was Lester's car or someone else's. She didn't want to chance it. She figured it could have been another trick from the Bible-thumper. Now, fearing that this guy, likely having been responsible for the pounding on the doors, and more likely than not, the same guy who was in the house pounding on her bedroom door, could have gotten in with his friends. Maybe they just wanted to scare her, or maybe more, it didn't matter. She just wouldn't take any chances now.

That has to be him, she thought to herself. *What if he has friends with him ... what if that's him trying to get me to go outside ... what if ... what if?*

BOOM! BOOM! BOOM!

As the knocking sounded from the side door of her garage apartment, Madam Delevingne jumped again, dropping her cheap dagger as she did. "WHO IS IT?!" she yelled, as she quickly picked up the counterfeit dagger off the floor and lifted it above her head.

"It's me, Madam!" The familiar voice sounded from the other side of the door. "I got here as fast as I could … are, are you okay?"

"*YES!*" she snapped back. Madam Delevingne was still frightened; thinking it could still be someone else out there, someone, like the Bible-thumper playing tricks on her, but it sounded like Lester, so she sheepishly unlocked the doorknob's thumb-lock, and then pulled the deadbolt back. Now raising the dagger with her right hand above the door, she slowly turned the doorknob with her left hand and carefully looked out the crack. Not knowing what to expect, there he was, a welcome mixture of a half-assed, greasier version of Tom Petty and some dirty tweaker from the city. It was Lester Gnaws, her newly acquired slave; *Rommar the Initiate Elect* — her newly acquired tool.

"Hello?" a nervous voice sounded.

"Jesus Christ, it's about fucking time, Lester!" she belted angrily.

"I'm sorry, Madam, but I didn't know how to get around all the construction … I had to backtrack a few times … sorry about it. I … I saw your car. Maybe I could—"

"Okay, okay, never mind that now! We need to get outta here, and now!" "Is, is everything alright here … you sounded so upset," Lester asked.

"Yeah, I'll tell you about it in a minute, just let me get my shit together, and we'll get outta here. And you're sleeping here tonight too, so make plans for that, Rommar!"

"Okay! Plans made ... I'm here," he said, now with puppy dog eyes staring back at her. The angry woman ignored the man. She just continued to stuff things into her large duffle bag, now cramming in various items of an occult nature. From little brass and tin boxes of seeds and herbs to various articles of clothing, and other knick-knacks, Lester Gnaws couldn't decipher. Regardless, Madam Delevingne was oblivious to her swain's child-like love, even though the man just stared down at her as if she were touched in the head. He didn't care, and she just wanted to get the hell out of there — and fast.

"Hey, do you ... do you hear anything strange?" the nasty woman asked.

"Strange, Madam?"

"YES ... like footsteps or voices ... shit like that?"

"Ah ... no ... no, I, I don't hear anything ... what do you hear?" Lester inquired; his head, now tilted to one side.

"It, it doesn't matter," she returned sullenly, almost embarrassedly. "I think I'm being played. When we get back later, you and I are gonna search the place, okay?"

"Ah, yeah, okay, sure," Lester said carefully. He didn't want to chance angering her, but he had to know what was going on. "What ... what happened here tonight, Madam?" he asked.

"Never mind, Lester ... let's just get outta here!"

Now with her oversized sack filled with the tools of her wicked trade, Madam Delevingne ambled to the side door and pushed Lester forward to imply that they needed to hurry. And as they bounced out of the doorway, she turned and locked the door with lightning speed. Then, she looked around her entire surroundings, first staring at the bushes, and then towards the back of the house, and in between old Arnie's barn. She checked the tree line behind that, and even up towards the second-floor windows. She scanned the front area too, where she had run like hell less than an hour before, but there was nothing there. Even the sky seemed normal. It wasn't as gloomy as it was before; it wasn't a greyish-green or a murky, blood-red. It wasn't as dark as outer space, or as she had surmised earlier that night

— as being as black as a raccoon's asshole.

Now, there were no weird, glowing eyes, whatever they were; those horrible yellow orbs that had chased her. For the moment, everything seemed normal. Even the air was crisp and only slightly breezy. And the night air smelled natural too, like pine, and for a moment, she thought she could detect the delightful fragrance of the Texas Mock-orange blooming in the summer night. Everything seemed normal.

✠

Madam Delevingne and Lester Gnaws bolted to the car. The silver, beat-up, 1999 Ford Mustang was a welcome sight, especially knowing that her car was dead in the middle of the street.

"Do you want me to look at your car, Madam? I'm pretty good at—"

"No, Lester," she said, cutting the man off in mid-sentence, though now, in an almost kindly manner. "Maybe later, Lester. Right now, we just need to get outta here. I just want a go."

As Lester started his car, Madam Delevingne told him to try calling her on her cellphone to see if it worked. As he pulled the device from his back pocket, Lester located her number on his speed dial and punched in her name. He just stared at his phone now, waiting to see her name appear. A second later, the lyrics to Alicia Keys *Girl on Fire* had begun to sound in Madam Delevingne's hand. And as her favourite old ringtone eerily sounded from the cellphone, she just stared at it as if having been punched in the stomach.

"Is it going through?" Lester asked cautiously.

"Yeah … it's working again, Lester, but—"

Just before she could complete her thought, the cellphone once again said *Goodbye* and then shut down.

"I, I just don't get it, it worked before," Madam Delevingne said, now looking as confused as one of the Three Stooges trying to figure out what a cellphone even was.

"Madam?"

"Okay, okay, let's just forget about it for now, Lester, let's just go. Now's a good time, Lester!"

As he backed up and began to shift into drive, they slowly drove over the gravel road where she had fled earlier. Madam Delevingne scanned the trees where those deep yellow flashing eyes had peered down on her. They passed the barricades with their blinking, amber lights, which were all working perfectly now and bright enough to light the entire road. And then they passed her car, with its driver's side door still open. Now, the old Forenza had looked as dead and as deserted as any other heap of junk on the side of the road.

Once they passed the old Suzuki, with Lester driving delicately past the barricades and the construction equipment, Madam Delevingne turned to look out the rear window. She just stared at her car, which now seemed much closer than it felt when she was running away from it less than an hour ago. Now, her car just sat there as dark and as forgotten as a tombstone; lifeless and barren. And just as she was starting to look away, the car's hazard lights began to flash, flashing three times in succession. On the third time, the lights went black again, and her cellphone immediately vibrated in her hand, making her jump almost out of her seat as it did. She looked at the phone with questioning eyes as it came back to life, as it offered the cell's logo and the word *Hello*. And once again, there was a text message waiting to be read—

Wise men learn many things from their enemies, it read. This was followed by the name 'Aristophanes,' the 5th- century Greek playwright. Nevertheless, Madam Delevingne could only stare at the phone, but slowly lowered it to her side a moment later. Her face was expressionless.

Now, Lester turned to look at the woman he loved with just the hint of worry, but had turned away quickly before she could spy such a questioning look. He loved her, but he knew full well that she was volatile and quite often, vicious. Besides, he didn't want to risk losing the woman of his dreams.

Now, as distant thunder sounded again, along with the dull flashing of lightning in the next county, a cold streak of sweat ran down Madam Delevingne's face. And as she turned in her seat, she just stared at the dark road ahead of her, as those strange words began to echo in her head over and over again.

NOS AUTEM VENIO AD TE — NOS AUTEM VENIO AD TE ....

CHAPTER TWELVE

The Scales of Reckoning. A Day of Judgement
Friday, July 3rd, 12:01 A.M.

"The great deceiver knows that one of his most effective tools in leading the children of God astray is to appeal to the extremes of the paradox of man …"

— *Dieter Friedrich Uchtdorf, Quorum of the Twelve Apostles,*
The Church of Jesus Christ of Latter-day Saints

It was going on a minute after midnight when Lester's Mustang entered the front entrance to the Baytown Nature Center, at the end of Baytown Drive, and then down Boise Avenue. When they made their way to the end of Boise, Lester turned out his lights and slowly pulled up and parked on the shoulder of the old cement road. There were several other cars already there, so Lester pulled in slowly, just behind an old, beat-up minivan. He knew it had belonged to his friend, Herc Benet. And with the odd selection of beat-up vehicles in front of it, such had been obvious that the Order of Magnus Datha had assembled. Now, the unholy battle would begin, and the vengeance upon the heated enemy of their beloved mistress would commence.

Madam Delevingne got out first, quickly surveyed the area, and then headed for the tree-shrouded entrance that people usually took to reach the waterline. Even though the Baytown Center wasn't their typical place for working magick, she always remembered her chosen domains, and where she could ditch if the cops arrived, or where to squat and not be seen. It was the wisest thing to do, and Madam Delevingne was, after all, the wisest of them all.

The others were already in place, waiting to be led to the assigned location for working the blackest of magick. She surmised that their mother group in Ohio was probably already assembled and already in meditation. She figured that she'd have enough time to give the coven a run-down on the mysterious Bible-thumper, and launch their attack at the third strike of the witching hour; exactly twenty-three minutes past midnight. This would continue until at least 3:00 a.m., when the witching hour would begin the wane into the last of their intentions; until her enemy would receive his or her just reward.

As the witching hour was the peak time for seeking vengeance, a time that always worked the best for her, she had counted on the mystic phenomena. She knew that with full submission from the universe, destroying her enemy, and with complete impunity, she would be victorious. Now, she couldn't wait to get started. Once the black mass ended, and the deed was done, they would feast at the local Denny's or at the Village Inn. It would be their treat, of course. After the celebration, she'd go back home *with* Lester, at least for the rest of the morning, and contemplate future plans of ill repute. They'd both check out Arnie's house to find out how someone had actually broken in, or even if anyone could have gotten in, and then call the police to report it. It would all end well, she knew that much for sure, just as she knew that whoever he was would get his *just desserts* — he would pay with everything.

✠

Lester and Madam Delevingne made their way down the dark paths of Brownwood Drive and then onto the dirt and clay pathways under the cover of darkness. When she looked up, the clouds that had threatened the ritual were now almost completely gone. Now, she could actually see the clouds parting as if some great wind was blowing them away. This was the first time she felt better, more complete, and most of all, secure in her plans.

"I have my armies now, *Bible-man*," she muttered under her breath. "And now, your god won't stop us from ripping your heart out, you son-of-a-bitch."

"Yes, Madam, we'll kick his ass for sure," Lester returned, knowing instantly that he shouldn't have said anything, as if Madam Delevingne had even wanted his reassurance.

"I didn't ask, Rommar!" she barked.

"Ah, yes, Madam," he returned sheepishly.

Using the light from his cellphone, he watched as his mistress checked her phone too. It worked, and she quickly scrolled down her messages only to find none. She checked the Hollow Cauldron's website too, but there were no messages there either, and no one left any money in her Patreon account. Then she checked the last quote she had received as she was leaving her garage apartment. It came from a private number.

"Fuck … something's wrong with my fucking internet. I'll have to look into this later," she murmured, thinking that she should have gotten at least a few messages by now; at least one love letter from an admiring fan. She turned on the light on her cellphone and shined it around. The place was as dark and as creepy as any horror movie set, but this was perfect for that night's mission — perfect for setting the stage.

When they reached the clearing, the faint light of a small fire could be seen, along with the shadowy silhouettes of five human forms lingering in the glow of the fire. They stood about in a semi-circle, talking in low mutters. And when they detected the lights from the approaching cellphones, they spread out just in case it was the police. But once Madam Delevingne and her swain had entered from under the canopy of draping ivy and leaves, the assembly quickly formed before them with gasps of delight.

"Oh, grand leader; Prime Hierophant of the Order of Magnus Datha," a short, misshapen woman croaked from beneath her dark-brown hood. "Oh, most profound of the Order of Pry Thealemè Ex Mortis ... patron of the grand, Ordo Tenebris Lux, our most beloved," she continued. She was one of the most feared of Madam Delevingne's followers: Member-Elect Grizzela. She held the sacraments and their Guild's *Book of Shadows*. Behind her stood an unmistakable shape: the massive girth of an obese man. This was none other than Cron, the most loyal of lackeys.

Next to Cron stood Pentia and Sombra, two of the Order's elects, both wearing dark-brown cloaks with black mantle hoods. They stood next to Grizzela as if her private attendants. Next to them stood Ka'nar, who tightly held the

Guild's sacred athame, along with a simple black box that held that which only the elect of the Order had known. And though his pitted and pockmarked face could be seen beneath the lower extremities of his hood, his expression had nonetheless highlighted an angry demeanour and a constitution of determination and hatred most sublime.

In the next few minutes, Madam Delevingne took her time to slowly review her cultists. When done, she nodded her head in pleasure. "Kras Mala, our Supreme Elect, our Master Level Elect, and Kid'en'el are at their homes tonight," she said in a proud and commanding voice.

"They will pray with us at the hour of destruction … at the hour of our retribution!" she barked.

Now, the assembly stared on in a perceived reverence, though the light of the glowing campfire had obscured the faces under those dark hoods. Their silhouettes seemed to glow in the strange darkness, making the assembly appear as evil as the heart of their mistress, creating an image that might have very well made even the heartiest of men shudder. Such was the intention.

Madam Delevingne raised her hands as if to have the crowd lower their voices, and then she smiled slightly. "We must also give reverence for our fallen sister, our Mala Medea-Loc, the High Priestess of the Second Order of Daelemarr," she said cryptically. "Known to the mundane as Thomasina Barros, she has since descended. Yet, her spirit is here with us … she aids in binding us as one … and in making us strong!"

The gathering swayed in reverence for their fallen sister, with their hands held over their heads or in front of them, as if mocking the evangelical witnesses of God. Like those from a church revival, they were proud and secure in their faith — their faith in Lucifer — their faith in Satan.

"We are also aided by our sisters and brothers of The Silver Twilight Oasis," Madam Delevingne continued. "They are, as we speak, gathered in full regalia and in ceremony!" She chimed this last passage with a particular glee, a particular pride that only made her grimace more pronounced, and with a cryptic sense of malicious satisfaction.

✠

Once the opening invocation of intention was finished, Madam Delevingne walked forward and into a thicket of shrubs. Grizzela followed, as was the custom. There, Grizzela would help Madam Delevingne in preparing for the ritual. She'd slip out of her clothing, which would be gathered up and placed in a black satchel, and then she would be anointed with the sacred oils that were kept in the black box.

Once she was dressed in the unholy sacraments, which consisted of a black robe and cowl, along with a dark yellow sash, the polar opposite of royal purple, the colour associated with Christ Jesus, Madam Delevingne would begin the sinister ritual. Now, she smiled and raised her hands above her head.

"It is done," she chimed as she returned from the thickets. "So mote it be!"

"So Mote It Be! So Mote It Be! So Mote It Be!" the coven returned gleefully.

Now, Madam Delevingne nodded and smiled, her yellowed teeth glaring like a sick animal preparing to strike. Her sash was a dull, mustard hue, the colour of the eerie sky she had witnessed earlier that morning. She wore leather sandals and the *Carcanet of Spite*, the silver necklace with black stones surrounding it, along with a large Andesine gemstone at its centre. At the centre of that, an altered version of a unicursal hexagram was etched in silver. It is an icon, and with no uncertain doubt, an unholy relic representing the darkness that surges unseen within all of us, a darkness that surges in the vile Madam Delevingne.

The Carcanet of Spite would be the only ceremonial jewellery she'd wear during the high ritual; it having been passed down to her by Kras Mala, whose mundane name was Janet Florence Schroll, the ancient member who was allegedly gifted the Carcanet necklace from none other than Charles Milles Manson on August 10th, 1969. The curious good even has the name *Charlie*, crudely scratched on the reverse side of the cursed necklace. Understandably, it is Madam Delevingne's most prized possession.

Now, as Grizzela finished the anointment rite, the hunched, little woman applied the facial paint, which consisted of the crushed powders of dried berries and Limonite, along with a mixture of shea butter and goldenseal to create a thick, ochre-coloured paste. When it was finally applied, covering her forehead to the bridge of her nose, cheeks, and ears, the pigment from the ferric oxide and goldenseal matched Madam Delevingne's sash perfectly, giving her a unified look of demonic menace. It made her partly obscured eyes take on an equally demonic look.

When they had finished, Madam Delevingne stepped out of the thickets, with Grizzela fast on her heels. She held a brass censor she had stolen from Saint Margaret Mary's Catholic Church in Cedar Park. It smouldered with the resins of camphor and Dragon's Blood, filling the atmosphere with its noxious fumes. Then, she motioned that they all continue through the nature center's dark woods in order to reach the assigned destination, until they would come upon the old Brownwood subdivision where the ritual would take place.

The 'Brownwood,' as it's called today, was once a community that thrived on the three bays: the Crystal, Scott, and Burnet Bays. And long before it was a useless five-hundred-acre peninsula that served as a glorified bird sanctuary, it was known as the Brownwood Home Community, a post-World War II housing development; a well-to-do establishment formed by business moguls and the captains of industry of the day.

The Brownwood once housed Baytown's elite, which had fared well until Hurricane Carla slammed into it on September 11, 1961, taking a toll on its sturdy, though nonetheless fallible design. By August 1983, when Hurricane Alicia hit, it spelled certain doom for the already dilapidated homesteads. The water surges were too much for the construction, despite its sturdiness. And as such, the community and its once beautiful homes were permanently floundered, becoming a legal battleground and an eyesore at the same time.

After a series of mandatory evacuations and a slew of lawsuits, with the last of the residents having moved on, leaving their once beautiful homes forlorn and forgotten, Brownwood became a ghost town literally overnight. And though the majority of the three hundred homes were torn down, with the debris and rubble from the houses cleared decades ago, only the foundation of a single homestead remained, becoming a secret place for fisherman to cast their rods during the daylight hours. For a select few, however, it served for much darker purposes once night fell.

Although the land had been cleared years earlier, having been reclaimed by nature in the process, it had nonetheless become a dark and foreboding place. The locale would acquire a woeful reputation as the years went on, one of crime and illicit behaviour, becoming a haunt for drug dealings and lasciviousness. It would become a beacon for evil, a haunt for wickedness and debauchery. And it was perfect for criminal activity — it was perfect for rituals and black masses.

✠

Madam Delevingne knew the area well and had held many rituals there over the years, just as many other covens had done for the last few decades. When she was tight with Roddy Clinson, her former boy-toy. They'd go to the old foundation in the dead of night to consummate their lust for life, and other dirty deeds of a more nefarious order.

There, they'd drink, smoke weed, and fuck like rabbits. It was an era when she'd practised her newfound craft of the witches; when she learned that the old gods didn't care about her transgressions, when she had learned that if you wanted something, you didn't beg for it — you simply took it.

In those fledgling years, she had learned that she was, in fact, a goddess in her own right, and worthy of greatness, and that such was sacred to her. And where Crowley had his sacred places; his places of high ritual; whether Blythe Road in London, at his Boleskine home in Scotland, or even in the more obscure locales like the Boca do Inferno in Cascais, Portugal, and especially his Abbey of Thelema in Cefalù, in the Province of Palermo, Italy, Madam Delevingne had her special places too. Without a doubt, the Brownwood was her most revered, though little- used place for high rituals. Here, she would offer her odes and debts to her dark lord once and for all.

For hate's sake; for unholy revenge, Madam Delevingne would get even with the Scripture-touting online harasser. She would utilize the surroundings and the wicked lusts of her coven to bring the man down, and she would be victorious. Now, the vile woman had her plans and her armies in place. In the blackness of her heart, she knew she would have her vengeance.

✠

Once they passed the highest point of ground, just past Crow Road, around the old, rusty gate on the path, and just past the Tracey Seine Boardwalk that leads to the pristine shores of Crystal Bay, the coven made their way past endless patches of basket flowers, and the scurrying armies of mud crabs on the shore. They finally came upon the riprap and broken concrete slabs from an old boat launch from decades earlier. The uneven, mould-covered concrete structure jutted out at least twenty feet from the shore. Beyond that, they made their way to Wooster Point, just as Crow Road intersects the now-dead and forgotten Bayshore Drive and Mapleton Avenue. It was here where the ritual would commence.

This location; this unholy pit of forgetfulness and bad memories would be the last battlefield of the arrogant, and far too self-assured Bible-thumper. It would be here where an unseen foe would fall, and where his errors against the great Madam Tarja Delevingne would be consummated — where he would pay for his most unforgivable transgressions.

As they reached the area where they would set to rite, everyone had noticed that the sky was starless and dark. Now, in the thickets of the night, there was a curious haze hovering low in the sky, like a thin negligee keeping all the best secrets secure. It offered just a hint of what was yet to come. As Madam Delevingne entered a section of the old home's foundation, she stood at the edge closest to the bay waters. With only her blasphemous Carcanet necklace sparkling in the night's gloom, she alerted her coven to enter. Now, as they gathered around her, she lifted her hands above her head and spoke—

"Here, close to the foundation where we stand, lay a tiny graveyard, the once Wooster burial grounds," she echoed as if she were a museum docent. "Now buried under the choppy waters of the bay, after years of forgetfulness … here, tonight, it lies, resting beneath, facing the waters of Scott Bay, a graveyard of more than a century past!" Her voice, now rising to a tide of authority, and then ebbing to a subtle note of respect and awe, had indicated to the cultists that their mission would be both necessary and blessed.

Madam Delevingne smiled and nodded her head. "In these watery graves lie the bones of a witch; fellow of a sisterhood that would have embraced us," she continued. "It is she, Ednetta Collander, who embraces us tonight … giving us power, and strength! We assemble in order to fight an enemy that has done great harm to us … who has secured his place in the realms of annihilation … therefore, let us proceed to that struggle!"

When her hurried monologue had ended, she led the coven to where the remnants of a great swimming pool had once rested. The uneven, ceramic-tiled depression was partly filled in with dirt and sand from the bay, exhibiting only the chipped blue and white tiles of its inner circumference. It was here that the ritual would take place, a location that harboured a view of all three bays, and which would offer the black moon's full strength for the ritual.

Madam Delevingne, a great boaster, and aficionado of Baytown's folklore and history, both within reason, knew how to embellish such legends with her own style of bullshit. The graves she spoke of, its most famous being Ednetta Collander, were nothing more than a simple woman who had unfortunately died at the age of forty-three in 1959. She was neither a witch nor a devil-worshiper, but the falsified story sounded good, and Madam Delevingne was sticking to it.

Now, she gazed over to where another grave had once rested. This was where a young boy named Martin Elmar Wooster, for whom the graveyard was named, had rested. He, too, was just a poor unfortunate to have gone to that great beyond by means unknown. Outside of that, the graveyard served little purpose, besides the fact that most of the bodies had all been relocated, meaning that few, if any, cadavers actually resided under the dark waters of the three bays. Despite such inconsistencies in truth, however, the ploy always worked, and the coven followed without question or disruption. Now, the deed had begun.

CHAPTER THIRTEEN

It was a quarter after midnight when Madam Delevingne stood at the centre of that decrepit pool of yesteryear. There, she prepared for the obscene ritual. The others,

Grizzela, Pentia, Sombra, and Ka'nar formed the outer arch of the circle, while Cron and Rommar took post at the rear. There was no space unoccupied, though the missing members had surely made a dent in what they were accustomed to, especially in not having the proper number of thirteen members. The other six members had departed the coven a year or two earlier, forming a noticeable divot, though, for Madam Delevingne, this made little difference. She knew there were enough members to stop one inferior, Bible-toting zealot — more than enough to destroy him.

Now, Madam Delevingne motioned for Grizzela to bring one of the larger, ornate black boxes to her. From there, she would lay a thin line of black salt around the entire inner circumference of the pool, and then, using two ritual censors with tiny holes in it, she would pour the contents of four of the small glass bottles into it. This would ground and protect the location with Satan's unholy blessings. She smiled as she did, knowing she had gotten away with robbing Saint Joseph's Catholic church with flawless skill. And indeed, she had done so.

In an instant, she recalled plundering the church on Carolina Avenue with two of her acolytes, pilfering the blessed sacraments as the priest left for lunch. A slanted smile had risen on her warped face. Now, that greasy smile gleamed as best it could, despite the rotting yellowness of what was left of her jagged teeth. She had been victorious.

✠

Retrieving the tiny bottles from the black box, the ones that held the oils and dried herbs, she added the oils to one of them and several pinches of powdered herbs to the other. There was henbane, one of snakeroot, and another one of aconite. Grizzela lit the powders, and once the herbs began to smoulder, she added a few drops of the black banishing oil. This was followed by sprinkling the remainder of the oil over the broken and mouldy cement walls of the antiquated pool. When finished, Madam Delevingne began to read from their coven's Book of Shadows, which was handcrafted from a large sketchbook that she had covered in artificial material to give it the look of leather or animal pelt.

"Now, she held the book high above her head, while still being able to read the words within. And with that, Madam Delevingne embraced the attention she now commanded from the cultists and began to recite the odes of the goddess with a zeal that could shame any Catholic priest. Her diction was flawless.

"As with the first woman to praise the goddess, to praise the Lords of Darkness, she had bequeathed unto us the truth … and it is for our sake that this truth falls upon us in service!" she bellowed gleefully. Now, with her voice getting louder and louder, she began strutting before the assembled cult members, her hands waving with an arrogance that could inspire any banana republic dictator into emulation. Madam Delevingne's eyes were wide with hatred, so wide, in fact, that the cultists actually began to fear her.

✠

Madam Delevingne lifted her hands in front of her face and continued her opening benediction of hate. "To our Mother Astarte; to the goddess Anuit ... we beg favour in our quest for unholy revenge!" she screamed at the top of her lungs.

"So Mote It Be!" the cultists chimed, their hands raised in exaltation.

"To the King of Tyre, we praise thee! And with a sharp knife we cut deeply into the flesh ... the middle finger of your left hand in devotion to our master and to our mistress! Eat the pain ... eat the pain!"

"So Mote It Be!" the cultists returned.

"Thee, I invoke, the Bornless One!" Madam Delevingne continued. "Thee, that didst create the darkness and the light ... Thou art Asar Un-Nefer!

"So Mote It Be!" the cultists chimed with glee, "So Mote It Be!"

"Hath of great torment and pain, I bequeath unto you! Bring forth thy destruction ... bring forth thy death, Oh Lord of Light; Oh Lord of Darkness, I beseech thee! Bring forth, oh goddess of Datha ... Magnus Datha! The destruction of the enemy ... she brings death and destruction to the fiend at the gates of our sanctuary!"

"So Mote It Be, Madam! So Mote It Be!" the cultists chimed again.

Now, as the moon appeared to become brighter, bright enough to see that the winds were beginning to pick up, Madam Delevingne used nature's odd behaviour as a sign to step up her act, and to use every ounce of her skills to provoke her coven into a frenzy. Such would aid in convincing not only her followers but herself as well. Her hatred for this unknown person; the unknown Bible-thumper, the assailant who threw the first punch, had to be punished. And he *would* be punished. No matter what, he or she had to pay for such insolence. She believed it was her right.

"*AR-O-GO-GO-RUU-ABRAO!*" she cried. "Thou spiritual Sun ... Satan ... Thou Eye, Thou Lust! Cry havoc! Cry aloud! Cry aloud! Whirl the Wheel, oh my Father, oh Satana, oh Sun! *SOTOU! SOTOU!* Thou, the Saviour of the forlorn, the outcast! Oh, thou, the Saviour!"

"So Mote It Be! So Mote It Be!" the cultists chimed in a frothing frenzy, So Mote It Be! So Mote It Be!"

As Madam Delevingne screamed as loud as she could; remembering the offences of the Bible-thumper who so enraged her, she looked upon her tiny army with lust so great that she found herself laughing, proud, and with delight, her eyes blazing like that of a crazy woman. As she stared down at her coven, she realized that they respected her — that they loved her.

In a second, Madam Delevingne had realized that such love would have been an alien realization; an alien emotion only a few years earlier. And with those passing visions of her memory, she remembered. She had been abused as a child, sexually abused by her own father; forced into fellatio as his friends watched with lustful glances, and leering eyes, and then to be shared among them like some filthy sex doll.

Her mother, the mother that she had so admired and respected as a thief and confidence artist, had left her alone with that monster, that son-of-a-bitch that violated her day in and day out for five straight years. There was no justice for the young Julianna; no love, nor respect. And so, she had fled to her safety among the outcasts, and devoted her life to fight for depravity and evil, vowing to rage against the church — against God.

Now filled with a seething hatred, Madam Delevingne's smile and laughter subsided into a grimace of hate befitting any respectable worshiper of Satan. Her instant memory of those events had scorched her heart until finally, it had become black and dead. Now, her memories were filling the landscape of her thoughts; her eyes bulged once again in rage as she read from the Book of Shadows. She became what she loved the most — pure, unadulterated evil.

The coven continued to sway in a manner befitting a love-in at Woodstock. Now, as the cultists twisted and vibrated in a foul, abominating zeal, they swayed with lust and rage that had shone in their eyes. Their hands rose higher and higher as they swayed from left to right, their faces emulating those of their mistress. Cron and Rommar looked at each other as if brothers, knowing full well that their place in the Order was secure. The others knew that for once in their lives they had belonged to a family tighter than any mundane family could ever have embraced. Now, they embraced Satan's perceived love for them — they embraced their hatred for the Son of the Hebrew God.

☦

As the time had reached the designated hour of 12:13 a.m., Madam Delevingne had noticed that the winds were blowing heavier now and that the night sky was casting an eerie glow over the scenery. The small, sheltered picnic tables that stood only a dozen or so yards away began to take on the shimmering luminescence from the moon's demonic shadow, a glow that created the strangest of images. In her own right, Madam Delevingne knew that this night was not only sacred to her but blessed by her gods. As such, she was prepared to offer *all* for them.

This was a time that would not only cement her coven's love and admiration for her, but also that the mysterious *Bible-thumper* would be paid what was due him. Madam Delevingne would have her revenge, growing more powerful each day that followed. Now, the coven lowered their hands with lust and hatred in their eyes.

"The Hebrew pillars shall fall!" they screamed as loudly as they could. Madam Delevingne offered a sinister grin in response to her coven's zeal and participation.

"*THE MATSTSEBAH OF BAAL SHALL RISE!*" she screamed in return. *MRIODOMI! MRIODOMI! MRIODOMI!*"

"And thou, the sea ... thee Abode!" the cultists returned with joy, "*RUUT-ABRA-IAFF!* Oh, *SATANAS! SATANAS!*"

Madam Delevingne had lowered her hands halfway and then bowed her head.

"Thou the Wheel, thou the Womb that containeth the Father ... *IAFF! IAFF!*" she cried in a low, guttural voice. She had been in some form of perceived prayer, and it had appeared as genuine. Now, thunder echoed in the distance as she continued. "Oh, great Babylon-Bal-Bin- Abraft! Babylon! Thou Woman of Whoredom ... Thou Gate of the Great God of Mirth! And thou, Lady of the Underworld of the Path! ASALL-ONN-AI! Hail, thou, the unstirred! Hail, Sister, and Bride of Woe, of the God that is all and is none, by the Power of Eleven, I beseech thee!"

As Madam Delevingne chimed her odes to the dark prince and to a goddess of her own design, she offered her hands held high above her head, as her head now hung low, as she consummated her odes with reverence and fury. For sure, as Aleister Crowley himself, the patriarch of their craft, had recommended, such a dual regimen of faith in practice was that of magick. And such as it was to its beholder, as well as to the unity of the Microcosm with the Macrocosm at its goal, Madam Delevingne had understood this and had prepared for it. Now, she knew that Satan himself had favoured her quest to destroy her enemy. Now, she smiled down upon her coven, her eyes red and glossy with hate.

As she watched the cultists continue to sway in a perverse sense of servitude, Madam Delevingne had, for a moment, seen a dark man standing behind the picnic shelter. For a second, she thought she saw two yellow points of pale-yellow light, as if there were eyes glaring at her. And the figure was as black as pitch. But when she blinked her eyes and looked again, the dark man was gone.

✠

By 12:23 a.m., the moon was becoming darker and darker, now earning its evil reputation of being called a black moon. Madam Delevingne's eyes couldn't deny what she was viewing. The clouds that had parted and made clear the moon's unholy light only thirty or so minutes earlier had once again chosen to retake the sky's circumference. It seemed as if the entire night was being lit by arrant flashes of lightning in the distance, and the clouds were becoming fuller and denser too, now with only the flashes of the quickly approaching lightning giving shape to them.

In seconds, the wind began to pick up with such strength that Madam Delevingne's robes began fluttering wildly in the wind, almost to the height of her raised arms and hands, exposing her nakedness beneath. She began to tilt, though she held her stance, having to use all her might to do so. The coven also swayed with the wind, even though they were now kneeling on the earthen interior of that ancient swimming pool, swaying back and forth like stiff reeds in a hurricane.

At its centre, the pool had created a small amount of shelter from the winds, creating a kind of suction. It held the cultists close to the earth. Now, it was easy to see that the winds were now taking on a far more active role in the night's ritual. Both Sombra and Pentia had to hold tightly onto the wicked Grizzela, whose tiny frame and weight were obviously being pulled and lunged from the force of nature. Ka'nar and Rommar, both lightweights, had to straddle heavy chunks of concrete boulders to avoid being lifted by the winds. Cron, however, didn't seem to be affected, though as his hood had since been blown back, his prematurely grey hair seemed to be alive, as if the massive man was being electrocuted.

Now, as the lightning began to flash with more and more voracity, Madam Delevingne was no longer able to hold her authoritative stance and quickly realized that the ritual had to be hurried. And so, with her hands still raised above her head, she yelped the final words of the invocation in order to close the ceremony. Now, the deed was soon to be accomplished.

"Bring death to the Christian invader!" she belched with rage. "Bring destruction to he or she that brings disgrace upon us! Destroy! Destroy! Destroy!"

By 12:39 a.m. on the stroke, Madam Delevingne's fanny pack began to vibrate, which she had belted beneath her vestments. She groped for it, despite having a cellphone or any such device on her body being forbidden during any ritual. Nonetheless, she continued to yell to the coven, even above the now rising howl of the winds, as the bay waters crashed behind her.

"Lower your head in respect to the unholy coven!" she commanded, hoping to sway the group from not seeing her cellphone. "*LOWER THY HEADS!*"

In the few moments it took for the coven to obey their mistress's commands, Madam Delevingne quickly looked upon the face of the phone. She squinted to read the words through the beaded rain that obscured the screen—

And it shall come to pass in that day, saith the Lord God, that I will cause the sun to go down at noon, and I will darken the earth in the clear day: And I will turn your feasts into mourning, and all your songs into lamentation...

In what took only a few seconds to read, Madam Delevingne remembered that Bible quote from her early years at the Saint Philomena School for Girls, wincing as she did. And though the passage was a little different from her Catholic Bible, she recalled that passage all the same. She remembered what the nuns did when unruly girls behaved unruly — when they used such a passage to redirect them into fearful submission. Her eyes were bulging to their limit now, exposing to all that the enemy; the unseen Bible-thumper had sent yet another message.

Madam Delevingne, now in a fit of utter rage and hysteria, had pitched her cellphone as far as she could towards the picnic tables ahead of her and then raised her arms as high as she could possibly lift them. As she raised her voice from a loud command to an almost blood- curdling scream of rage, Madam Delevingne's greenish- yellow teeth gnashed together in an erratic way, now with frothy spittle exploding from her gaping mouth as she did. She had continued to belt out odes to Lucifer in one final crescendo of hate—

"*IEOU-PUR-A*! Thou fire! Thou six-fold star initiator compassed about with force and fire!" she screamed at the top of her lungs. "*IOU-PUR-A* ... vide supra! Sun, Lion, and Serpent, hail! All Hail, thou Great Wild Beast!" Though her words were illegible, they were nonetheless words from the very breaths of her soul; breaths to entice that angel of darkness.

"*SO MOTE IT BE*!" the cultists yelled out, "*SO MOTE IT BE*! *SO MOTE IT BE*!" Thunder clapped again and again as Madam Delevingne twisted and turned in a frenzy, and with spittle still flinging from her dripping mouth, commenced with her final invocations—

"I command thee! *ABRASAX*! *ABRASAX*! He who rules the three-hundred and sixty-five regions of the aeon spheres; he who ascends to the unknowable God Vide Supra! Vide Supra!" she screamed at the top of her lungs. She would continue to pant like a laboured beast as she did, staring maddingly and with vicious intent. Her eyes were red, and her mouth filled with those decaying, yellowed teeth, had continued with her odes of hate. "Vide Supra! Vide Supra!"

Now, with the crescendo of thunder and the crashing of the lapping waves upon the shores of the bay, the cultists could hardly be heard. Nonetheless, they too screamed in favour of their mistress. "So Mote It Be, Madam! So Mote It Be!" the cultists continued to scream in unnatural fervour, "So Mote It Be! So Mote It Be! So Mote It Be!"

✠

Within moments, the winds were practically like those of a hurricane, actually beginning to lift Grizzela off the ground. The other coven members stood up now, practically in unison, and held on to each other for support, as Madam Delevingne looked at them with an expression of confusion and rage intermixed with a question. The coven continued to chant along with their mistress and without hesitation.

"Oh, hear the Infernal Names of Abaddon, of Kali, of Sekhmet, and of Dagon! Drink from your chalice," she screamed, her voice now sounding like a frog croaking. "Drink from your chalice! Clockwise! Clockwise! Turn and point thy athame! Thy cane, and thy sword to the four quarters! Call forth the Princes of Hell! Satan from the north! Lucifer from the West! Belial from the south! Leviathan from the east! So Mote it Be! So Mote it Be!"

Now, as the hour was nearing completion, Madam Delevingne hurried to culminate the ritual. "*SABRIAM*! Ho Sangraal! Ho Sangrall! Oh, Babylon! For mine angel pouring himself and herself forth within my Soul! Destroy my enemy! Destroy our enemy, I beseech thee! Oh, Satan, my Lord! Lust of the goat! Lust of *thhh* ... *theeee* ... *AAAAAAAAAARRRRRRRRRRGH*!"

Just as she was about to bring the final incantation to a close, Madam Delevingne found herself being lifted upward, as if the heavy winds were lifting her off the ground. At the same time, she could hear what sounded like some gigantic animal, or a herd of animals, roaring or galloping above her head, and from all around her. Now, there was growling from everywhere, and from every aspect of her hearing. The growling, such as it was, had been as loud as the horn of some massive oceangoing vessel, with its vibration so great, the cultists could feel it under their feet. For the vile Madam Delevingne, she could only look down at her feet as they dangled and kicked.

The coven gasped in disbelief. They too looked around, trying desperately to figure out a reason for their mistress being lifted off the ground.

Though everyone knew the winds couldn't have created such an effect, they knew there must have been a sane answer for the event, so they all looked around frantically in order to find the reason for the vision. And then there were those sounds! Those God-awful sounds!

✠

Madam Delevingne's sandals fell to the earth below, one by one, as her legs flailed in fury. In a second, she was floating six or seven feet off the ground, hovering in place as if being held by some unseen tether. Some of the coven members fell to their knees, while others stood in place, trying desperately to stay steady from the intense winds and the stinging spray from the bay waters as it sprayed against their faces. A second or two after that, the coven turned and began to run for the shelters a dozen or so yards away. That is, all except for Rommar.

Pentia and Sombra, still holding onto Grizzela with all their might, had actually lifted the miserable old woman from under her arms and carried her towards the shelter, while Ka'nar ran ahead of all of them. Still clutching his athame, he looked around for any unknown assailant. He had instantly remembered the strange, Bible-quoting enemy his mistress had so hated and had thought the man, or whoever it was, might have been responsible for the strange events, but no one was there. And with the storm raging as it was, along with the darkness of the hour, he wouldn't have seen anyone anyway. Now, he too bolted for the picnic shelter.

Meanwhile, Pentia stared at her mistress as she ran, tripping over her robes in the process, forcing them to fall to the ground in an almost comedic fashion. Cron, being the heaviest among them, hobbled as best he could. But instead of running for safety under the shelter, he headed for the adjacent wooded area, where several thick oak trees had swayed the least. Rommar, however, had remained near Madam Delevingne, or more appropriately, beneath her.

Now, the majority of the coven had interlocked with each other; embraced each other in a haphazard manner, huddling together like a clump of black and brown scraps of cloth, like so many dirty rags intermixed with the terrified faces and bulging, pleading eyes beneath their now visually animated hoods. Fear had taken the place of pride, and terror in place of hate. Some of them were now clenching as tightly as they could to the wooden picnic tables, while others gripped the heavy stone arches of the shelter, all of which had been bolted to a sturdy cement foundation with precision, riveted by huge iron bolts.

The coven members, Sombra, Pentia, and Ka'nar, were embraced together, their eyes as wide as the hubcaps of an old Buick. Sombra, her facial expression now looking like Munch's famous painting *The Scream,* was now pointing to the sky above where Madam Delevingne had hung in an otherworldly haze of swirling mist, water, and the whirling sand and debris from the ruins below. Sombra couldn't scream or make any sound at all — none of them could, though grunts and gasps were faintly heard, even though an ungodly loud, almost locomotive-like thunder had filled the air.

When everyone gazed at the image, looking above Madam Delevingne's head, at least fifteen feet above her, everyone saw what Sombra had been trying to scream at. Now, about ten feet above Madam Delevingne hovered two light-red or orange-coloured orbs that seemed to oddly pulsate. And the coven watched through the haze and mist of the maddening storm as those orbs, those basketball- sized balls of iridescent light, seemed to radiate with a rage all their own.

The two glowing orbs seemed to be getting darker and darker, like that of a radiant orange that had begun to turn, like that of oranges that had gone bad, only now with a strange luminescence of the blazing sun. Everyone had realized that the otherworldly luminescence had looked oddly familiar to them. They looked like eyes.

Grizzela, now crying like a spoiled child, her miserable and vile demeanour now long-departed, had now sported the facial expression of a condemned prisoner being led to execution. They had all succumbed to a fear that they had once considered only for others; only for the weak, and those they hated. This day, the mighty cultists of the Order of Magnus Datha would know what fear was, even if it would only last a few moments more. Regardless, each of them had known their fate, even when they could not find escape — they knew, all of them, that death was very, very close.

✠

Cron continued to lie flat on his massive belly while he clung to the thick trunk of a huge oak tree. Now, he spouted the chants more like a Christian than a Satanist. He blubbered like a little child; the tears flowing almost as much as the pelting and stinging rains that had now covered the entire view of the bay like a grey mass of deadly clouds. He was terrified beyond comprehension. Now, at that moment, he was truly sorry for his sins.

Madam Delevingne, still suspended in mid-air, had now appeared like a vision of the ancient texts she had thought herself an expert in. And it didn't take long for her to finally realize her fate. Like a woodcut from a fifteenth-century manuscript of magic, she hovered seven to ten feet above the dirt-ridden circumference of the old swimming pool, with Rommar still beneath her, his hands outstretched as if a father trying to save his child from drowning. He was yelling to her, but the tremendous crashing and swooshing sounds that encompassed the area were so loud that his voice and the voices from the terrified cultists would not have been heard that night.

"Madam … Madam Delevingne! Take my hand!" Rommar screamed!

Madam Delevingne had heard the voice of her newly acquired paramour, her newly acquired slave, calling out to her. But she couldn't speak — she couldn't even utter a word. She just floated with her arms straddled to her sides, her face turned to him with the unmistakable appearance of intense pain and terror. She outstretched her hand to him, but he couldn't reach her. At that very moment, Rommar held out his hands for her to take. Then, an almost ear-shattering screech blared from the sky above them, as if all the angels in heaven had shouted all at once; as if every wild animal on the earth had all roared at the same time.

Madam Delevingne's face; her typical expression of rage and hatred had dissipated into that of a child who was lost in the crowd of a busy city. Fear was her god now, her arrogance replaced by an unspoken regret. Now, as Madam Delevingne began to reach down to Rommar, and just as he was about to grasp onto her hand, and into the safety of his loving embrace, the man was lifted up in a second's notice and was whipped from the ground and out of her sight. He was flung out to the bay waters with one tremendous swoosh. Rommar was gone.

✠

Despite the intensity of their obsequious respect for their mistress, for Madam Tarja Delevingne, the once feared cultists of the Order of Magnus Datha had chosen to stay where they were, in the perceived safety and reassurance of the sturdy steel and wood shelter. Instead of helping her, they cried out for their mistress to come down, as if she were somehow controlling the act of levitation. And that was as far as they would go for their beloved mistress, and as much as they would offer her. Instead of sacrifice, they had chosen betrayal.

"Jesus! My Jesus ... Forgives me? Pleassee, I begs of youz ... Jesus! My Jesus!" Cron begged as loud as he could, forgoing his training as a student of the occult, and his *forever* servitude to the dark lord. "Jesus! Jesus! I rezz...I rez-nounces the Satan and all hiz workz! I swears of thee, Faddah ... I promises ... I swears I ... I serves you, my Faddah for herez-on-innns!"

The Fat Man, still lying on the ground, his head buried in the wet grass and mud, lifted his gaze to stare upon the supernatural visage that had once been his mistress. He just watched with his mouth agape, his eyes wide and unblinking, despite the stinging rain. Madam Delevingne was now suspended in mid-air like a ragdoll in a hurricane. Now, the other coven members shouted as they embraced each other, whimpering like frightened dogs being led to euthanasia. And though their fear had rarely been observed by the average, mundane human on any average, mundane day, their fear was omnipotent this early morning.

Thunder boomed again, and again as the coven members cried with regret. They cried for calling on something they now knew they shouldn't have called upon, knowing full well that demons and devils were real after all. Now, they could only watch as Madam Delevingne, their mistress and leader of one of the most public covens in the

United States, began to rise higher and higher into the air, as if by some great, unseen hand. They watched as her arms and legs were splayed outward, with only her face staring down at them.

It had been made clear, the coven; Madam Delevingne's prized and beloved cultists could only watch in horror as their leader cried for help, and as she begged for mercy, as she prayed to her infernal gods.

While under the shelter, Sombra, Pentia, Ka'nar, and Grizzela just watched as Madam Delevingne begged and whimpered with arms reaching to them for rescue. And though the mist of the raging storm had impaired their vision, for the most part, they would still be able to watch their mistress die.

In what would only later be recounted by Cron, who still gibbered and begged for the forgiveness of God, he, too, would witness the obliteration of Madam Delevingne and the self-believing image of a mighty cult; the cult of Magnus Datha. Now in a state of surrealistic shock, his eyes stared without blinking as Madam Delevingne was slowly being dismembered. First, her vestments; the black robes and cowl were ripped off her by some unseen force; the belt of her hidden fanny pack being snapped, all as if made of tissue paper, with her yellowish-ochre sash wafting to the ground like an insane butterfly fluttering out of control in a storm. The vision was simply insane.

As the tempest blew with a crazed whir of rain and debris, which twisted in a crescendo of tornado-like beauty, Cron had thought he saw a dark image; an image or an outline like that of a large man standing behind the old pool, behind and below Madam Delevingne. At first, he thought it might have been Lester, but the image didn't even slightly waver in the storm, and it was unlike anything he had ever seen before. The image was as black as tarpaper, and it was unmoving, despite the intense winds. For an instant, he thought he saw two glowing pin-pricks of light, like a tiny set of eyes, where eyes would have rested in the black shape of what had to be a face. They were as bright and as yellow as the midday sun.

As soon as Cron witnessed the weird visage, the uncertain apparition quickly faded from sight. And just as the image had faded away in the stinging mist, Cron looked upward to witness Madam Delevingne's arms and legs being slowly pulled away and out from her body, as if some gigantic, invisible playground bully were pulling the legs off a frog. The screams that the vile woman had uttered were like no screams Cron had ever heard before. The deep, guttural shrieks of someone being bitten in half by a massive shark, or as if being eaten alive by a pride of starving tigers, the shrills of pain and horror were beyond comprehension.

Cron watched the phantasma of gore from his supposed safe spot beneath the cops of trees. He could only hold his breath in shocked terror. He couldn't even move, the mass of his body feeling as if something had been holding him down, as if something as heavy as a small car had been placed on his back. He didn't fight the feeling, instead holding onto clumps of weeds as support. He was incapacitated. He could only watch helplessly as it dawned on him that Madam Delevingne had looked as if her arms and legs were overcooked chicken, as her legs were being slowly pulled out. It appeared as if she were dying in slow motion.

✠

Another ear-shattering crash of thunder boomed overhead, just as the coven watched the flesh of Madam Delevingne's arms being pulled apart in segments, with pieces of reddish-yellow flesh falling to the ground; as clumps of fat and tissue splashed as it hit the murky, rain-filled pool below. And as her bodily tissues fell to the earth, Madam Delevingne's bowels had opened as her body relaxed; as she fainted from what could only have been tremendous pain. Then, she released a steady torrent of urine, followed by loose faeces being ushered out of her like mud from an overfilled storm drain. Then, her body went limp. A second after this, she opened her eyes and screamed a gurgling, blood-soaked shriek of death that no witness would ever forget.

"*SATAAA! MASTSSS … Ma …* masster!" she cried as a thick, saliva and blood-like substance bubbled from her mouth; her eyes rolling to the back of her head, her limbs, what was left of them, falling one by one to the muddy, sludge-filled swimming pool below her. The image was surreal as those torn appendages landed in the sludge with a splash and a thud. "*SSSSAAAATTTHHH-h-ah … aataa … Nnnn … Aahhh, oh, I, I*—"

Those being her last, human-like utterances, Madam Delevingne's back had arched forward, and then back again, along with a sharp, snapping sound that was loud enough to be heard by the coven members as they watched in horror. Now, the coven's eyes were affixed on the supernatural opera of gore, but they were, all of them, silent.

Madam Delevingne's stomach region began to appear as if it were being pulled outward to give the impression of instantly becoming pregnant; the skin being stretched and stretched outward until it was obvious that it had ruptured. This was evident by a small, dark-red blast of spray shooting out from her midsection. A second after this, her stomach returned to a relatively similar size as before. And just as this occurred, Madam Delevingne let out a screech-like scream, with her head lunging forward as if inspecting her stomach and then falling to her chest, and then to its side, and then back again.

At this point, and now in shock, Madam Delevingne just lingered in some ether of semi-conscious alertness. Her back still arched outward, and with her stomach appearing to be separating before the coven's eyes as if being vivisected by unseen fingers, the coven could only watch in horror as their mistress died slowly, and most painfully. They watched as the skin was slowly being ripped to the sides of her body, taking on the appearance of the skin from a grape being gently pulled from its flesh. The image was simply horrible, yet mesmerizing to watch.

Now, the cultists watched as their mistress's intestines began to slowly unravel, like a pumpkin's innards being scooped out by some invisible spoon; with so much gloppy, red, and pink-coloured entrails, they were ushered out, and to the ground below. Some of the entrails waved in the wind, dangling, swaying from their unearthly, aerial suspension. The limbless body, its head now dangling to one side and oozing a dark-red, almost blackish-coloured, stringy goo, had finally gone limp. The deed was done.

As Madam Delevingne's head hung listlessly toward the ground, now swaying in a semi-circle manner, blackish-red saliva dribbled from her nose and mouth. For a moment or two, she appeared to still retain life, but this had to have been the result of the torrential winds. And though a brief sound of something like escaping air had again authenticated the chance of life, this too was incorrect, having been nothing more than the swooshing of the trees.

Now, silently, the witch, the grand witch of Magnus Datha, was dead.

✠

Cron continued to watch the horror from his safe location under the sturdy oak trees. Now, instead of arrogance and hatred, the unfortunate composite of the once intimidating Madam Delevingne, he continued to pray and beg for forgiveness. He watched as the once mighty mistress was pulled apart like a fetal pig in a high school biology class; her intestines, appearing to be unravelling, had been tossed to the ground with audible plopping sounds. It gave a visual impression that Madam Delevingne was being held by some thin and curvy hose, like one of those collapsible garden hoses that stretch out when water flows through them. The image was utterly phantasmagoric.

Within a minute or two after that, Madam Delevingne's lifeless body lifted up again, another twelve or so feet higher. It looked as if it were being inspected by that unseen force. The reddish-orange orbs, those basketball-sized, luminescent eyes that had so terrified the coven, were indeed inspecting what was left of the grand witch of Magnus Datha. Her body, turning to one side, and then to the other, with only half of one leg remaining, had wagged listlessly as the body turned. The open gashes where the other limbs had once occupied had now proclaimed to the remaining witnesses that such was the reward for Satan's service.

Now, only what looked like a yellowish-white femur jutted outward as if having been snapped like a chicken bone during a feast. It oozed something that looked like thick syrup, a bloody syrup that had frozen into a semi-hard shaft before it could reach the ground below. Cron, still hidden between those sturdy oak trees, just watched in horror as that rigid strand of coagulated blood and gore swayed in a semicircle, and then in the opposite direction, like a grisly pendulum predicting a doomed future. A second or two after this, the remains of the once mighty Satanist, the grand High Priestess of Magnus Datha, fell into the bloody sludge below with a dull thud and a splash.

Madam Delevingne's coven watched as the glowing orbs had simply faded into nothingness. They continued to huddle under the heavy wood and steel roof of the shelter, now praising Satan once again. They begged the dark lord to spare them, begging Lucifer to forgive them for their lack of faith. They huddled and chanted, praising the Sultan Demon for his perceived greatness and kindness. Cron, however, continued to cower and beg, choosing to remain secure in the thickets, under the great oak trees. He continued to beg for the forgiveness of God, the Hebrew God, the Christian God that Madam Delevingne had so despised.

In the time it took for Cron to achieve this realization, the storm, its winds, its sheer force of power had risen to such a crescendo that the air had become a torrent of stinging droplets that felt more like a thousand needles hitting him. It was as if a thousand hypodermic needles were now piercing his flesh all at once. Regardless, Cron had shut his eyes and continued to pray to God for forgiveness and salvation. He begged for mercy.

"LUCIFER! LUCIFER!" the cultists screamed in unison, their voices echoing in a fearful stress, was in fact one last effort of obscenity to appease the fallen one. The remaining coven members had commenced their chants in hopes that Satan would deliver them.

"LUCIFER! Oh, Dark Lord, save us! BEELZEBUB! Master of the Air and Light, protect us! BELIAL, oh Great Demon of the sea, deliver us … oh, mighty BAAL save us!"

They chanted and prayed. They begged and raged with hatred on a person none of them had ever known. Such didn't matter, whoever it was, he or she was the enemy of their mistress after all; an enemy of the great Madam

Tarja Delevingne. Their fear now replaced by rage once more, they believed that with a renewed faith in their false god, they would be spared; that they would be victorious.

As the cultists continued to chant and beg, the storm began to rise, rising much higher in voracity than only moments before. Now, with its howling winds screaming to the point of shaking the now tree-bent woodlands around them, Cron could only continue to pray and beg. The winds were so strong that clumps of foliage had even lifted out of the ground, only to be tossed into the whirling, debris-filled air like so much dust. This had enticed the coven's chants to grow louder and louder. And as the earth seemed to shake as they cried to their unseen master, Cron just prayed to God as he lay there, shimmering, shaking with regret for his many sins. For the first time in his life, and with reverence and obedience, Cron had given himself to the Father, the Son, and the Holy Spirit.

In a moment of clarity, the man who called himself Cron had now abandoned the false moniker and begged that God would spare him, that *He* would spare Hercules Reginald Benet for his transgressions and wrongful inequities. He believed that God would forgive all who obeyed *His* commands, and that forgiveness was assured, so long as all believed that Christ Jesus was and *is* the Son of God. Hercules Reginald Benet was, at that moment, reborn in the faith. In a second, and despite the raging storm around him, he felt a tremendous weight being lifted from his body. Herc Benet's fear had also lifted, instead, embracing a sense of belated joy, despite the horrors he had witnessed that early morning.

As he revelled in his newly found joy, Herc began to hear what sounded like wood being crushed as if a bulldozer was trampling over a house. As he turned to look at the picnic shelter, he watched as its roof began to lift, and then slowly began to be ripped off the heavy wood pylon beams, leaving twisted metal brackets and splintered shards of wood where the roof had once rested. The roof, still intact, minus a few shingles having been blown off by the mighty winds, had continued to lift up at least forty to fifty feet high. At first, Herc had thought that the roof had been caught in a tornado, but then he soon realized that the entire rooftop was even and still, regardless of the powerful winds. The sight didn't make sense.

Now, as that roof just continued to hover in midair all by itself, what sounded very much like an extremely loud fog horn, or perhaps the horn from some massive ocean liner, had begun to sound. And a second or two after this, there was a tremendous screech. This was followed by the roof being lifted up another five feet or so, only to come smashing down on the now-open shelter, crashing into, and crushing everything into an explosion of wood shards and splinters. The force had blasted the wreckage in all directions, with the sound so deafening that neighbourhoods a mile away had heard the commotion.

The force from the rooftop's descent had created an air mass so great that it had blown Herc Benet into a roll that had sent him at least ten feet away from his oak- shrouded sanctuary. His mass of blubber shifting on the ground as he tumbled had created an amazingly similar, though quick-paced image of a flesh-coloured blob, like the titular monster from the 1950s film of the same name. The image contained equal measures of levity and horror at the same time.

Herc was a naked mass of shivering flesh now, all that emanated the sounds of whimpering and tearful outbursts as he looked away from the decimated structure. His body shook, and understandably so. Now, he just watched as the storm lifted in less than a minute; the winds dying down to a standstill, with the stinging rain having been reduced to a few errant droplets that plinked into the pooled water below.

All was quiet now. And all but Hercules Reginald Benet, were dead.

✠

Herc Benet continued to lie in the mud and leaves, now observing the once hearty wood shelter, a shelter that had been reduced to a flattened heap of wood debris and human waste. The mass of wood shards now stood no more than two feet off the ground, two feet from the concrete foundation that once supported it. No sound came from the debris, but a shallow pool of murky water had formed a gruesome tributary around the foundation. The water was red.

As Herc slowly got himself onto his knees and then pushed himself upward and onto his feet, the massive man just stood in a daze. He wobbled from left to right, as if intoxicated. And though he didn't move from that spot, he inspected the mass of debris where the hefty shelter had once stood, hoping to find life there, but he didn't. Herc Benet knew that no one other than himself had survived the storm. He had been the only one to survive God's wrath.

As he stood in place, Herc began to hear what sounded like muffled music, but he remembered that he didn't have his cellphone with him, having left it in his minivan earlier that night. He looked around, and in the bushes until he finally spotted a dim light glowing from the gravel trail ahead of him. The faint glow was coming from Madam Delevingne's cellphone, exactly where she had thrown it during the ritual when the woman's enemy had sent his last message to her. Now, Herc slowly ambled to where the light was coming from and listened as he recalled a familiar tune echoing from the now waterlogged cellphone.

When he picked it up, he just listened to the tune as it continued to play. And then, silently, he began to read the final message on the screen—

"For her sins have reached unto heaven, and God hath remembered her iniquities. Reward her even as she had rewarded you, and double unto her double according to her works: in the cup which she hath filled fill to her double…"
— Book of Revelations, XVIII: V-VI

✠

Now dazed, naked, and shaken, Herk Benet held Madam Delevingne's water-soaked cellphone, having read the passage in its entirety, but he continued to listen and ponder as the music played on. It was indeed a familiar tune to him, though it was an older tune. Herc remembered it being popular in the 1980s. It was a tune that described regret in one's life; regret of one's sins. And as he listened, barely making out the words, the tune had come back to him.

The singer had expressed that he was looking back on his life with a sense of shame and that he was always the one to blame. And as the antiquated tune hissed and crackled, the voice seemed to warp to a seemingly dying gasp of breath—

It's ah, it's ah, it's ah … it's ahh sssssiiiiiiiinnnnnn.

Now, as the music eerily crackled as it echoed from the cellphone, with the backlight glowing in spurts, going in and out of view like a live wire spurting sparks, Herc continued to stand in place as he just watched the phone shimmy in its ghostly hue. He tried desperately to regain his bearing on what had just taken place, though he was unable to find such a bearing, or even recall what he had always conceived as sanity. Now, he wasn't even sure of his sanity. How could he?

Herc Benet, now shaking and trembling, had finally come to the conclusion that he had wasted his life. He had come to the realization that his arrogance, as unfounded as it was, had left him empty and naked, but that God, being the only true light in the universe, had forgiven him all the same. And within the very second that he had come to that conclusion, another message popped up on the cellphone's screen. Herc read it, and then quickly dropped the phone into a puddle of muddy water. He ran away and through the woods, running as fast as his obese and naked body would allow him to run. He ran away screaming, crying, and begging for forgiveness.

Now, a long drumroll of ominous thunder rumbled across the sky. On the water-soaked ground, the cellphone lay in the water; its face glowing with one final message—

"And, behold, the veil of the temple was rent in two from the top to the bottom; and the earth did quake, and the rocks rent..."

— *Matthew XXVII: LI*

PART III
CHAPTER FOURTEEN

**FBI Field Office, Jacksonville, Florida,
Conference Room #5**

Monday, July 6th, 9:15 A.M.

Assistant Director Margaret Fanning and Assistant Special Agent in Charge Scott Howington sat tense that early morning. Now, the large monitor glowed ominously in the conference room as a light rain fell across Northern Florida. The morning had been dark due to the black clouds that raced across Jacksonville's skies, promising for a wet day, but it would be far more than inclement weather that threatened the days ahead.

The man on the monitor, a distinguished-looking gentleman in his fifties, sat perfectly still behind a large, mahogany desk. He offered the appearance of a man who had seen more than he had wanted to, exhibiting a singular ruggedness that seemed to quench an otherwise privileged upbringing with an education in posh universities or who had hobnobbed with stately politicians or society's elite. The man may have appeared brutish, but that couldn't be further from the truth.

Noah Elijah Mateo, the Executive Assistant Director for National Security, was the go-between for the Director of the Federal Bureau of Investigation and every branch in its hierarchy. Noah Mateo, a former Marine with the Special Operations Forces for close to twenty years, was also a seasoned cop with the Baltimore Police Department's Special Weapons and Tactics Division. Mateo is no-nonsense and direct in everything he does, but the purpose of the day's transmission had irked him. It was a case that made no sense at all, and the Bureau wanted answers. Today, he was on a mission.

✠

Since the early days of 1994 to the present, a series of highly bizarre homicides or otherwise odd deaths have plagued the FBI and other law enforcement agencies to the point that two separate task forces having been assigned to investigate the deaths. And though this occurred close to a decade before Noah Mateo even joined the Bureau, he has since been put in charge of a now larger-than-normal case file known simply as: 'Conundrum Folly.'

Today, Noah Mateo and the Chief Directorate of Intelligence, Ellen Horwitz, faced the Assistant Director of the North Florida Field Office and her second in command. The reason for that morning's meeting was strange and complicated, though both A.D. Fanning and A.S.A.C. Howington had been aware of the homicides and the almost non-ending list of events that had followed the Conundrum Folly casefile. What they didn't know before this day, however, was that the Bureau's most recent person of interest had lived in their state. In fact, the man lived less than thirty miles from Jacksonville.

Instead of an elaborate group of assassins attached to some organized crime syndicate, or a terrorist cell operating in the Sunshine State, the alleged culprit was a lonely, middle-aged man, a security guard who walked a silent beat in a forlorn and dying shopping mall just northwest of Jacksonville. The man wasn't ex-military, nor was he on any watchlist outside of the Bureau's inner offices, where, as of late, he has been of singular interest to every agency in the United States and abroad. The man wasn't considered a clear or present danger, yet at the same time, everyone with a title and a rank wanted to know who the man was. Everyone had to know.

✠

Static fizzed across the monitor of the dark, fifth-floor conference room, just as the Directorate of Intelligence, Ellen Horwitz, sat down next to the Executive Assistant Director. They had both exhibited expressions of urgency, and perhaps worry too, though A.D. Fanning had been accustomed to such facial cues by her colleagues and superiors. This was simply a fact of life for the FBI today; a fact that hadn't improved since the domestic terror attacks of 2024, a day that shook the nation, a day that shook the world.

"Good morning, Margaret," the rough-looking man said. This was followed by a half-hearted attempt at a smile. Mrs. Horwitz, however, offered no expression, save that of a persecuting stare that probably terrified her children.

"Good morning, Noah. I trust we have an issue before us," A.D. Fanning asked politely.

"I suppose you could say that, Margaret, though I doubt you're completely unaware of the situation outside of it being in your 'limbo files.'

"I see. And which one are you referring to, Noah?"

"That would be case file number zero-six, thirty sixty-four-dash-P.A.B. It should be in the grey section of your back files by now."

"I'll get right on it," A.D. Fanning said. This was followed by offering A.S.A.C. Howington a stressed glance, a now fully understandable look that instantly had her second-in-command begin jotting something down on his legal pad.

"Margaret, once you get to it, I want you to keep in mind that the first official investigation into our P.O.I. wasn't handled by Bureau standards, and wasn't nipped in the bud, or otherwise dealt with by your predecessor. As such, the gentleman of our inquiry was mistreated. Certainly, the first investigation had gone south very quickly. And though our P.O.I. was not officially implicated, more paranoid minds had considered him the root cause all the same."

"I understand," A.D. Fanning returned. "What happened, Noah ... and why is this person of intense interest now?"

"Long story short, Margaret, and you'll get the gist of this as soon as you read the docs, but our person of interest was, shall we say, mistreated. Scratch that ... he was treated less than properly by two of our former agents."

"I … I don't understand, what agents, Noah? My agents?"

"No, no, Margaret, this is just about two years prior."

"Who are they?" A.D. Fanning asked with a furrowed expression.

"Stand by," the Executive Assistant Director said, just as he whispered something into Mrs. Horwitz's ear. "I'm having something sent to your office email. You should get it in a few seconds." Now, in the time it took for A.D. Fanning to bring up her inner office email server on her laptop, the email from the Washington office had popped up on her screen. She could plainly see that there was a large PDF and a Word document file, along with twenty-three photo attachments to the email. She opened it and downloaded each attached photograph.

"Come through alright?" Noah Mateo asked. His expression was as deadpan as a corpse.

"Jesus, Noah … what the hell did this?"

"What you're looking at are the remains of those two agents. These were posted to the Jacksonville office about a year before you took command, Margaret, but be advised … this is officer's only information. Please don't share these with any of your agents, except for Mister Howington here, or your S—A—C, of course."

"Right, right. Ah … Mister Howington is acting Special Agent in Charge at the moment, Noah, so you can share whatever you need to with him."

The Executive Assistant Director nodded in confirmation. "I understand," he said flatly. "Take your time with these. I'll explain as best I can, Margaret, but I can only assure you, none of it will make any sense."

Now, A.D. Fanning found herself in a silent state of existential shock. Each of the twelve photographs showed the impossible. The first eight had exhibited what had looked like a massacre, where the person or persons, or an animal for that matter, had been squashed into a reddish-black paste. Even the bones, if they were, indeed, bones, had been pressed so deeply into the wood floor that the dark marrow of the bone had become paper-thin. The only thing that would separate a human from an animal was the blood-soaked clothing that had become a part of the floor itself. The image was simply impossible.

The remaining four photographs showed a man around the age of fifty or older. He was as thin as a scarecrow, with hollowed, sunken eyes and stubble covering his face, as if a forgotten man. The name below each photo read: J. Everson, FBI. Walter Reed Psychiatric.

A.D. Fanning had remembered reading the name when she took control as assistant director of the Florida field office. And it only took a second to remember reading the disciplinary notations on the man. She remembered thinking, *Oh, thank God he transferred to another field office.*

Now, she realized that any information regarding an inner-office transfer of both agents had been a falsehood. Why, however, had yet to be answered.

"Margaret? Are you okay?" Executive Assistant Director Mateo asked?

"Yes, yes, of course, Noah," she returned sullenly. "These are our agents? How ... how is it we haven't been apprised of this?" She asked. This time, her expression was less than understanding.

"Margaret, the director felt that under the circumstances, the events that took place before your command of the North Florida office weren't vital," he stated flatly. "However," he continued, "he thinks that the P.O.I. is much more than he seems at the present moment. Now ... be advised. Our person of interest, a Mister Patrick Allen Bush, had been lighting up the scoreboard, if you take my meaning."

"I think so," A.D. Fanning said. "The man is implicated, so something ... something like the death of one of our agents, and ... and that he may have had something to do with this, Mister J. Everson. Is that about right?"

"You hit it on the head, Margaret." Mister John Everson was a hard case; a man with a very bad attitude that could alienate the pope at communion. In short ... the man was a straight-up asshole of the worst order, if you take my meaning."

"I see," A.D. Fanning returned with a slight grin. "That's why we kept him on the payroll, I suppose."

The Executive Assistant Director smiled and then chuckled ever so lightly. "I get your point, Margaret, but as you remember, the madness of twenty-twenty-four, and the all-hands-on-deck events that followed had us missing many details, and in need of agents, despite any reprimanding that might have been missed. That said, what you see before you, and all of what you'll be reading in the coming days, are all attached to this one man. Seriously!" He said this with a dying smile that just as quickly turned into a humorless expression. "No joking, Margaret," he continued. "This Patrick Bush is something else, and he needs our full attention. But there's more to this. Much more."

"I don't understand, Noah, what else do I need to know?"

"Well, for one thing, this guy, whoever he really is, has just exploded in every arena, from the military to the top echelons of power. Now … this Bush character travels, and has been listed as a frequent guest to some pretty big names and titles in China and Russia, and throughout Europe. He's been investigated by M—I—Six and others throughout Europe, only to come back clean."

"So … so that's good!" A.D. Fanning said.

"On paper, yes, I suppose that would be considered a good thing, but the inquiries have been continuing since ninety-four, and they're always loaded with more questions. The man is just too close to our enemies, Margaret, so much so that the CIA has been involved. Director Warren and the others feel that the man needs another look-see, from a federal point of view. That said, I'd like your best agents to take that look and offer the very best surveillance available. Bush will be notified, naturally, but not until we gather a little info from our friends at the Agency. And this comes from the top."

"I understand, Noah," A.D. Fanning returned, now with an expression to match a marble bust of Ludwig Von Beethoven. "But I'm curious … why am I only now getting this information?" she continued. "These files you sent me, the first set, anyway, are dated eight, twenty-three, two-thousand and twelve, with the rest following up to twenty-twenty-one. I don't understand this. Just seems I would have seen this in our active logs."

"Well, normally you would have. It's just that it's been kept on the low, which is also the director's choice. This Bush character is like the name on the file … he's a conundrum."

"What exactly is he being implicated in, Noah? I read here that he's connected by way of direct interaction with said victims, but that he's never been discovered anywhere near any of the crime scenes, either before, at the time of the deaths, or afterward. It reads that his alibis are airtight."

"Correct, Margaret, but the majority of these victims have received minor threats from Bush each and every time. I say minor because said threats are always Biblical in nature, meaning that he warns them that something bad will follow should they not obey the Lord's commandments. Yes, they're minor threats, but threats all the same."

"I see," A.D. Fanning said softly.

"Margaret, think of Islam, and their attacks on the U.S. over the years. There's a reason for this, and it's not always because we have interests in the Middle East or their territories. We, as a nation, and indeed, all of Western society, simply do not mesh with theirs. Plus, the fact that we have had more positive dealings with Israel and the Jews in general, as compared to Islam, only compounds the situation. And what do they do? They threaten us for our evil ways. So, much like our Mister Bush, he nonetheless poses as a viable threat. And it is this reason the Bureau is obligated, primarily so due to the fact that he's a citizen of the United States."

"Of course, I get that, Noah. And I trust because he's involved with outside personalities, whether good or bad actors, the CIA has an interest?"

"Partially, yes. But I don't doubt for a second that it's all that straightforward. I'm sure they have other, undisclosed reasons for their interest. But, if you scroll down to page seventy-eight on your PDF, I think you'll see some of our issues. Let me know what you think of that, Margaret?"

Now, A.D. Fanning scrolled down to page 78 and quickly read it. "Good, God!" she exclaimed. "He's got a net worth of close to forty-eight million? But it says he's a security guard at a shopping mall, up in … up in Garver Town. This doesn't gel, Noah."

"That's just the beginning of the strangeness, Margaret. He's much more interesting. Take your time and read over everything, and get back with me when you're finished. Director Warren has set up a meeting scheduled for this week or the next, just not sure of the exact date yet. Now, they'll be several guests from our military present there, as well as a representative with military intelligence from the U.K. He's an expert in physics."

"Physics?" Margaret asked in understandable confusion. "I don't get it, Noah, why physics?" The question seemed appropriate, though for the Chief Directorate of Intelligence, the question had been pertinent all the same.

"Because outside agencies, primarily ours, have determined that Mister Bush has been closely involved with aspects of advanced physics that are deemed dangerous," Mrs. Horwitz said forcefully. "And because he's playing footsie with some of China's and Russia's top scientists, we need to make sure he's not working on something quite deadly here, on U.S. soil," she concluded.

"Yes, that said, I'm sure you can spot the importance here, beyond the orchestration of over a hundred and twelve possible connections to highly bizarre deaths across the U.S. alone," the Executive Assistant Director added. "And that had been in three years. Anyway, we need to make sure Mister Bush is simply a harmless religious nut, and not the dangerous kind. Yes, it's possible he's just that, a harmless zealot, and nothing more. But … but if you'll take a quick look at the copy of the CIA's findings from two thousand and eight, which is … I think on page eighteen … yes, pages eighteen to twenty-three, you'll see what we're talking about."

A.D. Fanning quickly opened that Word document and scrolled down to that page. Then, she turned her laptop so A.S.A.C. Howington could see.

"Cult activity," she read aloud. "Society of Rood? I never heard of it," she said.

"Neither have I. Do they have ties here in the U.S., sir?" A.S.A.C. Howington asked the Executive Assistant Director.

"We haven't determined that as of yet, Mister Howington, but it seems plausible at this point. This will be one of your missions in the coming days. Now, if you'll enable your share-screen, I have some things to apprise you both on; things that you'll be covering at the meeting. Keep in mind, Margaret, what we're about to show you concerns details of two separate, recent incidents that took place in a neighboring city of Chicago, and the other in Baytown, Texas, near Houston. Those field offices are on it, respectfully, but because our person of interest is in your neck of the woods, you have the lead in this, and this is also from the top."

"You have my complete attention, Noah," A.D. Fanning said, just as she exchanged a glance with A.S.A.C. Howington.

"Good, Margaret, that's very good. I can't imagine anyone better to oversee this thing and to take it to the right place. Just understand that what we're about to show you constitutes the very word, insanity. What you're about to see is simply the latest collection of similar events that number in the thousands, worldwide."

"Thousands?!" A.D. Fanning exclaimed. Her shock was understandable, though she couldn't understand why such events had been kept secret. What would follow would take the concept of madness and impossibility to a whole new level. For the FBI, they were about to venture into the realms of both madness and impossibility at face value.

✠

By the time it took for Executive Assistant Director Mateo to transmit the collection of crime scene and coroner photographs to the Jacksonville field office, the storm that had been brewing over the Sunshine State had become a full-fledged thunderstorm of epic proportions. And though the lights did flicker several times, the already dark atmosphere in conference room number five became darker, save that of the redness of the gore that had now overtaken the monitor.

Now, the 65-inch VIZIO monitor glowed with the carnage of two souls that had barely made news headlines, or which had scrolled across the FBI's inner-office database. The deaths had been a secret — but why?

"Take a look at Batch Number eleven-forty-twelve, Mrs. Fanning," the Chief Directorate of Intelligence said. "These are the remains of a Mister Nathan Nicholas Prud, a former professor with Nimbus University near Chicago. And as you see, he had been man-handled by something that could *not* have been done by a man, wouldn't you agree?"

A.D. Fanning just stared at the images and then advanced to the next photo. "This is incredible," she mumbled, now astonished by what she was witnessing. A.S.A.C. Howington said nothing, but his expression foretold a silent repulsion that couldn't be denied. "Um, minus the ... the ah ... the gaping gash in the victim's chest, it looks as if the man may have fallen from a relatively high location, possibly could have rolled over uneven terrain as well. Is it ... is it possible—"

"This did not occur from any great height, Mrs. Fanning," Mrs. Horwitz interrupted. "This occurred within the confines of a small nature preserve, in a county about sixty miles from Chicago. And he was discovered by a county worker at the park, having witnessed the man enter the park, and apparently had become like this in less than an hour's time. He was discovered off a wooded path between a thicket of rather large trees and the marshlands. He wasn't dropped by any aircraft, as our preliminaries have already confirmed, nor was the body relocated from another location. This appears to be the Dekalb County medical examiner's opinion as well, though that is the extent of such an opinion. He still hasn't concluded a cause on the record; no logical cause, leaving the case open in his jurisdiction. What you see here, all forty-three photographs, constitutes the mystery at hand. But this guy isn't alone."

Now, Executive Assistant Director Mateo leaned in to the monitor, offering a grimace that had convinced both A.D. Fanning and A.S.A.C. Howington that the mystery, as Mrs. Horwitz had put it, was about to become far more involved.

"The next one is a bit worse," the man said flatly. This was followed by a photo of Juliana Addams, the self-styled witch and devil worshiper from Baytown, Texas. Now, the Assistant Director and her second-in-command could only stare at the carnage. They couldn't even respond to the gore that appeared on the monitor.

"What ... what in the name of God could have done this, Noah?" the typically stalwart woman asked.

"And that, Margaret, is the million-dollar question," the man stated emphatically. A moment or two later, the monitor advanced to yet another series of photographs, this time, taken by Special Agent Keith Straub, a medical examiner out of Quantico, Virginia, and from another medical examiner from the Houston Coroner's Office, a doctor named Tumin.

"This is obviously not a death by misadventure, is it?" A.D. Fanning asked sullenly.

"No, Margaret, not by a long shot," the Executive Assistant Director said. "What did this is still a matter of debate, though there is a witness."

"And?" A.D. Fanning asked, now with an expression of being utterly amazed.

"The event, which you're going to read about, involves the mangled or otherwise mutilated bodies of six individuals, including Miss Addams here. The survivor of this ordeal is a man by the name of Benet, a Hercules Benet, also from the Baytown area. His testimony, thus far, is incredulous to say the least. But, there is camera evidence saved on an attached MP-four file, and a few JPEGs too. Just take your time with these, Margaret, and remember, all this should be kept low for the time being, until the meeting. We're trying to confirm safe travel for our British guest."

"Right," A.D. Fanning mumbled. "And who is this person, exactly?"

"A man by the name of Grange; Doctor Erick Grange, Ph.D. He's extraordinary, according to a few agents who have worked with the man, from our London attaché office. In fact, the agents at our legat had insisted that our growing list of victims coincide with England's list of victims, concluding that there's no fluke here. There's a connection between these and those in the U.K. and throughout Europe. You'll read about this too, but for now,

I need you to prepare for the meeting, which, like I said, should be Monday or Tuesday, around the fifteenth or so."

"Next Monday or Tuesday, alright, I'll leave these days open. In fact, I'll keep the week open for this," A.D. Fanning murmured as she jotted down the dates in her yearly planner.

"We'll let you know," the Executive Assistant Director said. "And like I said, we're going to need a few of your best agents, which, according to our data … let's see here," the man continued as he rifled through a stack of papers on his desk. "Ah, yes, Richard Thyssen and Peter Wellington. I think they'll do. At least this is Director Warren's feelings. Oh, plus you'll be getting some new blood for this one, an on-loan agent, alright?"

"Oh, I see. And who's this agent?"

"A young woman by the name of Vass, a Monica Vass. She's quite exceptional, has top scores at the academy, and is profoundly talented. I've attached her CV, deportment, and ratings, all listed in the addendum section of the PDF."

A.D. Fanning nodded as she continued to write in her planner. She smiled ever so slightly when writing the name Peter Wellington down. A.S.A.C. Howington simply grinned at the name being mentioned.

"You find something amusing?" the Directorate of Intelligence asked, now with raised eyebrows.

"Not amusing, Mrs. Horwitz," A.D. Fanning returned, "it's just a little odd, that's all."

"Odd?"

"Yes, odd. You see, Agent Wellington has had a few reprimands, mostly before my watch, but as of only a few months ago, he's been … how should I put this? A little pressing in the amorousness department with some of our female agents."

"I see. Well, nevertheless, the director feels the man is a good fit for this mission, so we'll keep him all the same," the stern woman said curtly.

"Will do," A.D. Fanning said. "I think we're ready for this, and will keep our calendar open for the meeting. Is there anything else we should plan for, and special guests I should know about?"

"There's a complete list in the addendum section of your PDF," the Executive Assistant Director said. "Your friend Alex Brenner will be there to represent the Agency, as well as representatives from various branches of the military, which includes direct contacts with the NSA and other intelligence agencies, but most of all, at least one of them will be reporting back to Damer herself."

"The president is interested in this?" A.S.A.C. Howington blurted.

"That's correct, Mister Howington. Though her interest appears to be her own, we should assume that everything you say and do will be funneled right to her, so let's keep everything as official as can be. You know how much she dislikes any kind of authority other than her own." Now, the Executive Assistant Director exchanged glances with the Directorate of Intelligence, and then cleared his throat. "My apologies," he said. "Let us simply follow procedures, and to the letter, shall we?"

"Naturally, Noah. You can count on us, as always.

"Excellent, Margaret, excellent. Now ... there's just one more thing before I let you go. We don't have a bead on this thing as of yet, but it's important. Please, just listen and keep your eyes and ears open ... okay?"

"Ah, of course, Noah, what is it?"

In the moments it took to fully describe what Executive Assistant Director Mateo was apparently dreading to say, the storm had picked up in its veracity. In seconds, the skies had become as dark as pitch, with bursts of lightning flaring in crescendos that made the federal office shake and shimmer. The mood had taken on the distinct feeling of dread now, and as the temperature fell to a chilly 60 to 55 degrees Fahrenheit, A.D. Fanning and A.S.A.C. Howington remained silent as the man on the monitor spoke.

For a second or two, both could see the fear in the Executive Assistant Director's eyes, despite having been a tenured police officer in one of the most dangerous cities in the world, and despite having been a combat Marine of great distinction. It had been obvious that what the man had to say had irked him; confounded him, though he believed — the man believed what he was saying.

✠

In the four to five minutes it took for the Executive Assistant Director to explain his concerns, A.D. Fanning had concluded that the man wasn't only telling the truth, but had feared dealing with the FBI's person of interest.

And though it wasn't commonplace for any federal agent to fear the unknown, let alone scuttlebutt of the supernatural, this federal agent had. This was apparent by his behaviour and by the shakiness of his voice. The man was unnerved by Patrick Allen Bush, the Bureau's newest concern, albeit a somewhat hidden concern.

Executive Assistant Director Mateo explained that the name Patrick Bush had indeed been a name spoken of in the backrooms and smoke-filled offices of the world's highest examples of law enforcement, that from the United Kingdom and throughout Europe, his name and the mysterious Society of Rood had been investigated by their top agents, only to yield hearsay and unfounded conjecture. That is because the deaths associated with this shadowy cult, now considered a religious sect of ancient stature, as according to Alex Brenner of the Central Intelligence Agency, the nature of said deaths has been considered rendered by what six out of twelve Pentagon thinktanks referred to as: *Mors per exotica mensuras.*

The Executive Assistant Director explained that the Latin meaning had equalled to "Death by exotic means," and that the recorded number of deaths associated with Patrick Bush and the Society of Rood, having numbered to six-thousand, four hundred and eleven from April, 1994 to the present, respectfully, had been authenticated by the top intelligence agencies around the globe. Whether the Central Intelligence Agency, England's MI-6, Israel's Mossad, Germany's Federal Intelligence Service, or India's Research and Analysis Wing, the name Patrick Allen Bush had been mentioned in one way or another, and had been investigated.

Other agencies, such as Russia's Foreign Intelligence Service and China's Ministry of State Security, had deemed the man an ally to what these countries had referred to as 'research and development' and to 'commerce.' Certainly, praises that had garnered more concern than respect from opposite nations had been a key factor in prolonged investigations, despite the man always being found guiltless.

Now, as the clock turned to 10:15 a.m., the Executive Assistant Director turned and whispered something to the Directorate of Intelligence. A second after this, the stern-looking woman got up and left the room. And a second after that, the man leaned in to his camera as close as he could, and quickly scanned his surroundings. Then, he hit a switch on his desk, effectively ending the recording section of his daily log. He did this so that the following statements would not be recorded in the daily minutes or reach his superiors. Now, he took a deep breath and offered his most sincere feelings on the Patrick Bush case.

"Margaret?" the Executive Assistant Director said quietly. "What I'm going to tell you and Mister Howington is for your ears only, understood?"

"Of course, Noah," A.D. Fanning said cautiously, while A.S.A.C. Howington simply nodded in confirmation.

"Two things," the unnerved man on the monitor continued. "First, what you're both going to take away from the upcoming meeting is going to confuse more than answer questions. Brenner and his cohorts with the Agency have their own agenda. This is painfully obvious, but in spite of this, and because you're friends with Brenner, I'm asking you to play dumb, at least dumb enough to relax him a little. You get my meaning, right, Margaret?"

"I think so," she returned, complete with a look of total despair. "Why, Noah … why the cloak and dagger?"

"Well, let's just say that ninety per cent of what you're going to hear is old news, even if it's new to you both. Brenner knows this, and he's not expounding on anything, so we're going to be cautious on our end. Plus, my counterpart in the U.K. has given me a lot to chew on. He's positive that this Bush character is working on something that isn't just responsible for all the deaths recorded around the globe, but that the man is working; is working with this cult, I should say, in order to do much, much worse."

"I … I don't get it, Noah, how? Is this the part you said has to do with physics? I don't understand," A.D. Fanning said in a whisper.

The Executive Assistant Director sat back in his chair and scratched his chin. He looked perplexed. "We think so, at least … at least this Doctor Grange has hinted at as much," he said. "Just what exactly, we don't know yet. He's not giving any solid info. That said, when he arrives, give him anything he wants, okay?"

"Okay."

"The plan is for Doctor Grange and Agent Vass to tail Bush when he goes to an upcoming opera. That information is in the packet our courier will be delivering in a day or so."

"A packet, right," A.D. Fanning said with a confused expression. She could only exchange a glance with A.S.A.C. Howington, but it was obvious she was overwhelmed by the information.

"Don't sweat the details right now, Margaret," the man said. "There's a complete rundown in the packet, tickets and a few credit cards … for the opera in Palm Beach. When you read it, you'll understand. Anyway, Director Warren and Mister McFarland from British Intelligence are working on something, so don't be surprised by what comes about in the days ahead. Believe me, Margaret, this thing is bizarre, and I'm lowball'en that sentiment by a mile."

"Jesus, Noah, what the hell is going on here?"

The Executive Assistant Director offered a stressed expression as he scanned the room again. "Yeah … hell is right. And that brings me to the last part, so listen well, both of you," he said. "This Patrick Bush … he's behind most of what's been going on for the last three decades. I can't prove it; in fact, no one has been able to do that … at least officially. Regardless, we know it all the same."

"Noah, just tell us. We'll keep this to ourselves, I promise, but … but we have to know." A.D. Fanning offered her most concerned expression now, despite feeling a tinge of fear herself. "Please, Noah, I've known you for years, hell, we shared an office when the Hoover complex was still being used, for Christ's sake. You know you can trust me … and Scott here is as company as a company man could be!"

"Yes, yes, I know that. It's just that I don't want to sound like an idiot, that's all."

A.D. Fanning sat back in her chair and smiled. "Are you kidding me?" she said with a brief exhale that sounded suspiciously like an aborted giggle. "I watched you lose money hand over fist betting on the L.A. Clippers again and again. No matter how many times I tried to save you, you always went right back to handing out your hard-earned dough … ya' dolt! Now that was idiocy."

"Nice, Margaret," the Executive Assistant Director returned with a grin. He, too, sat back in his chair and relaxed, at least a little. "Alright … you got me," he continued. "Okay then. Here's the deal. Bush is a monster, Margaret. He's a bona fide monster with some kind of power that has been alluding us and … and everyone since the nineties."

"Noah … our P.O.I. is not a monster," A.D. Fanning said with a judgmental expression. Even A.S.A.C. Howington just stared at the man with raised eyebrows. "Seriously," A.D. Fanning continued. "You better not be playing a game with me. We have history, Noah, having saved your butt on more than a few occasions, but if you're punking me, I'll strike back, and it will sting for years … you got me?" she concluded with a smile. Even A.S.A.C. Howington didn't know what to think. Was she kidding, or was she serious?

Everyone knew that it was practically impossible to know if the assistant director was playing with you like a cat would a hapless mouse, or if she was propping you up for the kill. Now, the atmosphere in the cold conference room was thick with doubt.

A.D. Fanning had her ways of terrifying her subordinates when she was mad, but this was Noah James Mateo, Executive Assistant Director of the FBI, head of the Intelligence Branch; Strategic leader of the FBI's intelligence program, overseer of integrating intelligence and operations across the entire span of the Bureau. The man didn't play games. He was as serious as a brain aneurysm.

"Okay, Noah," A.D. Fanning said. "Let's get to it, shall we? I don't care if you tell me that Bush is an alien from Alpha Centauri or if he was once a woman and then became a man, I want to know the details. If my office and my agents are walking into some kind of trap, we deserve to know. Now spill, Noah!"

For the briefest moment, A.S.A.C. Howington wished he were anywhere else than in conference room five. He couldn't tell if all of the banter was staged or serious. That is, until the man on the monitor leaned in and nodded. There was no smile, only the most deadpan expression that could be imagined.

"Okay, here it is, Margaret ... Mister Howington. Here's the truth as a very small handful of us have come to see as fact," the Executive Assistant Director said. He was serious, and both agents of the North Florida field office had known it. "Patrick Allen Bush has somehow harnessed a power we simply don't have a name for, outside of what Senior Special Agent Bryon Glick had referred to as being *magic*," he said.

"Magic? Like David Copperfield magic?"

"Negative, Margaret, like Merlin the Magician kind of magic. Like *The Lord of the Rings* and *The Hobbit* kind of magic, like Darth Vader kind of magic, and pure craziness like that. Now ... I realize how stupid that sounds, but out of the nine international agencies I've been working with, all of them have offered a similar response."

"Okay, okay, magic then," A.D. Fanning said, now with the slightest tinge of sarcasm. "This just tells me that this cult Bush is involved with has found a way to screw with people's minds, Noah. It's not the first time."

"No, no, Margaret, it's not that simple. Some of the top minds have been looking into this since at least twenty-ten, and that was just a new file being dated for review. We've been looking into this guy since nineteen-ninety-four, if you can believe that. Tell you what, check out Agent Darlington's files on Bush ... listed as case number B-Twelve in the cold files."

"B-Twelve? There's no such thing, Noah."

"They can be found on our database. Just look in the cold files," the man said firmly. "You'll find it under the letter X. I think that may have been a little joke by our Agent Darlington."

"Like the TV show?" A.D. Fanning returned sarcastically.

"Yeah, like the TV show. It was a hot programme back then, and Darlington always had a flair for the dramatic. Anyway ... just read it, and then bury it back where it was found. I ... I know you'll find it, Margaret."

"This is all so crazy, Noah. Yes ... yes, of course, I'll read over it. But this has all been documented and cleared by the director, then, so what's the big deal? I just don't get it—"

"It's just observations, Margaret, and nothing else," the man said. "The agent did his job, and maybe a little more. But when you read it, you'll understand why he retired shortly thereafter. But, and I can't stress this enough, but do not under any circumstances share any of it with anyone outside of your A—SAC here. Do you understand, Mister Howington!?"

"Yes, sir, I understand," A.S.A.C. Howington returned. For a moment, he thought he was back in the army, or at North Georgia Military College. For a moment, he felt a pang of fear himself, realizing that the whole affair had been true and on the up-and-up. That the truth truly was stranger than fiction.

"Alright then," the Executive Assistant Director said solemnly. "I'll accept that, Margaret, but please, for friendship's sake, please … do not trust your gut feeling about this Bush character. He's a monster, Margaret. He's powerful by means none of us understands. Hell, you could watch him for three-weeks straight and he'll not do so much as wink at you, but his enemies will start dying one by one right in front of your eyes, and the only thing you'll get out of the guy is a smile … as if he knew you were watching him the whole time. He knows, Margaret, somehow, he knows!"

A.D. Fanning could only shake her head in disbelief at the man's outlandish comment. "Jiminy Crickets, Noah, do you know how that sounds?" she said, followed by a chuckle.

"Oh, yeah, I know how it sounds. But here's the deal regarding my obviously bat shit sounding comments. I've been privy to a few highly outrageous videos of no less than five victims in the past three years, all firmly resting in our off-limits files. Five victims, Margaret, five people who were alive one moment and dead the next."

"You saw this … five people dying right before you?"

"I did," the now numb-looking man returned. "We watched as a cloud of smoke formed out of nothing, in the centre of a massive parking lot, in the middle of the night. Then, with that smoke beginning to descend to the earth, this cloud, which formed out of itself, got bigger and bigger. Then, we watched as two men were lifted up, and torn in two by unseen hands, or whatever. They were ripped in pieces, Margaret, and with absolutely no logic behind it whatsoever."

A.D. Fanning exchanged a glance with A.S.A.C. Howington and then looked back at the man on the monitor. She had known Noah Mateo since 2010 and had worked directly with him since 2016, back in Washington D.C., but he had never acted like this. He was no nonsense; *Balls to the Wall*, as he liked to say when a case had exceeded its expectation. He wasn't a fool, and he wasn't touched in the head, but today she didn't recognize the man. He was animated with what could only be perceived as insanity.

"These guys were known combatants of an Iranian terror cell stationed in Philadelphia," the Executive Assistant Director continued. "The field office there had a solid bead on this cell for almost eight straight months, with four agents from D.C. working the case. Well, while on a stakeout, six of our agents watched dumbfounded as these two shitheads were lifted in the air, I don't know, maybe six to ten feet, and a second later, they're literally ripped in two, one in half, and the other right down the middle. I about soiled myself when I saw this, Margaret, and you can believe me when I tell you I've seen a lot."

A.D. Fanning could only glance over to A.S.A.C. Howington with an expression that held fifty percent being played, and the other fifty percent as if having been slapped in the face. Her second in command hadn't looked any different, though he kept his eyes on the man that filled the monitor, waiting for a smile or a laugh. But there were neither. There was only a grimace where an otherwise contented expression once was.

"Noah, I … I believe you all saw something—"

"No, Margaret, the videos had been taken on the best quality equipment the Bureau has, and not only that, but video cameras from an adjacent parking lot and a shipping and receiving centre had caught the same thing our agents had. Quantico checked the video files for any kind of secondhand tampering, only to conclude their authenticity. It happened, Margaret, and you and Mister Howington here are about to see it directly. That's why I've been cleared to pass on the latest video to you … compliments of Director Warren.

"You, you're serious," A.D. Fanning mumbled. "Okay then, Noah, we'll take a look. But, but why do you think Bush is involved with … with what you and your agents had witnessed?"

"Because for a week before the incident, Patrick Bush had sent several emails to them, these two men ... the two leaders of that terror cell. Those emails were written in perfect Persian Farsi, or ... or Perso-Arabic script, I should say. Anyway, the man had requested, no, no he had *ordered* both men to cease and desist their activities, and to come to Christ Jesus. This, Margaret, is a common factor in each and every incident with the name Patrick Bush attached to it. There are no coincidences, Margaret, it's fact."

"Okay, Noah, we'll put our best efforts towards this," A.D. Fanning said. "But I don't suppose you'd send those videos to us, would you?"

"I'm afraid I haven't been authorized for that, Margaret, but the video file we are sending shows a similar event. It's not as clear as our other saved footage, but you'll see the facts soon enough. Now ... I have to sign off. We'll be in touch, though. Maybe after the meeting, we'll catch up. I've a crazy schedule, so I'll I.M. you when I'm free, okay?"

"That's fine, Noah," A.D. Fanning said. She was stunned by the information, and though it had at first sounded like a crock of bullshit from a man she had always remembered as having a healthy sense of humour, she knew that he was dead serious today. "Okay, Noah, just keep me in the loop, and be sure to transmit any information I'll need for the coming week. Okay?"

"You got it, partner. We miss you here, Margaret. If you ever get tired of the constant sunshine and those damned beaches, you let me know ... I'll get Warren to ship you back home to the rain and snow A-SAP!"

"Nothing doing, buddy," A.D. Fanning returned with a half-smile. "I'll talk with you soon." And with that, Executive Assistant Director Noah Mateo arched forward to push an unseen button, followed by a royal blue screen, and the official logo of the FBI at its centre. Now, A.D. Fanning and A.S.A.C. Howington sat in the quiet room with only the sound of rain pelting on the large, picture windows. The room was still cold; dreadfully cold.

✠

Assistant Director Margaret Alice Fanning had heard a lot in her tenure as an agent with the Federal Bureau of Investigation, but today had been the dealbreaker to anything even remotely resembling the law. Now, she could only stare at the wallpaper on the large monitor. She just stared at the official logo of the FBI, as the blue field behind it had made the room glow in the darkness. She found herself exhausted. She wanted to go home.

Now, as she packed up her yearly planner back into her valise, she stood up and walked over to the door, and flipped the switch to the overhead lights. The gaudiness of the fluorescent lights made her squint. A.S.A.C. Howington did the same. He continued to sit, as he too found himself numb to the information.

"What the hell is going on?" he mumbled loudly.

"I don't know, Scott, but I've a feeling this thing is about to go nuclear," the assistant director returned. And then she smiled, ever so slightly. "Let's go check this video out," she continued. "I want to see this thing for what it is. I just don't trust it."

"You think it's AI?" A.S.A.C. Howington suggested.

"I doubt Quantico or the boys at the lab are gonna miss something like that. They'll break everything down pixel by pixel to find out. No … I doubt it's artificial intelligence, in spite of it taking over the world."

A.S.A.C. Howington nodded to the comment. "You're probably right," he said, now standing up quickly and pushing in his chair. "But I'm sure something was missed," he continued. "It's something simple, I'm sure of it. Either way, I'm curious about this Baytown video."

"I as well," A.D. Fanning said, just as she was about to leave the conference room. Then, the lights flickered three times, and then went dim, much like street lights do at night, when a flash of lightning confuses its sensors that it was daytime. Now, the large VIZIO monitor flickered as well, with its official-looking FBI logo and bright blue background going black. This was followed by something popping up on the screen. It looked like an antiquated music video.

"What the hell's this?" A.S.A.C. Howington said, now pivoting to look at the image. The screen had become a series of deep reds and blacks, with a silhouette of some Spanish architecture in the background. This was followed by white letters spelling out: Capitol Centre, Largo, MD, March 21, 1977.

"Ah, we must have a glitch," A.S.A.C. Howington murmured. "The storm, I guess."

"Yeah, I … I suppose," A.D. Fanning returned, now peering out the large picture windows. The rain had continued, as flashes of lightning glared towards the north of the state, towards the tiny hamlet of Garver Town.

A most familiar tune began to play. It was *Hotel California*, by the Eagles. And as the stage began to be overtaken by an aqua-coloured light, it became clear that it was the titular band of the past playing out their signature tune. Now, A.D. Fanning and A.S.A.C. Howington watched stunned as Don Henley sang; as Don Felder, Joe Walsh, and Randy Meisner made history. Indeed, the tune had been intoxicating to both the assistant director and her second in command. They were, for a moment, mesmerized.

✠

As the famous song of the 1970s faded to black, the monitor simply turned off. This was followed by the lights coming back on, as if someone had hit the switch to do so. Then, just as it had sprung to life, the monitor went black, having shut down all by itself. Now, the assistant director turned to face her second in command with raised eyebrows.

"Okay, that was weird," she said as she looked at her watch. "It's going on eleven-thirty, Scott. Why don't we head for lunch? After that we'll go to my office and watch this damned video. I don't know why, but I have a pain in my gut, and I think it's coming from this case," she concluded.

"Agreed," Howington said flatly. Then, he turned and gazed out the large picture window, and looked down on the east parking lot, then out towards the beach. The rain had made it foggy, and almost surreal, like a black and white piece of art, like what indie photographer Michele Palazzo might have taken. He felt a chill run down his back as he turned to face his superior. "Do you think Agents Thyssen and Wellington are a good pick?" he asked suspiciously.

A.D. Fanning took a deep breath and then exhaled loudly. "Yes," she returned. "Richard Thyssen will be able to dig something up on this Patrick Bush, if there's anything worth finding. He's got that gentle touch, you know? He's certainly the typical example of the good cop. And Wellington, well ... he's talented, there's no doubt of that, despite his somewhat juvenile antics from time to time."

A.S.A.C. Howington chuckled at this, having been the one to cosign the man's disciplinary report. "I suppose," he chuckled again. Now, looking somewhat disgusted, A.D. Fanning said nothing more and then turned to leave the room. Howington followed, switching the lights off at the same time.

Now, the two left the room, leaving a dark circumference with only the occasional flash from distant lightning to offer a temporary glow. And just as thunder echoed throughout the room, shaking the entire building with a light hum, both the assistant director and her second in command heard the now familiar tune of the Eagles once again. They both stopped and turned to look back into the dark conference room, a room that had now taken on a bluish glow.

Huh, *Hotel California* again," A.S.A.C. Howington murmured. "Strange. Must be receiving a signal from somewhere. Must be the storm."

✠

The assistant director and her second in command tried to make sense of that morning's meeting. They would try to put the pieces together while they had lunch, and they would watch the video again and again. They wouldn't be able to explain what they would see, of course, but both would quickly realize that the name Patrick Allen Bush and the mysterious Society of Rood had promised for a lively investigation. They couldn't explain it, but both had secretly dreaded what was coming. They feared for the future.

EPILOGUE

FBI Field Office, Jacksonville, Florida
Margaret Fanning's Office

Monday, July 6th, 1:15 P.M.

"Fate whispers to the warrior, 'You can not withstand the storm.' The warrior whispers back, 'I am the storm."

— Unknown

Assistant Director Margaret Fanning and Assistant Special Agent in Charge Scott Howington had just returned from lunch. They figured eating something might help them figure out the insanity of their impromptu meeting with the Executive Assistant Director that morning, but that wasn't the case. Now, the two had just as quickly returned to A.D. Fanning's office and prepared themselves for the information sent by the E.A.D. They had no idea what they were in store for.

A.D. Fanning signed in to the FBI's encrypted email and quickly brought up the file attachment that Executive Assistant Director Noah Mateo had sent her. Despite having been one of her closest confidants, her old friend had nonetheless placed a series of clearance protocols on the email and its attachments. Now, she read the brief notation, which was listed as 'Eyes Only.' This made her frown, especially when accompanied by the words—

"What the hell, Noah? she mumbled to herself. "We just had a super, top-secret meeting less than an hour ago. Cripes, what's with all this cloak and dagger nonsense?"

Now, the assistant director shared a glance with A.S.A.C. Howington and then began downloading the attachments. The digital multimedia container format files were larger than normal, so she opened the Word document and decrypted it. She read the brief notation by the Executive Assistant Director.

"Margaret, what I'm about the share is to be kept for you, and you alone. Please, do not share the following information with anyone, except your acting S.A.C."

A.D. Fanning could only stare at the command for a second, and then continued reading.

"Beginning around June of twenty-sixteen," the message continued, "we had noticed the presence of a possible impostor appearing around some of our crime scenes, primarily those regarding our P.O.I. Though the man has only identified himself with osculating aliases, he has never been apprehended or otherwise questioned. The description of the man is as follows: Tall, around six-one, thin, with full, grey hair. He's around fifty-five, maybe sixty years of age. He tends to wear somewhat outdated clothing and old, aviator-style sunglasses. This gentleman is often accompanied by one or two younger men, roughly late twenties or early thirties. They all flash badges with realistic IDs, complete with an official hologram logo, which places this firmly in the federal crime arena. The short and skinny of this, Margaret, is that we have a few impostors spooking around."

A.D. Fanning felt a cold chill run down her back now. The fact that there were phony federal agents poking around her crime scenes was bad enough, and certainly, such a thing didn't sit well with her, especially those with the name Patrick Allen Bush attached to it. Now, she sat back in her chair and took a breath.

"Something wrong?" A.S.A.C. Howington asked.

"Ah, no … no, just thinking about something," she said softly. "Just waiting for these damned files to load. They're taking forever." She leaned in and finished reading the message.

"Margaret, we believe these impostors may be black ops, maybe *Agency* men. And though we only have a few images, they're ambiguous enough to fit almost any category, so much so, in fact, that our biometrics give us around twenty possible matches, with half of those coming from abroad, and a third of the remainder dead. And yes, we followed up; right up until Director Warren put a stop to it. Now we're ordered to abandon this and simply observe and report. This goes for you and your agents. *IF* you spot these gentlemen, we want you to observe, report it to me via official methods, and then return to the first objective. *DO NOT ENGAGE.*"

A.D. Fanning couldn't believe what she just read. Now, the cloak-and-dagger agenda was beginning to make sense. But who these men were and why they were involved with this case had remained the question; a question that had come from the top. Moreover, she received a gag order regarding these gents, and to downplay it, too. She couldn't believe it, especially when the Bureau's person of interest had been at the core of these events. It was maddening.

✠

A.D. Fanning closed the message and saved it to the locked file icon on her desktop. She made a copy of the MP4 collection that was now downloaded and then placed it in the file folder. Though these files were considerable in size, she knew she had to save everything. She knew that she would need them again, especially as the 'Conundrum Folly' case was just getting revved up for an entirely fresh investigation.

Now, she opened the first file, 'Batch Number 66-06-P.A.B., Image numbers 1-23.' Then, she transferred the file icon to the large wall monitor across from her desk, got up, and pivoted it about twenty degrees out so her second in command could see clearly. Then, she sat back down. She wiggled her mouse and opened the first of the 19 images and the four remaining video clips from the Baytown, Texas Incident. She couldn't explain it, but she felt apprehension as she opened the first crime scene photo.

"Can you see alright, Scott?" she asked her second in command.

A.S.A.C. Howington got up and moved to a chair closest to the wall. "Ah, yes, I can see clearly," he said.

Now, A.D. Fanning hit the play icon under the video clip. "We'll start at the beginning, with the first clip," she said. The image showed a lime green background, with darker aspects that must have represented something moving down what looked like a nature trail. After a moment, the entire screen flashed, as if lightning had struck the ground, but a moment later, it became apparent that the light was either a flashlight or a cellphone light being turned on. And as the screen leveled out and focused, the images of six to seven human shapes proceeded down the foliage-lined path.

"Huh … this must be Addams' cult," A.S.A.C. Howington quipped. "I see that the cameras are animated," he continued. "That's an interesting place to play Harry Potter. I wouldn't think the city would pay for that kind of tech in such a desolate location."

"Well, the report said that these cameras were placed there by an independent group; a wildlife organization trying to save some rare birds," A.D. Fanning returned. "Okay, here's the next clip. I think … I think this is at the scene itself. Yes, there's the old swimming pool that Noah highlighted. Interesting."

"That's where the bodies were found?" Howington asked.

A.D. Fanning nodded in confirmation. "Just Addams, actually. Most of the cultists were discovered crushed under one of the picnic shelters, and another was found floating way out in one of the bays. His body was filleted, according to Noah."

"And one survivor?" A.S.A.C. Howington asked.

"Right, just one, just Hercules Benet. He was the only one to survive the ordeal."

"I see. Did the Executive Assistant Director send any files yet, electronically?"

"Negative. He's going to have those files sent by the Houston field office via courier. Should be here by tomorrow morning or early afternoon, according to Mateo. Okay, that's it for clip number two. Let's move on to the next one, shall we?"

Now, as A.D. Fanning advanced to the third video clip, the images immediately began to shake and shimmy, as if from hurricane-like winds. This, along with the cultists buckling and pivoting, had been proof enough, though the presence of rain was also seen. Seconds into the clip, the unmistakable flash of lightning was detected, along with the blackish image of a man or woman at the centre of the old swimming pool. This person, presumably Addams, had arms raised high and was screaming something to the others. There was a lone figure standing next to this person, while a rotund figure ran out of sight.

"Okay, okay," the assistant director mumbled. "This must be Addams … at the apex of the pool. And the large one, that has to be Benet. He supposedly took shelter under a nest of trees. Wait, wait a second?" she yelped, just as A.S.A.C. Howington stood up and walked up to the monitor.

"What the hell?" he asked unblinkingly. "What the hell is that?"

In what would seem to last for several minutes, the scene, which had begun as any other nondescript example of crime evidence or a similar scene that *should* have been nestled firmly into the arena of law enforcement, had quickly turned into something else. Now, both the assistant director and her second in command had found themselves mesmerized by what they were witnessing. Despite the graininess of the recording and the colour differences that made it hard to see, they were seeing something that shouldn't have been there, something otherworldly.

Now, as a cool waft of air passed by them, they knew that their mission had just become more difficult. They had witnessed the impossible. They had witnessed the insane.

✠

The image that played out on the monitor had shown what had to have been a vortex of wind, as if coming from a waterspout or perhaps a micro tornado. Such a concept had been voiced by A.S.A.C. Howington, who had witnessed similar events of nature in the past. In spite of the rarity of such a thing, it was a plausible explanation for what was occurring, at least in theory.

Now, as A.D. Fanning froze the image, then advanced the video clip frame by frame, she stopped as a tiny, white number instantly appeared next to the anomaly on the screen.

"This must be Quantico's doing," the assistant director mumbled. She walked back to her next, bent down, and read over the attached sheet in the email. "Right, Mateo says here that this was overseen and analyzed by our people at our lab in Quantico, signed by Unit B, and that they placed numbers next to areas to be scrutinized. Their findings are on page twenty-two of the attachments."

A.S.A.C. Howington offered his superior a furrowed expression and then nodded in confirmation. "The C.J.I.S. uses the latest version of the Next Generation Identification Systems, which means they have the identities of these people," he said flatly. "They're also in the know of what this thing is above Addams. What does it say about that?"

"Apparently, they don't know yet. What they do know is that there is an electrical charge around that thing, whatever it is. The stills were overseen a second time by the Criminal Justice Information Services, but the only thing confirmed are the faces of the cultists, which were also validated by N.C.I.C."

"It's amazing they can figure out those faces in such darkness and such an environment," ASAC Howington mumbled.

"Yeah … but they're using the latest technology, Scott. The System and Facial Analysis, Comparison, and Evaluation Services Unit has its stamp on this, too, so what we're seeing is still the best example."

✠

Once A.D. Fanning and A.S.A.C. Howington inspected the video clip to its end, they were able to see what had looked very much like a massive shape that had spanned at least fifteen to twenty feet in height and width, but which was observed morphing in shape, sometimes reaching what had to have been thirty feet high. The only thing that had confounded the FBI and its associates had been the fact that the *thing* was largely transparent, save that for a slight variation in temperature and consistency, which the FBI had determined as being electrical or electromagnetic in nature. Outside of this, there simply was no logical explanation for the odd image.

Understandably curious, A.D. Fanning continued to advance the images one frame at a time, reading every explanation that the lab results could offer. By the time she reached number twelve on the clip, she stood back in what could only have been horror on her face. Now, where there had only been a ghostly whitish-blue haze surrounding the weird image, had taken on a new item of strangeness. At the apex of the translucent image had appeared what looked suspiciously like eyes. Though not resembling human eyes, or those of any known animal, the things had looked like eyes all the same.

"What ... what are those supposed to be?" A.S.A.C. Howington asked. The tone in his voice had become darker, sullen, as if he felt afraid of something. Certainly, this was an emotion uncommon for the man. He had seen a lot of terrifying things during his many years with the Bureau, but this image had frightened him.

"I don't know what that is, Scott," The assistant director said. She returned to her desk, sat down, and began reading over the report again. "It says here that frames twenty to twenty-eight are positive for electromagnetic radiation," she read aloud. "Moreover, according to a Doctor Philip Tomes, one of the FBI's experts, a physicist at George Washington University, well, he says that by using something called E.M.I.R., or Electro-Magnetic InfraRed technology, his department was able to determine that whatever this thing is on the video clips are radioactive in nature."

"Right," A.S.A.C. Howington returned forcefully. "I remember courses back at North Georgia that covered this. E.M.I.R uses multilayer metal and polymer film to absorb electromagnetic wave energy and then converts it to a heated source. This is how they can pick that radiation up on their infrared equipment. That means that something tangible is behind that ... that invisible image on the nature preserve's film."

"I guess that makes sense," A.D. Fanning said with a quiver in her voice. "But the report also states that this Doctor Tomes and his lab used electronic image sensors to follow up on their tests. These had included C.M.O.S. and C.C.D. sensors, whatever those are. There's a lot of scientific jargon I can't make heads or tails of, but wait, he also states that there is evidence of high-energy particles and ultra-high-energy, most likely having been sourced by cosmic rays."

"Cosmic rays? That's incredible," A.S.A.C. Howington said. "So, whatever this thing is ... it's radioactive, at least somewhat. So, what can it be? This can't have anything to do with Patrick Bush, unless he's created it."

"Hum, I wonder," A.D. Fanning murmured to herself.

"Wonder what?"

"Bush is a physicist, Scott. He has his doctorate in it, along with another discipline regarding some kind of advanced geometry. He's top scores according to Mateo, so maybe ... maybe he does have something to do with this. Maybe he's had help from this Society of Rood. Maybe. Let's finish this, and then review the photographs. We'll call it a day with this. I've got a few calls to make anyway."

"Roger that," A.S.A.C. Howington said. He couldn't take his eyes off the video clip that glowed on the monitor. The animated images that had shaken and had shaken like a quivering child in shock had unnerved him. None of what they were looking at that afternoon had made sense. How could radiation as a source of power be able to straddle or otherwise capture a person, let alone destroy them in the manner that had killed Juliana Addams and her devil cult?

For the assistant director and her second in command, the enigmatic Patrick Allen Bush had taken on much darker overtones. Was he something beyond what the law could deem as being 'illegal?' And the shadowy cult he belonged to, a reality that had confounded him, had only forced him to question his own reality, if but for a moment. Regardless, there could be no doubt. The mystery of the Conundrum Folly Case was growing exponentially.

Now, they both needed to know more. They simply had to.

✠

As A.D. Fanning and A.S.A.C. Howington continued to watch the remainder of the video clips, both could only watch in horror as the vile Juliana Addams was literally gutted like a fetal pig before their eyes. And because the three main cameras at the Baytown Park had been mounted high on telephone poles, they were able to see every angle. And with the aid of the FBI's laboratories in Quantico, Virginia, they were able to see what no other would have; what none other *could* have.

From the inexplicable death of the cult's leader, Juliana Addams, also known as 'Madam Tarja Delevingne,' along with her temporary lover, one Lester Gnaws, their deaths had been the linchpin to a far deeper problem for the FBI. For though there had been ample proof that the victims had indeed died by inexplicable means, there appeared to be little hope of finding any reason in support of finding a logical answer.

For Lester Gnaws, also known as 'Rommar,' he would be flung out of the grainy image so quickly that the only evidence that this occurred was the natural effect of a solid object moving by fantastic speeds. This was discovered by the tangible, photographic wake that followed the man's body out of the frame. As for the other cultists, their demise had been recorded on the second camera. These images had been the most horrifying.

Now, A.D. Fanning and A.S.A.C. Howington watched in shock and awe as those silent, though nonetheless pleading souls beneath what looked like a sturdy picnic shelter had lifted off its support beams, then having been thrust down upon them at an immeasurable speed. Even the camera had vibrated by the force of this event, with its picture fizzing and sputtering as if it were hit by a solid object. Despite this, however, the two federal agents just watched silently; their eyes affixed and unblinking.

Although they had no explanations for the strange video clips, the photographs wouldn't prove explanatory either. Now, as they scanned over the photos, all of which had been heavily scrutinized by the FBI's top forensics experts, none had a fixed or logical answer for the events. What was available, however, was the physical evidence; the squashed and mangled cadavers of Juliana Addams and her wayward devil cult.

✠

The first photo stood out like a green light on the monitor. Out of the twenty-three photos, eight had been altered by the FBI's forensics team from the main lab in Quantico. The now highly regarded Unit B had served as the Bureau's newest branch, having been instituted in 2026 to investigate crimes using artificial intelligence. They were experts at determining if even the slightest amount of A.I. had been used in the photos, as well as in the video clips. There was no interaction. Now, A.D. Fanning and A.S.A.C. Howington would witness the truth.

The first fourteen photographs had seemed almost routine. Each had evidence of the cultists having been there, which was authenticated by the latest biometrics overlay systems used by the FBI. It showed the faces of the men and women of the cult, as well as details that would have been expected at that late hour. Whether insects flying around or the raindrops that sporadically fell, to the highly detailed shots of the heavy rain and lightning, Unit B had outdone themselves. Once they reached the fifteenth photograph, however, the concept of science and the law had gone out the window.

Now, what was displayed on A.D. Fanning's office monitor showed a detailed example of the gathering at the Baytown Park's ruins, where an old, dilapidated swimming pool had remained. Here, Juliana Addams was seen talking or directing her unseen cultists, while behind her lingered a mass of indescribable shape or origin. And beneath the six-paneled images was a notation, signed by Special Agent Marci DeWitt, FBI, assigned to Unit B. Her notation is as follows:

"Thermal infrared resolution indicates an amount of data unseen with this type of spectrum analysis," the handwritten notation read. "Moreover, the detail captured by our thermal imaging equipment has identified an unknown source at the crest of these photographs, though we are unsure of the consistency of said object. We have applied various heat and structure-determining tests, but they have reported that the object is both physical and non-physical in nature, and that it tends to fade in and out from one frame to the next. This tells us that the object might be gaseous in nature, though that hypothesis is not warranted at this time. We currently do not have an explanation for this. However, we have been ordered to perform a second investigation by the Directorate of Intelligence, FBI Central, Greenbelt, MD. Please refer to the full report for complete analysis and professional opinion."

— *Special Agent M.H. DeWitt,*
FBI Lab #6, Unit B."

A.D. Fanning turned in her seat and pulled up the document sent by Executive Assistant Director Noah Mateo. She read over Special Agent DeWitt's personal observation and opinion, but this didn't help. She explained that by using '160 x 120 type apparatuses, with a thermal array of 160 x 120 sensors or *pixels*,' as she described it, that it had made a baseline thermal image of everything in the Baytown Park that night, including Addams herself, the cultists, the trees and even the rain as it descended to the earth. This was normal, considering. What the agent wrote following this, however, had caused the most unrest with the assistant director.

Agent DeWitt's comments advising her superiors that by applying a higher thermal resolution, as seen in photographs seventeen to twenty-one, had offered her and Unit B's forensic experts a look into something that had escaped any logical explanation, as according to the agent's own words.

"What we found had not been clarified or had otherwise offered any explanation of said images, or what these images may represent," the notation read.

In short, Unit B was unable to empirically identify any source of the photographic anomalies. That statement, along with the advice to review the data and that a second analysis was to be issued, had been troubling to A.D. Fanning.

Now looking perplexed, she stood up and walked over to the monitor. And with her remote, she advanced the photos. From one thermal photo of Juliana Addams commanding her cultists one minute, to being lifted into the air the next had been unnerving, especially as the so-called *object* behind her had been at least twenty feet high, almost obscuring the camera's frame. The colour saturation of the images were no less discernible. The object had now taken on vibrant hues of deep purples and violets, offset by what could only have been two gigantic eyes, the shade of burnt oranges. This image had been too much. Incredibly, it was a shape that suggested a living thing.

"I think this will do for now," A.D. Fanning said sullenly. She almost appeared sad or defeated. "I think we'll call it a day, Scott, and let you get back to your duties."

"Affirmative on that," ASAC Howington returned. "I still have to go over the details with Myrna, and clear a schedule for this big meeting Mateo was talking about."

A.D. Fanning nodded silently. And then she looked at the man. "Right, that … that's a good idea. I'll keep you advised on that date once it's set up in Maryland. Oh, one more thing, Scott."

"Yes?"

"After reading over the docs Mateo sent, he advises an interview for our preliminaries, here in Florida. And though the Houston field office had already done this, we're authorized, which means it's an order. As such, I'm sending you out tomorrow morning."

A.S.A.C. Howington nodded with raised eyebrows. He appeared somewhat shocked by getting the chance for a field assignment again. "Right, sounds like a plan," he said enthusiastically. "A standard investigative interview, or a full-on Behavioural Analysis?"

"I think a B.A.I. would be best, Scott, but I'll need a detailed 302 when you get back. This doesn't have to be an overnighter, but you're cleared if you need it."

"Understood," he said, now checking his wristwatch for the time.

"Go on home, Scott. Get some rest, I'll arrange a flight for you myself, and text you the time and gate, alright?"

"Sounds good, boss. I'll see you when I get back." Now, A.S.A.C. Howington left the office without fanfare and slowly shut the door. He, like his superior, had had a full day, even though it wasn't even four in the afternoon yet. They were both spent. They were exhausted. They were both intimidated by this Patrick Bush, the recipient of the now-infamous Conundrum Folly Case. Though they both knew the strangeness was only beginning, there was nonetheless a feeling of exhilaration. They were both more than ready to figure the case out and put that winning feather squarely in their caps.

✠

Assistant Director Margaret Fanning sat back in her chair and fiddled with the computer's mouse. She closed the Baytown crime scene photos while ignoring the DeKalb County crime scene and autopsy photos. She had enough for one day. Instead, she opened the P.O.I. folder. Now, she brought up one of the twelve photographs of the FBI's weirdest persons of interest — Patrick Allen Bush.

The first photos were taken during the late 1980s to the early 1990s. From 1984 to 1990, respectively. They showed a young man ready to learn, as his curriculum vitae had clearly proven. The photos dated 1992, however, had shown a man who had changed significantly, both in demeanor and appearance. And though A.D. Fanning hadn't read the entire case file as of yet, she knew the man had gone through something very bad. This, she had promised herself, was to be open-minded before judging too harshly.

By the time she opened the other photos, those from the early 2000s to the present, had displayed a man who had seen it all. Though he didn't look like a madman, not appearing depraved like the others had, not like George "Machine Gun" Kelly, or Louis 'Lepke' Buchalter, nor the arrogance of John Dillinger, there was nonetheless something not right about the man. And though he didn't give off crazy, outsider vibes like Theodore Kaczynski or even Jim Jones, something about the man had made all the right people suspicious.

In truth, Patrick Allen Bush looked rather average, if not a bit sad. The man had looked calm and scholarly, like a college professor, though the kind of college professor that everyone knew could be dangerous if he wanted to be. This was the bone in Margaret Fanning's cerebral throat. She understood the matrix of criminals; the fabric that forced such people to do what they did. And when she looked in the eyes of this seemingly nondescript man, she knew he *could* be dangerous, very dangerous.

Now feeling a little dizzy, most likely from not having enough caffeine that morning, A.D. Fanning closed the file and reduced that back to a desktop icon. Then, she turned to look out the large picture frame window. The clouds were still dark, and to the northwest, a storm was pounding the landscape from Fernandina Beach past Hilliard. The lightning show was impressive, and made the steadfast assistant director glad it wasn't in Jacksonville.

"Alright, enough of this," she mumbled. She was just about to get up when her cellphone rang. The sound of the beep-like alarm was muffled because she had put her cellphone in her desk drawer. Regardless, it was a sharp beep designed specifically to wake people up or to get them motivated. This was why she chose that app. But now, for some reason, it gave her a start. "Alright, alright, just wait a second. Okay, who's this?" she mumbled even louder. She entered her passcode and opened it. There was a text message waiting to be read. She opened it.

"For hee is the minister of God to thee for good: but if thou do that which is euill, be afraid: for he beareth not the sword in vaine: for he is the minister of God, a reuenger to execute wrath vpon him that doeth euill."

— Book of Romans XIII-IV,
KJV, 1611

"What the hell ... what is all this?" A.D. Fanning murmured loudly. She checked who might have sent it, but the number had been listed as unknown. Now, she tried redialing that number, only to receive static in response. Then, just as quickly, a staticky tune began to play—

On a dark desert highway ... cool wind in my hair ... Warm smell of colitis, the staticky song played. A.D. Fanning just stared at her phone now, shocked by the familiar tune.

"What in God's name?" she yelped. "Who the hell is this?!"

Now, as she examined her cellphone yet again, this time opening the 'trace-a-call' icon, she followed by hitting the tab to trace the last caller. It had been a recent app developed by the Bureau for the instant identification of any caller and their location, whether from a cellphone or by computerized means. Every agent had it today, and it had always worked flawlessly. That is, until this day.

"Whaddoya mean no network?!" she yelped. "That's impossible, we can pick you up on the moon, if need be, why the hell aren't you functioning?" The assistant director just shook her head in defiance. Then, a photo came up on the cellphone's text space. It was a deep red photograph with a black silhouette of a building in the background, like an old Spanish Mission. And then it hit her. It was the same image that she and her second in command had seen earlier that morning, in conference room five. It was the same music video, the same Eagles concert from the 1970s. But why?

Now, Assistant Director Margaret Fanning put her phone down on her desk and then swiveled back toward the picture window. And without emotion, she just listened to the staticky music. She couldn't say a word. She just listened as a wave of icy coldness ran through her body like a cold knife. For the first time in years, she felt afraid. Something was coming — something wicked.

... Welcommme to the Hotel California ... oh, such a lovely place ... oh, such a lovely face.

The Muzac Man returns in 'Welcome to Garver Town.'
Coming soon to Retailers and Audiobook

Bio

Thaddeus Hawthorne Grey, Ph.D., is a former deputy medical examiner and funeral director. He has taught courses in physical anthropology, anatomy and physiology, embalming techniques, and chemical procedures in medical examination and the art of human preservation. Now semi-retired, he works as a consultant with private law enforcement agencies in Virginia, West Virginia, and Washington, D.C. When he has time, he writes for pleasure. Thaddeus lives in Groningen, Netherlands six months out of the year, and in Point Pleasant, West Virginia, and in Northern Florida during the winter season. He and his wife, Gwendolyn, live with their two Bombay cats, Grimalkin and Tanith.